LOVE AT
Full Tilt

LOVE AT
Full Tilt

JENNY L. HOWE

Delacorte
Romance

Delacorte Romance
An imprint of Random House Children's Books
A division of Penguin Random House LLC
1745 Broadway, New York, NY 10019
penguinrandomhouse.com
GetUnderlined.com

Text copyright © 2025 by Jenny L. Howe
Cover art copyright © 2025 by Leni Kauffman
Map art copyright © 2025 by John S. Dykes
Interior carousel ornament by juliars/stock.adobe.com
Interior emoji art from stock.adobe.com

Penguin Random House values and supports copyright. Copyright fuels creativity, encourages diverse voices, promotes free speech, and creates a vibrant culture. Thank you for buying an authorized edition of this book and for complying with copyright laws by not reproducing, scanning, or distributing any part of it in any form without permission. You are supporting writers and allowing Penguin Random House to continue to publish books for every reader. Please note that no part of this book may be used or reproduced in any manner for the purpose of training artificial intelligence technologies or systems.

Delacorte Romance and the colophon are trademarks of Penguin Random House LLC.

Editor: Hannah Hill
Cover designer: Ray Shappell
Interior designer: Cathy Bobak
Production editor: Colleen Fellingham
Managing editor: Tamar Schwartz
Production manager: Tracy Heydweiller

Library of Congress Cataloging-in-Publication Data is available upon request.
ISBN 978-0-593-80910-5 (tr. pbk.) — ISBN 978-0-593-80911-2 (ebook)

The text of this book is set in 11-point Sabon MT Pro.

Manufactured in the United States of America
1st Printing

The authorized representative in the EU for product safety and compliance is
Penguin Random House Ireland, Morrison Chambers,
32 Nassau Street, Dublin D02 YH68, Ireland, https://eu-contact.penguin.ie.

Random House Children's Books supports the First Amendment and celebrates the right to read.

This one is for sixteen-year-old Jenny:
Here's the book you needed.

VALYRAD'S FLIGHT
VALE OF VILLAINY

ATALANTIA

THE CURSED APPLE

ALISTAIRS LABYRINTH

DUDLEY'S TAILSPIN

PHOENIX'S LANDING

CASTERMAN'S CAROUSEL

LAST STEPS

REDDINSHIRE CASTLE

STARSHATTER HOTEL

From: LeanneS@fablelandmarketing.com
To: LiaBaker418@gmail.com
Subject: Welcome to the Fableland Superfan Scavenger Hunt!!

Dear Lia,

Congratulations! You are among the 100 people accepted into Fableland's Superfan Scavenger Hunt, part of the resort's month-long 50th-anniversary celebration.

As a participant, you and up to two guests will receive complimentary park tickets and on-property resort accommodations for the duration of the scavenger hunt (June 19 through June 25), as well as a number of other surprises! We hope that, in addition to your participation in the game, you and your guests will take in all that the parks have to offer. *(Please note that you will be responsible for all meals, transportation, and amenities beyond those described above or affiliated with the contest.)*

Through the Superfan Scavenger Hunt, you and our other superfans will showcase your in-depth knowledge of the parks by deciphering a series of clues that will take you from Casterman's Carousel at the center of Phoenix's Landing to the uncharted dungeon halls of Vale of Villainy, and everywhere in between.

The winner of the Superfan Scavenger Hunt will win a cash prize of $50,000 and a golden ticket to Fableland Resort (free access to the park for you and a guest for life, with no blackout days or fees).

Fableland would not be the world-class resort that it is today without its fans, and we look forward to welcoming you as you help us celebrate fifty years of magic and wonder.

Fall into your imagination!

Leanne S.
Fableland Marketing Division

CHAPTER 1

June 18

Logan Airport
Boston, MA

Fableland Resort was the brainchild of Fable Industry's CEO Sam Casterman. After years of entertaining children of all ages with his company's animated films, Casterman wanted to create a place where they could go into the movies and be a part of the action. In his most famous interview, Casterman proclaimed, "Sometimes we need to close out the world and fall into our imaginations. Our resort will bring imagination to life." And for the past fifty years, Fableland has been doing just that.

—*Fableland, 50th-Anniversary Documentary*

MOST PEOPLE LOVE ROLLER COASTERS FOR THEIR BEGINNING. That climb up, up, up as anticipation squeezes your veins and clicking tracks creep you ever closer to that first gravity-defying, stomach-wringing drop.

I prefer the end. When the brakes squeal and the car jerks to a stop and, for a fleeting second, silence settles over the world. It's a moment of perfect peace. One that reminds me that, even after being twisted and turned and thrown upside down, I'm okay.

I would do just about anything—even give up breakfast, my favorite meal, forever—if I could be listening to the screeching melody of those brakes right now instead of my mother's list of every possible disaster that might befall a barely eighteen-year-old girl in Florida without her parents.

"Don't go out alone at night. Don't talk to strangers." Mom huffs a breath like she's been running in place for the twenty minutes we've been standing at airport security. She lowers her head to dig through her purse. "And don't get into cars with people you don't know. Not even with that Dryve app all you kids are using." Extracting a tissue, she blots her nose. Tears shine in her eyelashes.

She can't cry in public. Not again. I run my hand over my stomach as if that will somehow unravel all its knots.

Mom squeezes the straps of her purse. "We hired you a driver to get from the airport to the hotel and back again at the end of the week. There should be no reason for you girls to leave the park."

"But we won't know the driver. How can we get in the car with him?" The words slip out before I can stop them. I smile to indicate it's a joke, but my mom's porcelain skin has found a new shade of white.

Dad frowns, the lines at the corners of his mouth so deep that

I can see them beneath his dark-brown beard. His tanned cheeks have gone red. "Amelia. You haven't gotten on the plane yet. This trip could still be canceled."

Crap. I better not have just torpedoed six days of parental freedom.

I grab his arm and make my blue eyes Fableland-princess wide. "I was kidding." You'd think they'd be used to my terribly timed sense of humor by now.

Facing my mother, I fold her into a hug. I'm barely five four, yet she makes me feel like a giant. Everything about her is so small and fragile. "I won't leave the park. I swear."

I don't understand the things that stress her out, but she can't help it. My grandmother says she burst from the womb anxious.

Mom tightens our hug. "Look out for each other, okay? And check in all the time."

I nod against her shoulder.

"No boys," Dad growls.

I salute him. "You got it."

It's an easy promise to make. My two best friends and I aren't heading to Fableland—the best amusement park in the world—for some vacation fling. I have a contest to win and a huge cash prize to secure.

I slip my hand into my pocket, my fingers curling around the pointed end of a folded sheet of paper. The first clue for Fableland's 50th-anniversary Superfan Scavenger Hunt popped into my email last night, one minute after midnight. Instead of sleeping, I spent the next few hours poring over the notebooks I'd organized for the trip, ensuring they were as thorough as possible. Every piece of information I could glean from the Fabler

Fanatics' Forums (F³ to its members) is sketched between the college-ruled blue lines in my neatest handwriting.

It doesn't matter that I've never set foot in any of Fableland's parks before. I know each one, inside and out. I can recite every Fable Industry movie by heart. I've read Sam Casterman's biographies so many times I've lost count. I've even dabbled in a little *Sunspark* fan fiction (Elorra and Oliver are OTP forever).

With Tess and Issy at my side, there's no way I won't win. Getting into this contest is fate, a tiny slice of Fableland magic that came bursting into my life at the moment I needed it most.

My fingers itch to glance at the clue again. *Just* to assure myself it's real. But my phone chirps with a text message from Tess before I can get the paper out of my pocket.

Tess
WE'VE GOT DUNKS AND DONUT HOLES. WHERE ARE YOU??
(2:40 PM)

Issy
I made sure they didn't put any jelly ones in the box!
(2:41 PM)

Lia
Still going through the mom checklist.
(2:42 PM)

Tess

(2:43 PM)

Issy
Hugging you virtually until you get here and I can hug you for real.
(2:44 PM)

Lia
I think we're winding down.
(2:44 PM)

Tess
GOOD BECAUSE WE NEED TO GET OPERATION FREEDOM UNDERWAY. IT'S OUR LAST HURRAH BEFORE COLLEGE, BABBBBBEEEEEYYYYYYY.
(2:45 PM)

 I eye the growing security line behind me, something hot and uncomfortable burning in my chest. From the moment I told my friends I got into the scavenger hunt, they've been more concerned about celebrating graduation than winning.

 But I'm not going to college. While they head off on a new adventure, I'll be living at home, working at the family furniture store, and suffering through lists like this with my mother daily. Fableland's contest is my one chance to change that. The prize money could give me a true taste of freedom. An opportunity to make some choices for myself, for once.

 "I should get in line if I'm going to make my flight," I say to my parents.

 Mom glances at my flip-flops. "Where are your socks?"

 "In my bag."

 "Lia, they make you take your shoes off." She squeaks out the words, a telltale sign she's about to spiral. Her cheeks pull in as she sucks their insides between her teeth, and there's no question she's making lists in her head of worst-case scenarios for going barefoot in an airport.

I angle my arm into my carry-on bag and fish around for my balled-up ankle socks. "Here, look." I toss them up and down like I'm juggling. "I'll put them on when I get to the front of the line."

A sigh whooshes from her lips.

This is why I haven't told her about the money yet. I don't know how she'll handle the possibility of me leaving. But that's a bridge to blow up when I win. For now, I'm happy to let my parents think the prize is a bunch of merchandise and one-of-a-kind swag. Thankfully, neither of them understands the workings of the fandom forums I frequent well enough to verify that.

I reach for her hands. "Everything will be fine, Mom. Just six days, then I'll be home."

My mother smiles. "Have fun." I know she means it, but her eyes are so wide she looks like someone's forcing the words out of her mouth.

I kiss her on the cheek and give Dad a hug, then wander to the end of the security line. My parents draw back a few feet and wave until I disappear into the crowd.

Laughter and chatter and the loud chew of X-ray conveyor belts usher me forward, and I suck in the longest breath, letting it fill my chest.

For the first time in weeks, I feel like I can breathe.

"Finally!"

Tess tackles me when I reach the gate. I swear she was a

linebacker in a former life. Tiny body, so much power. I have to brace myself to keep from toppling backward.

Her white skin is flushed with excitement, and her platinum-blond waves seem to have a life of their own. They crowd my face and smother my greeting as she squeezes me, but I'm too grateful for her apple-scented perfume and the way she hugs, like she's the only thing keeping you from dropping off a cliff, to do anything but laugh.

Issy's right behind her and envelops us with her tall frame, closing our perfect little circle. Her long dark hair is piled on her head in a topknot, and her olive-toned skin practically glows against the vibrant turquoise of her T-shirt. As always, she smells like the vanilla she dabs behind her ears every time she bakes. "You okay?" she asks me quietly. Her favorite phrase. She could be moments from drowning and she'd be yelling those words at everyone onshore.

I nod. "I am now."

There's nowhere I'd rather be after enduring a Mom Checklist than with Tess and Issy. They know I won't be able to sit still for a good ten minutes, my whole body humming, itching to move, like I'm trying to find an exit in a room with no doors or windows. Usually we'd go for a run, or have an impromptu dance party, or throw ourselves on Issy's trampoline, but the airport offers no such amenities, so they trail me as I pace circles around the rows of chairs.

The three of us have been certified ride or die since the second week of kindergarten, when Adam Schumacher dumped a jar of green paint over Issy's head, and Tess and I doused him in pink and purple in retaliation. None of us were allowed outside for recess the entire week, but it was worth it. The strongest friendships are born of petty vengeance.

We've been through all our best and worst times together, and I don't know what's going to happen when they leave for college. Will we still be *us* if our lives are no longer following the exact same trajectory?

My carry-on hits the floor with a *thump*, and I sit down in the middle of a row of empty seats. Tess flops into a chair across from me.

Time to stop worrying. I've seen what it does to my mother, how her thoughts transform the smallest issue into a black hole that swallows everything around it. I refuse to get caught up in that cycle. In mere hours, I will step into my favorite place on earth with my two best friends, and in six short days, I will win enough money to change my life. There's a smorgasbord of good stuff staring me in the face. A buffet of joy, if you will. I'm going to focus on that.

Taking a slow, deep breath, I silently recite the first clue of the scavenger hunt like it's a reset code: **Find the place where toast becomes bread and always adorned will be the royal head.**

Issy perches beside me and drags my carry-on between us, letting out an exaggerated huff at the weight. "What do you have in here? Bricks?"

"Among other things," I quip. Yanking the zipper down, I heft out a stack of five composition notebooks and set them in her lap, then pull the flap further open to get the manila envelope full of images and maps, which I offer to Tess, along with a Fableland visitor's guide. "This is most of my research."

The scavenger hunt was open to any member of Fableland's three biggest fan forums who is over eighteen. Everyone who got in was practically raised on Fable Industry's films and some of them visit the park multiple times a year. I need to be prepared.

Concern pulls at Issy's mouth as she skims the first notebook, pausing here and there to read a page. "You can recite most of this from memory."

"And you've read this"—Tess brandishes the guide's well-worn spine—"enough times that it's begging for death." As if agreeing, one of its middle pages flutters to the floor.

I snatch it up and fold the glossy paper delicately in my lap. "The more information I have, the better."

Issy wrings her hands on top of the stack of notebooks. "Lia," she says carefully, "you know we want you to win, right?"

"But you have, like, a one percent chance," Tess adds. "The odds aren't exactly in your favor."

Issy smacks Tess on the arm. "What Tess is *trying* to say is that we don't want to see you get your heart broken if, for some reason, things don't work out. We want you to have fun on this trip. We're going to your favorite place on earth!"

My chest tightens, but I refuse to let their words in. I *can* win this scavenger hunt. I *will*.

My whole life, Fable Industry has been a sanctuary. When I was little, its animated movies were a place of happiness and love where good always conquered evil and life made sense and even the darkest corners of the world held a spark of magic. As I got older, and my mom's anxiety worsened, I'd escape to those movies, or online to the lists upon lists of Fableland's myths and secrets. Reading about secret menu items and hidden spaces and fabled surprises—like the unicorn kept among the horses on Casterman's Carousel or the fountain so full of rings from every couple married in the park that it overflows with circles of gold, not water—helped remind me there was still magic out there.

"People beat bad odds all the time." Pulling a sudoku book out of my bag, I wave it at Tess. "I'm a puzzle master. And I practically have a PhD in Fableland. I mean, I had the first clue figured out in ten minutes." I didn't even have to consult my research.

Issy angles herself to face me fully. The airport's fluorescent bulbs illuminate the caramel highlights in her hair. "Just remember to have fun too, okay? If you want, we can find all the *Sunspark* Easter eggs and pretend we're in seventh grade again fangirling over Elorra and Oliver." I purse my lips, and Issy's hands squeeze into fists like she's afraid she's upset me. Her thumb fusses with the thin gold flower-chain ring on her index finger. I'd given both her and Tess one for Christmas in middle school, but Tess stopped wearing hers ages ago.

Tess nods emphatically, her long hair bouncing around her shoulders. "We *have* to go to that shop in Vale of Villainy with the weird food." She grabs my arm and shakes it. "And our hotel has that space-grotto-themed pool. How hot will we look lying out under the stars?"

I have to swallow the urge to remind her that most people don't see my plus-size body as *hot*. "I want to do all those things," I say instead. "But I also want to win. You know what this could mean for me."

"Real freedom," Issy says, echoing my mantra of the past few weeks.

"We just don't want you to be disappointed," Tess insists.

I appreciate their concern, but that scenario—and any other where the scavenger hunt doesn't end with me winning the money—doesn't exist. If I don't consider it, it can't happen. I plan to sway the orbit of the universe with my eternal optimism.

The power of positive thinking and all that.

Before I can respond, a woman's voice bursts from the overhead speaker. "Ladies and gentlemen, we will now begin boarding flight 327 to Orlando, Florida. Any passengers who have requested extra boarding time may proceed to the gate area." Abandoning our seats, the three of us cram together at the corner of the gate to wait impatiently for our boarding group to be called.

I let out another breath. It's almost here. Six days of freedom. Six days to win this contest. No parents. No curfews. No worries. A smile takes over my face. It infects Issy next, and then Tess.

We leave our questions and worries at the gate. Shedding them like an old skin or an outdated outfit.

When the gate agent invites everyone else to board, Tess lets out a squeal. We brandish our boarding passes and step onto the bridge, our steps shaking the flimsy structure as Tess proclaims, "Let Operation Freedom commence!"

CHAPTER 2

June 18

**Starshatter Hotel, Fableland
Orlando, FL**

Nothing helps you beat the heat like Fableland's new Cartography app. Blending the wait time updates that have become a staple of amusement park apps with the latest in crowdsourcing and mapping features, Cartography will, quite literally, plan your day for you. Just tell it what rides you can't miss and where you want to eat and shop, and it will map the park to ensure the shortest wait times and least amount of walking. All you have to do is let GPS lead the way!

—BuzzTech's Top 10 Apps List

* * *

"HOLY CRAP, LOOK AT THIS PLACE."

Tess stops beside me, taking in the large banquet hall with her jaw hanging open. Issy flanks her, eyes wide as planets. Above our heads a sparkling blue, white, and gold banner (Fableland's signature colors) welcomes Superfan Scavenger Hunt contestants.

In the information packet I'd received, the welcome event was described as a small gathering to give contestants a chance to meet and learn the basic rules of the scavenger hunt. I'd expected some appetizers, a few small tables to sit and eat at, and some Fableland employees floating around, greeting newcomers and handing out guidelines.

I should have known better. Fable Industry never does anything "small." Especially not to celebrate a milestone anniversary.

Booths have been set up throughout the space. Each offers different Fableland merchandise, from mugs to clothing to enamel pins and stickers and key chains to posters and artwork, all special editions available only for this event. Tables fill the center of the room, their round tops draped in delicate gray cloths and decorated with blown-glass planets surrounded by tea lights. A buffet with nearly twenty different chafing dishes and every kind of salad, bread, and dessert you can think of stretches in front of a large stage.

If this is a taste of what's coming this week, it's going to be more than I could have dreamed of.

"What do we do first?" I ask.

"Merch," Tess declares at the same time Issy says, "Eat."

I, of course, want to head straight for the contest info booth. The details of the scavenger hunt have been kept securely under wraps for the past few months. No one on F³ has uncovered any hints about the rules or how you win. I'm dying to hear more so I can strategize.

I wish Tess and Issy were as invested in me winning. But I don't need them to read a pamphlet. I can handle that on my own. "Divide and conquer?" I suggest.

Tess runs off toward the enamel-pin booth. Meanwhile, Issy has her phone out and is already recording for her foodie YouTube channel as she makes her way to the buffet.

I head left to the information booth. A girl with a blond pixie cut and a purple uniform that looks like a space suit sits behind the table. She checks my name off a list on her tablet, then smiles and hands me a small booklet and a large pin.

"Directions for downloading the app are on page one. You'll need your phone to compete in the scavenger hunt, so make sure to keep it charged or to visit one of our many complimentary charging stations in the parks."

My parents recently upgraded my phone because the old one could barely hold a charge for a few hours. I know it's so they can keep better tabs on me, but right now, I'm grateful. It will give me an edge to have a battery I can rely on.

The girl points to the pin in my hand, which takes up most of my palm. It's circular and has a yellow background with a white rendition of Percivel Night's insignia—a crescent moon with a sword struck through it—at the center. The word *Superfan* is written below the symbol in fancy blue lettering. "Make sure you wear that at all times in the parks. It's how we'll identify you as part of the contest."

I nod and secure the pin to the strap of my tank top as I step aside. After downloading the app to my home screen, I fill out all the necessary information to sign up. As soon as I'm done, I open it and poke around, hoping to discover more surprises, but there's not much there. Just another place to find the rules as well as the first clue.

Every time I inhale, a new delicious smell invades my senses, and the excited chatter around me has gotten louder as more people arrive. The sounds thrum through my bones like the bass of a really good song.

I'm surrounded by so many people who love this place as much as me. Some of them look my age, others older. One of the tables is occupied by a group of girls talking loudly and laughing over half-full wineglasses. I see parents doting on their kids as they fill their bags with merch. Couples wander the room holding hands. At the buffet, Issy is trapped behind two college-age guys with their contestant pins fixed to the sides of their baseball caps who are stacking their plates dangerously high with food. Everyone's wearing Fableland-themed clothing or singing along with Fable Industry's signature songs blasting from the speakers.

How am I here? At *Fableland*? And not even as a guest, but as a *VIP*. I can't wait to try everything at the buffet and grab any *Sunspark* special edition merchandise they have.

It would be cool, too, to meet some other contestants. Make a few new friends who understand how I feel about this place and its movies.

But first, I need to figure out how I'm going to win.

My eyes scan the rules as I make my way around the edge of the banquet hall.

It looks like there will be three clues a day. Each will lead us to a new location, where there will be a QR code to scan. Beyond that, there doesn't seem to be much to the rules. Just the basics: no getting hints or help from the staff, no interfering in someone else's attempts to scan the codes or get around the parks, absolutely no violence or misbehavior.

The most important thing, though, is that timing matters. Each day there will be fewer and fewer people moving forward. I memorize the numbers, whispering them to myself.

> Day 1: 95 people
>
> Day 2: 70 people
>
> Day 3: 60 people
>
> Day 4: 50 people
>
> Day 5: 25 people
>
> Day 6: 1 winner

Tess and Issy aren't contestants and they can't win the prize, but I hope they'll be willing to prioritize the scavenger hunt for me over everything else we want to do. There should still be plenty of time to explore, even if we're chasing clues in the morning. The marketing team wants contestants to spend time in the parks and blast social media with photos and updates. At least, that's what the handbook says.

I'm trying to come up with ways to convince them of this when I'm suddenly no longer vertical. My hands and knees hit the floor with a painful *thump,* and I can't help but groan. Hardwood and bare skin are not friends.

Sitting up, I glance around to see what I tripped on. A guy occupying the table closest to me has his chair pushed out to accommodate his long, long legs.

My cheeks go up in flames. I was pretty focused on my phone, and I must have caught my foot on the leg of his chair when I walked by.

I clear my throat. "Uh, sorry about that."

He doesn't react. His whole body is curled in toward the book splayed open in his hands.

I cough this time.

No response.

Now I'm staring. And still sitting on the floor. I can't help it. The more he seems not to notice, the more openly I gape at him. His stillness is like the eye of a hurricane, a blip in the Matrix, so out of place in the noise and color and commotion around us.

"You might want to push in your chair." I usually have a quiet voice, but I say it as loudly as I can. What Tess would call "with my whole chest."

That finally breaks the guy's trance, and he turns to me. He's got one of those faces that should be staring out at you from a big screen or brooding in the shadows of those paranormal romances that make Issy die from swooning. All square jaw and cheekbones and a straight nose and sun-kissed skin. His mouth has a natural downturn that makes him look like he's constantly ruminating on something. When his eyes meet mine, they shine like shards of glass. I can't tell if they're blue or gray or a really unique shade of brown.

I have to swallow a frustrated sigh. Of course he's ridiculous levels of hot. We normal-looking people have situational awareness. We know where to put our chairs.

"Why are you on the floor?" There's no judgment in his deep voice, just confusion.

"I think you mean, 'Are you okay?'" I mutter as I climb to my feet. I'm not proud of the way my entire body short-circuited the moment he looked at me. I should have stood up ages ago. "That's typically the response when you trip someone."

"I didn't—"

I point emphatically at his chair. Although he stays silent, a chastised look settles across his brow as he glances behind him. He runs a hand idly over the open pages of his book, the cover flat against the table so I can't see it.

I cross my arms over my chest. "What are you reading that's so interesting?" Imagine being so oblivious to what's happening that you aren't aware of crowds of people falling over your chair. (To preserve my dignity, I refuse to believe I'm the only one to do so.)

He peers down at his book, and his jaw tightens. I wonder for a moment if he's not going to tell me. Like it's somehow too personal or top secret.

But then Tess calls my name. A second later, she's at my side, her arms weighed down with overflowing tote bags. She waves them at me. "This was all free!"

She zones in on the guy at the table, and a mischievous grin spreads over her face. That expression means nothing but trouble.

"Well, hello," she says. "Who's this?"

I'm already spinning her around and pushing her away. "Another contestant."

He doesn't have any swag bags and his pin is fixed low enough on his shirt that it's barely visible. Almost like he doesn't want to be here.

Still, I turn back. I can't help it. He's a superfan, like me. The first one I've encountered outside the internet since middle school. Our eyes meet, and the intensity of his gaze jolts my heart out of rhythm.

"I'm Lia," I say. My wild pulse almost makes me stumble over my own name.

"Mason," he says softly. Then he's immersed in his book again like he never looked away.

His name echoes in my head as I shepherd Tess toward Issy, who has found a table near the entrance. I don't know why I can't stop thinking about it. It's not that unique a name, and it's not like he did anything but give me a nice introduction to the floor. Besides, I'm not here to meet someone. I'm here to win a contest that could change my life.

And Mason is one of the people standing in my way.

I manage not to think about him again until I'm sitting with my friends, the heaping plate of food in front of me making my mouth water. I survey the crowd, trying to identify who might be my biggest competition. The nonbinary person with the Percivel Night tattoo on their shoulder? The couple wearing matching Dudley the Raccoon headbands? The team that looks like a mom and a daughter quizzing each other at the table behind me?

The superhot guy with no chair etiquette?

My gaze flicks in the direction of Mason's table, but it's empty.

"I thought the app did all that?" Issy says.

An hour later, we're finally settled into our room for the night, our stomachs full to the brim and one of the queen beds smothered in swag. Issy and I have collapsed on the other bed, while Tess lies among the maps she's strewn over the floor.

Tess scoffs. "Cartography's for amateurs."

"Or people who want to get around the parks efficiently." I flash her a smile as I get up and wander over to the window.

Our resort is named after the Starshatter, a ship from Fable Industry's blockbuster animated film about two kids and their dog who befriend an alien and save the galaxy from annihilation. The hotel has been constructed in its likeness, with a glass dome ceiling tinted and strung with twinkle lights in the shape of constellations so it feels like we're floating in space.

"This is not about efficiency." Tess has her tongue jammed between her lips and she's poring over the map for Phoenix's Landing—Fableland's oldest and most iconic park. Her pen hovers an inch above the glossy paper as she sketches invisible lines over the images. "This is about immersion. We only have six days and we're doing it all. At every park. So I'm trying to find the best way." She narrows her eyes, then scribbles something in the notebook beside her. Lying on her stomach, her legs bent at the knee, she gives her right foot a little kick every time she gets an idea.

"You know we have to head to Dudley's Tailspin for my first clue before we do any of . . . this." I point to her plans with an open hand.

Tess spins one of her curls around her pen. "It's probably okay if you're not there *first* thing."

"It's not. The rules make clear that people are going to be cut every day. I can't chance getting to any of the clues too late."

Issy shakes her head. "I don't even understand how you figured this one out so fast. I tried searching those phrases online forever and got nothing."

"It's like a riddle." I lean against the window, its glass pleasantly cold from the air-conditioning. "Bread becomes toast in a toaster—"

"But what about an oven?" Tess suggests. "You can toast bread in there too. Or on a frying pan."

"Sure, but can you think of any significant frying pans or ovens from the Fable Industry movies?"

Tess shrugs. "I haven't seen any of the latest ones."

The answer's no. I've watched every Fable Industry movie multiple times, and I pored over my notes and checked F^3 the other night just to be sure. "The third Dudley movie has a toaster. One that time-travels. That would explain how toast becomes bread." From there it was simple enough. The clue is about the Dudley films, and the first one involves Dudley and his sidekick Squirt the Squirrel stealing back some crown jewels, which are something that would definitely adorn a royal head.

"Yeah, but how do you know we need to go to the roller coaster?" Tess points to the map. "That entire section of Phoenix's Landing is Dudley themed."

"Because that's the only place where both the crown and the toaster can be found together." There's a hidden elevator shaft in the queue for Dudley's Tailspin that houses every item Dudley and Squirt have stolen.

Tess makes a face and cuts her eyes back to her itinerary. My gaze follows hers to the maps, tracing over place after place that I've imagined for a decade. In the morning, they'll become real. My heart speeds up a little. It's like I'm standing in the same room as a celebrity.

There was a time when Tess and Issy were as wrapped up in Fableland as I was. By the end of sixth grade, we'd papered Issy's walls with lists of the parks' secrets and had watched every Fable Industry movie to the point that they replayed in our dreams. One rainy night in April, while the three of us were squashed onto Issy's bed watching the end of *Sunspark* for easily the hundredth time (Elorra and Oliver have the *best* kiss), Issy whispered, "We should do it."

Tess's eyebrows quirked. "Kiss?"

"No." Issy hit her in the face with a pillow. "Visit Fableland. Find Elorra's lab"—she jabbed her finger at one of the sheets of paper on her wall—"and the tree and the sunspark."

"And all the other Easter eggs," I added.

Tess's face went bright with scheming. "After senior year. A post-high-school-survival celebration."

Issy's grin spread wide. "A precollege blowout."

I cheered. Back then, I thought college was an option for me, too.

But as we got older, their lives got bigger. There were fewer movie nights and more parties. Issy repainted her walls a neutral cream and the Fable Industry memorabilia was replaced with food layouts from cooking magazines and recipes she wanted to try. Tess became a field hockey, softball, and mathlete star; Issy launched her YouTube channel and began staging most weekends in the fine-dining restaurant of a family friend. Every year, more paths opened up for them, while I dug deeper into Fableland as my parents hung up Employee of the Year plaques with my face and designed my "manager" apron and named a collection of bedroom furniture after me. All of it solidifying the one-way street I couldn't escape.

Now I'm the only one who still cares about the parks or *Sunspark* or any of it. I'm not even sure Tess and Issy remember that promise we made or realize that we're about to fulfill it.

I pin a smile to my face and try to pump enthusiasm into my body. It doesn't matter if we're here for the same reasons or not. We're at *Fableland,* and I plan to make the most of every second.

"I can head over to Dudley's Tailspin in the morning while you two ride the Moon Drop."

Tess gasps. "You can't skip the free fall!"

"Or the moon pies at the shop next door!" Issy adds. She shifts to the center of the bed and folds her long legs under her. "What if we wing it?" She traces the starred pattern of the comforter with her index finger, her eyes glued to the fabric.

From the look of horror Tess shoots her, you'd think Issy confessed to eating puppies. "Pardon me?"

"We can figure it out as we go. Hit all Lia's clues and see

everything in the parks. We're on vacation. We don't need to plan every second."

Tess's eyes are wide pools of mahogany brown. "You're a monster."

My phone beeps with a new message, so I leave them to bicker and curl up in an armchair beside the small desk. I don't need to look at the screen to know who it's from.

Mom
Everything okay?
(8:30 PM)

Lia
Yes. It's only been an hour. We haven't left the hotel.
(8:33 PM)

Mom
I know but I wanted to make sure you're still okay.
(8:34 PM)

Yep. We've only gotten mugged twice since we last spoke.

Everything's great! Our neighbors in the hotel have already offered us booze and drugs.

I erase both responses as quickly as I type them. My thumb jams so hard into my screen that my nail bends backward, a burst of pain racing to my knuckle. I wish humor worked for Mom as well as it does for me. It's like defusing a bomb, preventing my frustration from blasting out of my skin.

Issy walks over to the chair and curls up on the floor, then rests her head against my leg to stop its bouncing. She peers up at me. "Placate her. Then you can do whatever you want."

"Operation Freedom," I mutter as I type.

Lia
Yep. We're settling in to watch a movie and then get some sleep. Early wake-up tomorrow.
(8:40 PM)

Mom
That sounds fun.
(8:41 PM)

Mom
Make sure you call a lot.
(8:48 PM)

I know what a lot means for her. Every hour. More than that if I can. But it's not exactly a parent-free experience if I spend more time talking to my mother than going on rides.

My leg starts to dance hard enough that I knock poor Issy in the head. She doesn't move, only hugs my calf instead, like she can keep me still. Help me find some calm.

Rationally, I know my mom can't always control her bad thoughts. And I don't want her to worry. I want her to be okay. But I need a break. That's what this trip is supposed to be. A momentary oasis from that house where it feels like a hand is perpetually pressed over my mouth and nose. Stifling all my oxygen. Smothering me.

As I watch those three ellipses blink in response to her typing, no doubt to offer some other way to make sure I'm in constant contact with her, it feels like that hand is still grabbing for me, even hundreds of miles away.

Lia
I'll be okay, Mom. I will check in, morning and evening. I promise.
(8:53 PM)

Lia
I love you.
(8:54 PM)

Mom
I love you too, pumpkin. Kisses to the girls.
(8:55 PM)

Across the room, Tess watches me from her mess of maps. "Is the new medication not helping?"

I shrug. "It's gotten her panic attacks under control, but her compulsions are still there. Her doctor wants to give it a few more months before they try something else." Which means who knows how many more weeks of me shouldering all her worries.

I spend an unnecessary amount of time plugging in my phone before shoving our swag to the floor and flopping across the empty bed. My shoulders are so tense they're practically pinned together.

Issy's brown eyes are wide. "I'm so sorry, Lia."

I hold out my hands in a silent *oh well*. The soft light of the bedside lamp makes the sparkles in my silver polish glisten like the twinkle lights wreathing the Starshatter Hotel. "It's not your fault. It's not really hers either, which is what makes it so hard. I have nowhere to put all this. . . ." I shrug hard against the mattress.

Before graduation, I at least had volleyball. Games gave me something else to focus on, and spiking and serving the ball as hard as I could often felt like relief. Sometimes, I'd sneak into the gym early and kick balls against the wall until I'd worked up enough sweat to need a shower. Coach Christie caught me once, but she let me keep at it without a word. After that day, there was always an army of soccer balls waiting to greet me when I arrived in the morning.

But that's over now, and the only thing I can do with my anger is swallow it. Or try to drown it in the things I love. Like my friends. And Fableland. That's what I want to think about right now.

Tess lies back down on the floor and makes a show of gathering her notebook and crossing out tomorrow morning's itinerary. With a smile, she declares, "Dudley's Tailspin, first thing, it is!"

I let my mind wander as she revises her plans. I imagine the wind in my hair as we zoom around a roller-coaster track. I picture my arms in the air as we dip over one of those huge drops. I dream about the stories I've loved my whole life coming alive around me. That's all it takes to slow my heart, dash away my racing thoughts.

Fableland truly is made of magic.

Issy leans over the bed to peer at Tess's notes. "Do you really think it's wise to do Chester's Infinite Climb right after lunch?"

Tess has made a priority list for the morning (with my clues at the top), and the rest of the day is planned down to the minute. "Winging it" only goes so far with her.

"That thing has two massive drops and some wicked corkscrews," I point out. Even the "ride with me" videos make me queasy.

Tess shakes her head. "According to FableWiki, the line for

Chester is never less than an hour. We'll have plenty of digestion time."

I guzzle some water and settle into the wall of pillows I've stacked against the headboard. "If my lunch decides to revisit, I plan to make you the target."

Tess nods with exaggerated seriousness. "I accept this fate."

"I guess we're done, then, right? Tomorrow's all set?" Issy picks up the clicker and aims it at the TV. "This romance movie isn't going to watch itself."

"Wait. There's one more thing." Tess points a finger in the air.

"How is that possible?" Issy waves at the stacks of maps folded neatly next to my piles of research. "You've prepared for every possible scenario or alternate dimension."

"Seriously," I add. "I'm surprised you don't have an action plan for if Godzilla shows up."

"Kaiju attacks are obviously covered in my emergency protocol," Tess says. I can't tell if she's joking. "But we need a plan for when one of you meets someone. Do you want chaperones? Space? Do we initiate girl code?"

"Tess," Issy groans.

"I know. I know. You like being 'chronically' single." Her sigh is long and dramatic. "But let's be serious. We're on vacation, and this park gets an average of fifty thousand visitors a day. Odds are, at least one of you is going to stumble upon someone . . . interesting." She waggles her eyebrows with that last word.

I snort. "Girls like me don't meet people just walking around." Which was exactly how Tess met her current girlfriend, Grace. They were at Target, both of them in the office supply aisle, Grace looking for planners, Tess searching for the best pens. Their eyes met, and that was it. It's been almost a year, and they're still going strong. They're even going to try to make it work at different colleges.

But people don't see me the way they see Tess and Issy.

"What do you mean 'girls like me'?" Tess demands, as if we haven't had this conversation a million times.

I pick at an invisible piece of lint on my leggings. "Fat girls."

"Screw that, you're not fat," Tess says with a scowl.

Issy reaches across from the other bed to squeeze my arm. "Lia, you know I hate when you use that word. It's so ugly. And so not true."

Except it is. I *am* fat. My body has fat on it. And when they insist otherwise—like they always do—it feels disingenuous, whether they mean it to or not. Just like when we go shopping at straight-size stores and they ask me if I found anything cute, when they *have* to be aware that nothing in the store fits me.

I swallow against the words bubbling up my throat. My friends mean well, but they've been thin their whole lives. They don't understand what it's like to live in a body that is viewed as too much, as unhealthy, as gross. It's so rare to see someone who looks like me on TV or in a movie or a book who isn't trying to lose weight or always stuffing their faces. Even in my favorite Fable Industry movies, the rounder characters are always the butt of a joke or the villain.

If I win this money, I want to get a job in the company's film division and find a way to pitch a story about a fat princess with the brains of Elorra and the style and confidence of Regina from *Percivel Night*. I want little kids to see that plus-size people do more than eat or trip over themselves or make jokes. We can be love interests. Heroes. Geniuses. We can go on quests and solve riddles and vanquish the villain and save the world as well as any thin person.

We can get into contests and win.

"The last thing I need right now is some kind of vacation fling. I can't let anything derail me from this contest."

"Okay, but what about that hot guy you were talking to at the welcome event?" Tess jabs her hands onto her hips. "You weren't exactly in a rush to get away from him."

My back stiffens. "I wanted to know what he was reading." And how he managed not to notice that I fell over his chair. Dwelling on how attractive Mason is and how tall he must be and how his eyes are all the colors at once is not going to help me win. "Plus, he's going to be my competition."

"Rivals to lovers!" Issy yells, thrusting her hands into the air. I toss a pillow at her head.

Tess sighs and unfolds herself from the floor. "I think you're putting too much pressure on all this. You have a solid job waiting for you. No student loans. No rent. No matter what happens, you're good."

I fight off a cringe. "I don't want that to be my forever, though." I'm not sure I even want it to be my right now.

"What do you want?" Issy asks quietly.

"This." I wave around me, hoping it's enough of an explanation for now. I never talk about this out loud. I rarely let the thought pass through my own head fully formed before chasing it away. It feels like such a betrayal of my parents, to not want this thing they've worked so hard to give me. But I don't. "So no hot strangers for Lia."

"Or Issy," she echoes.

The smirk on Tess's face tells me she's not done. "Not even if it's the Elorra or Oliver performers?" she asks with a wink.

This is what I get for admitting to them that I thought Elorra was pretty hot for a cartoon. Beyond labeling myself "not quite straight," I'm still figuring things out, but Tess is convinced I'm one Elorra cosplayer away from my bi-awakening.

She looks primed to keep this conversation going into infinity, so I kick out my legs and grab for the remote. "Don't we have a rom-com to watch?" According to the description, this one has some of my favorite things: a second-chance romance, academic rivals, and book nerds.

I'm convinced there are few things more attractive than a person who likes to read. It's never been lost on me that both Elorra *and* Oliver have countless books crammed in their pockets and jackets the entire movie. Sure, Oliver stole his, but all the same. Hot.

The thought only causes my mind to drift back to Mason and *his* book. I shake my head to chase him away. I meant what I said. No distractions.

No plans but winning.

CHAPTER 3

June 19

Phoenix's Landing, Fableland
Orlando, FL

      ELORRA
Love gets in the way of more-important stuff.
[Off-screen in the laboratory, explosion.]

     QUEEN MAE
(cringes at the sound while waving away some smoke)
Maybe a distraction would do you good.

—*Sunspark (00:10:21)*

"WHAT DID PEOPLE DO AT AMUSEMENT PARKS BEFORE CELL phones?"

Tess swipes her finger across another row of jewel-toned

candies on her screen. When the person in front of her inches forward, she matches their pace by sliding along the metal railing.

It's been half an hour, but the line for Dudley's Tailspin still snakes around two more corners before entering the first indoor queuing area.

Above our heads, large fans spray mists of water to battle the heat, and the roof provides some sanctuary from Florida's sun. The railings that hem us in are crowded on all sides by carts overflowing with luggage and plastic taxicabs and cars. *Dudley's Tailspin* was one of Fable Industry's first movies—it featured an anthropomorphic raccoon thief turned hero who steals planes to thwart heists—and the whole ride is themed like an airport. The roller coaster has a nose capped with a propeller and wings as if it were a plane, and it's supposed to do enough tight barrel rolls to make you feel like you're flying.

I watch one of the cars zoom past before disappearing toward the sky. "Die of boredom?" I suggest.

Tess huffs appreciatively without looking up.

Beside her, Issy is absorbed in her social media, her red nails flying across her screen's keyboard. She's cultivated quite a following since she launched her Issy Will Cook Anything video series, and no doubt she's in the middle of some heated debate about the best method of hacking up a chicken or some other food-related thing. Ever since she started the series, she's been so much happier and more confident. I wish it were something I could share with her, but opening up a pudding cup without tearing the foil is Michelin-star-level cooking in my house.

As we fall back into silence, I resume my search of the walls, corners, anything big enough to hold the elevator shaft that conceals Dudley's stash. The problem is I don't know exactly what to look for. I may have studied every secret in the four parks that make up Fableland, but I've never seen them with my own eyes, only in pictures online, half of which are so zoomed in it's impossible to tell where in the queue the photo was taken. And the rest are so grainy I'm convinced they were shot with a potato rather than a camera.

"Do you see it yet?" I push up on my tiptoes to peek over the supertall dad standing in the next row.

"See what?" Tess asks.

"The elevator. Dudley's stash." I wave my hand at the queue. "The whole reason we're here." Every second that we're stuck in this line, my heart slams a little faster against my rib cage. It feels like it's beating in time to all the seconds I'm losing as we wait.

The reasonable part of me knows that we entered the park the minute it opened, and the odds that ninety-nine people got here before us are slim to none, but it's hard to be rational when it feels like your entire life is on the line. I'm desperate to scan that QR code and set the contest in motion.

"Shit. Right." Issy jams her phone in her pocket and glances around. When Tess doesn't do the same, she gives her a kick in the shin.

"Good God, woman, let me finish this round," Tess mutters. Her small mouth dips into a frown as she rubs her ankle with her free hand.

Their apathy causes a twinge in my chest. I cross my arms to chase it away.

When we finally pass over the threshold into the first indoor queue, we're assaulted by color and music as various animatronic versions of Dudley and Squirt trample suitcases on the luggage claim conveyor belt, hop the security line, and scuttle across the tarmac toward an unattended plane. The cool fingers of overworked air-conditioning trace across my skin, helping dry up three pools' worth of sweat.

More metal railings guide us forward. My eyes strain to see past everyone ahead of us in line. I wish I was taller. Or everyone else was shorter. Or they made comfortable sneakers with four-inch heels.

It takes some jumping and impressive tiptoe balancing, but eventually I catch sight of an elevator shaft on the opposite side of the room. Our timing could not be more perfect, because as I watch, its two doors yawn slowly open.

I strangle a squeal of excitement and dig for my phone. My pulse has ramped up, making my hands shake. This is it. The first clue.

"Let's go." I wave at Tess and Issy.

Tess peers up at me. "Where?"

"I found it." I point toward the elevator.

Issy claps her hands. "Oh my God. Go get it!"

"You're not going to come?" I frown.

Tess shakes her head. "We need to keep our place in line. We didn't wait over half an hour to not go on the ride, right?"

She has a point.

Issy grabs my arm and gives it a shake. "We need to hear all about it when you get back. Every. Detail."

I can't linger any longer to see if they'll change their minds. If the doors to the elevator close, I don't know when they will open again. It could be ten minutes. It could be an hour. From what I've read, the elevator was built to be as chaotic as Dudley. I can't chance wasting that kind of time.

The railings that herd the crowd through the room are tightly packed, so the only way to reach the elevator is to get to the walls. My muscles tense as I look around for an exit strategy.

The space between the railing's bars is too thin for me to squeeze through, but the railing itself is a little too high to climb over without it turning into a spectacle. The last thing I need is to become a meme or go viral because someone recorded me clumsily vaulting over it or getting stuck between its bars. I hate that being plus size means going unnoticed until you don't want to be. Anything embarrassing becomes twice as funny to the rest of the world when you're fat.

Thankfully, there's a break in the bars up ahead, so I creep forward, apologizing to every person I bump into as I hold my breath to make myself as small as possible.

The moment I'm free, my heart starts screaming in my chest.

This is actually happening. It's real. Money, new future, here I come.

The elevator doors are still open when I make it across the room, but there's someone already there. He's crouched near the right door. I spot the QR code as he scans it. At the beep of his phone, my stomach drops like I'm in a free fall.

I saw all the people at the welcome event yesterday. I know I'm not in this contest alone. But seeing someone else in action—seeing them get to the first QR code *before* me—ignites a bonfire of panic in my chest.

I'm already losing and I haven't even started yet.

I don't want to be a creep, but I can't help inching closer to him. My hands itch as if I'm going to break into hives if I have to wait a minute longer.

Finally, after what feels like the length of two Fable Industry films, the guy rises, his body unfolding until he reaches his full height. As my eyes drift over the backward baseball hat and then his face, recognition kicks me in the teeth.

I can't stop the gasp that rushes from my mouth.

He glances over at the sound, and a small smile lifts his lips. "Hey. Lia, right?"

Why does he remember my name?

My brain turns to mush and churns out the first coherent thought I have. Which, let's be honest, is not actually that coherent. "Find the place where toast becomes bread and always adorned will be the royal head."

One thick eyebrow creeps up his forehead. "Yep, you found it."

I can't believe I just recited a random riddle to him like some off-brand version of Romeo. Squatting to scan the code, I try to laugh, but in my head it sounds like a nervous cackle. "Sorry. That was weird." I shrug. "I guess I didn't realize how worried I was about getting the first clue until I got here."

"Makes sense." His voice is so soft I can barely hear it over the noise. "There's a lot riding on this."

He has no idea.

I aim my phone's camera at the black-and-white square. Above me, Dudley yells his various catchphrases at Squirt as he teeters atop the pile of stolen goods. My hands tremble and it takes me a minute to hold my phone still enough to catch the code. Being here, so close to the stories that have given me solace my whole life, makes me feel light and heady, like I can't quite anchor myself to the ground.

Finally, there's a telltale beep, assuring me I've captured the code, and I stand back up. The Scavenger app blinks, setting a buffering wheel spinning. A second later, an icon that looks like a scroll with the number 2 at the center appears on the screen. I click it, the gears in my head whirling before I even see the words.

Find the ball of fluff with the sparkle inside.

A smile overtakes my face. Another easy one. Obviously, it's Smokey, Princess Regina's dog from *Percivel Night*. At the beginning of the movie, Smokey swallows the Reddingshire jewels, then runs away, forcing Regina to leave in search for him, just days before her coronation.

I cast a glance over my shoulder. Reddingshire Castle, with its white marble turrets, spikes high into the bright-blue sky, the park's welcoming beacon. According to my notes, Smokey's in there, but the accounts as to where are conflicting.

"You good?" Mason's voice breaks through my thoughts. When I turn my gaze back to him, he nods down at my phone.

"Oh, uh, yeah," I mumble.

"Did you figure out the clue?"

My first instinct is to admit I don't know where to find Smokey, but then it hits me. Mason is my competition. Just because he's attractive enough to make my brain malfunction doesn't mean I should share my secrets. We're not on the same team.

I tip my chin up. "Obviously."

I should have brought my notebooks with me. I thought we'd have time last night to work out the clues, and I can't remember where the different forums said Smokey could be found. Some are more legit than others.

Mason has one of those heavy gazes that settles right against your skin, and he hasn't looked away from me yet. My expression must betray my worry because he asks, "You okay?" His voice brushes against me like a flutter of wings.

"Yep. Just strategizing." I put on a smile, even as my hand grips my phone a little harder.

Tess has begrudgingly accepted that this scavenger hunt is going to clash with her plans, but I can't imagine she and Issy are going to be jazzed about spending the day wandering one of the park's least exciting attractions in search of a small animatronic dog. It's another unpleasant reminder that we're not at Fableland for the same reasons.

Mason's head tilts. His expression is stoic and impossible to interpret through my haze of worry. "Have you been here a lot?" he asks.

I shake my head. "This is actually my first time."

"You must be some superfan to win a spot in this contest without ever visiting the parks."

I shrug. "You just had to answer some questions and be one of the first one hundred people to submit the correct answers."

He reaches for the back of his hat and idly adjusts the brim against his neck. "The questions weren't easy."

"I guess I know a lot about this place."

I hate being humble, but most people side-eye an eighteen-year-old—practically an adult—who still loves cartoons and make-believe as much as I do. The negative attention I get for my body is bad enough: I don't need any additional grief for my interests. So with everyone who's not Tess and Issy, I tamp my enthusiasm down to a low rumble, even if it feels like I'm tamping down my soul a little too.

Mason smiles. It's far from mocking, just a shy curling of his lips. A dimple flares in his cheek, and another set of wings takes flight in my stomach.

Maybe he doesn't think I'm such a dork. I mean, he's in this contest too. He must understand the magic of this place.

His eyes are still pinned on me. I'm not sure I've seen him blink.

"Well"—I wave to the elevator doors, which have begun to slide closed—"good luck?"

I turn away, but his voice freezes me in place. "Do you want me to show you?"

I look back at him. "Show me?"

"Where to find the next clue?"

I smile tightly. "No thanks. Like I said, I'm good."

This guy. First he manspreads all over the welcome room. Now he's assuming I have no idea where I'm going (sure, it might be true, but that's beside the point). Didn't he marvel at my knowledge of the parks a second ago?

"*Super* superfan, remember?" I point to myself. It takes an absurd amount of effort to sound breezy.

He pulls his cell phone out of his pocket and checks the time. It's the model of phone I had years ago, when I got my first one in junior high. That unreadable expression has returned to his face. "Maybe I'll see you there, then."

My eyes drift back to the line for the ride. Tess and Issy have barely moved forward a few feet. They're going to hire top-notch assassins to take me out when I tell them we have to go.

"What?" Mason asks.

"My friends are still in line." I sigh.

"You know you get unlimited front-of-the-line passes for you and your guests as part of the contest, right?"

My gaze snaps back to Mason's face. "What?" I studied all the information I got about the contest. Read every email a thousand times. How did I miss this?

He steps closer, his shadow swallowing me. "It's in the app. Click the icon that looks like a gift box. Something new pops up in there after every clue. The passes are for clue one."

I still want to kick him for second-guessing me, but now I want to hug him too. Tess won't be able to complain, no matter how much time I need to find clues, if we're able to walk onto any ride she wants. "Thanks." I smile for real this time. Mason didn't have to share that with me. I would have found the rewards eventually, but he could have secured himself a lead for a little while.

And he offered to help me find clue two. It's like he doesn't know what a competition is.

He nods. "You're welcome, Lia."

I fight off a shiver. "I guess I'll see you around."

"I hope so," he says. Then he wanders off, leaving me staring at his back, wondering if he meant it.

CHAPTER 4

June 19

**Phoenix's Landing, Fableland
Orlando, FL**

One of the first attractions open to the public in Phoenix's Landing was the walk-through of Reddingshire Castle. An exact replica of Princess Regina's home from Fable Industry's first major blockbuster, *Percivel Night*, this attraction allowed fans to experience iconic scenes from the film happening around, above, and below them as they made their way through the castle halls. While by modern standards the animatronics seem hokey and out of date, they were state of the art when the park first opened, causing some park attendees to pass out from fear or surprise.

—Fableland, 50th-Anniversary Documentary

IT'S BARELY TEN IN THE MORNING, BUT THE AIR BRIMS WITH THE scents of cinnamon and cotton candy and buttery popcorn.

I can't help but inhale as I herd Issy and Tess through the exit of Dudley's Tailspin. Our feet clap loudly against the metal steps, almost drowning out their excited chatter about the ride's most epic twists and turns.

"What about you, Lia?" Issy's brown eyes are wide. "This must have felt huge. You just rode your first Fableland attraction!"

"It was amazing!" Hopefully, neither of them can tell how badly I'm faking my excitement. I barely remember the ride. Even though it's been less than fifteen minutes since I left Mason at Dudley's Stash (thank you, front-of-the-line passes), in my mind, hordes of scavenger hunt contestants have already found the three clues and secured their places for tomorrow.

Two people scurry by us, contestant pins prominently displayed on their shirts, and my stomach drops further. They're headed straight for Reddingshire Castle, which is where we need to be.

I pause for a second. "Is it okay if I focus on the next two clues before we hit more rides?" Before either of them can answer, I hastily add, "With our FOTL passes, we won't miss out on anything because of wait times, and I'll be able to enjoy myself so much more if I'm not worried about getting the clues on time." I concentrate on Issy so I can avoid witnessing Tess's expression. None of this was in her itinerary. "Five people are going to get eliminated today. That's five percent of the contestants." Maybe appealing to her love of statistics and numbers will soften the blow.

But when I finally sneak a look at her, Tess's gaze is caught by something over my shoulder. "Hot guy," she mumbles.

At least she didn't point.

"Tess, if I don't want to go on any other rides until I find the clues, then I definitely don't want to chase some random dude around the park."

"He's not random. You were talking to him yesterday at that welcome thing."

My body (or my lizard brain or whatever part of me refuses to listen to the logic in my head) betrays me, and I whirl around before I can think better of it. We've started walking again, and I find myself looking at Mason.

He's beside the red-umbrella-capped popcorn cart across the street, leaning against a fence. His baseball hat is spun forward, and his short sleeves are rolled up against the oppressive Florida sun, exposing solid biceps.

My heart pounds like the drum section of a marching band. What is he doing? He should be getting the second clue by now. Unless he's already finished for the day. Ushering me one step closer to elimination.

I grab Tess's arm and turn us around. The last thing I need is for him to see us gawking.

On my other side, Issy mimes a scream. "I'm about to watch a romance novel unfold."

"No distractions, remember?" I say. "This is not Operation Suck Face. It's Operation Freedom."

"But you do, don't you? Want to suck his face?" Tess's grin widens to the point I could count every one of her teeth.

God, please let her not start listing other body parts to suck. "I don't even know him."

"We can fix that," Issy points out. Beaming, she pretends to strut toward him.

I yank her back beside me, shaking my head. I don't have time for this.

As I hurry ahead, a sourness fills the pit of my stomach. We have to pass by Mason to get to the castle. It's the only way without backtracking.

He's probably going to gloat if he sees us.

And see us he does, because he falls into step with me as soon as we get close. Almost as if I were who he was waiting for.

"Uh, hi," I mutter.

He's just stuffed a handful of caramel popcorn into his mouth and greets me with a sheepish, closed-mouth smile, his cheeks bulging like a chipmunk preparing for winter. It's cuter than I want to think about. Despite his height and broad shoulders, there's something boyish about him. Sweet. Like he has no idea how good-looking he is.

Or maybe he's one of those rare people who doesn't care.

"What are you doing here?"

"Obviously, I'm practicing for Squirt's eating contest," he says once he swallows. Though he doesn't open his mouth, his smile gets bigger somehow, and that steady gaze of his is locked on me.

"That contest was canceled five years ago after a kid almost died from an undetected corn allergy."

Smooth, Lia. Nothing says calm and collected like well-actually-ing a guy while simultaneously exhibiting your deep well of useless Fableland factoids.

"Poor Jimmy Anderson." Mason shakes his head.

"You know him?"

Mason nods. "I'm from Orlando. Jimmy and I grew up on the same street. His mom never let him eat junk food, so he'd never had popcorn or corn on the cob or even corn syrup. He had to lie his way into the contest."

"What?" Issy gapes at him. "How could someone live without having had popcorn?" From her sigh and the distant look in her eyes, you'd think we were talking about star-crossed lovers.

Mason hooks a thumb at the nearby cart. "Best in the park right here."

"I need some of that." Issy digs for her wallet until Tess gently slaps her hand down.

"No. We might be able to stick to our schedule if we hurry." I don't miss the way she glances at me like I've just canceled prom ten minutes after she arrived. "Take some of his and let's get moving."

Issy and I burst out laughing as we watch Tess's small form march ahead. "Did she really offer me his popcorn?"

Another closed-mouth smile pulls at Mason's lips. "I'm pretty sure she didn't offer."

Everyone keeps up a brisk pace, so it's not long before we reach Reddingshire Castle. By then, there's nothing left of Mason's popcorn but the dregs of unpopped kernels. The moment he offered us the open bag, the three of us descended with grabby hands. I hide my last two pieces in my palm like they're rare treasures. I've never tasted anything with such a perfect mixture of salty and sweet.

Mason remains by my side while Tess and Issy flit ahead, their heads pressed together as they examine Issy's phone.

"Are you already done?" I ask. He still hasn't explained why he waited for me, and why he's stayed with us.

"With the clues?"

I nod.

"Nope."

"Then what are you doing here?"

He shrugs. "Making sure you know where to go."

"I'm starting to think maybe *you* don't know where to go, and you're hoping I'll fix that for you." I smirk at him.

"I know Smokey is in Reddingshire Castle."

A small buzz of triumph flits through me. I'm two for two on these clues. "Then do you know what the word *contest* means?" I joke.

"It's still early. No need to start crossing swords yet." Mason balls up the empty popcorn bag and tosses it into a nearby trash can. His eyes, which in the sunlight I can now see are a deep grayish blue, narrow slightly. "Honestly? I was thinking maybe we should team up."

My feet freeze to the asphalt at his words. "What?" I tilt my head. "Like form an alliance? What are we, on *Survivor*?" That seems like a recipe for disaster.

A girl around my age with dark-brown skin and waist-length braids crosses in front of us and hurries toward the FOTL queue. A contestant pin is secured to one of the raccoon ears on her headband. Another person ahead of me. Another chance to lose. The muscles in my shoulders yank a little tighter.

Mason and I watch her disappear into the attraction. "Aren't we?" he mumbles. "I bet the clues are going to get harder and more people are going to get cut as the days go on. We'll have a better shot getting to the end if we work together."

I hate that he's not wrong. And it's not as if Tess and Issy have been much help. If I didn't know better, I'd think those two had never watched a Fable Industry movie in their lives, never mind once been superfans themselves.

But what happens when we get to those final days? It doesn't matter how much Mason helps me (or how hot he is). I won't let him win. I can't. I *need* that cash prize. Does he feel the same? Is he prepared to lose to me?

I can't bring myself to ask. I want to win too bad to talk him out of this. If even one of the ninety-nine other contestants roaming this park isn't my competition for a little while, it feels like a leg up.

I need every extra leg I can get.

"Okay, so if we do this, you get access to all my superfan knowledge. But what do I get out of the arrangement?" I guide us toward the castle, my feet picking up speed. I need that second clue cleared.

His hand catches my wrist. "I'll show you."

At his touch, I stop short, and my heart hiccups in my chest. He lets go a second later, but the feeling of his hand pressed to my skin remains long after it's gone.

You'd think I'd touched a live wire, not another human being.

I try to shake off the sensation. I hardly know this guy. I should not be this . . . *aware* . . . of him. It will only throw me off my game. That's the worst thing that could happen. I have to stay sharp. On top of things.

Mason nods for me to follow, then heads away from the castle entrance.

Tess and Issy fall back to join me as I stare after him. "Ah, the boring tour is this way," Tess says, pointing in the opposite direction.

"I know how to get to the clue faster," Mason calls back.

That's all the three of us need to hear to hurry in his wake.

The castle's shadow spills out around us as we circle the building, offering a momentary reprieve from the sun. Pointed gold-and-blue flags wave from the top of the turrets, Percivel Night's crescent moon insignia emblazoned at their center. *Percivel Night* was Fableland's first epic fantasy, and this is the castle where Percivel finally defeated Ike the Sorcerer. As Ike's spirit dashed holes in the black cloud he'd cast over the kingdom, Percivel scaled the tallest tower and reclaimed the castle for his love, Princess (soon-to-be queen) Regina. Somehow they've managed to make it look just as imposing and otherworldly as it does in the animated film.

Mason stops at a door on the castle's far side.

Issy's face blanches as we approach. "Wait. It says Employees Only."

He shrugs. "My friend works here." He pulls his phone out of his pocket and shoots off a text. A moment later, the door opens.

The guy exiting looks about our age and he and Mason nod

at each other. The guy takes a moment to make sure Mason catches the door before he walks off.

"Is that your friend?" I ask.

"Carter?"

I nod.

"No. He's inside." Mason gestures for us to move through the entrance.

Tess, Issy, and I cluster around the threshold like a bunch of novice vampires waiting to be invited in. "We really should get permission or something," Issy whispers.

"What if there are cameras?" Tess clutches my arm, her fingers digging into my skin. "I can't afford to be bailing myself out of Fableland jail. Or worse, real jail."

Mason shakes his head. "They're not exactly Big Brother here."

"Bullshit. Big corporations are the biggest Big Brothers. You never know when they're watching you. *Or*"—Tess thrusts a finger in the air, her rising voice bouncing off the walls of the corridor in front of us—"they've got you brainwashed."

Mason eyes her, his lips pressed shut, almost like he's wondering how he ended up with such a group of dorks.

I push forward into the hallway. "Those 'cameras' "—I throw some air quotes around the word—"are more likely to get a good look at us if we keep standing here."

As my friends follow me, Tess nudges Mason in the arm. "Lia knows *everything* about this place. If she says there are cameras, then there are definitely cameras."

She's being purposely ridiculous, but I think she meant that first part. I hug my arms around my waist. Lately, I keep letting myself forget that my friends love me, even if we aren't always into the same things anymore. They might not care as much about Fableland and its secrets, but they still care about me.

Mason and I take the lead as we walk deeper into the building. "So if you live nearby and your friend works here, you must come all the time?" I ask. Imagine getting to spend every day surrounded by great rides, amazing stories, and the most delicious food. It must be like living in a different world.

His brows draw together in concentration, and the natural downturn of his mouth deepens. "I used to. Carter's uncle is a bigwig in Fable Industry, so he gets us season passes and VIP status and all that."

"The dream."

He shrugs. "It's nothing special. Just a big theme park."

My mouth falls open. *Just a big theme park?* Is he serious? "This is *Fableland*. The most innovative resort in the world."

Mason looks at me, lifting his shoulders in another shrug.

More words fizz in my mouth and burst in my head. After years of living with my mom, I can't stand silence. It's too cavernous and open, too much space that can be filled by worries and anxieties and panic. Already, I can feel myself wondering if he thinks I'm strange and awkward, if we're going to be too late to find Smokey, if the laugh Tess and Issy are sharing behind us is about something I won't understand.

"What are you doing in this contest if you aren't a fan?" I blurt out.

"I'm here for the same reason everyone else is. That cash prize."

I bristle. I want to insist I entered the contest for the magic, not the money, but that would be a lie. Or a half one, at least. I care about the parks—I can't wait to see every part of them—but I need that money, too.

The hallway branches off in three different directions. The corridor straight ahead and the one on our left look like they lead deeper into the attraction. To our right, the hall slopes up and around a corner. Deep rumbles and muffled voices spill from that direction.

Mason leads us toward the noises. They grow louder and more intense with each step we take.

"I figured my backstage info might help me win." He gestures ahead, his gaze settling on my face. "Or help one of us win."

"Prove it." I grin. "Tell me something about the parks most people don't know."

He doesn't respond for a long moment. Then he says softly, "There's a secret tunnel system under all of them. It's where employees take kids who get separated from their parents."

My eyes widen. "What? Why? What do they do to them?"

A surprised laugh escapes his lips. "Keep them safe until they find their parents."

"But why *underground*?"

"To maintain Fableland's reputation as a shiny happy place."

"I'm not sure murder tunnels inspire shiny happiness in anyone."

Another laugh. "No one's been murdered."

"As far as *you* know." I shudder. I don't actually believe anyone's been killed at my favorite place on earth (if they have, don't tell me), but I like Mason's laughter more than I should. It changes his face, his whole demeanor, as if he's coming back to life from a century-long sleep.

We reach a door at the end of the hall a minute later, and I have to fight off a squeal. "It's so cool that you get to do this all the time," I say.

"Do what?"

"See the insides of the rides and stuff. How everything works." *Have magic flickering beneath your fingertips,* I want to add.

"These days it's mostly computers and programs."

"All right, Ebenezer Scrooge."

"I love Christmas. I'm super holly jolly." His voice is flat, but one corner of his mouth quirks up.

"Well, this place is Christmas on too many espressos. So you must love it too." I don't know why I'm so desperate for him to admit it. Maybe I don't want to feel like the only one who cares about this place anymore. It would be nice for someone else to get it for once—to understand me—and for whatever reason, I want it to be him.

If he responds, I can't hear it because the door in front of us has opened, and Percivel Night's voice screams out: *I may be small, but I am mighty! Heroes come in all shapes!*

This is one of Percivel's most famous lines from his climactic fight with Ike the Sorcerer. Goose bumps pop up on my arms as I listen to him repeat the words over and over on a loop.

When I was a kid, I used to believe him. Percivel is one of the few characters in Fable Industry's repertoire who doesn't adhere to stereotypical ideas of what a hero should look like. He's short with a round little belly and a pug nose and a blond widow's peak so sharp that he appears to be balding. When I dressed up in armor I constructed out of tinfoil for career day or tried to beat the boys on the monkey bars, when I answered questions in class and didn't worry about being wrong, when I marched up to Jackson Redmond in third-grade gym class and asked him to be my swing dance partner in front of all my classmates, I didn't think the way everyone laughed at me had anything to do with my fat body. How could I when Percivel had said heroes come in all shapes?

It would be another two years before I realized that my shape didn't count. That was when Jackson started oinking at me during recess because his friends thought it was funny. And when Tess and Issy left me alone on the bleachers during the upper-elementary-school Halloween party to slow dance with some sixth graders. And when our gym teacher, Mr. Alexander, accosted me for stopping to tie my shoe in the middle of stretching by asking if my backside was too heavy to lift off the ground.

Discovering you don't fit in is a lot like realizing that the rest of the world is painted in Technicolor while you're drawn in black and white. You're duller and less important, but somehow you stand out, in all the wrong ways. I didn't see reflections of myself anywhere anymore. Not even in my beloved Fable Industry movies. I had to start drawing my favorite characters on my own to make them look like me, because no one else ever would.

I took those drawings off my walls a long time ago, but I still look at them often. I even tucked a few into one of my research notebooks before I left for the airport yesterday. Hopefully, someday, Percivel's words can actually ring true. And if I win this money, maybe I can be a part of making that happen.

Mason's still standing by the door, talking to a tall, lanky white guy in a red Fableland shirt with the name CARTER on a name tag where a right pocket would be. After another minute, he turns back to us.

He has to lean close so I can hear his soft voice over the noise, and his hand hovers at the small of my back as if he means to usher me forward. My body anticipates his touch like gasoline thrown on a flame, every inch of my skin suddenly hot, hot, *hot*, but his palm never finds the fabric of my shirt.

Instead, he explains, "Take a right out the door, and you'll see the scene you need straight ahead. I'll follow you," he adds, when I can't quite tear my gaze from his fast enough.

With a nod, I force back my shoulders and head toward the animatronic display at the end of the hall. Tess and Issy are close at my heels.

A crowd has just moved on to the next area, the perfect time to sneak in and find the QR code. But as I get closer, I'm struck dumb by how . . . well, *real* . . . the scene looks. Ike and Percivel are currently fighting in Regina's bedroom on their way to the roof, and every detail from this moment in the movie has been captured. Regina's favorite golden brush with its missing ruby sits askew on her vanity, knocked out of place by a misfire from Ike's wand. One of the thick cream-colored curtains has a tear from the rod to the floor, where Percivel rode his sword down the fabric to avoid one of Ike's spells. Two of Regina's hairpins stick out of a portrait of Duke Hasslington (she refuses to marry his smug ass), his fate from her last fit of boredom. Percivel stands at the foot of the canopy bed, sword brandished in his right hand, his left keeping him balanced on the footboard, and Ike bounces from toe to toe on the top of a steamer trunk, his wand aloft to release a dangerous spell.

The lines they rehearse are plucked right from the movie.

Face it, Percivel. You're no match for me. Regina and her kingdom are mine. Bend your knee and you can join us . . .

. . . as the court jester, of course.

The only joke in this room is your face, wizard. I may be small, but I am mighty! Heroes come in all shapes!

"Holy shit." Tess stops beside me. There's nothing to separate us from the scene but a small, knee-high barrier. If we reached out, we could touch Regina's bedsheet. "This is *wild*. I feel like I'm *in* the movie." She rests her head against my shoulder.

Issy loops her arm through mine. "Right? It's almost like it might pull you in if you touch it." She leans forward a little as if to test her theory. She's wearing the same expression she gets whenever she perfects a recipe.

We probably have only a few minutes to find Smokey and the QR code before the next group of people pushes through, but I don't want to move. Joy pulses through me at my friends' reactions. For a second, it's like we're back in Issy's room, making promises about this very trip and speculating about the *Sunspark* sequel that never happened. I wish I could freeze this moment, this second when we're us the way we used to be. Trap it in a jar. Keep it close to my heart.

But then Mason's shadow falls over us, and I remember why

we're here. I hurry forward, determined to scan the code before him, even if it is by only a few seconds. Who knows if that might matter later?

Clearly, I'm excellent at this alliance stuff.

My eyes pan over the display, quickly locking on the white shih tzu curled up under Regina's bed. It's the one detail out of place. Normally, we don't see Smokey in this part of the film. He's missing until the battle is over and he rushes out of the basement, toward his owner.

Kneeling down, I reach over the barrier to scan the code beside the dog's wagging tail.

As I hover my phone's lens over the black-and-white square, I can't help but use my other hand to pat Smokey's head.

CHAPTER 5

June 19

Phoenix's Landing, Fableland
Orlando, FL

Park: Phoenix's Landing
Ride: Squirt's Wicked Whirl
PUKE-O-METER: 🤮🤮🤮🤮🤮

—*Fabler Fanatics' Forum, the Puke-o-Meter Scale*

"**Ride the mythical creature that started it all.**"

A smile pulls at my cheeks as I read the final clue for the day. A new horde of guests has pushed toward the display of *Percivel Night*'s iconic battle, and Tess has to guide me through them by my elbow so I don't get trampled, because I can't tear my eyes from my phone.

My heart thuds with excitement and relief. I don't need Mason to figure out this clue or find it.

According to Fableland legend, the carousel in Phoenix's Landing sits on the exact spot where Sam Casterman got the idea for opening the parks. Among all the beautiful horses on the ride, there's one white-and-silver unicorn with Casterman's signature on its belly. Supposedly, it's a perfect reproduction of the one he sketched on a napkin. His first concept for the park.

The mythical creature that started it all.

"I know where we need to go next," I say.

"Let's get out of here before we worry about that," Tess mutters. She's still pulling me by my arm like my feet don't work.

My whole body is a fizzy, shaken-up bottle of soda. Knowing with certainty the answer to the third clue, and where to find it, means that I've almost finished the first day of the contest. And I'm still in it. Every step, every clue pushing me closer to a cash prize that can change my life.

Issy's hand digs into the back of my shirt so she doesn't lose me and Tess in the crowd. She keeps peeking over her shoulder like she's afraid the police are going to nab us for line cutting at any second. Mason trails after her, and I can feel his gaze on me.

When we reach the door, another Red Shirt has taken the place of Mason's friend. They've got a deep tan from the Florida sun, and their rainbow-colored hair cascades over one shoulder; the other side is buzzed and speckled with yellow polka dots. A sparkling Christmas tree earring hangs from their exposed ear even though it's the middle of June, and immediately I wish this person were my friend. AIS, their name tag reads. Even their name is awesome.

The blond guy, Carter, is waiting for us outside. As soon as we step into the sun, Tess points at him and Mason. "How is this legal?" she asks, twirling her finger in the air. "You've got a guy on the inside."

"Carter hasn't given me any answers," Mason explains.

Carter smiles widely. He has a narrow, welcoming face, big hazel eyes, and one of those sideswept boy-band haircuts, the straw-colored strands lifting in the slight breeze. "Just a shortcut to one. There's nothing in the rules about that." He and Mason shift their eyes to me for confirmation. Obviously, they assume I have the rules memorized or something.

I wish they weren't right.

I shrug.

Tess isn't done with her interrogation. "But you have a connection. And *so* much more access."

Mason's brow furrows. "How is that any different from the people who come here once, twice, three times a year? Or the ones who pay for VIP tours and all the add-ons?" He pauses to take a breath, then scrubs at the back of his neck with one hand. "I've never worked here. I'm not related to anyone in the company. I'm not breaking any rules."

"That sounds pretty reasonable to me," Issy says. She hip-checks me gently, and I nudge her back, grateful. Tess has a tendency to try to blow up anything she doesn't understand. And for whatever reason, those bombs are often aimed at me. But Issy is always on my side. Always ready to defuse them.

Tess frowns, but she drops it.

Mason takes advantage of the momentary silence to introduce us to Carter. "This is Lia"—he points to me, then to Tess and Issy—"and her friends."

Tess jams her hands on her hips. "Oh my God, you don't remember our names, do you?"

"Sure I do." He turns to Carter, his mouth hinting at a smile. "That's Jess and Bitzy."

Tess growls, her small, round face scrunching, but she's fighting back a laugh.

I smother my own grin. "Where to next, *partner*?" I ask.

Mason lifts an eyebrow like he expects me to share the answer. There's a playful glint in his watercolor eyes. Obviously, he's figured out the clue, too.

I tip my chin up, my mouth pressed in a tight, unyielding line. No way am I going first. I get the sense he's thinking the same.

Carter claps his hands. "While these two continue their staring contest, let's Dog Shack it up. I've got an hour for lunch."

Tess shakes her head. "It's not even ten-thirty. We're not scheduled to eat until"—she swipes open her itinerary on her phone—"one-forty-five."

Carter brushes his sweep of bangs out of his eyes. "All the good combos will be sold out by then."

"We're not scheduled for hot dogs until Thursday anyway."

Carter clearly gives out smiles like they're as free as oxygen. He basically hasn't stopped grinning since we met him. But at Tess's remark, his already wide smile manages to grow larger. "Do you have your bathroom breaks scheduled, too?"

Tess's hands snap into fists, and I can see a lecture on the benefits of preparedness brewing in her eyes.

"Hold on. We've got to get the final clue first," I point out. Why does everyone but me seem to keep forgetting we're in the middle of a scavenger hunt?

"You've got plenty of time." Carter waves a dismissive hand. "I've seen maybe eleven or twelve people this morning, including you all. You could spend the entire afternoon eating hot dogs and fries and still be secure for day two." He fixes us with a pleading look. "Trust me. These hot dogs are a worthy side quest. Finnigan's Dog Shack has the most unique options anywhere. You have to try the Buffalo dog. Or the Grandma's Kitchen Sink dog. Or the Cereal dog—"

"No one needs to try the Cereal dog," Mason pipes up.

Carter frowns. "Dude. It's an experience."

"Froot Loops and powdered milk do not belong in a hot dog bun."

Truer words have never been spoken.

But of course, Issy is swayed. Nothing piques her interest like wild food combinations. "That settles it," she says. "We have to go to this Dog Shack." She grabs Tess's arm and shakes it. "It's the perfect content for my channel, right? My viewers have been begging for more weird food videos ever since we did the brownie experiment."

"The what?" Carter asks.

"Issy decided we should spend a Friday night seeing how savory you can make a brownie before it's gross," Tess tells him. "Bacon worked great, and black bean actually wasn't so bad. Zucchini made the brownies moister without affecting the taste. Potato chip was also a win. But then Is went off the rails, trying taco meat and chicken and soy-marinated shrimp, and well, I spent a lot of time staring at the inside of a toilet after that." She tips up her chin. "But I tasted every batch."

Carter shakes his head. "There is no scenario on earth in which shrimp should be involved in dessert."

"That was actually better than the taco meat, believe it or not," Issy points out. "Which blew my mind. I'd figured since mole sauce uses chocolate, the taco meat might be a winner." She chews on the inside of her cheek as we walk, clearly reworking the recipe in her head. Issy never gives up on a dish—no matter how bad—until she's perfected it. That's how we ended up eating hamburgers with peanut sauce for a month sophomore year.

My stomach practically groans at the memory.

Though we never actively agreed to it, we're all ambling in the direction of the Dog Shack.

I sigh. I would have liked to get to the carousel before lunch, even if Carter says we'll be fine, but Finnigan's is on the other side of the park, sandwiched between Squirt's Wicked Whirl and Dudley's Tailspin. Finnigan is a dachshund in the Dudley movies who owns a restaurant. Thankfully, he doesn't serve hot dogs. That would feel mildly cannibalistic.

Mason's eyes search my face. "Carter knows how bad I need to win this thing. He wouldn't take us on a field trip if he wasn't sure we had time."

"Don't you want to finish as soon as possible, though?" I glance away from him and watch the crowd. I can't help but scan each person we pass for a contestant pin.

"A few days from now? Sure. But today it doesn't matter if we're one or ninety-one. There's no extra prize for being the fastest."

I shrug. The information packet we were given did encourage everyone to enjoy the parks and document their time on social media. The daily eliminations are the only indication that timing is important. But every second I'm not working toward winning feels like the cash prize is slipping further out of my fingers.

My elbow bumps Mason's, and we both jump away, mumbling apologies. The brush of his skin sizzles hot on my arm, and I rub at it to chase the sensation away.

It normally takes me weeks, even months, of hanging out with someone to feel this tuned in to them. It must be this resort. Being at Fableland is like leaving the normal world behind. It changes all the rules.

"Did you really eat brownies with shrimp in them?" Mason asks me. His expression is almost painfully impassive, like he doesn't want me to think he's judging me if I did.

"Good God, no." The intensity of his gaze makes my skin flush. "Tess literally turned green."

Mason shudders.

"Issy doesn't only make gross stuff, though," I assure him. "Her aunt Kamila and her grandmother own this restaurant where they make the most amazing Puerto Rican food, and they've taught Issy all their recipes. She's planning to get a business degree and then go to culinary school so she can take over for them. Until then, she does foodie stuff on her YouTube channel, Issy Will Cook Anything. You should check it out. She's *so* funny."

Pulling out his phone, Mason opens an app and types a note. Like he's actually going to look up Issy's channel. "You should make sure to take her to the Land of Plenty in Hero's Quest. It's this pavilion—"

"Where they re-create food from the movies! It's definitely on our list. And Tess's schedule." Issy hasn't stopped talking about that exhibit since she booked her plane ticket.

My eyes hang on Mason's face a little longer than I mean to. It's so . . . nice . . . to be around someone who knows the parks the way I do. Who can immediately come up with places to go based on someone's interests and doesn't treat me like I'm immature or straight off another planet because this is what I care about.

Even though it's early for lunch, a line snakes around the Dog Shack. Tess groans and starts editing her itinerary.

Carter has his phone out, too, the screen bright against his tanned skin. "Do you guys use Cartographer?"

Tess sneers. "We're not amateurs. We don't need an app to map the park."

"Sure, oh wise one." He sketches a bow. "But you can also preorder your meals so you can spend that time going on rides instead of waiting."

Even Tess can't deny the brilliance of this. Along with the rest of us, she downloads the app.

Mason lingers near me. "What are you getting?"

"Not the Cereal dog."

"I'm *so* getting that," Issy declares.

I mime my cheeks filling with vomit, and both she and Mason laugh.

"The Barbecue dog's good, if you like pulled pork?" Mason offers.

The large menu is giving me serious decision fatigue, so I'm grateful for the recommendation. I add it to my order with fries and a frozen cola (the nectar of the gods) and check out. "Looks like my food will be ready in a half hour," I announce when the confirmation screen appears.

"Perfect." Carter thrusts a hand in the air, his index finger pointed up like a sword. "This gives us a chance to ride Squirt's Wicked Whirl at least three times."

I thought I'd read enough about Squirt's Wicked Whirl to be prepared for it.

A tiny ride that packs a punch. Five vomit emojis on the puke-o-meter. Everyone says not to be deceived by the small, compact structure or the seemingly simple restraint system.

From far away, I can see why people underestimate it. Unlike Dudley's Tailspin and a lot of the other roller coasters at the parks, whose tall, looming tracks arch and swoop and curl toward the sky as if they mean to burst through the clouds, Squirt's Wicked Whirl is a rectangular set of rails with multiple levels. The drops aren't steep. There are no upside-down loops or barrel rolls, nothing to steal your stomach. Just a lot of small hills and sharp corners.

And yet, as we make our way through the FOTL queue, screams fill the air from the riders. Louder ones than I remember hearing on Dudley's Tailspin earlier.

Carter studies our surprised expressions with glee. "This ride is a total dark horse. No one expects it to be as fun or as terrifying as it is."

"I love that you think fun and terrifying are somehow things that are supposed to go together," I mumble.

Beside me, Mason huffs a small laugh. It's so light it could have wings, and I imagine myself catching it between my hands and hiding it away in my pocket.

Serendipitously, the cars for the ride hold five. One lone seat up front, and two doubles. Carter jumps into the single seat, and Tess and Issy grab the middle row, leaving Mason and me to fill the back.

My heart leaps against my rib cage. I'm going to have to sit next to him in this tiny car, where our arms and legs will be flung together. Where I can't guarantee I won't strangle his bicep if the drops get too intense. We're going to be sharing air. Space. Gravity.

Suddenly, I'm too aware of my size. Despite Mason's height and the broad stretch of his shoulders, I take up more room than he does. I fill the seat differently, my stomach bunching around the seat belt, which, thank whatever higher power is out there, snaps into place.

Does he notice?

Does he care?

I know I shouldn't. My body is my body. I don't spend my time counting calories or dreaming of being smaller. I exercise because I enjoy playing sports. I like the way my heart dances steadily when I run, how my blood pulses warm in my veins. I like to feel the muscles in my legs burn after a good workout. I like knowing my body is strong and capable of the same things other bodies are.

But I also know I don't fit the way the world wants me to. And that this is usually the first thing people see when they look at me.

I breathe in and squeeze my arms as close as I can to my sides, trying to make myself smaller, to take up a little less room. Mason's expression is gentle, a smile hanging on his lips, as he looks over at me. There's none of the judgment I get everywhere else.

This will be okay. The same way it's been since I ran into him at Dudley's Tailspin. It's ridiculous to think that going on a ride together would suddenly change the way he sees me.

We both reach up at the same time to pull down the over-the-shoulder harnesses. Mine clicks once into place. Mason's clicks twice.

When I peek at him, I see that his harness is pressed against his flat stomach, while mine hovers closer to my chest. I bear down on it a little harder, but it bounces back up.

My pulse quickens. Maybe it's broken? That happens all the time at places like this. With so many people on the rides, there must be a ton of wear and tear. A little less discreetly, I shove the harness down. Panic starts to bubble, viscous and bitter, at my center, and I can feel my cheeks growing hot.

This stupid thing has to lock. It has to fit. It *has* to. I cannot be too big for this ride. Not with Mason and Carter here. I can't. I just can't. . . .

I'm fighting with the harness roughly enough now that Mason notices. My arms hurt from shoving it down, and tears burn at the corners of my eyes.

"These things can be so stupid," Mason says softly. He reaches over to give me a little more leverage. With his help, the harness pushes deeper into my stomach, but the telltale click of the lock never comes.

The ride's attendant approaches, making his rounds to ensure everyone is secured.

He checks Mason's harness and nods, then eyes mine. "This needs to go down more," he says. He's barely looking at me. He must do this so often every day that he stops seeing the people he engages with. His name tag reads MIKE.

"I think it's broken or something." I hate how much I hope that's true. How much my voice begs him to agree.

"Nah, sometimes they just need a little extra encouragement." He grips the sides of my harness and thrusts down.

It jams into my stomach hard enough that I have to swallow a grunt, but I still don't hear a click.

"Ah . . ." Mike keeps pressing the harness down and bounces against it, trying his damnedest to force the mechanism into place. His eyebrows knit together, and his mouth twists in a frown. When our eyes meet, I'm pretty sure he is actually seeing me for the first time.

He takes a reluctant step back and grimaces. It's obvious he doesn't want to say the thing I so desperately don't want to hear.

At this point, we're holding up the ride, and this has invited an audience. People waiting in the queue are standing on their tiptoes to see what's going on. Another attendant is heading our way. Tess and Issy have turned around in their seats, their faces full of questions.

I can't bring myself to look at Mason.

I wave Mike off and shove up the harness. My hands are shaking as I try to release the seat belt. I have to clench them into fists once, twice, three times before they're steady enough for my fingers to fumble with the button.

Rising to my feet, I mumble, "I'm going to . . . um . . . wait . . . out . . . outside." The tremble in my voice brings more tears to my eyes, and my stomach is a pit of snakes, writhing, churning, squeezing.

I don't care that I can't go on this ride. It happens. But I didn't need all these witnesses. It's like a neon sign screaming, *Hey, look at the fat girl,* at a time when I don't want to be seen.

I don't wait for Tess and Issy to reply before rushing for the exit.

CHAPTER 6

June 19

Phoenix's Landing, Fableland
Orlando, FL

[drafts][Fabler Fanatics' Forums]
Fat Unfriendly Rides at the Parks

Date: June 19
Forum Owner: LiaLuvsOliver

I feel like it might be useful to have a forum where we can warn fellow Fanatics about rides that may not be friendly to their bodies. I just had to get off a ride because the harness wouldn't lock and it was pretty mortifying. No one else should have to go through that if we can help it.

I'll get us started:
Squirt's Wicked Whirl . . .

I'M STILL SHAKING AS I SIT DOWN ON A CURB OUTSIDE SQUIRT'S Wicked Whirl.

My phone is clutched so hard in my hands that my knuckles are white, but I keep typing, filling up paragraph after paragraph in a forum creation page on Fabler Fanatics.

I've been fat my entire life. I'm well acquainted with the realities of living in a world where average means half my size. When I was in middle school, I stopped going places for fear I wouldn't "fit." I spent most of seventh grade missing parties and trips to the movies and into Boston, all my friends but Tess and Issy drifting away from me because I was never there. Yet, for everything I lost, the world didn't change. Better to smile at myself in the mirror and give the world and its ridiculous notion of "average" the middle finger instead.

But none of that means I want to announce to a bunch of strangers that I'm too big for a safety harness. There should be better protocols in place than a small warning sign that requires you to carry around a tape measure or a set of seats outside the ride you'd have to make a spectacle of yourself to use. We should be able to determine, privately and without shame, if a ride will work for our bodies.

I hear footsteps but don't look up until two beat-up running shoes stop in front of me.

Glancing up, I find Mason staring down at me. His hands fuss with the buttons on his shorts' pockets, and his mouth and eyes are soft with what looks like worry. "I'm sorry you had to deal with that. That kid was probably new. I bet he has no idea what he's doing."

I shake my head. "It's fine. It's just physics." I don't need anyone to make excuses for my body. I'm not sorry I'm fat. I don't want him to be. I dig my hands into the hem of my shorts so I can't fold my arms. Can't try to disappear. "Those cars are tiny, and they whip around fast. It makes sense that to be safe, they may not be able to accommodate every body shape."

It wouldn't kill parks like this to be more size inclusive, though. Surely the vehicles could be made bigger or there could be fewer seats in them.

Mason's gaze is always intense, but it deepens as he peers at me. Like he's staring at the ocean and can't see the bottom. "Want to find that last clue?" he asks.

"Absolutely." I climb to my feet. I'm so ready to put an end to this conversation. "Just give me a second to text my friends." Dusting dirt off my ass with one hand, I use the other to open a group text with Tess and Issy.

Lia
Heading to clue three. I will be back by lunch. Feel free to
ride Squirt as many times as you want.
(11:44 AM)

I barely have time to look away before I hear a *ding*. Then another and another and another.

Tess
That's what she said.
(11:45 AM)

Issy
Lia, I just punched her in the arm.
(11:45 AM)

Are you okay?
(11:46 AM)

Tess
That was total bullshit. Want me to find a manager? Or have a word with that attendant when we get back to the front of the line? There is no reason why that harness shouldn't have locked.
(11:46 AM)

Lia
I just want to get the next clue.
(11:47 AM)

Issy
We could come with you?
(11:47 AM)

Lia
No. Enjoy the ride. Exploit our FOTL passes for all they're worth. 😊
(11:48 AM)

Issy
I don't want you to be stuck alone . . .
(11:48 AM)

Tess
She's not alone. She's got Mason. 😉
(11:49 AM)

(11:49 AM)

(11:49 AM)

(11:49 AM)

My face ignites like a bonfire, and I quickly pivot so Mason can't see our conversation. While the string of emojis might look like nonsense to anyone else, it's Tess's shorthand for safe sex. Whenever any of us goes out on a date, she fills our chat with some version of this (replacing the eggplant with another doughnut for her). *She's the worst,* I groan to myself, even as I'm laughing.

Lia
I'm doing whatever the text-message version of hanging up is.
(11:51 AM)
See you at the Dog Shack in a bit.
(11:51 AM)

I contemplate turning off my phone or throwing it in the nearest water feature as I shove it in my pocket. Rationally, I know Mason can't have seen the texts, but worry still ropes my muscles into knots. My eyes avoid his face as I say, "Shall we?"

He crosses his arms. "Lead the way."

I head in the opposite direction of Casterman's Carousel, curious if he'll stop me. I keep my face trained forward so he can't spot my grin.

I don't know why I'm being so stubborn. He was the one who confirmed the last clue was Smokey. It shouldn't be a big deal for me to admit what I think the third one is. Plus, we're supposed to be working together.

But it's kind of fun, seeing who will give first. Like a game within the game.

Mason only lets me walk a few feet before he says, "You know the carousel's in the middle of the park, right?"

A little thrill fizzes through me. Not just because he caved first, but because I was right. Again. I raise an eyebrow. "I was checking to make sure *you* knew that."

He huffs a laugh as he walks away, forcing me to scurry to catch up.

It's a short walk from Dudley's metropolis to the center of the park. Here, the streetlamps lining the road give way to trees frosted with twinkle lights. Behind wrought iron fences, flowers bloom in every color, some real, some glass sculptures fixed with LEDs to make them glow. The grass under my feet seems greener, the sky over my head bluer, the sun's rays gentler, like I've stepped out of the real world and into a fairy-tale forest.

"Do you come here a lot?" I ask him as we weave through the crowds. There seem to be three times as many people in the park today.

Mason shakes his head. "Not anymore."

Every time a family with screaming toddlers streams by us, Mason veers toward me. The closer he gets, the more his scent—something wintry like mint or eucalyptus—fills my nose, and it's too much like he's a part of this fairy-tale setting. Part of the park's magic. I study the flowers intently, using them as an excuse to widen the gap between us.

"I almost got a job here with Carter, but . . ." He pauses, like he's considering how much more to share. I get the sense he's not used to talking about himself this much. "I get paid more doing construction."

"Do you like it?" I ask.

"I like working with my hands, I guess. But it's hot and tiring." He shrugs. "It's a job."

I understand that apathy more than he knows. It's how I feel every day about working for my parents. I clear my throat. "You have this," I say, flourishing my hands to indicate the park, "in your backyard, though. It has to be amazing to come here whenever you want." So many questions bubble up to my tongue. *What has surprised him most? What is the most magical moment he's had? What's his favorite thing to do here?* But his expression hardens, and he shrugs again, popping the words before they leave my lips.

Ahead of us, the trees part to expose the umbrella-shaped canopy of the carousel and then the team of horses dancing beneath it. The sides of the roof gleam with bright-white lights that are dotted among gilded mirrors framed with gems. Beneath the mirrors scalloped panels painted the blue of a clear summer sky and decorated with white-and-gold scrollwork throw shadows across the horses. Each of the dappled creatures appears frozen in movement as a new set of riders climb on. Polished-gold rods lock the steeds to the floor, and around them chariots and carriages fill the gaps.

My legs itch to run toward the carousel, lured by the joyful organ music and the way its lights dance toward the sky as it begins to turn. For years, I've studied pictures of this ride, every time I couldn't sleep, every time my mother's anxiety turned my muscles to knotted ropes, every time I felt like my world might crush me with its smallness. Now here it is, sprung off my phone screen, larger than life. Overwhelming all my senses.

"Seriously, how can you shrug about *this*?" I wave toward the carousel.

Mason replies with another lift of his shoulders. "They're plastic."

Irritation rises in me, and I spin away from him and hurry toward the attraction. Some people would give anything to be able to come here whenever they want. Yet he's taking it for granted.

He has no idea how lucky he is.

When I reach the fence that separates the carousel from the park's thoroughfare, I take out my phone. For a minute, I'm alone, but then Mason fills my vision again. He leans back against the fence to observe as I fuss with my camera.

"I don't understand how you can know so much about Fableland if you don't care about it," I say softly.

He's quiet for a long time. When he does speak again, it's hesitantly. "When I was younger, I was obsessed with these parks. Carter and I practically lived here. But then I grew up and saw them for what they are. Just places. No different from or more special than any others."

My muscles stiffen. Every one of his words is wrong. Wrong. Wrong. "You really are just here for the money."

"It would change my life. And I know enough about the parks and movies to have a chance."

I cross my arms over my chest. This scavenger hunt isn't supposed to be some means to an end, like getting a loan from the bank. It's meant to be another slice of Fableland magic. A chance to make our dreams come true.

Mason takes in my frustrated expression with a sigh. "Lia, it's all a facade." He nods to the park's central crossroads. "Just a carefully constructed fantasy." It's like he can read my thoughts.

Bending down, he plucks a blade of grass from the other side of the fence. Before offering it to me, he drags it between his fingernails. When he stops, the tips of his nails are green, and the blade of grass is withered and browned. "In the summer, when the heat's too intense to keep the grass alive, they paint it. Every night."

I jerk my gaze from him back to the carousel. My insides have curdled like sour milk, but I fight to keep my expression even. This is not the version of Fableland I want right now. Not the one I *need*.

I get my phone and zoom the camera in on the horses as they rise and fall to the rhythm of the organ music. "There's nothing wrong with fantasy. It helps people."

I can feel his eyes roaming my face. When I don't look at him, he turns and rests his elbows beside me on the fence. "Is that why you spend so much time researching this place?"

For once, I'm the one who shrugs. A few minutes ago, I would have told him about my job, my mother and her anxiety, how Fableland gives me an escape. Everything. I was so sure he'd understand. Now, though, I'm afraid he'll think I'm childish. As silly as he seems to find these parks.

The realization leaves me hollow.

I close my eyes for a second, letting the carousel music wash over me as it reaches a crescendo. Obviously, I was wrong to think that we shared some secret understanding. But I don't need his permission, or Tess's and Issy's, to love this place. I don't need their support to win this contest. That I love it, that Fable Industry and its magic have saved me more times than I can count, is enough.

I'm enough.

Mason gestures toward the carousel. "Let's go, before the next ride starts."

There's a bunch of people at the FOTL entrance, and I vaguely recognize some faces from the welcome party. Thank God we didn't listen to Carter and take our time. Who knows how many contestants have already been here?

I look back at Mason, but he doesn't seem nervous.

The attendant lets a handful more people through the gate and onto the carousel. A bunch of them beeline for the center circle of horses. A girl who looks a little older than me, and has somehow managed to maintain a perfect topknot and an even more pristine layer of makeup over her bronzed skin despite the sweltering weather, pushes everyone out of her way to get there first. She doesn't attempt to apologize when one of the guys she bumps into trips and lands belly-first across one of the horses. She simply scans the QR code and, with a cheer, runs off to meet the guy waiting for her at the exit.

Mason and I exchange a look. "She seems fun," I mutter.

He laughs.

I assumed, given the amount of money at stake, I'd run into a few . . . driven . . . contestants, but shoving people out of the way on the first day is excessive, and definitely against the rules. *May she get stuck behind one of the huge park parades and miss a clue,* I wish silently.

The music fades as the carousel slows to a stop. As soon as the current riders vacate the horses, the attendant waves us through.

"Feel free to take a ride if you want after you get the code," he says as Mason and I pass.

I plan to do just that. Maybe on Casterman's unicorn if I'm lucky.

I pick my way around the carriages, chariots, and creatures, trying my best not to appear eager even as my feet trip over themselves. My fingers squeeze my phone.

This is it. The last clue of the day. I'm almost there.

The unicorn is tucked within the inside circle of horses. Its white body shines like marble, as if someone's sole job is to polish it daily. This close, I can see each individual sparkle in the silver mane and horn, and how the creature's eyes are a stormy gunmetal blue, just like Mason's. Following the curve of its gold saddle, Casterman's swooping signature cuts across the unicorn's flank.

Beside it sits the QR code.

My heart's in my throat as I bend to scan it. Before I do, I let my index finger follow the trail of Sam Casterman's writing. I picture him in his trademark fedora and vest, sitting in the back booth at some dim, smoke-filled restaurant (it was the 1950s, when I assume everything was covered in a blanket of cigarette smoke), sketching his dreams into reality.

Mason can think whatever he wants. I know these parks are bursting with magic. I can feel it swimming through my veins as I press my hand to the unicorn's mane.

My phone beeps, registering the code, and then my screen is filled with confetti. Once it fades, a new message appears.

Congratulations! You're the 20th contestant to complete Day 1 of the 50th-Anniversary Scavenger Hunt! Your first clue for Day 2 will become available at midnight EST. On Day 2, only the first 70 contestants to scan the three codes will remain in the contest.

Heat blooms in my cheeks, and my heart pounds as I read the words over and over. *Twenty* out of *one hundred*. Those are odds people could bet on (or whatever it is people do with odds).

And I did it myself. *Me,* probably one of the only Fableland fanatics who'd never seen the resort with their own eyes until today. I figured out the clues. The only thing Mason did was give us a shortcut to one.

Mason appears beside me, and the same burst of color fills his screen as he hovers the camera over the QR code.

I point to a nearby carriage. "Are you going to ride?"

"No. But I'll wait for you." He gestures with his head toward the fence that rings the carousel.

I don't bother to argue. Forget Ebenezer Scrooge. This boy is Fableland's *Grinch*.

I slide onto Casterman's unicorn and let the organ music wash over me. A grin spreads across my face. I don't need Mason to celebrate this win.

I survived the first day.

No. More than survived. *Thrived.*

A realization slams into me like Dudley's Tailspin as it crashes down the last hill. This isn't Fableland magic. It's reality.

I could actually win this scavenger hunt.

CHAPTER 7

June 19

Phoenix's Landing, Fableland
Orlando, FL

ISSY MORALES @ISSYWILLCOOKANYTHING
HELP ME PLAN MY TRIP! WHAT ARE THE BEST DESSERTS YOU'VE HAD AT FABLELAND?

"OKAY. I'M SORRY. YOU HAVE TO EXPLAIN WHY YOU HAVE A BOOK at an amusement park."

I approach Mason as I leave the carousel. He's leaning against the fence, one elbow slotted between the bars to keep him upright, his other hand balancing his book.

The Hammer of God by Arthur C. Clarke. It's dog-eared, the layers of the paperback cover peeling to expose its white insides. A few of the book's yellowed pages have lost their corners.

"Are you usually bored with this many people to watch?"

I throw my arms out for emphasis. He's so close that I almost smack him in the chest. I have to fight not to tuck my hands behind my back. "You brought one to the party yesterday, too."

He offers me the book with a shrug. "I always have one." His voice is so soft I can hardly hear him over the carousel music. "I do a lot of waiting. Reading passes the time."

The cover is warm, as if it's absorbed his heat, and for a second, I consider how this object sitting on my palm was just in his hands. We're practically holding hands, Six Degrees of Kevin Bacon–style. The thought sends my insides somersaulting.

To distract myself, I flip through a few pages. Pausing on one, I scan the first paragraph, but my pulse's hum in my ears makes it impossible to concentrate. "Waiting for what?"

"Rides. To work or whatever."

"You don't have a car?"

"I'm saving for other things."

"It sucks, doesn't it? Not to be able to get around on your own?" The idea of me driving triggered Mom's anxiety so much that Dad had to put plans of getting me a car on hold until further notice. One of the many ways I am trapped (literally) in that house. "I'm constantly depending on Tess or Issy to get places, and my parents always have to drive me to work. It's like, how are you supposed to feel independent? Or like an adult or whatever?"

I snap my mouth shut to cut off my rant. I don't want to keep dwelling on these things that already suck me dry.

I wave Mason's book at him. "So what's this about?"

"An asteroid on a course to hit Earth."

"So a lighthearted comedy, then."

His laugh is so real it hurts.

"Is it good?"

His eyes abandon my face to take in the growing line for the carousel. "So far. I like Clarke's stuff. There's a lot of actual science to his stories."

"Do you only read science fiction?"

"Yeah."

"But isn't that another kind of fantasy?"

"It's not the same. It's speculative. Things that *could* happen. Not things that never will."

"So science instead of magic."

Mason nods.

His book is still clutched in my hand as we wander back toward Squirt's Wicked Whirl, and I can't seem to stop skimming its pages, as if they might tell me more than a story. Spill some secret about Mason and why he's here, with me, right now. Why this tight, nervous knot in my stomach won't ease, no matter how much I want it to.

Mason's sweet. He's great. But he's not why I'm here. I need to win this money and embrace every bit of wonder the parks have to offer. I can't do that if he's constantly trying to convince me it's all fake.

I hand over the book, trying to let go of him and whatever his presence promises along with it. We can work together for the next few days to get ahead, but that's it. We're an alliance of convenience, nothing more.

Instead of putting the book in his pocket, he fiddles with the cover, his fingers pausing for a long time over a spot on the spine mine had clutched moments ago. "What about you?" he asks. "Do you read?"

Four separate snarky retorts pop into my head, but he's staring at me with so much earnestness—like the question really matters—that I can't sass him. "Like it's my job. I don't really have a favorite genre like you, but I guess I tend to gravitate toward mysteries. I like trying to guess what happens. Solve the puzzle before the characters do."

"Maybe that's why you're so good at this scavenger hunt. It's kind of like a mystery."

"Maybe?" I smile. I'd never thought of it that way.

He gives me one of his ghost smiles in return, and my fingers itch to touch his lips.

Just ahead, the brightness and noise from a nearby bakery catch my attention. Through its open door, I can see treats of every variety: chocolate, gummies, bars of rice crisps and marshmallow, cookies, cupcakes, and pastries. Old-fashioned striped candy sticks in flavors like root beer and licorice and cinnamon fill jars in the corners of the shop, and everywhere you look there's saltwater taffy, caramel apples, chocolate bars as big as my head. You could build the witch's house from "Hansel and Gretel" out of this place's stock. The smell of sugar and butter sticks in the air and fills my nose.

Mason waves me in and beelines to the counter, pointing to a dessert on display that's styled like Dudley the Raccoon's face. I recognize the dessert from the approximately forty videos Issy sent me in the weeks leading up to our trip. Apparently, it's some criminally delicious combination of cookie, caramel, peanut butter, and chocolate ganache, dusted with powdered sugar to create Dudley's masklike eyes. She'd have a fit if she knew I was within feet of one without her.

As Mason heads back toward me, dessert in hand, I snap a picture of the shop's sign with my phone so I can make sure Issy finds her way here. Mason has already broken the raccoon's face in half and offers me one end, the caramel and chocolate insides oozing over his fingers.

"We're going to have lunch in like five minutes," I point out as I accept it.

"Appetizer," he says around a bite.

"Appetizers are savory."

He shrugs. "I'm a rebel."

The powdered sugar dusting his nose and one of his cheeks suggests otherwise.

I cradle my half of the dessert in both hands, my insides feeling like they're performing loop-the-loops. Nothing about him is what I expected after our first meeting yesterday.

I'm almost relieved when I hear Tess's loud voice behind me. "Dude, you need a napkin. You've got sugar all over your face."

Mason's eyes pop wide, and he starts rubbing his knuckles across his nose, his cheeks flushed. He somehow manages to miss every bit of sugar. I reach up to help, but Carter beats me to it, slapping a napkin to his friend's chin.

As soon as I see Issy, I hand her my Dudley cake. I love dessert as much as the next person, but trying this means something to her in a way it doesn't to me. She should get the first taste.

Issy screeches and pulls out her phone. "Can you film me?" she asks Tess.

As soon as the camera is on her, Issy breaks into an enormous smile. "Hello, fellow foodies! This week, my content's going to be a little different. Instead of cooking, I will be tasting everything here at the amazing Fableland Resort!" She angles the dessert at the lens. "It only makes sense that I start with the legendary Dudley the Raccoon cookie bar!"

She divides the dessert into three pieces so Tess and I can try it, too, then has Tess use the flipped camera so we can all be in the shot for our first bite. The three of us simultaneously break out into obscene groans as we chew. There are few things as perfect as chocolate, peanut butter, and caramel together.

Carter's eyebrows creep toward his hairline. "Are you going to do this every time we eat tomorrow too?"

I shoot him a glance. "Tomorrow?"

"I have the day off and Tess here needs a lesson in properly navigating the parks." Carter smirks at Tess, who rolls her eyes hard enough to cause some damage.

"I already have Hero's Quest fully mapped out, but I'm happy to prove you wrong," she says.

Carter arches an eyebrow at her. "But what if the clues are at a different park?"

Tess's eyes flash with frustration.

"You know we have to be flexible," I remind her. "The riddles could lead us anywhere in Fableland." My voice is as gentle as I can make it. "We won't have the first clue for tomorrow until midnight, so we can't plan where to go until then."

This scheduling thing with Tess isn't really new. She's been our friendship cruise director our whole lives, planning out sleepovers, mapping our trips to the mall, organizing food orders, and even inventorying our dolls' wardrobes for maximum style options. But these past few months, her love of spreadsheets and schedules has become less hobby and more lifestyle. She broke down when our limo for the prom canceled last minute and we missed our restaurant reservations, and she ghosted Issy and me for a whole weekend over winter break when we ruined her minute-by-minute plans for a girls' night by suggesting we go see a movie instead.

I wish she'd tell us what's wrong rather than trying to fix everything by holding the whole world in a vise grip. But every time I've asked, she's sworn she's fine.

She's chewing on the inside of her cheek, her index finger tapping out numbers on her palm like a calculator. All signs that Tess is ready to blow.

But then she sighs. "You're really cramping my style, Baker."

She heads off toward Finnigan's Dog Shack before I can catch her expression to see if she's joking.

CHAPTER 8

June 19

Starshatter Hotel, Fableland
Orlando, FL

At Starshatter Hotel, you can truly get away from it all.
Hang from the stars and leave your cares behind.

—Fableland's "Escape Life" national ad campaign

MY BED LOOKS LIKE A SHINY, STAR-COVERED OASIS OF COMFORT as we push through the door of our hotel room.

It's a quarter to midnight, and it feels like we haven't sat down in at least five hours. My calves burn from overuse and despite Tess's meticulously coordinated sunblock rotation, the sting of a light sunburn stretches across my shoulders.

I flop face-first onto one of the beds with a loud groan. "I know we teased you about your itinerary, but I think we really did see every inch of that park."

"Of course we did. I'm a master." Tess pulls out her phone. "I can't wait to see Carter try to do better tomorrow. And *fail*." Her fingers flick at the screen as she scrolls. "Oh shit. Issy, did you just get that email too?"

Issy nods furiously, and they grab on to each other and bounce up and down on the other bed, their faces split by huge grins.

I pick up my own phone and stare at the blank screen. "What email?"

Issy stills. "The stuff we ordered for our dorm room shipped."

"Oh?" Normally, Tess texts me pictures of everything she buys. Including soap and tampons. She needs the strangest forms of validation.

Tess's eyes brighten, like pieces of polished mahogany. "We got matching comforters and towels and stuff."

"Not *matching*," Issy clarifies. "Coordinating. Different geometric patterns in the same color schemes." She pulls up images to show me.

They're really pretty. One set has chevron stripes in aqua and white, the other a checkered pattern in different shades of blue.

"Your room's going to look awesome." I force as much enthusiasm as I can into my voice, but my insides twist as if someone's wringing them out. They're doing things without me. Already. And there's still two months before they leave.

"Right?" Tess nods. "We did it the minute we got our roommate confirmation."

So, less than a week ago. While I was sitting at home doing nothing.

I look back at my own phone, as if there's tons of important stuff waiting for my attention, and the two of them take that as a cue to return to squealing. I blink away the burn in my eyes. I'm happy for them. I'm sure it will make college so much less terrifying having your best friend beside you. But I won't be there too.

And if I don't win this contest, I won't have any adventures of my own.

My phone rings. The sound scrapes claws down my back. My mother.

It's practically midnight, and I've been so distracted by finding the clues and Mason and everything else that I forgot to answer her texts.

I close my eyes and push a long breath between my teeth as I sit up on the bed. My free hand clenches into a fist. I'm not ready for this call.

"Hi, Mom."

"Lia, sweetie, I've been waiting all day to hear from you." Her voice teeters on the cusp of shrieky. No doubt she's pacing the living room, counting silently or cataloging every white object around her to ground herself like her therapist taught her. There've been so many times I've had to do it with her that I almost start now out of habit.

"Sorry. We lost track of time."

"Are you okay?"

"Of course. I'm just wiped from the day."

"Did you girls have fun?" She still sounds on edge. She's probably gripping the arm of the recliner.

"Tons of fun."

In the background, Dad's rough voice bursts through. "No boys?"

"Did you hear your father?"

"Yep."

"And, no boys?"

"Of course."

Lying to my parents makes me hot and out of sorts, like I'm losing my balance on a tightrope. It's probably because of those "we're so very disappointed in you" speeches I got as a kid. Anger is the flick of a match. It's a spark. Quick and fizzling, then it's gone. Disappointment, though—it lingers. Like a virus. Infecting everything else.

But if I admit to spending half the day with a guy they've never met, they'll be on the next plane down here to drag me home. Mom would pilot it herself if necessary. The only reason I was ever able to date in the first place was because my two high school boyfriends were sons of my parents' closest friends, and we were rarely left alone. It's a damned miracle I lost my virginity to Dan junior year. We told my parents we were looking for a piece of our chemistry homework in Dan's car, so we'd had to be quick about it. I bet you can guess how magical and romantic *that* was.

My mother taps what I imagine is her sudoku pen against the end table. "And you're eating, right?"

"Three meals a day plus tons of water."

I yawn. It starts out genuine, but I stretch it into something more exaggerated, opening my mouth so wide my eyes water. I feel like a jerk, but I know if my mom keeps going, her list of worries will carve a hole into what has, overall, been a really fun day.

"Sweetie, get some sleep. Maybe take it easy tomorrow. You don't have to spend the entire day at the park. Then you could check in more."

I strangle the comforter between my fingers, counting backward from ten.

"That's the whole point of us coming down here. To compete in this contest and see the parks. If we were going to hang around and sleep, we could do that in my room."

"I know, sweetie. I know. You're really far away, though. It's hard for me not to be certain all the time you're safe."

My hand hurts from how tightly it's fisted around the cotton constellations. "I'll give you a call in the morning, okay?"

"Okay. And maybe in the afternoon, too? And a few times in the evening?"

I squeeze my eyes shut. I can't spend all day at the park checking in with my mother. Who knows how much more difficult the clues will be going forward? I need to be able to give them my full attention.

My right flip-flop is hanging off my toe, ready to be shed. I kick it across the room so hard it slams into the balcony's sliding glass doors. Tess and Issy jump.

"What was that?" Mom asks, her voice tense.

"Just Tess," I lie.

"Is she okay?"

Okay. Okay. Okay. I hear the word so much it's grown fangs. I need her to stop.

"Yep. Just looking through her suitcase."

"Hold on, honey, your dad wants to talk to you." There's shuffling as they exchange the phone, and then I hear my father clearing his throat. "Lia."

"Dad."

"This is a little late to hear from you." I catch the subtext beneath what he says—*too late for your mother to handle.*

"Sorry." I hate apologizing for living my life like a normal eighteen-year-old, but it comes out all the same. Because as much as I don't want to check in endlessly, I also don't want them to be worried about me. "We were having fun."

"I know. And I want you to keep doing that. So, what if you check in at meals? Things will be calmer for you then, and your m—*we*—will get to hear from you more often."

It's reasonable. My dad is trying to compromise. To give my mother and me each what we need. But it still feels like shards of glass tear at my insides when I agree.

We say a quick good-night, and I hang up before Mom can get back on the line. She would have continued with the warnings and I . . . can't. I don't want those things to burrow under my skin and affect how I see the world. I know it can be dangerous and unpredictable and unkind, but if I focus on the possibility of car accidents and school shootings and everything else I can't control, I'd never leave my house. That's not how I want to live.

Issy peers over at me as I drop my phone beside me on the bed. Worry tugs at her face, but she knows better than to ask if I'm okay. "You get in a fight with your shoe?"

"I think I won."

She cracks a grin. "Come sit." Hooking her arm through mine, she pulls me beside her so the three of us are crammed hip to hip on the other bed. "You never told us what happened with Mason while we were on that ride."

"It was . . . I don't know . . . good?"

"You should have seen how fast he followed you after Safety Harnessgate," Tess declares.

"Really?"

She flashes a salacious grin. "It was like Oliver chasing Elorra when the pirates captured her."

Issy beams. "Nothing was going to stand in his way."

I shrug, trying to feign nonchalance. What they're saying doesn't mean anything. It can't.

Since sixth grade, when Tess declared herself in lust-love with Taylor Swift and I couldn't decide if I would marry Captain America or Oliver Cray and Issy wanted Cap and Bucky to realize their feelings for each other, the three of us would sit cross-legged in the middle of Issy's king-size bed every Friday night and eat popcorn mixed with Reese's Pieces and confess our secrets. It's where I first told them, the summer before senior year, that sometimes I think girls are more than pretty, and where Tess first cried about her parents' divorce, and Issy confessed how bad the sex with her sophomore-year boyfriend had been. For seven years, we've never deviated from this ritual, no matter what else between us has changed. But the thought of talking about Mason makes my throat swell until it's hard to breathe. As if telling them anything more will make it too real. Make Mason and me something we aren't and can't be.

"He's . . . really sweet. That's all. We walked over to Casterman's Carousel to get the code, and he bought us that Dudley cookie bar." I fall back on the bed.

"This sounds like a date," Tess quips.

"There was no date."

"Maybe not yet."

"Not ever."

"We'll see."

"Tess." I shake my head at her. My hands are fists on my thighs. "There's nowhere for this . . . *thing* with Mason to go unless I win, so I can't want it. I *can't* get attached. I don't need more pressure put on this contest." I squeeze my eyes shut. "I already can't breathe."

"Lia." Issy scoots close to me, and I sit up and rest my head on her shoulder. She has a calmness about her that always soothes me. Like the eye of the storm to Tess's hurricane. "It'll be okay."

"I need to focus on me and this scavenger hunt," I insist. "I need a future that's mine to plan."

Just then a loud trumpet sound erupts from my phone.

Day two's first clue has arrived.

It's a perfect reminder of why we're here and what's at stake. As I grab my phone and gather my research notes on the bed, I tell myself one last time that this whole day with Mason was no different from that blade of grass he showed me.

Shiny and perfect on the outside, with nothing substantial beneath.

CHAPTER 9

June 20

Vale of Villainy, Fableland
Orlando, FL

Brave ye be who take a bite. What's inside cannot be found by sight.

—The Curséd Apple's slogan

"IS THAT EVEN A REAL DOOR?"

Tess has her hands on her hips as she watches me mount a small set of rickety stairs. With each step, the stairs waver, like a slatted bridge extended over a wide ravine. Issy hisses the next time the staircase shakes, but I know from my time on F^3 that they won't fall. This is part of the illusion.

"That's the whole point," I say. "People walk right by it."

I was shocked this morning when Tess didn't fight me about starting our day at Vale of Villainy to chase the first clue:

Here the sweetest treat tastes of death. Dare to take a bite. But she's been as excited about visiting the Curséd Apple as Issy and me.

Originally, we planned to wait for Carter and Mason to join us when the parks open to the general public in an hour, but I'm so sure I'm right that we decided to go on our own. I've read more than enough about this candy shop and its deceptive treats.

I need to rely on my alliance with Mason as little as possible so it's easier when it has to end.

Issy glances over her shoulder. "Are we supposed to be back here?"

Other guests are wandering through this part of Vale of Villainy, but we're the only ones in the small alleyway. The sides of the buildings that surround us are themed like the rest of the area, with dark, medieval-looking facades and flickering candles in the windows. Crooked signs hang over most of the doorways, swaying in a nonexistent wind, as if no one has wandered this way in decades.

The only conspicuous thing about the Curséd Apple is that it *doesn't* have a sign. Its dark windows gape like lifeless eyes and cobwebs stretch across their sills. But at the center of its elaborately carved door, visible only if you know to look for it, is an apple split in two. When I reach out and push both pieces at the same time, the door pops open and sways smoothly backward. Welcoming, despite the darkness within.

Behind me, Issy squeals and claps, and Tess is already clomping up the steps, making the entire staircase shake. "This is incredible," she says, hip-checking me in her affectionately brutish way as she shoves through the door.

I have to rub away goose bumps from my arms, even though the air this morning is so muggy it feels like we're breathing in a swamp. My friends' excitement fills me up, and I want to hold this moment in my hands, freeze in place everything I'm afraid we're losing.

I let Issy slip through the door ahead of me. As soon as I step inside, the scents of chocolate and caramel and fruit overwhelm me. Squat black cauldrons turned upside down and circled by short stools serve as tables. Ancient bookcases display glass jars with questionable contents, like eyeballs and ears and strange-looking plants floating in murky liquid. Hung all over the walls are brooms and stuffed birds and wide-brimmed pointed hats. I recognize a black broom with purple straw as Magabel the Dark's from *The Witching Time,* Fable Industry's most popular Halloween movie.

Stretching wall to wall across the back of the room is a case full of desserts. Issy is crouched in front of it, hands splayed against the glass. Tess and I join her as a woman sweeps through a curtained door behind the display.

She's wearing dark robes that hang open to reveal a corseted gown of ebony silk. Her blond hair is braided and wrapped around her head like a crown of snakes, and her smoky eyes and deep-red lipstick stand out against her pale white skin. My favorite thing, though, is that she's the same size as me.

Proof you can be beautiful and powerful without needing to be thin.

Her dark eyes narrow as she takes us in. "The first brave souls I've encountered in a fortnight." She's not performing an accent, but she still manages to sound sinister.

Issy's face lights up. "Not a lot of people find this place?"

"None but a few, my dear."

Issy and Tess turn to me with wide eyes and the biggest smiles on their faces like we're twelve again.

"We each get to sample one, right?" I run my finger along the counter. The top shelf houses truffles in every color and variety, along with stacks of chocolate-covered caramels and crèmes. The next one has everything you could imagine dipped in chocolate or caramel or marshmallow: pretzels, graham crackers, fruit, cookies, some stranger options like jalapeños and butter crackers and bacon. The bottom shelf cradles what looks like pastries and uncut fruit.

"Ah. No." The woman waves an onyx-painted nail at me. "As my first customers, you get to sample them *all*."

Excitement buzzes through me. This is something I'd never read about.

Tess crosses her arms. "And how much is *that* going to cost?"

"Tess." Issy's voice is tense. She'd most likely offer up her entire college fund to taste these desserts.

"You risk only yourselves." A wicked, close-lipped grin spreads across the woman's face. "Here at the Curséd Apple, nothing is as it seems."

That's the beauty of the Curséd Apple. It's got layers of secrets. Finding it is exciting enough, but eating its candy is a whole other experience. Nothing in this shop looks like how it tastes. I've read about people ordering salted dark chocolate truffles that tasted like peanut butter and banana, and others who had white-chocolate-dipped pretzels that were actually shortbread. Someone ordered a chocolate jalapeño that turned out to be blown sugar with strawberry jelly inside; another bought coconut chocolate bark that was made with potato chips. Most of the surprise flavors are delicious, but now and then someone will get something disgusting, like mashed potatoes or meat or cheese. The Cursed Apple is not a place for finicky eaters.

We settle down at one of the cauldrons, and for the next half an hour, we try at least twenty different desserts. Issy acts as the photographer, snapping photos of each plate and then texting them to Tess and me. She's also recording videos of our reactions for her channel.

Of course, I nominate Tess, queen of shrimp brownies, to be the taste tester. "Don't," I say with a finger pointed in the air, "tell us what it is. I want to see your expression." Half the fun is watching her face change as she figures out the flavor. Twice, she spits her bite back out on the plate. The first time because she didn't expect a peanut butter cup to taste like raspberry and lemon. The second time because the crème in her truffle was gravy flavored.

Issy and I roar with laughter as Tess wipes her tongue on a napkin. "No one wants Thanksgiving with their dessert, thanks," she mutters.

Finally, the woman sets the last dessert in front of us. It looks like a simple mandarin orange. The exterior has the same feel as an orange peel, and when squeezed, it has the same consistency. There are wedges inside when Tess breaks it open.

"So help me, if this tastes like peas, I'm suing," she says, sending Issy and me into another fit of giggles.

Sucking in a breath, Issy wipes tears from her eyes. "I don't think I've laughed this hard since Tess wrote that *Sunspark* self-insert fanfic and was so proud of it that she read every line to us out loud."

Tess sucks in a breath, her fists jamming into her hips. "Isabel Morales, how *dare* you. We swore we'd never speak of that again."

My cheeks are hot from laughing so hard. "I'm pretty sure I can still recite from memory the part where you swing from the jib sheet to save Princess Elorra from the vicious mermen."

"Especially because you can't swing from a jib sheet." Issy cackles.

Tess's face scrunches up as she crams the first piece of orange into her mouth. "Listen," she says around her bite, "not all of us are rich enough to have been on a boat, *okay*? Thirteen-year-old Tess was doing the best with what she had."

Her throat bobs violently as she swallows, but when Issy asks how it tastes, Tess smiles and says, "Refreshing. It really is an orange."

Which is a lie that Issy and I don't discover until we've each greedily crammed two slices in our mouths. They're soft like mousse and taste like carrots, but without the spices and sugar that make carrot cake good.

We cough our bites into napkins at the same time.

Tess erupts into laughter. "Revenge," she declares. There's a sharpness to her voice that pulls my eyes to her face. Tess loves to joke around and tease us, but if we do the same to her, she sometimes gets upset. Like she's afraid our jokes have too much truth behind them.

I make sure to laugh along with her as I stand and take a big swig of water from my stainless steel bottle to wash the taste of the carrot from my mouth.

Issy follows me to the counter. She wraps an arm around my shoulders and rests her temple against the top of my head. "Thanks for making this happen."

"It was the clue."

She gives me a little shake. "I mean the whole trip. We needed it." Her arm tightens, pulling me closer. "I needed it."

"One last hurrah before college," I mumble. The exact thing she and Tess have been saying for weeks.

"No. Soaking up as much Lia time as possible." Her voice trembles. "I need reserves for when I can't hug you whenever I want."

I wonder if she knows how bad I needed to hear that. A tear slips down my face, and I pretend to scratch my cheek to wipe it away.

It's a relief when the woman wanders over to check on us. We've still got five whole days here, and all summer before Issy and Tess leave. I can't get this emotional already or I'll fall to pieces when they actually go.

Time to refocus on the contest.

At this rate, we'll be able to knock out the three clues before ten-thirty. Part of me can't wait to see the look on Mason's face when he arrives and we're already on to clue two. Maybe this time, I'll get to ask him if *he* needs help. The thought makes me giddy.

The woman smiles at me from behind the counter. "Do you dare to try another?"

I laugh. "Not today. But I can't find the QR code to scan."

I knew the second I popped a piece of the white chocolate truffle in my mouth and tasted that bitter burst of star anise on my tongue that I'd found the answer to the clue. White chocolate is the sweetest kind, and I honestly believe star anise shares a flavor profile with rotting corpses. Issy agreed that, of everything we sampled, the white chocolate truffle most closely matched the riddle. And as if to confirm it, when the woman set the dessert down, she said, "Fear for your life, sweeties."

Here the sweetest treat tastes of death. Dare to take a bite. There's no question we solved it.

But there was no QR code beneath the truffle, and I hadn't seen one anywhere in the shop as we wandered around. That must mean the attendant needs to direct me.

The woman's dark eyebrows arch. "What's that, deary?"

"The QR code. For the scavenger hunt."

"You're speaking in tongues."

Maybe since it's the second day and things are getting more difficult I have to make it crystal clear. "Here the sweetest treat tastes of death. Dare to take a bite. The white chocolate truffle with star anise. I ate the whole thing."

"I don't know what you mean. I barter not in death."

Though she stays in character, the woman offers me the slightest shake of her head before turning away. It's enough to tell me that she knows what I'm asking. That she understands exactly why I'm here.

And that I'm wrong.

CHAPTER 10

June 20

Vale of Villainy, Fableland
Orlando, FL

Any true foodie knows that some of the best restaurants in the country can be found at Fableland. From five-star steak houses to the latest in farm-to-table to quick counter service treats, there's something to satisfy even the most discerning eater. The resort's latest dining experience, Hellfire, opened in Vale of Villainy to rave reviews this spring. Not for the faint of taste buds, the restaurant specializes in intense flavor and bold ingredient combinations....

—*Restaurant.com, "Where should I eat this summer?"*

"WHAT DO WE THINK OF THIS?"

Tess preens in front of a full-length mirror, a maroon top hat covered in cogs perched on her head.

"Great if your plan is to become the hero in a steampunk novel," Issy says. She stands behind Tess, sporting the red cloak and furry wolf paws from *Run, Little Girl,* Fable Industry's "Little Red Riding Hood" retelling.

Issy had spotted the souvenir shop, with its homage to a bunch of the company's older movies in the display window, as we left the Curséd Apple.

I had my face buried in my phone, frantically Googling desserts at the parks while dodging texts from my mother, when Issy caught my arm and pulled me into the store.

"I've heard about this place," she insisted. Her wide eyes glanced around us. "Apparently you can find memorabilia here that's rare or even discontinued."

Which made perfect sense. The shop is named Clockbender, after the villain from *The Witching Time,* who used time magic to mess up history and confuse people's memories. Where else would someone find merchandise from earlier decades?

Since then, Issy and Tess have been wandering the aisles, screeching with joy every time they find another toy they'd had as kids.

I should be doing the same, but instead I'm glued to a bench by the door. My mind keeps rehashing what happened at the Curséd Apple over and over. How could I have been so wrong about that clue? And why can't I find any other answers on F^3? If I didn't think Tess and Issy would handcuff me to them, I'd go back to the hotel to consult my notebooks.

A lavender shirt flaps in my face. When I glance up from my phone, Tess is standing in front of me with her arms crossed. "Mason and Carter will be here soon. You guys will figure it out together," she insists.

"I don't want to need him to do this."

Working together is one thing, but depending on him? Not being able to solve the clues on my own? I refuse to accept that reality.

"Hey." She snatches my phone from my hand and waves it in front of me before handing it back. "We're practically standing in Issy's childhood bedroom. They have the Oliver Cray doll that parents just about murdered each other over that Black Friday when we were in sixth grade. And you're missing it all."

I groan.

"The parks have barely been open an hour," Tess reminds me. "You've got plenty of time to get your clues."

Except fifteen people will be eliminated today. And chances are, we're all feeling the pressure to finish fast.

I don't have "plenty of time" if I want to win. But giving my brain a break might help shake free some new ideas, so I stand up, giving in. *For now.*

Across from us is a shelf of chemistry sets based on Elorra's lab in *Sunspark*. My parents got me one for my tenth birthday, but I destroyed all the beakers in the microwave. (I had the power too high and they melted.)

I wander over and trace my finger along one of the boxed sets. "What if we're in the wrong park?"

"Carter would have told me when I texted him to meet us," Tess says.

"He and Mason could be wrong too."

Tess sighs. "Lia, there are like fifty places in Vale alone to get dessert. You've only crossed one off the list." She shakes her head at me. "Now look at this." Flicking out the shirt she's been carrying, she rests it over her chest.

Elorra is silk-screened on the front. The princess's copper curls are, as always, pinned beneath her tiara by four pencils, and she's holding up a beaker that's sloshing a bubbling black liquid all over the front of her sunshine-yellow gown. Beneath its lace hem, sturdy boots peek out.

It's everything we loved about the character as kids captured in one image. Tears prick at my lashes, and I have to blink them away. I will never hear the end of it if Tess sees me crying.

She places her hands on my shoulder blades and pushes me forward. "We're each getting one and we're going to wear them all day. Go get yours."

A giant smile spreads over my face as I beeline for the clothing section.

There's an entire rack of the lavender Elorra shirts. I flip through them, one by one, starting at the back, where the largest sizes should be.

The biggest I can find is an XXL, and when I hold it up in front of me, it's clear the shirt is woefully undersized.

My stomach drops, though I probably shouldn't be surprised. Stores love to offer XXLs and pretend they're body inclusive, when that's not even technically a plus size.

Two of the shirts tumble from the rack as I comb through them again. I count four extra-smalls, five smalls, three mediums, three larges, and one extra-large. Plus the extra-extra-large in my hand.

My gaze drifts to my friends, who are holding their shirts to their bodies and laughing, and my heart pitches into my throat. I don't want to tell them the store doesn't have my size. I don't want to miss out on this moment.

Squaring my shoulders, I examine the largest Elorra shirt again. Thankfully, the fabric is jersey cotton and has a good amount of stretch. I should be able to get it on; it just won't fit the way I'd want it to.

Whatever excitement I had about bonding with Tess and Issy has evaporated by the time I leave the register. I'm so tired of having to shop online and hope I pick the right size, or visit specialty stores that basically scream "Oh hey, you aren't normal, your body's wrong." Clothes that fit should be a right, not a straight-size privilege. Especially somewhere like Fableland that markets itself as a safe, fun place for everyone.

I refuse to let my body be the reason I miss out. I'm going to miss out on too many other things with Tess and Issy once they're gone.

Pulling the shirt over my head, I join them at the mirror. Tess has already knotted hers into a crop top, and she and Issy are posing and pulling exaggerated faces at their reflections. The best I can do is not cry. My shirt is stretched taut over my breasts and hugs every curve and roll of fat much more snugly than anything I would choose to wear. I like flowy peasant tops and swing dresses and cozy cardigans and loose shirts I can French tuck into my favorite jeans. Clothes that let me decide how much of my body I want on display.

Tess insists we need crowns and hurries off to find some, while Issy and I stare at ourselves in the mirror. "Look at us, we're so cute," she says.

I don't feel cute, though. I feel exposed. Still, I do my best to play along. "Tess would call us hottie magnets."

Issy's eyes skip past mine in the mirror, her face clouding over. "Ummm . . ." She drags the word out before clearing her throat.

"What?" I ask.

Determination tightens her jaw, and she swallows. She only gets out the word *I* before Tess reappears and, teetering on her tiptoes, jams plastic gold tiaras on each of our heads.

"Nobody is ready for these princesses," Tess declares as she snaps selfies of us from a million different angles.

Issy concentrates far too hard on securing her headpiece in her curls. Like she's trying to distract herself. It makes me wonder what she'd been about to say. "There should be more opportunities to wear crowns in everyday life," she quips.

"Oh my God, how iconic would we look grocery shopping in full regal attire," Tess pipes up.

"Trendsetters," I mumble. I want to be done talking about these shirts and get away from the mirror. Tugging on the hem, I turn away, letting my gaze roam the store. It immediately snags on Mason at the entrance, like some kind of hot-person radar.

At the same time, Tess announces, "Carter says they're here."

The sight of Mason reminds me of the clue and my failed guess and how many people might already be further along than us. My stomach thickens like a swamp.

What if Mason doesn't have the answer to today's first clue? What if he does?

I want to continue in the contest, obviously, but I hate the idea of being the only one who got an answer wrong. What kind of superfan am I if this guy who doesn't even like the parks knows them better than I do?

"Hey," Mason says as he wanders over to me. Already his gaze feels familiar. Comfortable. I hate it. I love it.

I nod in reply.

Carter claps his hands. "All right, supernerds," he says, addressing me and Mason, "guide us to the first clue."

His words are a knife stabbing at an open wound. Swallowing, I do my best to look smug, but I'm pretty sure my jaw is trembling. "What if I'm already done for the day?" I tip my chin up as if that will save my performance.

"Then you are either the world's best alliance partner or the worst. Depends on if you plan to share." Carter winks.

But Mason's watching me, those watercolor eyes tracking every fissure in my facade. "What's wrong?" he asks softly.

The words push out of my mouth before I can stop them. "I can't figure out the first clue. I thought it was one of the desserts at the Curséd Apple, but I was wrong." Panic scratches at my throat, and my hands clench into fists. "We wasted like an hour there. What if people are already finishing up for the day?"

It's like I've slid a stone out from the middle of a wall. Releasing that one worry sets the rest of them free in my head. Now I can't stop thinking about my mom and next year and how miserable I will be if I don't win this contest.

"No one can get the first clue until ten-thirty," Mason says. He's almost a head taller than me, and he hunches slightly so I can hear his soft voice.

"How do you know?" I'm as loud as he is quiet. Nothing summons my competitive side quite like the idea that someone knows something I don't.

He grins. "That's when the restaurant opens."

"Which one?"

He shakes his head. "You can figure it out. I need to know my alliance is with someone who actually knows their stuff."

I huff indignantly. "I knew every clue yesterday."

"Those were easy."

This time I flat-out squawk.

I'm still gaping at him as the five of us make our way out of the store. From the sly glint in Mason's eyes, he's clearly baiting me. Or possibly trying to motivate me? Either way, it works.

"Issy." I fall into step with her. I may know the movies and the parks, but Issy knows the food. She's basically been studying it since we booked our trip. "Mason says the first clue is at one of the restaurants here that doesn't open until ten-thirty. Any guesses to which one?"

She bites her lip, her brown eyes narrowing. "Chocolate that can kill you?"

"Yes." A less poetic paraphrase, but close enough.

She pulls out her phone and starts typing into the browser, her feet slowing to a stop. Multitasking has never been her strength, except in the kitchen. "Dastardly has that lava cake," she mumbles. "Lava can technically kill you. . . .

"Then there's Temptations. Pretty much everything on their menu is decadent. I know they have some chocolate dishes. . . ." Her voice trails off. Her fingers are moving even faster now.

"No. Wait." She glances up at me. A wide smile splits her face. "Hellfire."

"What?"

"It just opened. One of their most-raved-about desserts is called Death by Chocolate."

I actually scream, then throw my arms around her. "My culinary queen."

Issy beams, resting her temple against mine.

I don't know what I'm going to do without her next year. Except for my parents, no one else believes in me so unconditionally. I try to always do the same for her. Like with her cooking videos. I'm always the first to watch and share.

Arching an eyebrow at Mason, I say, "Death by Chocolate."

"Death by Chocolate," he echoes.

I can't help but pump a fist like the dork I am.

Tess waves her phone at me. "Hellfire is on the other side of the park from half the rides we want to start with."

I can't get into this with her again, so I wrinkle my nose apologetically. I can't commit to doing anything else until I secure my spot for tomorrow. She knows this. I refuse to have to repeat it.

Issy steps between us. "Why don't Tess and I go find the chocolate-and-banana Cronuts I need for my channel while you, Mason, and Carter get the clue. We can knock out two things on our list at once."

"Good plan," Carter says, spinning his hat around so the brim covers his eyes from the sun. "Except I'm going for the Cronuts."

No one else has any complaints, so the three of them head north toward Clockbender's Tower, while Mason and I turn east.

In the distance, the mountain peak from Valyrad's Flight cuts jagged edges into the bright-blue sky.

We're quiet for a few minutes as we dodge through the crowd. Ahead of us, I catch sight of a ginger-haired guy with a contestant pin speed-walking in the same direction, and my steps grow faster. Mason's long stride helps him keep up easily.

He yawns and rubs at his eyes.

"Sorry for being such a bore," I quip.

One corner of his mouth ticks up a little. "I picked up a few hours of work this morning stocking shelves for Carter's dad, so I didn't get much sleep. He owns a twenty-four-hour pharmacy and lets me come in whenever I want to make some extra cash." He's wearing a large silver ring on his index finger, and he spins it around as he talks.

"When did you go in?" I ask.

"About two."

"In the morning?"

Mason nods. "I wanted to make it a decent shift. I can't work my regular job while I'm doing this contest."

"I would have gone straight back to bed as soon as I clocked out." I'm a monster without at least six hours of sleep.

"I need the money," he says.

I don't mean to ask for what, but the words come out anyway.

"For college," he responds. "I have to pay for it myself, so I've taken the last year to work full-time and save up."

"So that's why you're doing this contest?"

"It would cover more than half my credits if I stay in-state."

My stomach tightens. I've been so focused on why *I* need this contest money that I haven't even stopped to consider that someone else could have real reasons to want it too.

"My dad thinks college is a waste of time." His eyes catch mine. "But it's not. Not for me, at least." Something sharp has slipped into his tone, and he presses out a breath like it's a weight in his mouth.

Then he clears his throat, and it feels like a door has shut between us. "That's . . . quite the shirt." He nods at me.

I tug at the T-shirt's hem, suddenly too aware of how closely it fits. Which then makes me too aware of everyone around us, and how thick the crowd is, and how people keep jostling Mason and me closer and closer together.

"*Sunspark* . . . is . . . was"—I don't even know how to talk about my best friendship anymore—"a thing with Tess, Issy, and me."

"I won't tell you, then, how much I hate that movie." He crosses his arms even as another small smile tugs at the corners of his lips.

Here we go again: painted grass, the sequel.

I mirror his body language but not his grin. "Please don't. That movie's pretty special to me."

He doesn't say anything else, as if he wants me to decide how much to share, but everything about him has softened. It urges me to keep going.

"Eighth grade was terrible for the three of us. All this bad stuff kept happening. Issy's favorite uncle died in a car accident, and Tess's parents got divorced, and my mom . . ." I shake my head. I don't talk about my mother's worst day. If I did, I'd have to remember it. "Anyway . . . we spent a lot of time hiding out in Issy's room watching Fable Industry movies. And most of the time, it was *Sunspark*."

His mouth draws tight, and he drifts a little closer to me. Though our arms aren't touching, I can practically feel his skin against mine.

"That's why you love this place," he says softly.

I nod. "It gives me somewhere to escape." I take a breath, preparing to tell him more.

But then a family with at least five kids pushes between us, laughing and talking as if we weren't there. Just ghosts they can walk through.

I get turned around dodging them, and by the time I'm facing the right direction again, I don't see Mason. He must have kept going.

He's so tall, and my body seems so attuned to his, that my heart starts to beat a little faster when I don't spot him anywhere.

I can get to Hellfire on my own. Cartographer is installed on my phone, and I know the parks' general layouts. But for once, I want to get to this clue with Mason. I want to help him get as far as he can in this contest too.

A warm hand wraps around mine, making me jump. I look up to see Mason beside me again, moving ahead to thread us through the throngs of people.

My pulse is galloping wildly, thrumming in my veins and beating at my eardrums. I should let go. Should scurry to keep pace with him.

But instead, I secure my grip. I hold on tight.

Just for now. Just until we clear the crowd.

CHAPTER 11

June 20

Vale of Villainy, Fableland
Orlando, FL

> OLIVER
> Milady, it looks as if you are in need of some saving.
>
> ELORRA
> (arches an eyebrow)
> You're the one stuck in a trap.
>
> —*Sunspark (00:40:05)*

IT'S ONLY TEN-FIFTEEN WHEN WE REACH HELLFIRE.

The restaurant is empty and quiet, except for servers setting up tables and noises coming from the kitchen in the back.

Ten or so contestants are hanging around in the foyer, scrolling through their phones or chatting with each other.

"I'm surprised there aren't more of us," I note. Secretly, though, I'm glad I might not be the only one to have made a mistake.

Mason shrugs. "Everyone gets so caught up in the lore, they forget about the food. Plus, this place just opened and it's super expensive." Tess has made it a point to express her distaste at the prices of the parks' food at every meal, so I can't even imagine what "expensive" must mean.

He starts to stride forward, but I grab his arm to stop him, letting my fingers linger for only a second before pulling back. Neither of us has said much since he took my hand to get through the crowd. Even once we'd cleared the worst of it, we held on for another beat before we glanced at each other sheepishly and let go.

The heat of his touch still sizzles against my skin like the embers of a dying fire.

"They're closed."

His eyes drift over me. "I know a guy who works in the kitchen. We can get a Death by Chocolate before they stock the dessert display. Save us some time."

"Isn't that cheating, though?" I'm not as scared as Issy is of breaking the rules, but the last thing I need is to get banned from the contest.

Mason shifts so he's facing me fully. "What do the rules say?"

I shove my hands on my hips. "I don't know why you're so convinced I have them memorized or something."

His head tips to one side, and he waits, calling my bluff.

My resolve lasts for about a minute; then I huff out a

frustrated breath. "All I remember is something about being able to find clues only during the parks' operating hours." In reality, I could recite the lines word for word, but he doesn't need to know that.

This Fableland fanatic has at least a small amount of dignity.

"The parks are open." He stands still.

He's letting me make the decision.

"As long as you don't think we'll get kicked out," I say.

"I think the worst that will happen is the code won't scan until ten-thirty."

He's probably right. Still, I bite my nails as I stare at the kitchen. What if this is a way to weed out cheaters? I don't want to win so bad that I disqualify myself. And Mason.

I look down at my phone. There's only like eight minutes until the restaurant opens.

You'd think we were consulting on how to defuse a bomb or rob a bank from how seriously I'm considering this. Yet Mason's eyes take me in without judgment. He's statue-still, his handsome face placid. If I'm annoying him, he's doing a great job of hiding it.

Finally, I sigh. He takes that as his signal to head for the kitchen.

Thank God, because if I had to say it out loud, I'd end up trapped in my thoughts all over again.

Wringing my hands, I bounce on my heels as I watch Mason cross the room. I feel like the lookout on a heist. All I need is some kind of secret whistle and an escape route. It's suddenly very clear that everything I know about heists I learned from Dudley and Squirt.

The double doors to the kitchen swing open just as Mason

reaches them, almost smacking him in the face. A couple emerges, the girl clutching a plastic bowl that cradles a chocolate bonbon about the size of a baseball. I recognize her from the carousel yesterday. She's the one who was pushing people aside to reach the unicorn first.

Her friend in tow, she breezes by Mason as if she hadn't been on the verge of concussing him. She spots me while she's spooning her first bite of the dessert into her mouth, and her eyes dip to the contestant pin on the hem of my Elorra shirt. A smirk spreads over her face as she pauses in front of me.

"I told you I'd be first," she whispers to the guy.

Something sharp and hot zips through me. Grudges aren't typically my thing, but now this girl feels like my nemesis.

"May you never have replacements when your smoke alarm batteries die in the middle of the night," I mutter at her back.

I'm not a Fableland villain, I don't know how to do vengeance, but I really, really want her to lose. At this contest. And at life.

"What's that?" Mason steps up behind me. In his hand, he's got the same bowl and chocolate bonbon as the other contestant.

"She's a jerk." I nod at the couple as they disappear into the crowd. I quickly recount her nasty attitude.

"So you cursed her batteries?"

"What's worse than a smoke alarm that won't stop beeping?"

"Fair." He hands me the dessert.

"We need to take her down." I don't want to lose this contest, but I especially don't want to lose to *her*.

Using the spoon, I cut the chocolate bomb in half and press one piece to the side of the bowl, revealing the QR code. Mason and I lock eyes. It's 10:28. Close enough. Neither of us says anything as we lift our phones at the same time and scan the code.

A new scroll appears in the app, and I click it open.

To solve this clue, you must reach the highest of peaks.

Although most people think Reddingshire Castle is the tallest building in Fableland, it's actually the mountain that houses Valyrad's Flight, one of Vale of Villainy's most death-defying roller coasters. At the top of the queue, there's a secret balcony with a statue of Valyrad, his demon wings spread to full span, overlooking the park. The very tips of his wings are, according to everything I've seen online, the actual tallest point in the park.

My eyes find Mason's. "Valyrad's Flight," we say in unison.

Activate Alliance Level Two. No more coy attempts at rivalry or teasing.

Ever since he grabbed my hand on the way to Hellfire, something's shifted. It feels like we're a team now for real. As if that small touch we shared was a strand of thread, stitching us firmly together.

At least until the final day.

But I can't think about that right now.

Mason eats his half of Death by Chocolate like it's literally his last meal.

Watching his eyes close in delight as he takes the final bite of mousse and cake makes my heart dance. "I'm guessing you've never tried one of these before," I joke.

"They're thirty bucks a pop if you don't have a contestant pin."

I shrug. "It's okay to have a treat now and then."

Every time my mom makes it through one of her bad anxiety episodes, we always go out and do something for ourselves. Get a mani-pedi, Thai from our favorite place an hour away, a new outfit from the little boutique on Water Street that has my size. Something to remind us that it's okay to find a little slice of happiness when life is tough. I want to believe that somewhere in her, Mom is thinking the same thing about my time here, even if it's too hard for her to voice it.

"Every dollar gets me closer to college," Mason reminds me.

Swallowing, I drop my gaze to my feet. His drive is something I don't understand. Outside of this place, of my wish to pitch the company a fat princess, I don't have a dream I'd make endless sacrifices for.

I don't even know how to want anything besides space from my parents.

A crumpled piece of paper tumbles by our feet in the breeze, and I catch it with my toe. "What do you want to do after college?" I ask, bending to pick the paper up and throw it away.

The main street in Vale of Villainy is this incredible reproduction of the village beneath Pillager's Peak from the *Valyrad* film. It's reminiscent of London in the 1800s, with Victorian houses stacked one next to another among shops and cafés, the sidewalks speckled with gas lanterns. Everything is swathed in shades of gray and black, as if the sun has stopped shining here, blotted out by Valyrad's evil and his wings. That effect doesn't need to be spoiled by litter.

A cast member dressed as a newsboy breaks character to thank me, and I shrug, my cheeks burning.

When I turn back to Mason, he's staring at me like I'm a stranger.

"What?"

"I've never seen someone do that before."

"Pick up trash?"

"Pick up trash *here*."

I shrug again, more as a defense mechanism this time. I don't know what to make of his consuming stare. "It's easy to leave places a little better than you found them," I say. Before he can say anything else, I rush on. "You still haven't told me. What comes after college?"

He's quiet for a moment, his knuckles brushing back and forth over the tip of his chin. I've noticed he does this a lot, stops to think before he speaks. Like what I'm asking is important enough to consider deeply. "I want to teach."

"Wow."

His jaw tightens, and a stoniness settles over him. "I know it's dumb."

"Are you kidding? That's the least dumb thing I've ever heard." My fingers twist into my shirt to keep from grabbing his arm.

His expression softens, the same way it did when I asked why he likes science fiction. It's as if no one has ever cared enough to learn what's in his heart.

"I'm betting from those books you carry around that you want to teach science." It would make sense with his whole vendetta against fantasy—wanting to study how the world actually works.

His cheeks turn red, but he's smiling. "I'm thinking maybe

I could use them to help with difficult concepts. I sucked at school, but reading those books helped me better understand things. Maybe . . . I don't know"—he shrugs hard like he's trying to chase away whatever this conversation is making him feel—"maybe I could help other kids who are struggling."

Something raw and real passes over his face when I say, "I bet you will."

My phone buzzes with a text from Issy. A picture of her, Tess, and Carter displaying their half-eaten Cronuts with giant smiles on their faces.

A knot forms in my stomach as I imagine Issy and Tess hanging the photo on their dorm wall. Another memory without me in it.

Lia
Nice! We're headed to Valyrad's Flight for clue 2. Meet us there?
(11:22 AM)

I can feel Mason's eyes lingering on me, so I do my best to ignore the sourness that overtakes me every time I think about next year.

"What about you?" he asks quietly.

"What about me?"

"Didn't you just graduate? What's next?"

"Working at my parents' store." I try (and, by his expression, completely fail) not to sound miserable about this prospect. "We sell furniture."

"Not your thing?"

I shake my head. "It's a good job. But I'm not . . . a fanatic . . . about furniture."

"In that case, you should come work here." The right corner of his mouth ticks up slightly, a flash of teasing in his eyes.

I laugh ruefully. "I wish."

"What would you want to do?"

My shoulders stick by my ears as I shrug. I've never admitted this out loud to anyone but Tess and Issy. "Create new stories. Ones that represent more people." I run my hand over the back of my neck, accidentally tugging some of my hair out of my ponytail. I try to laugh. "Now who sounds dumb? I don't even know if that's a job that actually exists."

"It does. There's a whole storytelling department here. They come up with the concepts that get turned into movies and rides and performances."

"Oh," I mumble weakly. He's made this silly idea of mine seem almost real. Something I could grab on to. Actually do.

Mason's gaze deepens, its touch heavy on my face. "And that's not a dumb goal at all."

I dismiss those words with another shrug. "It doesn't matter. My mom can barely handle me being in another room. Never mind another state." I force a smile as if this is all fine. Even if it is so *not fine* that it hurts.

"Where's home?" he asks.

"Massachusetts."

"That's far."

I shrug. "It's not *that* bad, but my mom . . . she's a worrier."

Up ahead, the entrance of Valyrad's Flight comes into view. The tension in my chest loosens at the sight of it. I don't want to have to explain that "worrier" is the world's biggest understatement when it comes to my mother. I don't want to keep thinking about her and next year when I'm in my favorite place on earth, doing everything I can to change my future. But if Mason asked, I'd end up telling him more. A simple look from him seems to unspool every thought I've keep tightly coiled and hidden away for so long.

Tess, Issy, and Carter are waiting for us by the ride's sign, and as we file into the queue (me first, followed by Mason and then our friends), they gush about the Cronuts and their soft texture and silky ganache so much that my mouth waters. Thank God Issy had some sent to the room for us to snack on tonight.

The FOTL section is moving quickly, and we make our way up a series of cavern halls lined with flickering torches that set the shadows dancing. Every few minutes the flap of giant wings fills the narrowing space between the stone walls, and blasts of wind buffet our hair.

When we hear Valyrad's baritone call out the first warning to turn back, I can't help but glance at Mason and grin.

The light in his eyes as he smiles back chases a shiver up my spine. He looks almost as excited as I feel.

I never want to leave. My heart squeezes at the thought of it.

Just before the loading area, a second corridor branches to the left. Small arrows are etched into the wall, barely visible among the claw marks that rip through the stone from ceiling to floor.

I wave for the others to follow as I take the turn. The corridor should angle up and end on a balcony with Valyrad's statue at its center. I remember reading about it on F^3.

We seem to walk forever in the near dark. After the third bend, Tess asks if we're lost.

I keep moving forward. I have already been wrong once today. It can't happen again.

Beside me, Mason's strides are as sure as mine. "Have you been here before?" I ask him quietly.

"When I was a kid." His mouth tightens for a second. "I had nightmares about this thing for a week afterward."

"No way."

"It's huge," he confirms. The way he spreads his hands to demonstrate makes our arms brush and neither of us steps away.

All the heat in my body rushes to that spot and stays there. I think the last time I developed this strong a crush on someone so quickly, I was eleven, and the guy was a cartoon character. It doesn't help that Mason looks a little like Oliver Cray.

I avert my eyes from his, afraid of what he might be able to read on my face.

Finally, the air-conditioned cold is met by a wall of Florida humidity. Sunlight creeps toward us from the opening ahead.

"Holy shit," Tess mutters as we step out onto the balcony.

Above us towers a fifteen-foot replica of Valyrad. His wingspan is easily the size of a large car, and they reach out past the railings, shooting over the mountain's peak and into the sky. Exactly as the posts on F³ promised. He stands facing us, as if he's just landed from flight. Although he's made of the same gray stone as most of the statues I've seen here, his feral expression and the bend and pull of his muscles seem so fluid that I almost believe he's real.

"Okay, I get the nightmares," I mumble.

Mason laughs.

Issy, Tess, and Carter are circling the statue, taking it in from every angle. I extract my phone from my pocket and snap a few pictures: one of the full statue and the rest of my friends' awed expressions.

At the same time, Mason and I step toward the QR code positioned at the center of Valyrad's chest. We almost bump into each other before he waves for me to go first. Queuing up the app and capturing the image feels like it takes an eternity. The whole time, I can feel Mason behind me as if he's pressed against my spine, even though there's enough distance between us to fit another person.

I could stand here for hours, admiring this statue, but four other contestants wander in and it's a reminder that I need to hurry. We rush to retrace our steps to the FOTL queue. At this point, the quickest way back down to the park is to do the ride.

The loading area is as well themed as the rest of the attraction. Stalactites jut from the ceiling like spears, and a cold wind whips through the cavernous space, blowing droplets of water from the icy stone into our faces.

This is one of those indoor roller coasters where your feet hang over the ride, and the whole thing begins with a ninety-degree drop into darkness. Each of the cars has wings as wide and jagged as Valyrad's that swoop over our heads.

Issy and Tess sit in the back of the car, and Carter takes the middle row, leaving Mason and me to ride in the front.

The seat fits snugly against my hips, and I'm relieved when

the harness pulls down over my head and snaps easily into place. I would have cried if I had to miss this after all the anticipation.

These few moments before a ride begins always fill me with a potent mixture of excitement and dread. My legs are currently dangling off the floor, and we're who knows how many stories up, and I have volunteered to be twisted and dropped and turned at high speeds *in the dark* with nothing but shoulder restraints of plastic and metal holding me in place.

Why do we love this so much?

Adrenaline pumps through my veins, and my shaky knee knocks against Mason's. My heart beats wildly in my chest.

He grins over at me. "Are you ready for this?" he asks.

I shake my head. "Absolutely not."

A second later, the lights dim and animatronic versions of Dahlia Penny and Valyrad appear on either side of us. They yell their iconic lines from the movie at each other, their voices cracking over our heads like thunder.

Just before the track creaks to life, Mason holds his hand out.

My eyes cut to the entrance ahead, waiting to swallow us whole. Then I weave my fingers through his.

A second later, the car jerks, and we're tossed downward into the dark.

I don't let go the entire time.

CHAPTER 12

June 20

Vale of Villainy, Fableland

Orlando, FL

At this point, Fable Industry movies are so synonymous with cinema gold that most people don't remember their one major flop. *Last Steps,* which premiered in 1996, was the company's final attempt at live-action films, and their only foray into horror. It tells the story of Debbie Lemon, a high school senior crowned prom queen just minutes before a zombie apocalypse descends upon her town. Pissed that she's had her glory stolen by a bunch of shambling corpses, she gathers a ragtag group of friends to enact some revenge. While the premise could have been fun, the movie is plagued by excessive gore and badly written jokes, resulting in an unsettling romp better suited for straight-to-DVD.

—*"Little Known Facts: Fable Industry,"* Film Quarterly

MY LUNGS ARE STILL GASPING FOR AIR AS WE STEP BACK INTO the sunlight.

I'm pretty sure I didn't stop screaming for the entire three minutes of that ride.

"Roller coasters in the dark should be outlawed," I mutter. I thought seeing the upcoming loops and steep drops was bad, but it is so much worse when you can't anticipate what's ahead.

"No way." The apples of Tess's round cheeks are bright pink with excitement. "That was epic."

Issy looks just as elated. "Should we go again?"

"Feel free, but Mason and I need to go get that last clue." It's getting close to lunchtime. Who knows how many contestants have already secured their place for tomorrow by this point?

"As long as you're sure?" Issy says.

Tess hooks her arm in Issy's. "They'll probably be faster without us anyway." She smiles and waves at me as she drags Issy back toward the entrance of Valyrad's Flight.

"Text us where to meet you!" Issy calls over Tess's head.

My stomach dips as they disappear into the crowd. I know I told them to go, but it feels like they've chosen the rides over extra time with me.

And we have so little time left.

I sigh. I can't focus on this right now. Not when I haven't finished the contest for the day.

Mason peers over my shoulder as I get out my phone, his shadow enveloping me. We were so absorbed in the statue and the ride that we both forgot to check the final clue for the day.

"'No one likes their summer drinks undead,'" I read.

The words blur as I scan them a few more times. Summer drink. Undead. Neither means anything to me.

My eyes flit to Mason's face. "Any ideas?"

He shakes his head, his mouth pulled tight.

"What's undead here?" That seems like the most important word to parse.

"There's the skeleton dragons from *Moonwatcher*, but that attraction is over in Hero's Quest." He scratches the back of his neck. "They don't seem to be having us park-hopping yet."

The two of us peer at Carter.

His hands fly up in surrender. "I'm getting out of here before I accidentally help you cheat." He and Mason share one of those elaborate fist bumps guys like to do. "I'm going to meet up with Isaiah for his lunch break. Let me know if you want to join us." His hazel eyes drop to me. "Or . . . not."

His boyish face is beaming with mischief, and Mason looks ready to kill him as he scurries off.

I cross my arms. "What do people drink in the summer?"

"Ice water?" Mason suggests.

"You know some yawners," I quip.

That little tick of a smile that tells me he appreciates my jokes passes over his mouth.

"Icees?" he tries again.

"Iced tea?" I offer.

Nothing is jogging my memory.

"Lemonade?"

"Wait." That word triggers something in my brain. I reach out an arm to stop Mason from saying anything else.

"When life gives you lemons," I mumble.

Mason's watercolor eyes pop open. "Use them to kill some zombies."

"Debbie Lemon."

We're already walking when Mason says, "The Last Steps walk-through is behind Hellfire."

"We're probably okay, then, right?" I ask. "A lot of serious Fableland fans don't even know about that movie."

"I'm honestly surprised it's a clue so early on."

"I went to my eighth-grade Halloween dance as Debbie Lemon," I admit sheepishly. It took my mom and me weeks to find the right prom dress (Debbie's is purple and puffy and covered in sequins, not exactly the style these days), and then to tear it up and cover it with red paint. Her anxiety had been less overwhelming then, and I still remember how much fun we had destroying that dress in the most artful way possible.

Mason's eyes are pinned to my face. "I bet you looked incredible." He's completely serious, not so much as blinking as he says it.

"It was a cool costume." I do my best to sound nonchalant, but every inch of my skin has caught fire. None of the guys I knew at school were ever so direct or sincere. I feel adrift, like a white-water tube headed straight for a waterfall.

As we cross through the middle of Vale of Villainy, where the crowd is thickest, I hear two dudes talking loudly behind us.

"Why do fat girls think they don't need to wear more clothes?" one of them says.

It takes one quick glance over my shoulder to know they're talking about me. They look like they're in their early twenties, both of them white, one with short blond hair, the other with brown waves to his chin. Their shirts have gym logos on them, as do the bandannas tied around their foreheads.

My heart's a hammer, and I want to use it on their smug faces. I'm wearing shorts that hit me at midthigh, and the Elorra shirt covers everything but my arms. I'm not flaunting anything. And even if I were, what I put on my body is no one's concern but mine.

I grind my teeth.

Beside me, I feel Mason stiffen, and his hands snap into fists. I touch his arm and subtly shake my head. Fableland has a zero-tolerance policy for violence. We're not risking our chances at the prize money over some fatphobic jerks.

"Seriously," the other guy replies. "No one wants to see that."

He's halfway through the sentence when two hands grab my ass hard enough to hurt.

I squeak and jerk away, heat flooding my face. Embarrassment snakes around my bones and coils tight.

The guys laugh like a pack of hyenas, and the blond guy steps toward me as if he intends to pinch my ass again.

Mason slips between us, his body a brick wall in the middle of the path. He's easily a foot and a half taller than the two guys and just as broad and muscular. His eyes flare wide. "Dude. What the *hell*." It's the loudest I've ever heard him speak.

My hands tremble, and I press them to my thighs to still

them. This is not the first time I've been ridiculed by strangers, and normally I would say something snarky and walk away. But this guy put his hands on me. I'm having a harder time shaking that off. I honestly don't even know what to do.

The two of them stare at Mason, bewildered. As if they have no idea what has him so riled up.

The blond holds up his hands. "All I'm saying is that fatties—"

Mason stalks forward another step. "Call her that one more time." His back muscles roll taut beneath his T-shirt, and tendons stand out in his neck. Everything about his posture screams predator ready to pounce.

This guy is about to throw a punch for me. The realization is enough to clear the panicked fog in my head. I clutch the back of his shirt and pull him toward me.

"Let's go," I murmur. "They're not worth it."

I feel those dudes watching us, hear them laughing. Nothing Mason does, nothing I say, is going to change their minds. Ignorance is thicker and harder than steel.

When he doesn't move, I release his shirt and plant the palm of my hand on his shoulder blade instead. "Mason."

That seems to snap him out of it. He looks at me. His eyes are the color of storm clouds. They flash like lightning.

"We have a contest to win," I remind him.

The way his face softens tells me that he hears everything I'm not saying in those words. That I don't want to be a spectacle, that I don't want to see what happens if we keep antagonizing those assholes, that I want to get back to why I'm here.

He nods, and we stride ahead, taking the first right into

another area of the park, even though it's not the fastest way to the Last Steps attraction. For the moment, I care less about being the fastest ones to the clue and more about putting some distance between us and what just happened.

Mason is keeping closer to me than usual, and when I tip my face up to peer at him, he lifts an arm and asks, "Okay?"

I take his wrist in my hand and pull it down, slinging his arm over my shoulders. His side is warm against mine, and for a second, I let myself press my cheek into his solid chest.

It feels safe here, with his strong body so close to me. Mason could so easily be one of those guys. But he doesn't see what they see when he looks at me.

He doesn't see a body.

He sees me.

"How are you so calm?" His breath stirs the soft hairs around my forehead.

I don't feel calm at all. My heart hasn't slowed, and I can't get the memory of that guy's rough hands on my ass out of my head.

I shrug beneath his arm. I don't know what to say.

"Does that happen a lot?"

"Not the ass-grabbing." This is the first time anyone has ever touched me anywhere but my arm or my shoulder without my consent. I want to shower, or maybe burrow into a hole in the ground, and I want to cry and eat two hundred bowls of ice cream, but I also want to throw up. Yet I also don't want to give those guys that kind of power over me.

Tess likes to say that only you get to decide how people make you feel. It's a sentiment I've cross-stitched on my heart (one day I'm going to put it on a pillow, too). And I've decided that no jerks are getting under my skin today. Anytime now, that will become true. I just have to wait long enough.

Mason's chin rests on top of my head. "I'm sorry," he says softly.

"When you look a certain way—one that makes people notice you—this happens. You must deal with some form of it, too, right? I mean, you're so hot." I'm too raw and frayed to hold my tongue.

Of course, the moment the word is out of my mouth I want to melt into the asphalt.

Neither of us is looking at each other, but he hasn't let go or run away. Nor have I died of embarrassment and faded into a ghostly form.

"Something tells me it's not the same," he says softly.

His words are like a warm blanket in the middle of winter. All I've ever wanted was for Tess and Issy to understand this way. To recognize how my experience in the world is different from theirs, rather than to dismiss me.

I burrow my face a little more deeply into his chest.

We're quiet as we make our way through the kiddie section of Vale, themed around Fable Industry's Western, *Annie DoGood*. Just past the saloon, the aesthetic shifts from the town of Homestead and its frontier vibes to that of an abandoned carnival. Most of the rides in this area are old-school: a Tilt-a-Whirl, some giant swings, two creaky roller coasters with wooden tracks. There's also a Ferris wheel with cars that twist and turn precariously in the wind. Off the main paths, the grass is overgrown and graffiti is scrawled across the benches and game booths.

Last Steps is tucked away in a corner, its sign one of those whiteboards with interchangeable black letters you sometimes see in front of schools announcing events. In fact, the whole attraction is made to look like a school: a long, wide brick building with almost all its windows broken. Bloodied curtains hang out of a few and red handprints mar others. Above the entrance, metal block letters once spelled out the school's name—New Cumberland High—but a bunch have been rearranged or removed so it reads HIDE and RUN.

Now that we're so close to the third clue of the day, I want to break the haze left by our encounter with those guys and get back to winning. But I can still feel their hands on my body, still hear every word they said.

I rush forward like I can outrun those thoughts, but Mason catches my hand and tugs me gently back toward him.

"You know you're beautiful, right?" His eyes sear into mine, and his voice is more resolved than I've ever heard it.

I shake my head. I don't want to dwell on what happened. I don't want to talk about it anymore. "Mason, it's—"

"Right?"

I sigh. "I know I'm not what those guys want me to think I am."

He hasn't let go of my hand and he draws me in a little closer, so our sneakers are toe to toe. "When I saw you at the welcome party, it was like staring into the sun."

"I hurt your eyes that bad, huh?"

He nudges my foot. "No, you were that stunning."

There's a lump the size of a baseball in my throat. I can barely swallow around it. "I felt the same." I can't help but add, "Even if I wanted to kick your chair for tripping me."

He grins for a second, but then it fades from his face. He squints, his gaze tracing the periphery of the Last Steps building. "Would it be too much"—his voice cracks a little—"if I texted you or something sometime?" He rubs his face with his free hand. "I know you're leaving in four days, and this isn't any—"

I interrupt him by making a production of digging my hand into my pocket for my phone. When the screen turns on, it's so covered in text messages I gasp.

Mom
I'm sorry I missed your call. Dad says things are going well?
(11:28 AM)

Mom
I really wish you'd let me know that you're okay.
(11:32 AM)

Mom
Sweetie, I think you need to start checking your phone more during the day. I don't like this.
(11:34 AM)

Mom
Lia. Please check in. Maybe a little earlier than yesterday.
(11:36 AM)

Mom
What are you girls up to today?
(11:38 AM)

They go on and on, a full map of my mother spiraling over the past half hour.

"Whoa," Mason says as he notes all the texts on my screen.

Normally, the idea of him seeing this would make me sick to my stomach, but there's already too much in my head. "My parents are super overprotective. I still can't believe they let me come here for a week without them." I swipe away text after text. "Sometimes, I think they opened the furniture store just to make sure they could keep me close." For the first time since Mason and I met, I don't feel the impulse to say more.

"That has to be hard."

"I feel like I'm going to spend my whole life being smothered by them. And then I feel like a jerk for being mad that my parents give a crap about me. There's no way to win."

I type out some responses to my mother to avoid looking at Mason's face.

Lia
Hi Mom. Sorry I missed you earlier too!
(11:55 AM)

Lia
We're having a great time, though it's been super hot today!
(11:57 AM)

Lia
We're about to go see one of the musical performances so I am going to turn my phone off. Call you tonight!
(11:58 AM)

Flicking open a new contacts window, I ask, "What's your number?"

He rattles it off, and I save it, then send him a message. After that, my phone goes back in my pocket.

I'm still feeling shaky, but I know I need to refocus on the contest. On money that can help me carve out some freedom from my parents. On the opportunity to share my ideas about more body-inclusive characters with Fable Industry. Maybe I could even join that storytelling department Mason told me about.

What if my stories could change someone's mind? What if I could help make sure one less person has to experience what I just did?

I peer up at Mason and push a smile onto my face. "Let's go hunt some zombies."

CHAPTER 13

June 20

The Last Steps Immersive Experience
Vale of Villainy, Fableland
Orlando, FL

DEBBIE LEMON
preens before a horde of zombies shambling toward her

"Don't you think chain saws make lovely prom accessories?"

—*Last Steps (1:24:18)*

"I PROBABLY SHOULD HAVE MENTIONED THIS EARLIER, BUT I MAY have wet myself the tiniest bit the last time I was at a haunted house."

I can't believe I just admitted that out loud, but as I read the terrifying warning sign at the front of the queue for Last Steps, it seems like good information for Mason to have.

Especially since, according to him, we're going to need to get to the end to find Debbie Lemon.

He snorts. "There's a bathroom near the fried dough stand." He points behind us at the double doors swinging shut, locking us in.

I narrow my eyes at him. "It was *not* my fault."

"I'm going to need more information," he says.

I sigh. "Two years ago, this production company put on a haunted house in an abandoned warehouse a few towns over from us. It was professionally done—actors and costumes and makeup artists, the whole thing. Tess and Issy wanted to go, but they didn't want to leave me out."

We shuffle forward in line, watching as groups of people disappear through the double doors at the opposite side of the room. "On top of the regular haunted house stuff, this place had floaters. They wandered around the people waiting in line and circulated in the warehouse, too. The three of us were going through a room made up to look like an abandoned hospital. Rusted metal-framed beds, syringes strewn across the floor, cracked linoleum, and flickering fluorescent lights. An old wheelchair in the corner kept rolling back and forth on its own. And in the last bed, as far away from us as possible, there was a lump under the sheets. It was quivering." I pause to meet Mason's gaze. "*Quivering.*"

He grins.

"So, like fools, the three of us wander toward it to figure out what we're looking at. It's too big to be a baby or an animal. But it's not big *enough* to be an adult. And when we get close, we realize it's moaning." I scrub my hands over my face as the sound plays in the back of my head.

"And we're so focused on the bed, we don't hear the floater come in. He comes right up to me and whispers, 'You're doomed.' I screamed. Oh my God, did I scream." I run my hand down my throat. "I swear I have scars from it."

"Okay, I would have punched the guy," Mason declares.

"I might have, if I hadn't been so mortified about wetting myself. A little. Just a little." I feel the heat in my cheeks. A few minutes ago, he said I was beautiful, and now I'm doing everything I can to torpedo that image.

"If it helps, I once nailed my boot to the floor at a construction site." From the gravity in his voice, you'd think he was in a church confessional. "It went through my sock too. It's a miracle I didn't get my own foot."

I laugh. It takes effort not to press my hand over my chest to stop my heart from wildly beating. This is the magic of Mason. No one else has ever made me feel so at home in my own skin.

The family of four ahead of us steps into the attraction, and I can see that there's nothing beyond those doors but darkness.

Mason and I scoot a little closer together as we approach the attendant. She's tanned and blond and dressed like a gym teacher: tight white tee, tiny green running shorts, a whistle around her neck. She's doing a terrible job of pretending she's not gawking at Mason.

My stomach ties itself in a bow.

The girl hands him a glow stick and shepherds us to the threshold. "Follow the white line," she says ominously. Then she shuts us in.

Without the ambient light from the entrance, the only thing breaking up the dark is the sickly green glow that halos Mason's left hand. He holds the stick out so we can find the line on the floor.

"Tell me more about this job with your parents." He's whispering, as if to avoid disturbing anything in the room. His voice is already so quiet that I have to lean in to hear him. A few strands of my hair feather across his arm.

I shrug, although I'm not sure he can see me. "It'll be the same as what I do now. Keeping the office organized, doing the paperwork for sales. Eventually they want me to become a salesperson." I sigh. "It could be worse, I guess. Tess is always reminding me I should be grateful."

The white line guides us around a corner, and the darkness thins as we cross into a high school gym. To our right, metal bleachers steeple toward the ceiling. Animatronic couples in flouncy pastel dresses and awkward tuxes hold hands or make out on the benches. A few people sit alone with cups of punch or stare, bored, at the crowd dancing on the basketball court. An old Whitney Houston song my mother likes to belt out croons from speakers in the corner of the room.

"You can be grateful and still not love what you're doing," Mason says.

"My father started plans to open the store a month after my mother found out she was pregnant with me because he wanted to build something he could leave me. He wanted to give me a legacy. The grand opening was on my first birthday. It was literally decided from birth that this is what I would be doing." I try my best not to sound bitter, but the words slice at my tongue.

Mason listens without pushing me to say more. I appreciate

it. I'm tired of defending how I feel about my future. I'm not like Tess. I'm not fixated on having stocks and 401-whatevers and all the other stuff she talks about like she's an accountant, not a soon-to-be college freshman. I just want to be happy. And to feel like the life I'm living is mine.

Mason and I pause when we reach the dance floor. The white line we've been following zigzags straight through the crowd. Goose bumps rise up on my arms and across the back of my neck. It's a tight squeeze in spots and who knows what's lurking in there.

"This is messed up," he mutters.

I smack his arm. "You've been here before."

"It doesn't make it any less creepy."

I groan. At this rate, I'm definitely going to wet myself again.

And the worst part is, we have to go single file. "I'll go first," he offers.

"So something can eat me from behind?"

He laughs. So loud it echoes around us. My insides flutter, light and airy and manic, like moths are dancing in all my organs. Over the past two days, that laugh has become one of my favorite sounds. I want to hear it again and again, and a million times more. I want to be responsible for every one of them.

"Then you go first."

I squawk. "I'm not going to be some zombie appetizer."

He groans and rubs his forehead with his palm. "Lia, I can't do both."

I huff out a beleaguered sigh. "Fine. Go." As soon as he walks in front of me, I grab the back of his shirt and ball it in my hand.

You'd think being close enough to the animatronics that I can stare them in face would make them look less real, but between the costumes and the dim lighting and the whole atmosphere of the room, I have to search for clues—the way their chests don't rise and fall with breaths, the stilted manner of their blinking—to be certain they aren't people.

Identifying those tics makes me feel better for about ten seconds. But then I see them through the forest of bodies, a couple toward the edge of the crowd. They're people, not animatronics, I realize, as the guy spins the girl and dips her, and then they share a kiss. They must have been at it for a while now, because their labored breathing breaks through the piped-in music.

I wait for them to charge us or turn into zombies or something, but they keep dancing, and even though they're good, the whole thing feels creepier than any monster. It's like they're ghosts caught in an endless time loop.

My fingers dig more deeply into Mason's T-shirt.

Once we're past the dancing couple, we push through a wall of silver and green streamers back into darkness. I don't know how they do it, but the music fades out as well, so only our footsteps and breathing disturb the silence.

Forget his shirt. My hand clamps his biceps.

Mason raises the glow stick to illuminate my face. I see his jaw feather in the eerie light. The green turns his eyes into kaleidoscopes, a circle of gems refracting. "Will you share one of your stories?"

I choke on his unexpected request. "What?"

"One of the ones you want to pitch when you work here." The way he says *when,* not *if,* turbo-charges my heart.

"It's . . . um . . . not really fully formed yet."

"I don't care. I want to hear it anyway."

I haven't even told my friends this idea. Still, I can't say no to him. I don't want to. "Her name's Princess Caelyssa Whitepetal. She has a body like mine, and long golden-blond hair she keeps braided down her back. She's a ranger."

"Like a park ranger?"

I snort. "No. Like a hunter. She's a master at the bow and arrow. She can weave her way through any forest like it was her home. She has a unique connection with wildlife." I fall quiet. "That's all I've got so far."

His arm presses deeper into mine. "Keep working on it. I want to hear more."

At that, my heart pounds so hard in my chest I'm surprised it doesn't burst out. He keeps doing this, making everything that's always been so out of my reach feel suddenly attainable.

We've been walking down the same dark corridor for long enough that if not for the unbroken white line at our feet, I'd be certain we got lost. Finally, we reach a new set of streamers, and when we cross through them, we find ourselves back in the gym.

Only this time, the focus is on the makeshift stage opposite the bleachers. Toward the back of it, a DJ stands behind his turntables. At the front, beside a microphone, a pretty blond girl in a purple sequined dress flashes a five-hundred-watt smile as she holds a crown atop her head. The white-and-red sparkly sash across her chest reads PROM QUEEN. Her voice rings out against the high ceiling as she thanks everyone for voting for her.

She's clearly animatronic, as is most of the crowd, though Mason and I point out what look to be a few people among them.

I grasp another handful of his shirt when one of the humans turns around and I swear they have red eyes. We speed-walk our way to the next room.

And find ourselves face to face with a zombie.

I scream. The sound echoes off walls I can't see in the dark. I've stopped walking, and my mouth gapes, howling into the peeling flesh of this . . . thing . . . in front of me.

"Lia." Mason takes my hand. "It's fake."

"What?"

"The zombies." He points, and for the first time my vision moves beyond the creature in front of me. There's a whole horde, a symphony of gnashing teeth and wordless groans and shuffling feet that go nowhere.

I close my eyes and count to twenty, letting my heart slow and my breathing follow. When I open them again, I'm able to view what's in front of me clearly for the first time.

They're ridiculous. One has an eye hanging from its socket. Another has pulled off its own arm and is gnawing on it like a dog with a bone. One toward the back has a giant hole through its chest like it got in a fight with a cannonball.

There's nothing scary about this, I tell myself.

Mason steps a little closer. "You okay?"

I nod.

"We have to go through them, like the dancers," he says. "You ready?"

I'm not, but I nod again anyway. *You can do this, Lia.*

Mason's shoulders are taut, and his jaw clenches as we work our way through the group.

We're both tiptoeing, as if we might shake one of these things to life if we bump it. My muscles feel like shoelaces pulled too tightly, and I can't get a full breath into my lungs until I see the pack of zombies beginning to thin.

I drop my eyes to the white line and let my gaze cling to it like a lifeline. If I stare at my feet, then maybe everything else around us doesn't exist. It's like the whole "if a tree falls in the forest" thing. I just have to keep looking—

Six of the zombies break from their rows and rush at us.

This time it's Mason doing the yelling. "Shit!" he screams. Then he grabs *my* arm as if I'm going to protect him.

Were we not in a haunted house, and if my bladder were not seconds from forsaking me again, I would give this guy a lecture on why in situations where monsters are trying to kill you, it's okay to maintain conventional gender roles.

Instead, I just run, sticking to that white line like it's the yellow brick road and I'm Dorothy.

The next curtain of streamers might as well be the gates of heaven by the way I rush at them. Once safely on the other side, I slow down and pace in a circle. My heart is still in my throat trying to strangle me.

Mason stands wide-eyed beside me, huffing breaths.

"We're both chickens," I mumble, laughing despite my racing pulse.

He grins. "We're almost there. Two more rooms."

He offers me his arm, and I clasp it tightly as we move forward. This room looks like a parking lot, complete with life-size cars and streetlamps that climb to the ceiling. Zombies chase promgoers around cars and into the woods at the far end of the room. Others huddle over bodies splayed across the trunks and hoods of cars, feeding.

With only the glow stick and the dim light of the streetlamps, it's hard to tell which are real and which are robots, and *of course*, the white line leads us directly through the carnage.

I can hear the soft chuff of Mason's laughter as I curse under my breath.

"This place is supposed to be for kids," I whisper as we pass a particularly gory scene of zombies feasting on guy in a letterman jacket. The sounds are too authentic, and there's blood dripping on the floor. I'll be sending an angry letter to Fableland's CEO for whatever nightmares this provokes.

I'm about to say this out loud when one of the zombies turns its head and looks in my direction.

"Nope!" I yell. Then I'm shoving Mason in front of me.

We don't get too far before Debbie Lemon sprints out of the darkness and rushes at the zombie. Mason turns around to watch the fight, but I press my hands to his chest and keep herding him forward.

I need that damned clue and then I need sunlight. And some kind of palate cleanser. Fourteen puppy videos might help. Or a bunch of those soothing clips of people wrapping presents. I might have wasted too many hours on those during Christmas (and failed terribly at trying to replicate them).

We reach the final room, where Debbie Lemon stands on a pile of zombie corpses as the sun rises behind her. Her dress is ripped to shreds and covered in gore, her hair is a mess, and she's missing one shoe, but her prom queen crown sits perfectly straight on her head. In one hand, she holds a cup of lemonade.

"When life gives you lemons, use them to kill zombies," she declares. One of the zombies in the pile at her feet moans, and she dumps the liquid on its face.

As we step forward, I see the red-and-white prom queen sash has fluttered to the ground. It's a little too close to the undead bodies for my taste, but attached to its far end is the QR code.

I bend and scan it. Mason comes over to do the same.

As he reaches down with his phone, the nearest zombie juts out its head and snaps its teeth so close to Mason's hand that he yelps and falls backward.

I can't help but laugh. "Admit it, you peed a little," I joke as I help him up.

"That dude's lucky he didn't get a shoe to the face."

We hurry outside, and I take a deep breath of warm air. My heart is still racing as I check my phone for updates.

I'm definitely going to binge gift wrapping videos during lunch.

A similar congratulations message from yesterday pops up on my screen, confirming that I've made it through day three.

I can see the same banner on Mason's phone from where he stands beside me.

Then a new notification appears, announcing that we now have access to a leaderboard so we can watch in real time as contestants finish up the day.

I'm still hoping the obscurity of the three clues means we've finished at the top, but my heart drops when the board appears on my screen. I have to scroll more than once to find my name, all the way toward the bottom at sixty-six. Mason is right behind me at sixty-seven.

I swallow hard against the lurch of my stomach. We barely made it through. There are only three spots left, and they fill up as I stand there staring at my phone.

We could have lost. That can't happen. Not now. Not after Mason told me about the storytelling department. Not after I brought Caelyssa to life today.

"We were too close to getting cut," I say, looking over at Mason.

He nods solemnly. "Did you see who's number one?"

My gaze flicks back to my phone, and I search for the top of the list.

The face of that blonde from Hellfire stares at me from the first position. Beside her photo it reads ERICA K.

"Hell no," I mumble. "She's not winning."

"That means no rides, no food, no messing around tomorrow. It looks like the top ten contestants cleared all three clues today in an hour." He points at his phone's screen.

I don't know how I'm going to convince Tess and Issy.

But I stare up at Mason, determination on my face. "Then tomorrow, we do it in forty-five minutes."

CHAPTER 14

June 21

Atalantia, Fableland
Orlando, FL

My family's favorite story to tell is the day I got lost in Atalantia on my fifth birthday because I was following Lucy the Lobster. I saw her red claws waving in the air as she waddled through the crowd on the way to Neptune's Launch. *Seaward Bound* was my *favorite* movie as a kid, and for a long time Lucy had felt like my only true friend. She was the lone lobster hanging out with a bunch of fish. Just like I was the only Korean American in my class at school, in my neighborhood, pretty much anywhere I looked. Lucy understood what it was like to look different. I just wanted to give her a hug, and Mama wasn't moving fast enough. So I took matters into my own hands. . . .

—*Grace Choi, "Confessions," facelessinFableland.com*

Mason
Have you figured out the first clue yet?
(6:45 AM)

Mason
Carter and I only ever went to Neptune's Landing as kids. We were pretty convinced the rest of Atalantia had cooties.
(6:47 AM)

Lia
Why? Because most of the rides are from the princess movies?
(6:55 AM)

Mason
I was not a sophisticated ten-year-old.
(7:00 AM)

Lia
It's at the waterfalls next to the Seaward Bound ride.
(7:10 AM)

 I unraveled today's first clue in record time when it came in at midnight. **Even the cutest sea creatures have dark doppelgängers**—it was obviously a reference to the dancing shadows of Lucy the Lobster and her friends from the animated film *Seaward Bound*. According to F^3, they can only be seen from the very center of the waterfall. Which meant we were going to start our day in the park soaking wet.

Right now, I'm doing a poor job of texting and walking as Tess, Issy, and I head for the hotel shuttle. Atalantia opens early on Wednesdays for guests staying on-site and VIP visitors, and I plan to have us standing in front of the shell-encrusted gold gates at exactly eight.

When I met back up with Tess and Issy yesterday after lunch, I had not been prepared for how disappointed they'd be with me for doing the Last Steps walk-through without them.

"I know you've got this contest stuff, but this trip is supposed to be for us too," Tess had said, kicking a few stray rocks off the sidewalk. "We have *plans*."

I had to bite my tongue to keep from reminding her that she was the one who had all the plans. Issy and I had never agreed to anything. We just hadn't bothered to fight with her. "Tess, do you really want me to lose this chance for life-changing money because I might have to go on a ride or two without you?" I'd hoped that saying it out loud might help her hear how unreasonable she sounded.

Her mouth had puckered into a pout, and she crossed her arms. "We're supposed to experience it all together."

"Then stay with me while I do the contest stuff."

That didn't seem to satisfy her, so to make peace, I suggested that we get to Atalantia early today and find the clues immediately, and then we could go back to Last Steps, or follow Tess's detailed tour of Atalantia, or whatever she wanted to do. I even offered to search for the clues independently from Mason, so it was a day for just the three of us.

He and I agreed to keep in touch via text and share whatever clues we worked out so we'd stay even on the leaderboard, but our texting started long before we got day three's first clue.

I sent him pictures of everything we ate. He replied with photos of his dachshunds. I complained that Tess and Issy were going to drag me back through Last Steps. He answered with a picture of his boot with the hole in the toe. When he started his shift at the pharmacy last night, I got images of every shelf he restocked.

It was like he was making sure I remained part of his day, even if I wasn't with him.

As we climb onto the small bus, I read over his texts one more time. I can feel Tess's eyes settle on me, her gaze heavy with judgment.

"What?" I ask her, shoving my phone in my pocket.

"You've been on that so much lately," she comments.

My face heats. "I need it for the contest."

We sit down, me next to the window, Tess beside me, and Issy in the seat behind us.

"And for Mason." Her lips tip into a teasing smile.

I shrug. "We're just working together."

Issy leans forward so her arms curl around my headrest. "That's not how either of you look at each other." She arches an eyebrow meaningfully.

My shoulders lift again. I don't know what they want me to say.

"He lives around here, right?" Tess asks.

"Yeah." I look away from her to stare out the window. I can already see Atalantia's centerpiece, Ocean's Grace, the giant conch-shell castle from *The Sea Witch's Revenge,* stretching up toward the clouds, its pearlescent pink sheen winking in the sunlight.

Tess shifts beside me. "Have you talked about what's going on with you two?"

"We haven't talked about anything," I confess to my reflection. At least not anything related to the feelings I'm struggling to ignore. "He told me I was beautiful, that's about it."

"Aw, that boy is a walking green flag," Issy quips. "Total romance hero material."

"No kidding," I mutter. That's what's making this so hard. He's like no one I've met before.

"I get the sense he's not much of a talker, though." There's a laugh in Tess's voice that lets me know she's not being critical.

"But he's a total texter." I can't help but smile as I face them again and show off our string of messages.

For a few minutes, the three of us laugh over Mason's pictures, and I have to explain to them about the boot, and how I admitted to him what happened the last time I was in a haunted house.

They're both appalled at my honesty.

"You don't understand." I sigh, burying my face in my hands. "When I'm with him, I want to tell him everything. I want him to know every part of me. Even the embarrassing stuff." I groan.

Tess shoves her shoulder into mine and leaves it there. Her expression gets serious again. "Just be careful, okay? We're leaving in four days."

"I know." And I mean it.

I really do.

Until another message from him flashes on my screen and my heart takes flight.

Sprays of water still coat my forehead and cheeks from the Seaward Bound waterfalls when Issy and I stop and stare at my phone, trying to decipher the second clue.

We'd headed straight from the shuttle to the ride when we arrived at the park. Most of Seaward Bound takes place deep under the waterfalls, where a submarine travels an underwater track, but guests can also explore the small paths around the falls by themselves. If you're brave enough to cut straight through the splashing water to the center, you'll discover a small cave with a series of human-size shadows in the shape of lobsters, starfish, and seahorses dancing against the water's gurgling backdrop. After I'd scanned the QR code on the cave wall, Tess, Issy, and I stood there for a while laughing at the creatures' awkward dance moves. It was impossible to tell how the silhouettes had been designed and what made them move.

Another example of Fableland's magic. Let Mason try to explain this one away.

Then Tess got a call from her girlfriend, Grace, and wandered off somewhere quiet to take it, leaving Issy and me to work out the next clue on our own.

This pool of circles can never be broken.

"Pools?" Issy sighs, brushing wet strands of hair off her forehead. "Practically everything in this park is water related."

"Yeah, but they're not all pools." And most of them aren't circles. Or full of circles. I'm still trying to decide what that phrase means.

As I let my brain marinate on it, I check the leaderboard in the app. Since we gained access to it yesterday, I haven't been able to stop looking at it. It provides real-time updates on where people are in the process of searching, which is helpful but also incredibly stressful.

Sixty-six. That ranking from yesterday still haunts me. I lay awake half the night, tracing the patterns on the ceiling's plaster as I panicked. Only sixty people will get through today. If I stay where I am on the board, I'll get cut.

But for now, at least, I'm at the top of the list. Tess, Issy, and I were the first people to the waterfall, and I was the first to get the QR code, although a person with dark-brown skin, lilac hair, and a really excellent undercut scooched in after us to grab the code, too. According to the leaderboard, their name is Ember. They were in the top five yesterday too.

Definitely someone to keep an eye on.

I wish my head start was more of a comfort. But as another contestant jogs by us, I can practically feel my advantage slipping away. I don't know these parks the way other people in this contest do. Sure, I've studied every map I could find, but that's not the same as navigating them in real life. I'm not familiar with their contours, the places where the crowds tend to thicken and bottleneck, the shortcuts that let you avoid parades and other outdoor performances.

I fight off the itch to check the leaderboard again for reassurance. Instead, I turn my attention back to the clue.

Breaking the riddle up seems to be the best way for me to solve it. Since I can't puzzle out the "pool of circles" part, I shift to the other key phrase: **can never be broken.**

"What are things that can't be broken?" I ask out loud.

"My love affair with pork belly." Issy grins.

I snort. "Nothing is stronger than that."

Her mouth purses. "Metal? A lot of gemstones?"

"Maybe . . ." I bite my lip. So far the clues have been more abstract, so I try to consider less-literal interpretations. "Hearts? Promises? Vows?"

My brain zings, and for a second I can't keep up with the surge of thoughts that fill my head. Vows make me think of weddings and marriage. An event where you exchange rings. Where are there rings at this park?

I beam at Issy. "The Fountain of Union."

"Ah!" She claps. "Oh my God. Yes. All those rings. Circles that can't be broken."

The fountain has always been Issy's favorite Fableland Easter egg. Supposedly, every couple that gets married at the park tosses a set of bronze rings into the fountain and makes a wish for their future. There's an entire F^3 forum dedicated to the wishes people have made and whether they've come true. The three of us used to read them out loud like storybooks when we were younger, Tess trying to prove why every one was a coincidence, while Issy and I melted into the magic.

I pull up the map to see where we're headed, while Issy texts Tess to tell her where to find us.

"Hey, it looks like the fruit sushi stand is right near the

fountain, so we can film your video once we scan the code." There were a ton of comments on Issy's last video insisting she try the snack, even though it wasn't on her list. She's been stunned by all the extra engagement she's getting for her new content. Last night, she joked that maybe she should forget college and just travel the world eating food.

Tess practically had a brain aneurysm.

Issy smiles. "Then Tess won't have to worry about adding it to the itinerary later."

"And you can post it during prime viewing hours for maximum engagement." I laugh as soon as I hear myself. There's nothing like the girl with a hundred followers on social media trying to sound like an influencer.

"Want to be my marketing manager?" Issy quips.

"Oh yeah. If you need triangles stacked on top of each other for your graphics, I'm your girl." I took one design class in high school, and all I remember is how to move shapes around in the different programs.

Issy chuckles, but the light in her face quickly fades. "Do you . . ." She stops and sighs. "Do you find Tess more controlling than usual?"

I bite my lip again. Yeah, I get frustrated with Tess, but I don't want to pile on her. Especially when she's not here. "Why? What's up?"

Issy straightens her ponytail as she dodges out of the way of a large family streaming by. "Yesterday she tried to get me to approach, like, four different guys. I don't get it. Why is she pushing so hard for me to be with someone?"

Issy dated a lot in our first two years of high school, but she hasn't been out with anyone since the end of our sophomore year. Her last boyfriend had been a senior, and an asshole, so I assumed she needed a break after him. Plus, there's enough pressure at the end of high school with graduation and figuring out what's next. I don't blame anyone for not wanting to add relationship drama to the mix.

Issy's mouth screws up as if she's not done talking, but she only clears her throat, a pained expression taking over her face. It's the second time since we've been at Fableland that I've felt like she's holding back with me. Usually, the two of us are open books to each other.

Before I can ask what's up, she starts pacing.

"And this schedule of hers," she goes on. "If we needed to wait in lines, I would get it, but there's no chance we're going to miss anything. We can walk onto every ride."

"Yeah. It's been a lot." I scratch at my neck. "Even before we got here, she's been less willing to compromise." I want to ask if something happened, but part of me is afraid Issy knows something I don't. That there are already secrets between them they aren't sharing with me.

"I wish she'd tell us what she's thinking." Issy sighs.

"Me too."

Tess catches up with us on our way back to the center of the park. The Fountain of Union sits outside Ocean's Grace. Two lovers stand in an embrace at the center, one a human woman, the other an octopus-man hybrid. Two of his tentacles encircle the woman's waist and one brushes through her hair. A fourth cradles her cheek. Water trickles from their eyes like tears, washing down their bodies and into the crisp blue pool below them.

It's a reenactment of the final moment in *The Sea Witch's Revenge,* when Titania and Pericles kiss, uniting his undersea realm with her human kingdom.

The three of us stop in front of it to take it in.

Issy's eyes are wide, an amused grin on her face. "This statue is like three steps away from being a cover for one of those NSFW monster romances."

I laugh. *The Sea Witch's Revenge* has plenty of talking fish and upbeat songs, but the story is all about war and loss and what makes someone a monster. Tween Lia had a lot of questions about how exactly Titania and Pericles had children in the sequel that my mother lost her mind trying to answer.

Tess cocks her head. "Is it just me or does this tentacled man kind of resemble Carter?"

I cackle. "Oh my God. He does." I can't unsee it now. Pericles has the same narrow, boyish face and wide innocent stare.

"Wouldn't he and Is be adorable together?"

"Pericles? He's not real, Tess."

She rolls her eyes. "No, Carter."

"His boyfriend would probably disagree." Yesterday, Carter gave me his phone to take a photo of him holding three gigantic ice cream sandwiches, and the wallpaper on his home screen was a picture of him midkiss with a cute dark-skinned Black guy.

Tess groans. "Damn it. I was shipping them so hard."

At that, Issy's gaze snaps up from her phone, and she frowns, shaking her head.

I try to catch Tess's eye, but she's taking photo after photo of the statue and snickering as she texts them to someone.

Carter, I assume.

We slowly pace the circumference of the fountain, listening to it burble as we look for the QR code. Issy spots it first, secured onto the flowing curves of Titania's gown.

After I scan it, I stand back and take everything in again. The way the Fountain of Union is described on F³ and other sites, I'd expected it to be overflowing with rings. So many there wasn't room for water. But there are maybe fifty scattered along the floor of the pool. On the surface of the water, dead bugs and debris float by.

It's the first time something from these parks hasn't lived up to the hype. I was expecting something spectacular to memorialize magic, love, romance. Everything *The Sea Witch's Revenge* is supposed to be about.

I can't help it. My mind skips back to Mason and his blade of grass.

Taking a quick photo of the dirty water, I text it to him.

Lia
Well this is disappointing.
(8:45 AM)

Mason
Is that the fountain? That place is sad.... 😒
(8:47 AM)

Lia
Why do you hate Fableland so much?
(8:50 AM)

Mason
I know what it's like to have it let you down
(9:02 AM)

There's a story there, but I don't want to push for more than he wants to tell me.

He sends a photo of the gates as they open.

Lia
Hurry up. There are like twenty people with clue one already
(9:05 AM)

Mason
I can see that. Way to go number 1. 😊
(9:08 AM)

Lia
Why aren't you using the hotel rooms they gave all of us?
(9:10 AM)

If he stayed overnight, he'd be closer to the parks and able to take advantage of the early openings, which are only for guests staying at on-property hotels.

Mason
I can't leave the dogs. My father doesn't exactly take good care of them.
(9:12 AM)

Now I want to punch his dad. I send Mason the location of the first two clues. It's the best way I can think to help. Then I find my friends.

They're at the fruit sushi stand across the park's central square, both of them studying the menu like it's an explanation of nuclear physics.

My gaze drifts toward the fountain one more time, and I think of Mason's text. Shoving a hand in my pocket, I fuss with the ring jammed in the bottom. I brought it from home, meaning to make a wish in the fountain—even if it broke the rules. But as I turn to join my friends, I decide to leave it where it is.

I don't want magic to make my wish come true. I want to do it myself.

When I reach Tess and Issy, I blurt out, "If I win, I'm going to try to get a job here." I say it without conditions. Without hesitation. It feels like I'm finally grasping something. Gripping it firmly with both hands.

If I can share that plan with Mason, then I should be able to share it with my friends too.

Issy screeches and jumps up and down. "*Yes*, Lia. You love this place. This is perfect."

Tess arches an eyebrow. "To be with Mason?"

That thought occurred to me, too, but it's not where my conviction comes from.

"No. I want to add to this." I gesture around us. "I've been thinking of this story about a fat princess I could pitch someday. I love this place, but it could be so much more inclusive. What if I could help with that? If I win this money, I could do something good here."

"You'd *kill* at that," Issy says. Her eyes crinkle with joy.

"Yeah, you would," Tess echoes. But she's frowning as she taps my leg with her foot. "Just don't forget you're living a dream right now too, being here. Not everything is a fantasy."

She's not wrong, even though the timing of her reality check kind of sucks. For once, I can imagine a different future, and the possibility of it is close enough to grab. I wanted to relish that for a moment.

Shaking my head, I pull out my phone, ready to finish the day.

The next clue waits for me on the screen.

The sea contains many legends that live only in stories. But beneath the sink of an anchor this fantasy creature will come alive before your eyes.

I repeat the words in my head. The leaderboard sits open, and I watch as two contestants pop up into positions one and two. Already done for the day.

"The sink of an anchor," I mumble. "Fantasy creature." My pulse kicks against my veins, and my stomach ties itself in knots.

I have no idea what any of it means.

CHAPTER 15

Neptune's Bounty
Atalantia, Fableland
Orlando, FL

50th-Anniversary Scavenger Hunt Leaderboard

POSITION	NAME	CLUE NUMBER	TIME
1	Ember M.	Finished	10:30 am
2	Erika K.	Finished	11:02 am
3	Kaitlyn H.	3	8:25 am
4	Britney L.	3	8:30 am
5	Jenna M.	3	8:32 am
6	Lia B.	3	8:40 am

THE SEAFOOD RESTAURANT NEPTUNE'S BOUNTY SITS AT THE center of Fableland's award-winning aquarium, Neptune's Launch.

It normally has a six-month waitlist, but one of the perks of being in the scavenger hunt is the VIP access to restaurants and other amenities. Issy made us a reservation the day I got my ID number.

That's one of the only reasons we're following a host to a table right now.

After wandering Atalantia and doing endless research on our phones for over two hours, we are no closer to cracking the third riddle. We were all beginning to get cranky and tired, and the leaderboard hadn't moved in almost half an hour, so I agreed not to miss our reservation.

Clearly, this clue was a doozy.

I figured we can eat and regroup, and hopefully by then, I'll have come up with the answer. Or Mason will.

What I did not agree to was ignoring the leaderboard. Even though nothing has changed, I watch it like a hawk as we cross the dining room. A translucent dome arches overhead, and sunlight slices through it like gems, the layer of glass the only shield between us and the hundreds of fish and other aquatic life that dart about the blue, blue water.

"It seems . . . uncouth to have a seafood restaurant surrounded by so many fish," I point out.

Tess tilts her head so it angles up like mine. "Right?" Her mahogany eyes are the size of globes. "It's like, 'Behold, fish, your destiny.'"

"But it's so pretty." Issy presses a finger to a nearby tank, and a yellow-and-white fish races forward to kiss the glass.

We're led to a booth in the corner that's surrounded by water on two sides. It's one of the best spots in the whole restaurant, but my stomach curdles. Booths are not always fat friendly, especially somewhere like this where they're fixed to the wall and don't move. In my head, I perform some plus-size geometry. *How much space between the table and the back of the booth? Is that space wider than me? By how much?* There are few things more painfully embarrassing than not fitting somewhere. I had enough of that on Squirt's Wicked Whirl. Before I even sit down, I'm collecting excuses for why we need a different table. Anything to keep Tess and Issy from asking too many questions or making me explain myself.

My muscles are so rigid as I slide in, they're ready to crack in half. I have to fight the urge to shrink myself by sucking in my gut and lifting my shoulders. The surface is cold from all the AC, and my skin prickles as though every person in the place is scrutinizing me. It's such a relief when the table's edge only grazes my stomach that I almost burst into tears.

Issy flaps open her menu with a swift flick of her wrist, dragging my attention back to my friends. "If you both don't order seafood, I'm disowning you. Every year this place ends up on at least three 'best of' lists."

I push my menu aside with a grin. "Oh wise one, please tell us what to order."

Issy's face lights up. "Oh my God, seriously?"

"Yes, please." Tess lets out a dramatic sigh. "My brain's too tired to make a choice right now."

Issy claps her hands. "Eek! I feel like Gordon Ramsay or something."

Tapping her nose with her perfectly polished index finger, she surveys us, then cuts her eyes back to the menu. She studies its contents like her decisions will have global implications. "Tess, you enjoy some spice, so the shrimp Mozambique. And, Lia . . ." She pauses. "The backyard duo, because I've seen you eat scallops and shrimp and I know how picky you are about seafood."

"Works for me." My stomach growls in agreement, and we laugh.

"Their sweet and spicy cauliflower appetizer is supp—" Issy starts, but Tess immediately talks over her. "Hold up. This entrée is forty bucks." Her cheeks have turned bright red.

"I know, but it's supposed to be one of their best dishes," Issy notes.

"That kind of cash would buy all three of us dinner at home."

"But we're not *at* home. We're on vacation." Issy's voice has a little bit of an edge to it. "The point is to have some fun and splurge."

Tess's eyes narrow. "It's just food. It's not like we can take it home as a souvenir." She picks up the menu and gives it a cursory glance. "I'm getting the crab cake appetizer."

Issy shrugs stiffly. "Suit yourself. I'm getting the lobster mac and cheese. And *yes,* I know it doesn't have a price on the menu." In Issy's mind, a really good meal is more than worth the cost. For her eighteenth birthday, her mom told her she could have whatever she wanted, and she chose dinner at a five-star restaurant in NYC.

Thankfully, the server appears, defusing the tension between them. Issy orders for us, then rattles off a bunch of appetizers too. "My treat," she insists after the server leaves.

We settle into a normal rhythm again once we have our drinks. Issy frets about how she's going to admit to her followers that the fruit sushi they wanted her to try was, as she puts it, "less than delectable," and Tess waxes poetic about Atalantia's most popular roller coaster, which somehow manages to go underwater.

"It's obviously enclosed so you don't drown, but you're getting sprayed with water the whole time, and the cars slow down in the tunnels so you can see the battle between the humans and the krakens happening all around you. The POV video was epic."

"I refuse to watch those," Issy says. "It kills the whole surprise. Like reading the back cover of a book before you jump in."

"Except if you did that, you could probably avoid all those sobfests you end up reading by accident because you thought they were rom-coms," I point out.

"Those books should come presoaked with tears as a warning, not with cute illustrated covers."

"I think the back of the book *is* the warning."

Issy knows she can't fight with me there, so she takes a sip from her straw as she smothers a grin.

A few minutes later, our appetizers arrive. It takes two runners from the kitchen to drop off all the plates.

"Good lord, Is," Tess mutters, "did you order for three or three hundred?"

Issy already has a fork in her hand. "The portions aren't that big." She segments one of the marinated cauliflowers in front of her into smaller pieces. "Plus, who knows when I'll ever eat here again. I want to try as much as I can." She pushes a small dish of fried clams toward Tess. "Dig in!"

Tess and I don't need any more encouragement than that to fill our plates.

My phone buzzes on the table as I'm eating.

Mason
You're still at clue three on the board. What happened?
(11:38 AM)

I pull up the leaderboard to see that Mason is on the same clue. Only three more people have cleared them all for the day, so there are still plenty of spots open.

Lia
We haven't been able to figure it out.
(11:41 AM)

You either?
(11:42 AM)

Mason
I just got it. I was waiting for you.
(11:43 AM)

Lia
Why??
(11:44 AM)

Mason
We're in this together.
(11:45 AM)

I know you're having a girls' day but can you come to Neptune's Launch quick to scan the clue?
(11:46 AM)

Lia
We're having lunch at Neptune's Bounty. I'll be there as soon as we're done.
(11:48 AM)

My stomach somersaults. I thought the clue was super challenging, but it must not be if Mason figured it out so easily. It's not as if he's deep into the parks and their secrets. There has to be something obvious that I'm missing.

Or maybe my never having been here before is more of a weakness than I thought.

I shove my phone in my pocket and stab at a fried clam. For a second, I wasn't stressing about the contest, but now the pressure is back, pushing like a strong hand against my ribs.

"Still no luck on the clue, huh?" Tess asks. She doesn't give me a chance to answer before adding, "At least we won't starve as we wander around all afternoon while you figure it out." She smiles at me to signal she's teasing, but my hackles still rise.

"I'm sorry this contest is such a burden," I mumble.

Her smile falters. "That's not what I meant."

"Okay," I say. I know I should drop it, but I'm tired and stressed and I can't help it. "What did you mean, then?"

She shakes her head. "It just feels like you're treating this week as if it's the be-all and end-all."

"Isn't it?" I just told them that if I win the contest I'm going to come back to Fableland. For once, there's something *I* want, but it can only happen if I win that money.

"No." Tess's throat bobs as she swallows hard. "You don't need this contest. You can change things anytime you like. You just have to *do* something."

I cross my arms and slouch back in the booth. I can't believe the things coming out of Tess's mouth. Does she even hear herself?

"The money—" I start.

"Tess—" Issy pipes up.

"Is, you know I'm right," Tess says, her voice rising the way it always does when she's challenged. Then she turns to me: "That prize is just another excuse. Because if you don't win, then you can rationalize why you haven't changed anything. We've watched you do this forever. All those times you've hid behind your parents, your job, your body." She waves her hand between her and Issy. "We don't want you to hide anymore, Lia. We both know you don't need to."

Blood shoots through my veins like bullets. All this time, I thought my friends were doing their best to understand what it's like for me, even if they couldn't *truly* know what it is to live in my parents' house or to live in my body. But if Tess thinks things are that simple, then I guess I was really, really wrong.

I won't dignify her comments about the contest with a response. I'm not cowering behind the idea of winning this money. I'm doing everything I can to make it a reality, to make my dreams about working here come true. But what she said about using my body as an excuse, I can't let that go. Not this time.

I push my plate away. "I'm not hiding, Tess. I just know how people see me. Yesterday, while Mason and I were looking for the clues, some guys started making fun of me. I tried to ignore them, the way I always do. Do you realize how often people stare at me or make comments? You probably don't see it because I don't react. I don't let it get to me. I don't even tell you about it." I slide out of the booth and fish forty dollars from my pocket.

"One of those guys, he grabbed my ass. He was trying to put me back in my place. Remind me that, according to him, I *should* be hiding." I grind my teeth. Tears bite at my eyes but I blink them away, my eyelashes fluttering wildly. I didn't cry when it happened; I'm *not* crying now.

Issy mumbles, "Oh my God," and a million emotions cross Tess's face. So many that she can't speak.

"So please don't act like you know anything about what it's like to be me or what I should be doing." I throw my money on the table. I can't stay here. Not right now. I need a break. Some time for the sting of Tess's words to fade.

She wants me to do something. Well, here we go.

"I need some space," I say. "I'm going to finish the clues for today on my own." Then I walk away.

As I maneuver through the crowded restaurant, fighting back tears, staving off the urge to jam an elbow into the ribs of every person who rudely knocks into me, I reply to Mason.

Lia
I'm on my way.
(12:02 PM)

CHAPTER 16

June 21

Neptune's Launch Aquarium
Atalantia, Fableland
Orlando, FL

50th-Anniversary Scavenger Hunt Leaderboard

POSITION	NAME	CLUE NUMBER	TIME
3	Britney L.	Finished	11:20 am
4	Kaitlyn H.	Finished	11:29 am
5	Mason C.	Finished	11:43 am
6	Lia B.	3	8:25 am
7	Jenna M.	3	8:45 am
8	Rachel G.	3	8:57 am

I DON'T EVEN REALIZE IT'S RAINING UNTIL I SEE MASON PUSH through the aquarium entrance sopping wet.

He skids to a stop when he sees me sitting on a metal bench next to the dolphin tank. The glowing light from the water-filled tank highlights the blue in his eyes so they shimmer. The weight of his gaze on me is so familiar that something cracks in my center, and all the tears I've been fighting back burst out at once. I make this horrible noise, somewhere between a sob and a cough, inviting looks from the parents around me.

He falls into a crouch at my knees, the same way he did that day outside of Squirt's Wicked Whirl. I swipe my knuckles across my eyes to hide the tears he's already seen.

"You're soaked," I mumble.

"It's raining." A small grin twitches his lips, but his gaze remains steady on my face. His hands hover, close but without touching, and that widens the hole in my chest. A hiccup escapes my throat as I try to swallow it back.

"Are you okay?"

"Look, there's dolphins." I point over my shoulder.

I can't talk about anything real right now. Not until I can open my mouth without sounding like something possessed. My phone buzzes with another text from Tess—easily her twelfth one—but I don't respond. I don't even read it. Right now, the only thing I can handle is sitting on this bench.

Mason seems to understand because he settles beside me without another word.

My gaze chases the water creeping down his arm as it drips from his elbow to the floor. "You're still soaked." Apparently, emotional exhaustion is real, because I feel like I've just run a marathon, and my brain can't reach beyond the very obvious fact that he's wet.

"There don't seem to be a lot of towels around."

"Come here." I gather the end of my flowy tank top into a bunch and, careful to keep my stomach covered with the layer under it, wipe the wetness from his cheeks and brow. Leaning forward, he presses gently into my touch. The whole time, his eyes study me intently, like I'm performing surgery or building a bureau or something equally intricate.

When I'm done, I smooth my shirt down over my waist and turn away to watch the dolphins behind us. My fingers linger over the damp spots on my shirt's hem like they're a part of Mason I get to keep.

He faces the tank too, his hands fussing with his ring as they hang between his knees. "So, dolphins, huh?"

One swoops by us, as if summoned, rolling so its belly is turned to the glass like an aquatic dog looking for pats.

"That's Remy," I say.

"Oh?"

"After my dog. That's who he reminds me of." I glance over at Mason. The flickering water plays with the angles of his face, darkening the shadows beneath his sharp cheekbones and defined brow. None of it can dampen the light in his smile, though.

His phone rumbles, and he checks it before turning it off and putting it away. His brow creases, but all he says is "How so?"

"They're both big and whitish and love to swim. They also both like to come at you belly up."

Mason laughs.

"Remy's supposed to be a golden retriever, but I'm pretty sure someone swindled my dad and sold him a polar bear instead." I rub my chest with the heel of my hand, a small warmth glowing there. Remy's the one good thing about staying home. "Have you seen videos of polar bears rolling around in the snow? That's Remy, every winter. And he's one of those light goldens, so he's practically the same color as a polar bear, and he sleeps as much. If we could walk him without having to wake him up, I think he'd prefer it."

"Lia." I'm babbling, and Mason's tone tells me he knows it. "Do your friends know where you are?"

I close my eyes and shake my head.

"Tell them. They're clearly worried." He nods down at my pocket, where my phone is buzzing again. "You don't have to say anything else."

Sighing, I dig my phone out. I know he's right, but I hate giving in. It's like somehow we're playing by Tess's rules. *Again*.

There's so many messages, they cover my screen. Two are from Mom, the rest from Tess and Issy. Both of them saying "I'm sorry" and asking where I am over and over again.

I swipe open our group message.

Lia
I'm okay. Mason met up with me and we're going to get that third clue. Talk later.
(12:50 PM)

As soon as the message is sent, I switch off my phone. (Sorry, Mom.) I'm not ready to talk. Or to let go of the anger still sizzling beneath my skin. I have the right to be mad. For a lot of different reasons. But the minute I agree to talk, I'll lose that, and it feels like the only control I have left.

Standing, I press myself to the glass. Dolphin Remy swims straight at me and stops with his snout grazing the other side. I smile at him, but all I see is sadness in my reflection.

"We got in a fight," I say.

Even though Mason doesn't respond, I can feel him listening. He never tries to prove that he's listening, the way most people do, by talking more and *louder*. He just waits until I'm ready.

It takes another minute, but then the words tumble out. "We've been friends our whole lives, and for most of it, it felt like that would always be true. But lately . . . I don't know . . . we're out of sync." My mind drifts back to Issy this morning, stopping before she was finished talking. And Tess, so hell-bent on controlling everything lately. "It feels like we're being pulled in different directions or something, and all that exploded today."

I hold a hand up, palm facing the tank. Remy spins so he can flap his fin at me.

"Maybe he really is your dog." Mason's arm bumps mine.

I press both my hands to the glass, and Remy does a barrel roll, like he's slapping me a high five. He's trapped in there and yet he seems freer than I am.

"You'll work it out," Mason says softly.

I glance up at him. He's so tall I have to tip up my chin for our eyes to meet. "What if we don't?" That's my biggest fear. That something between Issy, Tess, and me will break too completely to mend. That today I helped loosen another stitch.

"You will. Just give things a minute to breathe."

We watch Remy take three more laps in silence. Then Mason

nudges me gently. "Do you want to explore the rest of this place? Or will Remy break out if you leave?"

I snort. Loudly. Then immediately rush into the next room so I won't have to look at Mason until the blush recedes from my cheeks. I don't know why I'm so uninhibited around him, but even as I pray to disappear, there's a big chunk of me that likes it. He's this reminder that it's okay to refuse to see myself the way the world wants me to: as too much and not enough, all at once.

Unlike the atrium, which is bright with sunlight from the glass roof and the wide blue tanks, this room is thick with darkness. The only glow is from the small windows encasing jellyfish that dot the space. The one that greets me as I enter has a collection of six iridescent purple blobs, their short, feathery tentacles trailing like bike streamers as they lope languidly through the water.

Mason steps closer to the tank, his fingers twisting his ring. The movement seems as unconscious as breathing. He must feel my eyes on him, because his gaze drops to his hand.

"It was my grandfather's." He walks over to the next display as he says it.

This one contains a whole horde of yellow jellyfish, their tentacles easily five times the size of their bodies. They drift diagonally across the tank, gooey leaves tossed in a watery wind.

A group of kids bunch around the glass, forcing Mason behind me. His wintry smell is everywhere, and I can feel the heat of his skin dancing across mine. All it would take is half a step back for my spine to be pressed against his chest. The thought makes my heart jump.

I peek at him over my shoulder, to find his eyes on me, not the jellyfish. "My grandfather died a year and a half ago, but I lived with him from when I was ten until he passed. He was the crankiest old bastard you'd ever meet. And he talked less than I do. But when he loved you, he loved you fiercely," Mason says. He twirls the ring again, more deliberately this time, as if he wants to make sure I see it. "He feels a little less gone when I wear this."

I turn to him. Out of habit, I open my mouth, "I'm sorry" poised on my lips. But they're such useless words in the face of loss, so I bite them back and rest a hand on his arm instead.

His eyes slip to it and then to my face. I let my fingers linger for only a second before pulling my hand back.

"I learned all my swears from him."

I grin. "When I was in junior high, my grandmother would sneak me books by some lady named Danielle Steel that I was *way* too young to read. I probably learned more from those books than any 'talk' my parents gave me." The words haven't fully left my mouth before heat invades my cheeks. *What am I doing? Why am I talking about sex with Mason?*

His eyebrows arch. "I'll have to check out this Danielle Steel person."

"There's no science in that fiction. Though she does have one book where the main character has sex with a robot...."

Mason lets out another of those unrestrained laughs, a smile lingering on his face. In the short time I've spent with him, I've begun to learn his smiles. They may all be small and closed-mouthed, but they have different shapes and cadences. His smart-ass smile tips up his lips on the right side of his mouth the tiniest bit higher and sharpens the angles of his face. His amused smile shines in his steel-gray eyes like a lighthouse in a hurricane. And his shy smile, the one I've seen most often, is practically a ghost. Flitting so quickly across his face you'll miss it if you aren't paying enough attention.

This time, it's me who finds a new tank. At the back of the room, it stretches from floor to ceiling, the brackish water behind the glass speckled with white jellyfish so small and bright they look like stars against a night sky. They're domed and spotted like mushrooms and could easily fit into the palm of my hand. Leaning into the glass, I count them, slow and precise, trying to stop my heart's rapid patter.

Being around Mason feels different today. Or maybe this is the way that it has always felt, but I'm too stressed right now about fighting with my friends to push it away.

He stops next to me, our shoulders close. His scent overwhelms the brininess of the salt water that laces the air.

"Why did you live with your grandfather?" I keep my eyes trained on the jellyfish as they dip and flow, dip and flow.

Mason's arm is solid as it rests against mine. He clears his throat, and when he speaks, his voice is so soft it hurts. "When my mom died, Pops fell apart. He never got himself right again. He'll tell you he sent me to my granddad because my grandma had died not too long before Mom and the old man needed the company, but really, I think Pops cared more about his grief and his gambling than me."

I tilt my head to see his face. Again, I want to say I'm sorry but don't.

"It's fine," Mason whispers, like he can hear my thoughts. "I was a hellion. Granddad straightened me out. I would have been a different person without him. I don't think I would have liked that person." His face is full of everything. I have to fist my hands to keep from cupping his cheeks. He pats his pocket, his palm thumping against whatever book has taken residence in there today. "He's the one who told me to use what I've got to help others. He believed I could be a teacher. So I'm working my ass off to save up money for college. And I'm going to do it. For Granddad." He's a little breathless from talking so much. "And for me."

My eyes sting. Everything he's saying, I want it for him. But I want it for me, too. Not to be a teacher, but to have dreams. To want to do something so bad that I structure my whole world around it.

"Why are you helping me with this contest?" I whisper. "You need the money too."

He glances down at me. In the dim light of the tank, his watercolor eyes look like shiny opals. They lock with mine, the intensity of his stare pinning me in place. "You're the first person since my grandfather who actually sees me."

My heartbeat is so fast, so loud, I can feel it thudding against my eardrums, tapping in my veins. "He's right, you know? Your grandfather."

Neither of us break eye contact. "Yeah?" Mason breathes.

"You've got that unbreakable patience the best teachers have. And you're smart."

He shakes his head hard. "No, I'm not. You should have seen my grades when I graduated last year. I probably won't get in anywhere. I'll have to start at community college and transfer."

I cross my arms and shift so my entire body is facing him. "Grades don't mean anything except that you know how to work the system. How to study or take a test or whatever. I got really good grades and I've already forgotten half of what I learned. But you're killing these clues. You remember everything. And you don't even like it here."

The throbbing mass of spotted jellyfish cascades from the top of the tank to the bottom, bathing us in shimmery white light. It frosts Mason's face and hangs ice in his eyes, and I get that feeling again, that he's accidentally stepped out of a fantasy world and ended up here. Like he belongs somewhere full of magic and endless daylight and flowers that blossom as tall as trees.

His eyes dip to my lips, and my heart shudders. If he tries to kiss me right now, I'm not sure I'll stop him.

"Thank you," he says.

"For what?"

He shrugs, then lowers himself onto a nearby bench. "Carter thinks it's ridiculous to spend all this money for school to get a job where I'll probably be making less than I do now." He scratches at the back of his neck. "And Pops, well, he thinks I'm too dumb to get into college, so it's a waste of time. He refuses to use a penny of Mom's insurance money on school." He sniffs and drags the back of his hand across his nose.

I inch toward him until our knees meet. For once, I'm the one casting a shadow over him.

"You know, assuming he hasn't already blown it all."

His shoulders bow under the weight of everyone else's versions of him. It's like he can't see himself through all the static.

But I do. Clear as day.

He glances up at me, and something in my face seems to shake him, because he tosses his gaze over my shoulder and coughs. "Have I ever told you this is my favorite part of the park? It's the only part of Fableland that's real."

His words sting. Because real is exactly what I don't want this place to be.

I ask him again what I asked him the first day we met. "What's wrong with a little bit of magic?"

He spins his ring, focusing hard on the action like it's a difficult task. "It's a promise. And promises are just lies that haven't happened yet."

In the end, those are the words that shatter my resolve. I want him to believe in something, to trust in something, even if it's just himself. But maybe for now, for this one second, it can be me.

I push forward until we're chest to chest and cup his face in my hands. For the first time since I hurried away from Issy and Tess at lunch, I'm not thinking about my friends or my mother or what's waiting for me at home. I'm not even running the third riddle through my head.

There's only Mason and his rainstorm-colored eyes and the way I want him to feel the magic of this park, if only for a second.

I want to be a little bit of magic for him.

Our lips are barely two inches apart when I pause. My knees are shaking. My hands are shaking. Every part of me is liquid.

Beneath my fingers, Mason's face tenses as if he's fighting to keep still. "What?" he whispers.

"I was . . . Is it okay if I . . . if I kiss you?"

His lips part loosely, his eyes unblinking under his forest of lashes. I swear the blue in them sparks against the darkness. He nods slowly, but the movement ricochets through my body, snapping my nerves until each one is raw and buzzing.

I run my palms along his jaw. There's a little bit of stubble, and it scratches against my skin.

Tons of people mill around us. Kids screaming. Parents calling their names. One kid bumps into our bench. Four toddlers kiss the glass of the jellyfish tank.

Yet somehow there's no one but us. We're trapped in this tiny bubble, hidden away from the world.

Mason waits. Patient as always. His eyes capture mine as I study his face. His hands search out my waist. Even through two tank tops I can feel their warmth, and it stirs me back into motion. I lower my face to his.

I don't close my eyes until our lips meet.

Just to make sure it's real.

CHAPTER 17

June 21

Neptune's Launch Aquarium
Atalantia, Fableland

Orlando, FL

Since its construction in 1982, Neptune's Launch has been celebrated as a premiere aquarium, on the cutting edge of animal rehabilitation and conservation education. But rumors of another aquatic life encounter in Neptune's Launch abound. Self-proclaimed park scholars have insisted for years that somewhere within the circular structure of Neptune's Launch lies a tunnel to its belly. That at its end sits a vast saltwater tank. And in that tank lives a mermaid. . . .

—*FablelandNow.com, "Fableland's Best-Kept Secrets"*

MASON'S LIPS ARE MAGIC SPELLS.

They melt against mine as soon as our mouths meet, and my body sinks into his. Every part of me aches to find every part of him, but I mobilize all my willpower to remain still. Only my fingers move, grazing the nape of his neck as if I might be able to memorize it like a map.

I part my lips the smallest bit, but at the same time, the rush of blood in my ears starts to thin, and I remember that we're in an aquarium teeming with little kids and probably *a lot* of disapproving parents. My mother would pass out if she caught me making out in public. Then I'd get a three-week lecture on sanitation and safety as she bolted the door of my room closed.

The idea is enough for me to pull my face from Mason's.

Invisible fire crackles between us as we separate. I never knew absence could feel so . . . *present*.

His eyes, sleepy and hooded, take me in, and his right arm hangs around my hips, one of his fingers hooked in a belt loop on my shorts. I still have a hand knotted in his shirt. I can't seem to let it go.

The air drapes heavily over us, weighty with significance. As if one tiny kiss has sent the entire world spinning backward on its axis.

His face is impossible to read, and a sudden rush of doubt makes me dizzy. Is he not feeling what I'm feeling? Was the kiss bad? I scoot back before the questions spill from my lips.

That wakes him from his daze, and he smiles. "Hi." His voice is fragile, and it cracks.

I force my eyes to meet his. "That was . . . wow."

Pink blooms in his cheeks, and his eyes skip back to the jellyfish tank as he stands. It takes him long enough to say something that my heart begins to sputter.

"This is now officially not just my favorite spot in the park, but in the whole world."

"What? This tank of"—I lean over and squint at the small placard beside it—"Australian spotted jellyfish?"

He huffs out something breathy that I think is meant to be a laugh, then tugs me beside him. "This spot on the floor, right here." His voice comes out husky but delicate.

"Yeah?"

"Yeah."

I want to ask him if he'll visit it when I'm gone. If he'll think about the kiss as much as I will. Because I'm leaving. It finally, really hits me. No matter what happens, I'm gone in three days. And the only way I can come back is if I win this contest and he doesn't.

The reality is ice in my veins. This is exactly what I've been trying to avoid. Wanting something else I can't have. Another thing that will slip through my fingers like air.

But it's too late. Now that I've kissed Mason, it would be impossible to pack up my feelings again and hide them away. My heart is Pandora's box, and I broke it open.

"Maybe we should never leave here, then," I say. Probably, that's the only way this thing between us could work.

He grins. "All right, but Remy might get jealous."

I laugh, and the movement of my shoulders rolls through his body too, like we're connected.

"Shit. Twenty people are done now."

After taking another minute to chase off the haze from our kiss, Mason dropped reality's hammer on us by checking the contest app on his phone.

There are only forty spots left. And it seems like people are starting to figure out the last clue. Even as we stare at Mason's phone, two more people move up the list.

Thirty-eight spots left.

Panic jets through my veins.

Mason must see it on my face because he asks, "Do you want me to show you where the QR code is?" When I frown, he adds, "You did the same for me earlier."

"I like puzzling them out myself." I'm too competitive for my own good, but it's in my DNA, the same as my light-blue eyes and dark hair.

"What do you have so far?"

"That it's got to be in here." Tess, Issy, and I deduced that by process of elimination earlier. We've looked literally everywhere else.

I also found a really old post on a different fan forum that talked about a secret mermaid in a tank somewhere in this building. "And that the fantasy creature is a mermaid."

Mason nods.

"I just don't know what the sink of an anchor means." I turn and glance around us. "There's plenty of water and fish, but nothing nautical themed."

"What about a hint?" he offers as we head back to the outer atrium. Neptune's Launch is set up like a series of concentric circles, almost like the spirals on the inside of a conch shell.

The outside loop is lined with tropical fish. They flutter and flit through turquoise water, darting in and out of fissures in the pastel-hued coral and the gaps between rocks and seaweed. Some of them drift along in schools so big they look like curtains of bright color swaying in an invisible breeze.

I turn my phone on so I'm ready to scan the code as soon as we find it. A strangled noise pushes out of my mouth when my screen lights up.

Mom
Where did you girls go for breakfast? What about lunch?
(12:25 PM)

Mom
Was it good?
(12:27 PM)

Mom
What are you up to now?
(12:30 PM)

Mom
It's been a while since you checked in.
(12:32 PM)

Mom
Missed call
(12:37 PM)

Mom
Missed call
(12:38 PM)

Mom
Missed call
(12:40 PM)

Mom
Lia, I am starting to get worried now.
(12:47 PM)

Mom
Please call me as soon as you see this.
(12:51 PM)

Mom
Your father says you are probably seeing a live show and that's why your phone is off so I am going to wait a little while and hope you check in soon.
(12:55 PM)

I try to keep the alarm from my face as I glance over at Mason. "I need to make a quick call," I say, stepping toward the railing.

Mom picks up on the first ring.

"Lia." Her voice has the cadence of a record being scratched. "I was so worried."

"I'm sorry. But I told you I can't have my phone on *all* the time." I stop myself before I say what I'm thinking: *I need to breathe.*

Mason appears next to me and slips his fingers between my clenched ones. He doesn't stop me from moving, just stands there as I stalk back and forth like a lion at the zoo. His face is unreadable, but his blue eyes are soft as they squint at me. He offers me an encouraging smile when our gazes catch.

I let his touch tether me here, in Fableland, in this moment.

I'm not at home. My mother can call all she wants, but that's the only thing she can do.

"I didn't know where you were, Lia." Her voice spikes. Her knuckles are probably white from how tightly she's clutching the phone.

My father would want me to agree. It's the easiest way to calm her down. But I'm not feeling easy today. I'm perched on the tip of a knife, my whole body alert in a painful way.

"You do know where I am. I'm here. At the park. I called you as soon as I turned my phone back on. I've been fine for three days. I am *still* fine."

"But I can't know that if I don't hear from you."

I inhale deep and slow, then let the air buzz out through my teeth. "Mom, you can't know where I am every second of the day. Unless you never want me to leave the house." I say it as gently as I can. I don't normally talk back this way, but placating her isn't working.

Her cough is phlegmy and fractured, like she's crying. My father's voice murmurs in the background. Without letting myself think too much about it, I step over to Mason and curl into his chest. Like he's a cave I can hide in.

Mom clears her throat. Coughs again. The sound makes me jump. "We can't keep doing this," she says.

"I agree." My voice is hoarse. My heart hammers against my ribs.

Mason's hand smooths my hair, and he rests his chin on top of my head. For a moment, I let myself believe that my mother no longer has the power to make my life explode.

Then she speaks again. "If you aren't going to keep your phone on, I'm going to have to come down there."

Forget an explosion. Those words are an apocalyptic event. *DEFCON 1. Code red. Avengers assemble.*

I jerk away from Mason and stride to one end of the hallway. "What?" I croak.

"I have to be able to talk to you when I need to, or I'm going to have to come down there."

I'm shaking. No, more than that. Quaking. As if it's the ground, not me, that's moving. "You can't be serious."

"I wouldn't make you come home, but I could stay, make sure you girls are okay." There's hope in her voice. She wants this to happen. Like I'm a little kid.

She can't come here. She can't come here. She can't come here. I can't speak, the words playing on an endless loop in my head.

My silence urges her on. "I could tag along at the parks. I used to love rides. We could even get cotton can—"

"No." The word rips out of my mouth.

"What?"

Above me, the sky spins. My muscles are ice, ready to crack. "Lia?"

My mother and Mason say my name at the exact same time. Echoes from two different lives yanking me in two different directions.

I close my eyes, keeping my back to Mason as I fist the hem of my shorts in my free hand. It takes me ages to find one steady breath. "You don't need to do that. Everything's fine."

"I can't know that if you don't answer your phone."

"I'll answer it." It feels like a concession. A million agonizing little sacrifices.

"You promise?"

My teeth grind. "Yes. But, please, Mom, give me some space, okay? I'm here with my friends. We don't have much more time before they leave for school. I don't want to waste it all checking my phone."

My stomach twists. But I can't tell Mom about Mason. About his watercolor eyes or his smile that folds my heart into hummingbird wings or how everything I want means he can't have what he needs and I don't know what to do with that.

I glance at him. He hasn't moved. His eyes still guard my face.

"I want you to check in every four hours." Her voice is firm. It hits me like a stone.

"Okay."

"I expect to hear from you at five. No later."

"Okay."

Get through four hours at a time. I can do that. I can keep her there. Keep me here.

"I love you, sweetie."

And I know she does. The walls that she closes around me aren't meant to be a threat. But that doesn't stop them from crushing me.

I feel Mason's shadow before he appears in front of me. "Is she always like this?" he asks softly after I hang up.

I nod.

"That's why you need the money."

I nod again.

He doesn't say anything else. Just takes my hand and leads me forward.

We make so many twists and turns I no longer know where I am. The whole time, I can't think of much besides our palms pressed together. It's like paying attention to your heartbeat or your breathing. As soon as you're aware it's there, it's all you can focus on.

We come to a stop at the far-left corner of the building, outside the seahorse room. There's no light here, just the wavering shadows from the room's interior-lit glass enclosures, and I can barely see Mason in the dark.

Mason lifts my hand and folds down my fingers so I'm pointing only one. Then he stretches it toward the wall.

Something's carved there: one line down, a swoop on either side.

An anchor.

I trace the symbol with my fingertip, as if I'm carving it myself. My heart clamors in my chest.

I try to pull the marking down or press it in—*the sink of an anchor*—but neither action works. It's not a button or a lever. Just some grooves in a brick.

Mason moves my hand down four rows, then two bricks over, his touch gentle. Our eyes lock over my shoulder, and together we push on it.

There's a click, and with a creak and a rusty rattle, the wall glides away, exposing a dark hole that barely clears my head. "Oh my God," I mutter. "How the heck did anyone find this? How did *you*?"

"For Carter's eighth birthday, his uncle took us around the parks, showing us all their secrets. He made us promise that we would never share what we saw with anyone else, or Ike the Sorcerer would come blast us from our beds with his fire spells." Mason shakes his head. It's there again in his face, the way this place has taken something from him. "I was so scared of Ike back then I believed him."

I peer into the opening. "You better sleep in fire-resistant pajamas tonight."

He laughs softly, then draws me behind him into a dimly lit corridor. A second later, the door slips shut.

The seashell sconces lining the walls produce the only light breaking up the darkness. The air is cool and smells of the ocean, as if we might wade right into it if we venture far enough. Beneath it, I catch hints of Mason's icy forest scent, and his heat finds my skin again as he takes my hand.

"Is this another murder tunnel? I'm starting to recognize a pattern."

His laugh echoes around us. "I can take your phone and scan the code if you want to go back."

"We're already in the murder tunnel. The damage is done." I grin. "Let's huzzah this." For the first two months of senior year, that was Tess's phrase.

My heart stumbles at the thought, and for the first time since our fight, I miss her. And Issy. They should be here, even if they don't care about Fableland. They would love the quasi-haunted-house feel of this tunnel. Tess would inevitably make ghost noises, and Issy would pretend to see something in the dark. . . .

The sound of our steps bounces against the walls. "There's not really a mermaid down here, is there?"

"Not a live one."

I jerk to a stop. "Do not show me a dead mermaid."

He snorts. "Murder tunnels, dead fantastical creatures. Where do you think you are?"

"Listen, we just met. I don't know what you're into." It's meant to be a joke, but it falls flat. Too much of a reminder that it's only been three days. And we only get three more. I clear my throat.

Not too far off, a soft glow spills from beneath a doorway. Mason pushes the door open, then waits for me to enter first.

It's like stepping out of midnight into afternoon. I gasp, trying and failing to look everywhere at once.

The space is twice the size of my bedroom at home, and everything—the walls, the floor, the ceiling—is painted ocean blue. The color has been deepened in places to create the illusion of shadow; in others, it's been blended with whites and light yellows to look like pockets of sunshine breaking through the waves. Coral in shades of pink and purple and orange threaded through with dancing stalks of muted green seaweed march across the bottoms of the walls. All the fish are sketched in motion so they look like they've been caught while scurrying away.

And among it all, glowing in the spotlight of strategically placed lights, floats not one mermaid, but a whole coven (or whatever groups of mermaids are called) in a range of skin tones and every hair color you could imagine.

It's not the mermaid in the tank everyone talks about online. But it might be better.

One of them is holding the QR code in her outstretched hand. I walk over and scan it. My heart settles for the first time all day when I hear the familiar trumpet sound that signals I've made it to the next day.

I'm number twenty-nine out of sixty on the leaderboard. Not the top spot I wanted, but after the day I've had, I'm glad to have gotten through at all.

Another notification pops up in the app, coupled with a siren sound. I open it.

Starting with Day 4, all contestants who rank in the top ten will gain access to daily hints.

My eyes widen at Mason. "Did you see this?" I ask, flashing my phone at him.

"The new rule?" He nods.

"We need to get into that top ten tomorrow." And every day after that. If I'd had hints today, I probably would be much closer to the head of the pack. Maybe even in the top three. We need anything that will give us an edge. "No more messing around."

"Got it. No kissing tomorrow."

I squawk. "What? No! We just have to keep looking for the clues while we do it."

"I don't know if I'm that coordinated."

We both laugh, even as a flush overwhelms my face. I can't believe that we kissed, and that now we're standing here talking about it.

How is this happening?

Returning my phone to my pocket, I spin around four or five times, trying to take the room in. It's impossible to catch every detail, no matter how slowly I turn.

"Casterman came down here every night for almost a decade to paint this." Mason mirrors my movements, as if he can catch whatever details I leave behind. "So much for a real mermaid, right?"

I look at him, eyes wide, mouth gaping. "You don't think this is pretty close?"

"It's just paint."

"Paint that looks almost *alive*." I hook my arm through his and pull him toward a blond mermaid directly in front of us. Her face has been crafted with such detail that I'd swear her eyes track us, and her twin blond braids dance out around her head as if caught in a current.

I point these details out to Mason. He doesn't interrupt once.

When I go quiet, his eyes drop from my face, and he inches closer to the blond mermaid. His gaze is such a physical, tangible thing that it leaves a hollowness in its wake. "Why do you believe in all of this so much?" He runs a finger along the mermaid's braids like he's trying to hold them still.

Shrugging, I rest my back against her fin. "I guess I needed something, and Fable Industry was always there."

"Like in eighth grade?"

"And every other time before and after that." I rub my arms even though I'm not cold. After all that Mason has shared about his family, I want to be as honest in return. But talking about my mother makes my stomach clench and the air feel thicker, like my words might summon her and her worries here to suck the breath from my lungs. "I told you my parents were overprotective?"

He nods.

"It's honestly so much more than that. My mother has

generalized anxiety disorder, and it makes her freak out all the time that something horrible is going to happen. Plus my parents thought they'd never be able to have kids, and then I showed up, and I was really sick as a baby and Mom just . . . she can't handle not knowing I'm okay at every second."

He frowns. "That sounds like a lot."

"She went on every field trip, chaperoned every away game for volleyball. Sophomore year in high school she pulled me out of school every time we did an active shooter drill." I sigh. "And then they just always assumed that I was going to work at the store and take it over and never even asked me what I wanted, and I sometimes feel like I'm going to live in that house, in that store, in that tiny little life, forever." I blow out a breath. I've never shared this much before. I'm talking fast, and my voice is shaky. Mason reaches for my hand.

"But this place, there's so much to it. All these secrets and stories and myths. It reminds me that my world doesn't have to stay that small."

His lips spread into a smile. "That makes sense."

"It doesn't sound childish?"

He weaves his fingers in mine, and his eyes cut back to the mermaid. Something in them has softened. "Not at all. Seeing parts of this place through you has helped me understand why people like it so much."

"You can't tell me this isn't amazing." I drag him to a school of angelfish on the opposite wall. "Imagine how long it took Casterman to do this."

I run my hands along the tile. Its surface is cool beneath the paint, like the ocean at night, and the brushstrokes bump silkily against my palm. "I love how there's always something more to discover here. Something new to each ride you take again, a surprise at every turn, even when you think you've found them all." I exhale up at the ceiling. "I knew I wasn't going to find a mermaid here, but I didn't expect to find *this*." I turn back to him.

To find you, I don't say, though I want to.

My heart stops at the feel of my phone rumbling in my pocket. If it's my mom going back on her promise to wait four hours to talk to me I might scream.

But it's more texts from Tess, apologizing again and asking if I'm going to be back for dinner.

Shaking my head, I shove my phone away.

"Your mom again?" Mason asks softly.

"No. Tess."

"You can talk to her if you need to."

"I'm still too mad." There's no judgment in his face, but I feel the need to explain anyway. "I have a lot of pent-up . . . I don't know . . . anger? Frustration? Since I can't really get mad at my mom for how she acts. So I tend to"—my shoulders stick by my ears when I try to shrug; I don't know how to explain this without making myself sound like the Hulk, smashing everything I see—"lash out pretty fast when I get upset. Without giving myself time to think about my reaction. I don't want to do that, so I try to walk away until I've processed. Until I figure out some way to defuse my feelings. Somewhere to put the stuff I can't do anything about." Tess might deserve my anger, but that doesn't mean I should make her my punching bag.

Mason eases away, then taps his stomach. "Use me."

I make a face. "What?"

"Get out your anger here." He pats his palm flat against his chest.

"I'm not going to hit you."

He smiles, his watercolor eyes alight with amusement. "Chicken."

My mouth falls open. "I'm not a chicken. I don't want to hurt you."

"I can take it." We're clearly clowning around, but something in his voice goes beyond joking. Like he means it. That he can take whatever I give him.

"Mason."

He gives me one of those "come at me" waves.

I'm laughing as I attempt to swing my fist and barely bump my knuckles against his (ridiculously solid) abs. That's as good as it's going to get, because I don't want to hurt him. It seems like so many people have already done that. I don't want to be next. Not even in a teasing way.

"That was pathetic," he jokes, catching my loose fist in his hand. He moves like he's going to demonstrate how to actually swing, but then he simply tugs me closer.

His gaze intensifies as I close the small distance between us.

For a second that seems like an eon, we lock eyes, lost in each other. Then we're kissing again.

If our first one was a soft summer night, this one's a hurricane. We slam into each other like we've found another place to put the feelings we can't control.

His mouth is urgent, and our lips part at the same time. My hands claw at his shirt to draw him closer.

He guides me backward until my spine meets the wall, then

props a hand flat above my head. The other arm curls around my waist, angling me against him. Sparks pop and sizzle everywhere our bodies connect.

We're both breathless, but we keep kissing, keep grasping at each other, as if neither of us wants to be the first to let go.

If at that exact moment another contestant hadn't pushed through the door, forcing us to jump apart, our faces the deepest shade of red, we might have remained there, tangled in each other, for eternity.

CHAPTER 18

June 21

Starshatter Resort, Fableland
Orlando, FL

The best thing about staying at a Fableland resort? Twenty-four-hour room service. During our last stay at the Starshatter, my pregnant wife was able to have a bowl of pickles and a hot fudge sundae delivered right to our room at three in the morning.

—HotelReviews.com

MY FEET BARELY TOUCH THE FLOOR AS I FLOAT THROUGH THE Starshatter Hotel.

The kiss Mason and I shared in front of the elevator still burns on my lips. And tomorrow, I will get to see him again. Kiss him again. Wander my favorite place with him again. That alone makes it impossible to convince me that Fableland isn't built of magic.

When I reach our room, I can hear the TV murmuring through the door. Sitting on a tray beside it are two empty bowls, clearly once filled with ice cream. The round glass peephole stares at me like a winking eye as I try to muster the courage to use my keycard.

I shouldn't be surprised they're still up: Tess and Issy are notorious night owls. But I was foolishly hoping I wouldn't have to deal with the fallout from our fight until morning. They're going to be mad that I spent the entire day with Mason. That I barely answered their texts. But I needed space to process.

The lock beeps as loud as a fire alarm when I use my card. The door pops open, and I stand on the threshold like a vampire waiting to be invited in.

Tess and Issy are propped up against the headboard of their shared bed, huddled under a blanket because Tess can only sleep in arctic temperatures. The TV flickers with the bright colors of *Phoenix's Landing*, Fableland's most famous animated film.

They both jump to their feet.

"Are you okay?" Issy asks.

Tess is quiet, her face drawn, but her eyes skim over me the same way my mom's used to whenever I fell off my bike. Assessing me for damage.

"I'm sorry I'm so late." It takes me two more breaths before I can force myself into the room. As soon as the door shuts behind me, I press my back against it.

Issy rushes forward to hug me. "You can't tell us some creep grabbed you and then disappear. We were *worried*."

"I needed to work through some stuff."

Tess drops back onto the bed. "We could have helped you." She takes a deep breath and lets it out slowly. "We've hardly seen you, Lia."

"I—"

"And please don't blame it on the contest. There's no way you were looking for the third clue this whole time. You'd be out."

My muscles stiffen, and a rush of anger blasts under my skin. Although I want to move past this fight, I won't do it by giving into Tess's accusations. Yes, I shouldn't have stayed out so long with Mason, but it is not as if she's been so perfect this week either. "The contest is the whole reason we're even able to be here, Tess. And it's not like you give a shit about Fableland anyway. It seems like all you want to do is celebrate that you're leaving soon."

Tess's eyes flash. "What does *that* mean?"

"All you talk about is going to Penn State and your plans with Grace and your dorm room. You don't care about being here. You don't care that you're leaving me behind."

Both of us look to Issy. Her face is pinched. "Don't look at me. I'm tired of having to be the peacemaker. I came here to be with both of you, but no one has thought about what I want either." There's a sharpness to her voice.

The three of us stare at each other for a minute.

"God, we've all kind of sucked lately, huh?" I mumble.

That breaks the tension and we laugh.

"I'm sorry we made you feel left out, Lia," Issy says quietly.

Tess frowns at me. "I didn't mean those shitty things I said earlier about you hiding. And I'm sorry for not shutting up about college. And for not making you feel like I care about this contest. I know it's important." She sighs. "I just . . . don't know how to help. I don't remember as much about this stuff as you two do. I thought I was helping by making sure we did everything." Her shoulders slump. "I want us to have the best time."

"I'm sorry I abandoned you guys." I slide down the door until I'm sitting on the floor. "I was mad and I didn't want to say something I'd regret. You know how I get." I glance at Issy. "Is, tomorrow we'll film all the videos you want."

"Abso-fucking-lutely," Tess declares. "And I'll try to help with clues. Or at least not make things harder by complaining so much."

"And I'll make sure there's plenty of us time."

"And no more running off," Issy says. "We've already lost two precious days of Lia."

I cringe. "I'm sorry. I really did plan to get back by dinner, but my mom totally derailed me. She threatened to come down here."

My words land as heavily on my friends as they did on me when Mom spoke them. Tess's mahogany eyes are wide. "Nooo," she breathes.

Issy joins me on the floor. "What happened?"

I want to pull my knees to my chest, but when you're my size, it's not as comfortable as TV shows make it look. I settle for crisscross applesauce. "I stopped looking at my phone after everything at lunch, and when I didn't respond she lost it."

Issy's brow creases, and Tess is still gaping at me.

"She's not coming," I clarify. "I managed to talk her down." I lean my head against the door, exhausted all over again by thinking about that conversation. "She wanted to stay with us. Go to the parks and everything. RIP Operation Freedom, right?" I try to laugh, but it comes out like some sort of weird choke instead. Issy flinches at the noise. "Can you imagine? Her following us around?" I press my hand to my chest and suck in a breath. None of the air catches in my lungs. I can't breathe again. "What if she actually does it? Comes down here?"

"But she's not." Issy's voice is firm. "That's what matters." She breathes with me, in and out, in and out. I wonder if she's counting in her head like I do with Mom.

"I don't think I could take it. Everything's . . ." I let my voice fade. I don't know how to tell them I can feel time ticking away like slash marks on my bones. Not only the days left with Mason but my time with my friends, this small snatch of distance I've gained from my parents. It's all going to end in three days.

The only way to stop it is to win the contest.

Tess stomps over and drops beside me against the door, jamming her shoulder into mine. Like she wants to remind me how solid she is.

"I really didn't mean to leave you hanging. You know I wouldn't do that. I . . . I don't know . . . I panicked after I talked to her."

We're quiet for a few minutes. Finally, I ask what I've been so afraid to since I walked in the door. "Do you both hate me?"

Tess smacks my arm. "Good lord. Don't be such a drama queen. It was one day."

"But didn't I break a friend commandment or something by hanging out with Mason all day?"

She frowns. "I think there are worse ones to break than hanging out with a guy."

"Like what?"

"Don't murder your friends?" Issy offers. "Don't get them sent to jail?"

Tess holds up a finger. "Unless you're going, too."

"Great, so I broke the third-most-important friend commandment."

"No way. Stealing would come first. And probably lying, too."

Issy nods. "Or going to a new restaurant without your BFFs."

"That's your commandment," I point out.

She laughs. "*Still*. It counts."

"And don't kill puppies or get a puppy and not let other people come snuggle it," Tess says.

"That seems more like a life commandment."

"Yeah, but I'd be more pissed if it was a friend—"

Issy holds up her hands in surrender. "Basically, what we're saying is that we don't hate you."

I bump Tess's shoulder and smile at Issy. "Thanks."

Tess bumps me back harder. "Did you have a good time with Mason, at least?"

I immediately burst into tears, a geyser of uncertainty and confusion. I don't even know why I'm crying, because we had a great day. But maybe that's the problem. Today was too good. He's too good. I want to keep whatever this is between us and I don't know how.

"Oh my God." Tess grabs my arm. "Did he hurt you? I'll kill him. I don't care how tall he is."

Issy scoots closer, so there's no more than an inch between our knees. Her lavender-and-honey perfume fills my nostrils. "Lia?" Her voice is as soft as the scent.

I'm sobbing so hard I can't answer them. It's like I've been feeling too many things over the past few days and now they're all trying to escape out of me at once. My body shakes, and I'm gasping like I still can't breathe. When I do force some words out, my voice cracks. "It's the opposite. He's so . . . kind and thoughtful and easy to talk to and he makes me laugh, and I know it's so dumb, it's been like five minutes since we've met, but I think I might . . . maybe . . . have real feelings for him. Like not just a crush."

"Oh my God," Issy coos, bracing her hands on her topknot.

"No. Not 'oh my God.'" I shake my head so hard it makes me dizzy. "I can't fall for him."

"Why not?" Tess asks.

"He lives here. I don't. The only way to change that is for me to win this contest. But if I win, Mason doesn't. And he needs the money as much as I do."

"So make the most of the time you have," Tess says.

"What do you mean?"

"I love you, but sometimes you get so tangled up in your own head that it freezes you."

I jam my arms over my chest. What Tess just said, it makes me sound so much like my mother that it ices my veins. I don't want to let my worries eat me up. I don't want to forget how to act, how to *do* something. That's the whole point of this contest—to go after something that could change my life.

"He and I want to get the clues even faster tomorrow. If we can make the top ten, we can get extra hints for the last days. Is it okay if I meet up with him in the morning? We'll come find you two as soon as we're done. Or just me, if you want."

Tess nudges me. "Duh. That's the most efficient way to do it. Clues come first."

"Then Issy's videos."

"And Mason is welcome to hang out with us," Issy says. "Carter's already told Tess he plans to harass her at lunch."

There are so many things that still need to be said: about the past few months, about how they dismiss my weight, about how much I feel the distance forcing its way between us. But today has already stretched on for eighty years, and they both look so serious, and I let them down, too. So even though it aches to swallow everything for the sake of someone else—the way I have to do with Mom *every day*—I smile. "Things are just changing so fast. It feels like we're spinning in different directions. I don't want us to spin away from each other."

Tess drags me into her compact version of a bear hug. "As if I would let you get away."

I laugh into the split neck of her old Waterville High Track T-shirt. "It *is* pretty impossible to shake you."

She squawks and shoves me hard enough that I fall over.

The air in the room is lighter as we settle in to finish *Phoenix's Landing*, as if our talk cleared away some of the cobwebs clogging the space between us. Like old times, we all cram together in one bed and spread a carpet of junk food in front of us.

CHAPTER 19

June 22

Fableland
Orlando, FL

The forecast for today is sunny skies, delicious treats, and a second helping of magic.

—Cartographer app weather widget

Lia
I'm ready whenever you are!
(8:20 AM)

Lia
I'm at the gate. This is where we were supposed to meet, right?
(8:35 AM)

Lia
Mason?
(8:45 AM)

Lia
I'm starting to feel like my mother now.
(8:57 AM)

Lia
Did I get the time wrong? I thought we wanted to be there at opening?
(9:04 AM)

Lia
Is everything okay?
(9:25 AM)

Lia
Two people have already finished the clues for the day. Only fifty people will make it.
(9:33 AM)

Lia
We're never going to rank in the Top Ten at this rate.
(9:44 AM)

Lia
Are you okay? Did something happen?
(9:46 AM)

Lia
I'm going without you.
(9:48 AM)

Lia
Can you meet me at the Fool's Gambit?
(9:48 AM)

Tess
Are you done already?
(9:49 AM)

Lia
He didn't show up.
(9:50 AM)

Tess
ARE YOU KIDDING ME?
(9:51 AM)

Issy
Lia, we're on our way.
(9:52 AM)

Tess
I'LL KILL HIS ASS.
(9:52 AM)

Issy
How do you kill someone's ass?
(9:53 AM)

Tess
NOW IS NOT THE TIME FOR SEMANTICS, IS
(9:54 AM)

Issy
Lia, are you okay?
(9:55 AM)

Lia
Not really, but I'm not losing this scavenger hunt.
(9:57 AM)

Tess
Do you think he's playing you? Is this his attempt to get you out of the contest?
(9:58 AM)

Tess

(9:59 AM)

Issy
Tess, let's not jump to DEFCON 1 just yet. Is he on the leaderboard? Is he getting the clues on his own?
(10:01 AM)

Lia
No.
(10:01 AM)

Issy
Then I don't think he's trying to trick you or something.
(10:02 AM)

Lia
That's true.
(10:04 AM)

But I can't wait for him anymore.
(10:04 AM)

I need this money too. I need to win.
(10:05 AM)

Maybe it is best if I do it without him.
(10:10 AM)

CHAPTER 20

June 22

Hero's Quest, Fableland
Orlando, FL

Of all Fable Industry films, *Sunspark* is easily one of the most beloved. The love story between the brilliant but chaotic Princess Elorra, who prefers to spend her days with her Bunsen burners and experiments, and the roguish former pirate, Oliver Cray, still inspires pages upon pages of fan fiction decades after its release. They're an unlikely team turned even more unlikely heroes, and fans have forever lamented that their story did not get a sequel.

—*Buzzworthy, "Fable Industry's Top 10 Films and Why We Love Them"*

ISSY, TESS, AND I BLOW THROUGH THE FIRST TWO CLUES IN no time.

They were both *Sunspark* themed, so it took us about five seconds to guess each one. It's been fun, getting excited again about this fandom we all used to be a part of, laughing over how we'd swooned for Oliver Cray and Elorra, how we'd dressed like pirate scientists in sixth grade for Halloween.

Still, I can't seem to stop myself from peeking at the leaderboard. I'm ranked at twenty-eight right now, with one last clue to find.

My stomach drops. So many of the contestants are faster than me. And they don't just know the lore; they know how to find the Easter eggs. Like that mermaid yesterday. I've read plenty about it on F^3, but I never saw anything about the anchor. There's no way I would have ever scanned that code without Mason.

I need those extra hints more than anyone else. And now I've lost them.

Tess snatches my phone out of my hand. "Excuse me. We are about to enter the sacred space of Elorra's lab. No stressing about boys allowed."

I reach for my phone but she doesn't let go. "I was checking my standing." And seeing if Mason was on the board, but Tess doesn't need to know that part.

"I'll return it so you can scan the code." She rests her arm on my shoulders and checks me with her hip. "Look where we are."

Hero's Quest is separated into four different environments— a forest, a desert, a garden, and a mountain range—each of which borders Wayborn Castle, the park's centerpiece. We're standing at the entrance to the garden, the various flowers and plants, most of which tower over us, bursting with color. The brass fences that separate guests from the flora fork at numerous points to guide visitors toward attractions.

"I thought you were over this stuff."

Tess shrugs. "This is *Sunspark*. We should always support ladies who love STEM, even if they're imaginary princesses."

Issy is practically bouncing out of her skin she's so excited. She used to insist that she and Elorra were the most alike, since baking and cooking are their own kinds of science. She points ahead. "Southeast corner of the royal garden, behind the rosebushes, right?"

I nod, then recite the clue again. "Though colors surround it, the lowest, dankest place is this light's home."

Obviously, we're meant to find the sunspark for the third clue. Elorra hides it in her lab after she accidentally creates the ball of radiant light with one of her experiments. Because it shines so brightly, she has to squirrel it away under one of her worktables, buried beneath animal hides and thick blankets.

We head toward an ornate archway in the shape of a crown that sits at the easternmost corner of this section of the park. It butts up against the side of Wayborn Castle, and down a set of partially hidden stairs, we should find Elorra's alchemy lab.

The sky is cloudless, the sun beating down on the pavement. Most people are lined up for rides or seeking out air-conditioning since there's nothing to do in this area except examine the greenery and walk through Elorra's lab. I'm honestly surprised they haven't torn down this attraction to build something that would draw a bigger crowd. Walk-throughs aren't exactly the thrills people are looking for these days, even if Fableland has a way of making them magical.

We're traipsing down the stairs to the basement when that overcompetitive blond contestant, Erica K., steps out of the exit. I recognize her and her smug expression from her picture. A little thrill zips through me. She wasn't in the top ten either.

As always, her makeup is perfectly applied, her hair pulled up in an expertly messy topknot. She's one of those girls who would be princess levels of pretty if not for the haughty vibe she gives off. It ruins the whole effect. Like biting into a beautifully crafted truffle from the Curséd Apple to find turkey gravy filling inside.

Her blue eyes dip to the pin on my shirt. "Still in it, huh?"

I tip my chin up. "Seems so."

"I'm Erica."

"Lia."

She glances from me to my friends. "I know we're supposed to be in competition, but if you're looking for the third clue, it's not here." She smiles almost shyly, as if she isn't sure she should be telling us this.

"Really?" My hackles rise, but I do my best to sound neutral. Three days ago, she was pushing people out of her way. Now she's giving fellow contestants advice? Doubtful. Not when the number of us keeps getting whittled down.

I grab my phone from Tess's pocket.

Erica smiles, and I swear she flashes her teeth in the process like a predator. "Yeah. I wasted twenty minutes trying to find the sunspark. It's not there." She sighs. "Now I need to regroup and try to figure out what I missed."

"Damn." Tess frowns. "We were so sure this was the answer."

That lion's smile returns to Erica's face. With a quick "Good luck," she waves and jogs back up the stairs and into the garden.

Tess turns to follow her. "I demand we come back here after we find the other clue. I want to see if the lab looks as real as the Reddingshire walk-through did." She's on the first step when my hand catches her wrist.

"Look." I hold out my phone. On the screen sits the leaderboard, with Erica at number twenty-six. It says she finished the clues for the day at 11:10, which was about five minutes ago.

Tess's cheeks flame red. "What an asshole."

"She's definitely been playing dirty every chance she gets." I don't understand why. I know it's not great to make assumptions about people you don't know, but nothing about Erica suggests she needs the cash prize the way Mason and I do.

"I hope she can never find chocolate when she needs some," Issy mutters. Her petty curses always involve food.

The three of us laugh. "An excellent punishment," I say.

We hurry into the basement of the castle. The first left turn opens into the laboratory, and instantly, it's like we've stepped right into the film.

I want to take it all in, but I also want to secure my place in the contest, so I make my way over to the second workbench and crouch to look beneath it. Sure enough, there's an old wooden crate covered with fabrics. Pulling them away exposes a mason jar so full of bright light I have to squint to look at it. It illuminates every crack and speck of dust in the stone floor. The QR code is pasted on the jar like a label, and I scan it.

Position twenty-seven. I scroll through the page. Mason still isn't on it. He hasn't even gotten the first clue about Elorra's favorite drink.

I hand my phone back to Tess before I give in to the urge to text him.

It's hard not to worry about him. Nothing about the guy I've been hanging out with over the past few days suggests that he'd ditch me. Or worse, pull an Erica and try to make me fail like Tess suggested he might have. Otherwise, why would he have confided in me so much? Why would he have kissed me?

I won't know the truth until I hear from him, and who knows when that will be. For now, I want to be in this moment with my friends.

All around us, the sparkle of Elorra's well-kept beakers and pristine test tubes winks in the light from the bare bulbs above our heads. Equations and notes are scribbled in chalk across the walls, and there are jewelry and fancy shoes discarded on shelves and under tables, where Elorra had shed them as she entered.

Tess has her phone out and is snapping pictures, the flash giving off intermittent bursts of light.

"It looks so . . . real," Issy breathes. "Like they pulled it out of the movie and placed it here."

"I can't believe there's actual sunspark." Tess flaps a hand in the air, hurrying over to the table where I'd scanned the code. I gape at the sunspark with her, really able to take it in this time. According to the movie, sunspark is a flower that has captured a ray of the sun. Its bud is a ball of yellow light about the size of a dandelion puff, with a delicate green stem. It floats in the jar as if the flower is not subject to the same laws of gravity as we are.

We go quiet for a minute as we admire it. Then I mumble, "The eighth-grade versions of us would be losing their shit right now."

"Fourteen-year-old Tess would be trying to steal this." Eighteen-year-old Tess attempts to uproot the jar, but it's bolted to the wooden crate.

"We can get our own," I say.

"What?"

"That was one of the attractions they added when they renovated Hero's Quest a few years back, remember? You can climb Sun's Peak at the other end of the park and pick your own blossom."

"Shit. That's right. We all begged our parents to take us that summer." She sighs dramatically. "Well, we better carbo-load before that. It's like a thousand stairs." Tess's stomach growls, and the three of us giggle. "Speaking of carbs, I'm going to go grab one of those funnel cakes from the stand next door. Don't do anything *Sunspark* related without me."

Issy has walked behind the center lab table and is gripping the wooden edge with her fingertips, her back to me. She watches Tess disappear up the stairs. I almost don't hear her when she clears her throat, the sound as soft and delicate as she is. "Can I tell you something while she's gone?"

I move to the opposite side of the table so we're face to face. A large Bunsen burner and a two-tiered rack of test tubes stand between us. "Of course."

"I've been trying to find the right time all week." She's squeezing her eyes closed like we've reached the top of a roller coaster's tallest hill. I don't think she realizes I spoke. "But we're never alone, or things are tense, and I promised myself I'd do this before we leave."

"Do what?" I ask.

Issy lets go of the lab table to cross her arms. Her index finger bounces against her elbow. "I'm . . . I don't . . . I'm aromantic." She huffs the last two words out in one breath. Her knuckles blanch as her fingers clench. "And maybe asexual too. I don't know. I'm still figuring it out."

She watches me carefully, looking scared. As if I might judge her or something.

As if it were possible to see Issy as anything but amazing.

I bump her wrist with my hand gently. "Thank you for trusting me with that."

Her face relaxes a little. "I know you're still figuring it all out too."

"I have literally nothing figured out."

We both laugh.

Issy closes her eyes again for a second and takes a deep breath. "Now I need to tell Tess before we're stuck together in a tiny dorm room. The last thing I want is her bringing home a new potential guy for me from every frat party she attends."

"Oh God. Could you imagine? Your very own collegiate version of *The Bachelorette*."

Issy cringes. "I would die."

I stare at the doorway. "Tess always seems to take the longest to adjust to new things, huh?"

Issy frowns. "It's not really a new thing, though. This has

always been me, even if I didn't have the words for it for a long time."

I wince. "You're right. I'm sorry."

She shakes her head. "It's fine. You're pretty good at letting people be themselves, Lia. Tess is . . . well . . ."

"Not?" I offer.

"We're talking about the person who put cat ears on her dog and refused to accept that Jellybean was a Jack Russell for two years."

When Tess decides something about you, there's no changing her mind.

"Lately, she feels this need to set me up every time she's in a new relationship. Like she can't do anything by herself." Issy picks up her phone and idly moves her index finger across the screen. When I don't say anything, she clears her throat. "You know, Tío found me crying after the Valentine's Day dance in seventh grade."

"The one where Tess kissed Carly Snow?"

Issy nods. "And you had your first real slow dance with Dan."

"And everyone was trying to get you to go out with Jason Moreno."

She rolls her eyes. "Even back then, when it was only holding hands and texting and writing each other's names on our notebooks and *saying* we were together—whatever that means when you're thirteen—I didn't want it. And I thought that meant I was broken. It was Valentine's Day and everyone else was pairing up. The whole world tells us we're supposed to want to be with someone." She swallows, her long neck tense with the movement.

"And I think, because everyone thinks I'm pretty, it means I'm supposed to want to be wanted or whatever. But I don't."

Her words strike me. Suddenly I remember all the times Issy has been whistled at or people have practically snapped their necks looking at her. All the guys who tell her to smile. All the servers at restaurants who have left phone numbers on our checks. How awful that attention must have made Issy feel when she didn't want any of it. And she never told us. Not once. The realization carves a hole through my center.

She offers a sad half smile, like she can read my thoughts. "When I told Tío why I was crying, he said that maybe I simply hadn't found the right person yet. And it was like something exploded in my body. I *knew* in a way I'd never really known anything, that no, that wasn't it. And when I told him, he kissed me on the head and said, 'That's okay, too.' That was the first time I found any peace with these feelings."

A tear drips from her cheek. I circle the table so I can carefully nudge her shoulder with mine. She does the same back, then puts a little distance between us. Because Issy likes her space. She needs it like my mom needs lists. Like I gulp air sometimes when I'm feeling smothered. I hope Tess remembers that when she and Issy are roommates.

"Do you know much about what's going on with Tess and her dad lately?" I ask. I can't help but wonder if that has something to do with her obsessive planning.

Issy shakes her head. "She doesn't talk about him much since the divorce. Why?"

I chew on my lip for a moment. A few months ago, Tess had asked me to take a trip with her to visit her dad's new house, about an hour away. She wouldn't tell me why she needed to go or let me go inside with her when we got there. After about ten minutes, she'd come running back out, her face blotchy and stained with tears. She'd refused to explain what had happened and made me swear I would keep our trip a secret.

But now, as I stare at Issy's worried expression, I wonder if it's no longer a secret worth keeping. Sometimes the best way to be a friend is to break a promise.

"She asked me to take a ride with her to go see him a while ago. I don't know what they talked about, but when she got back to the car, she was clearly upset."

"When was that?"

"Just before Christmas." I swallow hard. "And it feels like she's been—"

"So much worse since then."

I nod.

"Damn it, Tess." Issy pushes away from the lab table. "I wish she didn't lock up like a vault whenever something is actually going on with her."

"Let's go find her. Otherwise, she's liable to schedule the next ten years of our lives for us."

Issy lets out a loud laugh. "Lia," she says when she catches her breath, "do you have any idea how much I'm going to miss you next year?"

I lock arms with her and we head for the exit. "If it's anywhere near as close to how much I'm going to miss you, I do."

CHAPTER 21

June 22

Hero's Quest, Fableland
Orlando, FL

Hero's Quest is home to some of Fableland's most beloved rides. Guests have been known to spend the entire day queuing up to experience the same attraction two, three, even four times. Not that I can blame them. Who wouldn't want to chase down bank robbers in the back of a horse-drawn wagon with Annie DoGood or be pursued across the sea by dastardly pirates alongside Oliver Cray? Nowhere in the parks have I had more fun than my days at Hero's Quest.

—A Fan's Guide to Fableland

"SOMETHING SPAT ON ME!"

Issy swipes at the top of her head as we weave our way through the exit of the ride.

As soon as we left Elorra's lab, Issy and I collected Tess from the funnel cake cart, and the three of us headed for the first ride on her itinerary, Prehistoric!

"I'm pretty sure it was one of those giant frogs," I point out.

"Ew!" Issy starts wiping at her hair more frantically.

"Is, it was water." Tess rolls her eyes good-naturedly.

"Be glad you didn't get sprayed by the stink bug." I shudder.

"That smell was just *wrong*," Tess declares.

Prehistoric! is one of Fable Industry's most popular animated TV shows. It follows a motley crew of kid-age dinosaurs on various adventures. The ride is one of the newest attractions at Hero's Quest, and combines state-of-the-art magnetic cars with 3D and 4D effects (hence the water and the smells) to take guests on their own harrowing escape from an erupting volcano.

There's lots of spinning and sharp turns, and at one point, the floor literally opens up and you're catapulted toward a lava river until Harry the pterodactyl swoops in to save you. I don't think any of us were prepared for how much yelling we were going to do on the ride. My heart's still pounding a little from that last drop.

"Again?" Tess asks, her eyes flashing with excitement.

Since I scanned my last clue for the day at Elorra's lab, we decided to ride each attraction we pass at least twice, if not three times, thanks to our front-of-the-line passes. It feels like making up for lost time, for all the years we'd wished we could come to Fableland, for all the nights we'd dreamed of screaming our way through Annie DoGood's big carriage chase or crossing the vast ocean with Oliver and Elorra on the Fool's Gambit. My friends have that look on their faces again, that sparkle in their eyes that promises me they're going to remember this week for the rest of their lives, just like I will.

"Okay, but after that, lunch," Issy insists.

Her phone rings as we're about to step back into the FOTL queue. I watch her brow furrow when she sees what's on the screen and immediately accepts the call.

"Hi, Mrs. Baker."

Shit. Tess and I exchange a look. "What time is it?" I ask her. I'd muted my phone and given it to her after we left the lab so I wouldn't be so distracted by the leaderboard and Mason.

She glances at her screen. "Twelve-thirty."

Shit. Shit. Shit. I missed my noon check-in. And not just by a few minutes.

"Lia's right here," Issy says. Her dark-brown eyes pop open wide as she looks at me. "It's our fault. We've been on so many rides we lost track of time. But she's totally fine. We all are."

I wave for her to give me the phone. "I'm sorry. I'm sorry. I'm sorry," I repeat as I put it to my ear.

"Every four hours, Lia," my mother says. The edge to her voice carves itself into my skin. "That's what we agreed on."

"And I've been good about it, right?" This is the first check-in I've missed since our conversation at Neptune's Launch yesterday. I even have notifications set up on my phone. I just don't have it.

"I should have heard from you half an hour ago."

I blow a breath up at the sky. My skin is doing that thing again, where it feels too tight for my body. And it seems impossible to get enough air into my lungs. My eyes burn with the threat of tears. I can't do this anymore. I can't go home, where there's no escape from it. Issy and Tess press in on either side of me like they're columns holding me up.

There's so much I want to say. So many ways I want to push back. But all I mutter is "I'm sorry." My voice cracks. "I'll be sure to check in at four."

"I love you, honey," my mom says before we say goodbye. I know she means it. But sometimes it doesn't feel like love. It feels like pressure, pushing me down, compressing me until my bones snap loose from my skin.

I return Issy's phone to her. "Let's get lunch now," she suggests. Tess and I agree, but none of us moves.

Instead, we stand there, shoulder to shoulder, staring at the moss-covered cave that houses the Prehistoric! ride. After another second of silence, Tess hands my phone to me. Like she knows I don't want to ask for it. Like it's the lock to my cell.

I tap the screen. Ten texts and three missed calls from my mother stack one on top of the other.

Below them are messages from Mason.

Mason
I am so sorry.
(11:31 AM)

I had to take my father to the ER.
(11:32 AM)

I was so freaked out that I left my phone at home.
(11:33 AM)

He's okay but it took forever.
(11:35 AM)

I'm just getting to the park now. I'm glad you got the clues. It looks like I still have a little time to get mine
(11:37 AM)

Done. Thanks to your Sunspark obsession I rewatched it the other night. I don't think I would have figured these out otherwise.
(12:40 PM)

I can't believe I'm admitting this, but it's not such a bad movie.
(12:42 PM)

Please don't be mad at me.
(12:43 PM)

My heart thumps. His poor dad. And God, poor Mason. He must be so stressed out. I feel like a jerk for doubting him, even for a second. Of course he would never ditch me or try to cheat me out of the prize money. He was dealing with something real.

That thought has me rushing to check the leaderboard with shaking hands. Relief whooshes out of me when I see Mason has snuck in at number forty-eight. Two spots from elimination.

I show his texts to Tess and Issy.

"Why haven't you answered him yet?" Issy asks.

"Put the poor guy out of his misery," Tess adds with a grin.

"I will, I will," I say. I'm growing more attached to Mason than I want to admit. He's always there, at the edge of my mind like a phantom. But nothing about this contest, about Mason, has any guarantees. It's like I'm hanging off a cliff, clinging to multiple ropes that are all starting to sever at once.

I need something more solid to grasp.

Lia
I'm so sorry about your dad! I am so glad he's okay. And that you got all your clues! Sorry for taking so long to answer, I had the sound off on my phone.
(12:55 PM)

Mason
I bet your mom loved that.
(12:57 PM)

Lia
She only sent like two hundred messages! 😳
(12:59 PM)

> I look over at my friends. "I really need to talk to him."
>
> They don't ask me to explain. They just nod. "Take however long you need," Tess says.

Lia
Do you have time to talk?
(1:01 PM)

Mason
Want to get out of the park for a bit?
(1:03 PM)

Lia
Okay.
(1:04 PM)

Mason
What are your thoughts about pancakes?
(1:05 PM)

Lia
There's never enough of them on your plate.
(1:07 PM)

They are like little fluffy clouds from heaven that hug your tongue.
(1:08 PM)

I would eat them for every meal if that were an option.
(1:09 PM)

Mason
So what I'm hearing is that you wouldn't object to grabbing some pancakes.
(1:11 PM)

Lia
There are no circumstances under which I would object to pancakes.
(1:12 PM)

"Mason!"

A woman's voice breaks through the din of country music and sizzling meat that meets us on the threshold of the Breakfast Nook, the small café Mason drove us to after we left the park.

Her golden-blond hair is swept up on top of her head in a messy bun, and she's wearing jean cutoffs and a tank top with the restaurant's name across the chest. Her expertly applied makeup hides the lines around her eyes and mouth, so I don't notice them until she's standing right in front of us. But the way she smiles at Mason and gives his cheek a peck, it's clear she's my mother's age.

She shifts her hazel eyes to me, and her smile widens. "Who's this?"

Mason's hand squeezes mine. "Lia." His mouth tips up in a smile.

Every part of me sings.

He looks at me and ticks his head toward the woman. "This is Nora."

I can't think of anything to say that fits in this totally comfortable space between them, so I just nod.

"I'm assuming you're here to eat?" She's already digging under the hostess podium for menus.

"When am I not here to eat?"

This makes Nora laugh. It's a full-on witch's cackle, and I think I love her. She's like a preview of Tess in thirty years.

She leads us to a table for two by a corner window. The afternoon sun has turned the laminated wood of the tabletop toasty warm. After Mason and I sit, she places a menu in front of me. Only then do I realize she didn't bring one for Mason.

She catches me noticing. "He has graduated well beyond the menu." She absentmindedly pats his cheek as she says it.

If with everyone else Mason seems to curl in on himself or turn to stone, with Nora he blooms. His usually stormy eyes are the color of the daytime sky, and a smile hangs loosely on his lips.

I want to freeze this moment. Frame it.

"What can I get you to drink, sweetie?"

"Chocolate milk," I say.

Mason's eyebrows creep up his forehead.

"Chocolate milk is the perfect breakfast food companion. It offers a sweet contrast to the starchiness of eggs and hash browns while also complementing more dessert-like breakfast favorites like pancakes or waffles or French toast. Plus it's *chocolate*. It will never do you wrong," I declare.

"You've thought a lot about this."

I cross my arms over my chest. "I don't need to think a lot about it. It's obvious."

He laughs. "Fine. Give me one, too."

Nora's grin is big enough to crack her face. "No iced coffee?"

Mason shakes his head. "Apparently I've been doing this all wrong."

Nora ruffles his hair and flies off to get our drinks.

"See, you'd be lost without me." I can't help but smile as I flip open the menu.

"I have been," he whispers. "It sucked not talking to you all day."

The shift in his voice draws my eyes back to his face. A hundred feelings crash into my body at once, so I'm basically an emotional ten-car pileup. I slide my hand across the table to clasp Mason's fingers. Part of me is afraid he'll recoil here, outside the park, in what's clearly his real life, but his hand meets mine urgently.

"Who's Nora?"

"My mother's best friend."

My hand tightens around his.

Sadness clings to his edges, but he smiles at my surprise. "She's the closest thing I've had to a mom for the past ten years."

I search out Nora's blond hair across the room as she pours our milk at the counter. Over her head hang framed pictures of smiling people. Others decorate the walls of the café. When

I glance at the photo beside our table, I find myself staring at a younger version of Mason. He couldn't be more than five, and hadn't grown into his ears or long limbs yet, but that closed-mouth smile and the haunting intensity of his gaze are a mirror image of the boy in front of me. He stands between a younger version of Nora and a tall, dark-haired woman who looks about the same age as her. She's beautiful in the same way Mason is, otherworldly. Without hearing her speak or seeing her move, I get the sense that she was utterly graceful. My heart hiccups a little, and I can't help myself, I lightly brush her face with my fingertip.

I look up to find Mason watching me. His eyes are bright. His thumb sketches a circle across my knuckles that sends a shiver down my spine.

"Is that your mom?"

He nods. "That was the day Nora opened this place. Mom and I came to the Nook every Sunday for breakfast until she died. We always sat here." His eyes leave mine to find Nora. "She doesn't let anyone else eat at this table but me. It probably loses her so much money, but she refuses. 'That's Lily's spot,' she says. I think it's the only way she can think of to properly honor Mom." When he looks at me again, his eyes are glassy. I reach for his other hand.

I want to ask him so many questions about his mom, about Nora, about how long they knew each other, how they became friends, but I don't want to overwhelm him.

He inhales slowly and deeply. Then he raises my right hand to his lips and sets them gently upon my knuckles, and I die in five hundred different ways.

"On my days off, I come over here and stay all day. When Nora closes up at five, I'll wander the secondhand bookstore a few doors down for hours." He hasn't moved his mouth away from my hand, and every brush of it ignites my veins like a strike of a match.

"And then he calls me to open back up so I can make him an egg sandwich for dinner."

I jump as Nora appears before us like she's materialized out of thin air. I'd been so lost in Mason that the world faded away. Beside my elbow, my phone blinks with new message from my mother. Across the street, the blue lights of a police car parked on the side of the road flash.

I swipe open my texts. "Do you have an unnatural relationship to breakfast food I need to know about?"

Mom
I hope you and your friends are still having fun.
(1:48 PM)

Lia
This place is the BEST.
(1:49 PM)

Mason's eyebrows dance up. "This from the person who called pancakes heavenly pillows earlier."

"I said fluffy *clouds*."

He snorts. Or maybe it's more of a chortle. Either way, it's my second-favorite sound after his laugh.

My screen flashes again. I roll my eyes.

"Your mom?" Mason asks.

I nod.

Mom
What park are you in again?
(1:55 PM)

Lia
Hero's Quest.
(1:57 PM)

Lia
We're about to get on a ride so I will talk to you at 4.
(1:59 PM)

I don't dare not answer her, even though it's been barely an hour since she called Issy. She's too stressed out, and I'm still afraid she'll make good on her threat to come down here.

Flashing an apologetic smile at Mason, I shove my phone back in my purse. My mom can wait until four now.

Nora has her pad out like she's ready to take our order, but she's looking at Mason. "Has she met Waffles and Toast?"

"Excuse me, who are Waffles and Toast?" In my enthusiasm, I lean across the table, almost sloshing my milk everywhere.

From the glare Mason gives Nora, you'd think she pulled naked baby pictures of him from her pocket. He's still holding one of my hands, so I clamp down on his wrist with the other. "Tell. Me."

A blush has crept into his cheeks. "My dachshunds."

"Wait." My fingers cinch his wrist so snugly red marks are forming. "You named those adorable hot dogs after breakfast food?"

His lips curl into a sheepish grin.

"Oh my God, you're amazing." My voice is too serious, as if

I'm admitting something more than those words suggest. Heat flashes in my cheeks, and I want to drop my forehead to the table.

"I'll . . . uh . . . come back in a minute," Nora says. With a play at nonchalance, she lets out a low whistle and wanders away.

People leave and new ones sit at the vacated tables. We haven't even ordered yet. My mind fixates on that. Ordering's good. It's active. It will propel us out of this moment, push us toward a new one where I didn't basically confess how I feel about him.

I grab the menu again. Tess taught me that there's no situation you can't extricate yourself from if you just keep talking. "What's good here? Of course, you promised me pancakes. So maybe I should go with those." Then I start reading the menu out loud because I don't know what else to do. "The Cheesiest of Cheese Omelets. An Omelet Only a Meat Lover Could Love. Grannie's apple bread French toast. Cinnamon swirl French toast. Philly cheesesteak frittata. Okay, seriously, who the heck orders that for breakfast?"

Mason lets me keep going until I list everything on the page. Until my heart has flown up into my throat. Until my eyes water from concentrating so hard on the glossy pages or from the terror of not knowing what he's thinking.

It's been four days. He shouldn't be anything to me but a crush fueled by his perfect face and muscles. Yet when my mind drifts to Mason (which is basically all the time now), all I can focus on is how funny and thoughtful he is. How he pays attention. How easy it is to confide in him. How I want him to know me in every way possible. How brave and courageous and determined he is, and how all of that makes me desperate to change things I've always accepted. How I want him to win every bit as much as I want to.

How I don't want this to end just because I'm leaving.

I'd always believed that feelings like this took time. That they grew slowly as you discovered a person's secrets, as they gave you access to their tiny corners and hidden rooms, as that gradual openness made them new to you.

But maybe feelings can take other shapes as well. Fire. And lightning. Bright flashes that burn up the sky. Maybe they can snap into existence with the smallest spark, and flare every bit as brightly.

Maybe four days can be enough to know someone. Really know them. Care about them in ways you didn't mean to.

"Lia."

I force myself to look at him. I wish Nora would take our order so I can put some food in my mouth to shut me up.

"I've thought you were amazing since the first time you made me laugh."

"Yeah?" My cheeks find a brand-new shade of red, and my skin redefines the word *heat*.

"Yeah."

"Well, I've thought you were amazing since you snuck us into Reddingshire Castle."

His eyes have fallen from my face, and they scan the table as if he'll find what he needs there. The air between us tingles.

"But I'm leaving," I say softly. It's time for us to acknowledge this. To figure out what it means. What we're doing here.

Mason still doesn't look at me. "I know."

"In two and a half days."

He clears his throat. Scrubs a hand over his face. When he looks at me, he's grinning, but that smile doesn't dance in his eyes as usual. "Then we should make the most of them." He nods toward the menu. "Let's get your heavenly pillows. We've got more to do before I have to get you back to your friends."

CHAPTER 22

June 22

Outside Fableland
Orlando, FL

The road leading into Fableland does its part to set the stage for the world of wonder Casterman hoped his parks would be. Although it's located a mere half hour outside the hustle and bustle of downtown Orlando, the resort is cordoned off from the city by miles of forest mostly made up of Florida's thin-trunked longleaf pines. When guests turn onto the entrance road, they are surrounded by nothing but trees and the sky and sun, creating the illusion that they are leaving the "real world" behind and crossing into a magic realm where anything can happen.

—*Fableland, 50th-Anniversary Documentary*

WE'RE NOT EVEN HALFWAY ACROSS THE PARKING LOT WHEN THE clouds open up.

Torrents of rain splash down on us in an instant.

Even as we sprint, Mason's hand never leaves mine. Water streams in my eyes, blurring my vision, and the strands of hair that have come loose from my ponytail are slicked along my forehead. The soles of my feet slip across the soggy bottoms of my flip-flops, and twice, I almost tumble into a puddle.

Mason stops to let me in the truck first.

As I slide in, my wet legs stick to the leather seat, making an awful squeaking sound every time I move. I fold my arms as tightly as I can, trying to hold back the water pooling off me.

Mason gets in the driver's side and turns the key in the ignition. "Are you okay?"

"This truck isn't yours, right?" I remember him saying something about needing rides everywhere. "I don't want to drip all over it."

A small, derisive grin twists his lips. "It's Pops's. Drip wherever you want."

"Is he still at the hospital?"

"Nah, he just needed stitches. Cut open his hand making a sandwich half-drunk."

I frown. "I'm glad it wasn't anything more serious."

Mason's jaw ticks with tension. "By the time the nurse took him to get looked at, he was sober and pissed off. Had me drop him off with a buddy so he could go gamble for the next few days. Clearly not serious."

Whenever Mason talks about his father, his whole demeanor turns to stone. Even the boyishness of his face is gone, replaced by an emotionless mask. There's nothing I can say to erase that pain, so I rest my hand on his arm.

Like a reflex, the palm of his other hand settles on my knuckles.

Rain drums the roof like the entire percussion section of an orchestra is sitting on top of it. Outside, water falls across the windshield in curtains thick enough to obscure the end of the hood.

"We're going to have to wait this out," he says.

"Okay." I fight off a shiver. "We're in *Florida*. How can it be this cold?" It's like the water has seeped directly into my bones.

"Don't you deal with blizzards up north?"

"Yeah, but I'm not wearing *shorts*."

He leans over to fish something from the back seat of the cab. A second later, he produces a worn gray sweatshirt and offers it to me.

I'm afraid it might be his father's until I take it and catch that pine and ice scent I've come to associate with Mason. I pull it over my head with too much enthusiasm and practically strangle myself on the hood. Mason has to help me wriggle the rest of the way into it. If I wasn't so cold, I'd be embarrassed. It doesn't help that he's laughing when my head finally pokes out the top.

Once I'm settled, he bends over the console so he can flick open the vent. It's hard not to notice that he doesn't move back, leaving us close enough that our sides touch and his arm rests across my knees.

I let myself sink into him. "Sorry it took me so long to respond today."

"I was worried you were going to think I was trying to con you."

I tear my eyes from his face to stare out at the rain. "I didn't know what to think honestly. We both want to win this contest pretty bad."

He leans forward so I'm forced to look at him again. "I would never have told you about my grandfather if I was playing you."

I nod.

"And I never would have kissed you."

I sigh. "I don't know what guys like you go around doing with their mouths." People that look like Mason have never paid me any kind of attention before. And maybe that was partially my fault. I assumed they had a lot of opinions about plus-size people that I didn't want to hear, so I usually gave them a wide berth. I probably would have done the same with Mason if he hadn't insisted on us working together.

"Guys like me?"

I wave at him. "Movie-star types."

The apples of his cheeks glow red as he shakes his head.

"Dude, you could get a job as an Oliver Cray performer. You look exactly like him."

He folds his arms across his chest. "Now I'm wondering if you're conning *me*."

"Stop." I give him a gentle shove.

"Would you be bothering to associate with me right now if I didn't look like your cartoon crush?" He's grinning widely. For once, his teeth are visible. Two of the bottom ones are crooked, and it only makes him more perfect.

Every inch of my skin is volcano hot.

"You make me feel like the parks do." I can't believe I let those words out of my mouth.

The smile ebbs from his face, and he tenses against me. "I know I've told you that when we were younger, Tess, Issy, and I used to be obsessed with Fableland. But it wasn't just *Sunspark* or the rides and stuff. It was all the secrets too. We used to spend hours scouring the internet for information on them. Tess organized everything in binders. They . . . I don't know . . . grew out of it, I guess." I shrug. "I couldn't, though. This place felt like all I had left."

I explained how I'd once punched a hole in our basement wall when my mom was too anxious to let me go to a party. My fist went right through the drywall. I completely panicked and hid it behind an old painting. My parents never found it, but I knew I had to find a different outlet for those feelings. "All that Fableland research that helped me get here? It gave me another way to cope."

Silence spreads between us for long enough that I jump at the sound of Mason's voice.

"I know you think I hate the parks, but it's not that simple. I used to buy into them just like you do." I see him swallow. "Thanks to Carter, my whole family always had season passes, and sometimes, when my mom and I were bored in the evening and my homework was done, we'd come over and ride one or two things. Then she'd buy me cotton candy and drive us home and tuck me in. It all seemed—to use your word—like magic."

"Cotton candy is the greatest." It's the only thing I can think to say.

Mason smiles, but his gaze is heavy. "I haven't had any since she died. When she got sick, I did the things those Fable Industry movies told me to do. I made wishes, I tried to be as good as I could be, I believed, I worked hard. I did it all." His eyes sink closed as his jaw clenches.

"But she died anyway," I whisper.

He nods, eyes still closed. I don't know what to do, so I wrap my arms around his neck. A jolt rocks through me when he hugs me back.

"It was hard after that"—his breath is hot on my scalp—"not to see it all as fake. False promises. And then these other shitty things kept happening to me: Pops got mean, stopped talking, stopped caring, started disappearing, spending all our money, then Granddad got sick and left me too. It's hard to believe in anything after that. Except myself. I'm the only one who can make anything happen, you know? Magic and wishes and all that, they don't do shit."

He pulls away so we're face to face, our mouths mere inches apart. "These last few days with you, though"—he hooks his hand under my chin and draws me in for a slow, sweet kiss—"that's magic I can believe in."

Once the rain lets up, Mason asks if I want to meet Toast and Waffles before we head back to the park.

"Just to meet the dogs?" I ask hesitantly. I know he and I have spent a lot of time alone over the past four days, but going to his house feels like something different. More intense.

"We could have a snack?"

"You ate like three hundred breakfast items half an hour ago."

He chuckles. "Lia, we just met. I don't have any expectations. I just want to show you the things I care about."

He's so straightforward. No games. No guessing. It warms me like a blanket out of the dryer.

"Of course I want to meet them," I say softly.

It takes us about ten minutes to get from the Breakfast Nook to Mason's house. It's one story, with a green stucco facade trimmed in white and a front yard that's empty except for a giant palm tree near the entrance. The homes surrounding it look similar, though the colors vary and some have brick accents or bright flower beds. Kids are playing basketball in a driveway at the end of the street. When Mason unlocks his front door, two blurs of brown and black skid around the corner.

Their nails scrabble against the tile as their little legs scramble toward us. One of them is barking his head off, the other letting loose these mournful bays like he hasn't seen Mason in six years. As soon as they get close enough, they dive at our calves, tails swishing the floor as they scamper in circles, unsure who to greet first.

One is all black, except for clusters of brown at his neck and at the bottom of each of his paws, almost like he's wearing brown shoes and a brown bow tie. The smaller one's smooth, shiny coat is entirely the color of maple syrup. The loudest laugh escapes my mouth when Mason points at him and says, "That's Waffles." Because of course that's Waffles. It only makes sense.

I kneel down to pet them. With every movement, my damp clothes cling to me a little more uncomfortably.

Mason must notice me grimace because he says, "I'm going to find us something dry to put on." My heart skips at his words, though I'm not sure why. He let me borrow his sweatshirt in the car, yet this somehow feels more . . . intense. Like a new level in whatever this is between us. "Can you handle this circus?" he asks with a grin.

"Listen, dog chaos is the best chaos."

Waffles has rolled over on his back and cries loudly as he waits for belly rubs. Toast is licking my right ear.

A soft expression passes over Mason's face, and my heart squeezes. For the hundredth time, I wish I could freeze this moment and collect it, save it like a picture in a photo album. Or better yet, step right into it. I want to be a superhero whose power is to return to their memories whenever they wish.

His gaze clings to me as he tucks a loose hair behind my ear, his thumb lingering against my neck. My skin catches fire when he raises that hand absentmindedly to his mouth on his way out of the room.

By the time he returns, I'm sitting on the floor with both dogs in my lap. Toast is snoring. Waffles's cries have been downgraded to an occasional sigh. His ears perk up at the sound of Mason's footsteps, but he doesn't move.

Mason lays a pair of mesh shorts and a T-shirt on the back of one of the stools at the breakfast bar and gestures toward the opposite hallway. "Bathroom's down there if you can extricate yourself from those two and want to change."

"Nope. I'm sorry, I live here now."

"I'll get you some blankets."

"And maybe a fridge? I'll need sustenance to keep up these pats." As if to remind me of this, Waffles lets out a loud whine.

Mason rounds the kitchen counter and pulls a bag of treats from a cabinet. The moment he gives it a shake, Toast and Waffles take off in his direction.

I climb to my feet. "Traitors," I mutter.

Watching me gather up the clothes he left out, he directs me one more time toward the bathroom. "My room's down the other hall. On the left. Come find me when you're done?" His voice snags at the end, like he's afraid I'll get the wrong idea.

I don't. Or maybe I do, but I don't think it's wrong. That summons a blush to my cheeks as I squeeze his hand across the breakfast bar.

"So you can see all my books," he adds hastily.

"Be there in a minute."

Waffles trots at my heels. When I close the bathroom door, there's a *bump* as he flops down outside. A moment later, a tiny brown paw slides under the gap. Apparently, I have a guard.

It's been a good half an hour at this point since the rain has stopped, and my clothes are more damp than soaked, but they're still uncomfortable. The fabric of my flowered tank has lost its softness, and there's nothing appealing about wet denim. I actually sigh as I peel them off my body and drop them in the sink.

My heart thudding, I hold Mason's T-shirt up against me. Time for more plus-size geometry.

The width and height seem okay—the shirt hangs down past my knees and is wider than my waist—but I'm worried about the length. The shirt could still not have enough room for me, and that would suck, because all I want is to have something of Mason's dangerously close to my skin.

Counting quietly to three, I yank the shirt over my head. There's no resistance, and it settles easily against my frame. It feels weird but also perfect to be wearing Mason's clothes. That's something girlfriends do—or what I always imagined girlfriends would do. My last boyfriend was so thin I never bothered to borrow anything of his but a scarf.

I survey myself in the mirror as I shimmy into the mesh shorts. The shirt is white, and under the fluorescent lights, my black-and-purple polka-dot bra peeps through the thin material. Thank the higher powers I put on a cute one today, instead of my usual cotton racerback with the tears under the arms that I refuse to throw away because it's comfortable.

Waffles jumps to his feet as I open the door. Once I've dropped my wet clothes on top of Mason's in the dryer and set it for half an hour, the dog guides me directly to Mason's room.

The house is sprawling and airy. The kitchen opens to a dining room that opens to a vast living room, the back of which is a wall of glass doors looking out on an enclosed pool and patio. The floors are tiled like the kitchen, except for the carpeting that blankets the bedrooms.

Mason's door is open, and Toast is lounging on the bed, his tiny back legs kicked out behind him. Waffles brushes by me and, with a sharp bark that screams, "Look, I'm here," dives onto the comforter, only to immediately flop onto his side.

When he hears me padding across the carpet, Mason spins around in his chair. "All dry?"

I nod, my mouth dropping open as I gaze around me. Every wall is lined with fully stocked bookcases except for the wall with his bed, which is pushed up under a large set of windows. On the far side of the room, a tabletop has been built between two hutches and cabinets, a bridge offering more shelf space over his head. The opposite wall boasts floor-to-ceiling bookcases, and one final, slimmer bookcase sits in the space between the door and the closet.

"You sleep in a library."

He grins sheepishly. "I guess."

I run my hand up the side of the nearest set of shelves. It's been stained well, the varnish smooth to the touch, the honey color bringing out the muted grain in the maple. "Who stained this?"

"I did." His voice is so, so soft.

I glance over at him. "Are you kidding me?"

He shakes his head.

"My father's had to fire four different guys over the years for not creating a finish like this." I flatten both palms against the wood, admiring it one more time. "Want a job?" I joke.

He huffs out a laugh. "I don't love furniture any more than you do."

We're teetering on the edge of everything we need to be talking about without ever touching it. What happens on the last day of the contest? What is this thing between us? What happens when I leave? But I've already said too much today. I don't want to be the one to bring this up, to risk breaking these fragile moments between us.

His stare is so intense it's like fingertips pressing into my skin, and I have to look away. I study the bridge above his desk. "Did you buy this unfinished?"

"I built it. And all the bookcases too. A friend's father does carpentry as a side job and he taught me a thing or two over the years. And he's got a really good workshop." He says it hurriedly, like details will diminish his talent.

I pull my phone from my pocket. "Can I take a few pictures?"

He nods, but his hands grip his knees, his knuckles going white.

Turning my back to him, I snap some long shots and a few close-ups to capture the intricate details. I can already see my father's face when I show him. Full of wonder, like a kid setting eyes on their overstuffed Christmas stocking. He might even be so excited he'll forget (or at least forgive) how I stumbled upon this masterpiece. By leaving the park and hanging out with a strange boy—everything he and my mother told me *not* to do.

After taking one last shot from the door, I toss my phone on the bed—Toast pounces on it and smothers it with his tummy like it's prey—and approach Mason. Tilting his head back, he stares up at me, his mouth slack, his brow furrowed. I cup his face in my hands. "You're full of surprises, you know that?" He keeps showing me all these pieces of himself, and each one wraps a new string around my heart. Pulls me down deeper.

"Yeah?" He shifts his head to lightly kiss my palm. I ignite. A bonfire threatening to burn up his carpet, his bookcases, the entire room.

"Yeah," I whisper.

Sliding my hands over his short hair, I lock them at the back of his neck. His knees fall open to let me closer. There's a tingling in my lips, and something pulses at my center, and I can't think of anything but kissing him right now. It's this overwhelming need, a high tide rolling over me or an endless climb to the top of a roller coaster's first drop.

As our mouths meet, he bunches the T-shirt in his hands like he needs something to anchor him.

I've never had someone kiss me like this. Mason understands exactly when to interrupt his soft, gentle kisses with more-intense ones. When to part his lips enough for his tongue to slip into my mouth. When to pull away to catch a breath, and when to sink in deeper.

He tastes like maple syrup, and smells like a forest, pine and clouds and rainwater, and I can't get close enough, no matter how firmly I wrap my arms around his neck.

The chair he's in isn't made for two, and I end up awkwardly straddling his right knee. When I lean forward, the chair teeters on its wheels precariously before they return to the floor with a thud that sends the dogs zooming around the bed. Mason's lips are on my neck as he secures us both on our feet. Too many shivers dance up my skin for me to feel embarrassed about knocking things over. My fingers dig into the small of his back, clenching harder with every spark that flares under his mouth as it trails down my neck, across my collarbones.

When his lips find mine again, I kiss him once and step away. The fog clears from his rainstorm eyes, and worry puckers his brow. "Are you okay?" His voice is gravel, stones scratching stones.

I answer by gripping the hem of my shirt and slipping it up and over my head. It pools at my feet with a quiet whisper.

There's something in his face as his eyes roam my body that

seems as open and vulnerable as I feel. My heart wobbles in time to my knocking knees, but I fist my hands at my sides, refusing the instinct to cross my arms over my body.

I've never been this undressed with anyone but myself. Even the few times Dan and I had sex, it was always rushed and somewhere dark, and I still had half my clothes on when we were through.

There's nothing hiding me from Mason, and it makes me wonder what he sees. The way the band of my bra pinches my skin and creates new pockets of fat above and below it? The stretch marks on my abdomen? How my waist is not as smooth without my clothes?

He's so quiet it makes my heart stutter, and a hundred different worries flutter through my head. "Is this okay?" I whisper. What if he doesn't want to move this fast? What if I'm pressuring him?

The thought makes me want to hide, and I start to fold my arms over my chest.

He gently takes my wrists, and his eyes capture mine. "It's very okay." His voice is low, almost a growl.

Then we're kissing again, his hands on my skin. In my hair. He walks me backward—*step, kiss, step, kiss, step, kiss*—until the backs of my legs meet the mattress. I hear the dogs jump up and scatter, but I can barely process it as Mason's hands slide down my back and over my butt.

I pull away for a moment and he immediately mirrors my movement, concern on his face. "Slow is okay, right?" I say.

His watercolor eyes are soft as they take me in. "Slow is perfect."

Everything between us has happened at warp speed, like we're in a two-hour movie that someone is fast-forwarding. But I can't rush into this. I can't have sex with him. It will only heighten the draw I feel to him, and I can't give him any more of my heart. Not with two days left until I leave. Not with this contest looming, where, even in the best-case scenario, only one of us can win.

I angle up to kiss him again. I rope the hem of his shirt in my hands and then pause to gauge his response. I don't want to do anything he doesn't want to do.

He's quick to help, grabbing the shoulders of his shirt and shrugging right out of it. He moves to kiss me again, but I sit down on the bed and gaze up at him. My heart's slamming so hard my head is a little woozy, and I need a good deep breath. Plus, let's be honest. I want to see him the way he saw me a minute ago.

His body is muscular, but not in an "I spend all my time at the gym" kind of way. He's lean, but his chest and arms and stomach are firm and defined. And warm beneath my palm as I rest it lightly on his abdomen and skim it up toward his chest.

He's still as he watches me look at him, his expression illegible. He doesn't take a breath until my fingers trace the tattoo over his heart.

Always, it reads in black ink, the letters styled to look like roses.

"What's this?" I ask. I press my hand over it, as if I can stamp the word on my own skin.

"It's for my mom." Each word cracks against his voice.

My hands fall away from him, and I crush them in my lap.

He's standing over me, his fingers idly wandering through the ends of my hair, but his gaze stays locked on the tattoo. "Every night, when she tucked me in, I'd say, 'I love you,' and she'd say, 'Always.' It was our thing." He blinks rapidly, like he's clearing his vision.

I reach out and rest my hand on his stomach again. "You can talk to me about her, you know."

He feathers his thumb over my jaw. "She would have loved you."

"Really?"

"She loved mysteries too. And history. Anything that reminded her the world was never just what we saw on the surface." He combs his fingers through my hair. "And she had the best sense of humor. No one besides her ever made me laugh so hard, until I met you."

My heart has climbed into my throat. I swallow around it. "You look like her. From the picture I saw at Nora's." From what little I've seen of his house, there don't seem to be any photos of his mom here, like his dad is hoping to forget her.

"My grandfather used to tell me I was all my mother."

"I'm sure he's right."

Mason's gaze intensifies. "Do you think your parents would like me?"

"What?"

At my hesitation, he drops beside me on the bed. "I know they're strict."

I struggle to order my thoughts into something that makes sense. He's asking about meeting my parents. That has to mean he's thinking about what happens when I leave. My whole body feels light, like I've been pumped with helium. Maybe we don't have to have an end date. Maybe, if we both want it, we can make this thing between us something more.

Something *real*. It already feels that way.

I scrub a hand over my eyes, then turn so I'm facing him. It's supremely awkward to be talking about my parents when he's shirtless and I'm only wearing a bra on top, but here we are. "My dad would love you instantly. Mom would take time. Anything new is triggering for her." I brush my thumb across his lips. "But what she wants most is for me to be happy." The words are true, even if I don't always believe them. Even if she can't always do what would make me happiest. "And you make me happy."

My favorite smile finds his face. "I'm glad."

That's all he has time to say before we crash into each other again.

CHAPTER 23

June 22

Starshatter Hotel, Fableland
Orlando, FL

TESS RHODES @RHODIEGIRL
A WEEK USED TO FEEL LIKE AN ETERNITY.
NOW IT DOESN'T FEEL LONG ENOUGH.

"ARE YOU STILL LOOKING AT THOSE?"

Mason pulls the truck into the drop-off lane at the hotel and cuts his eyes to me as he puts the vehicle in park.

"Yep." I swipe my thumb across another picture of his bookcases and admire the next one that pops up. It's the long view. You can see Toast's stubby legs in the corner of the frame.

"For someone who hates her job, you get pretty worked up about furniture."

I place my phone back in the armrest of the passenger seat and face him. "I don't hate my job."

I must be frowning harder than I realize, because his brow furrows.

"If I had chosen it for myself, I might like it." Like everything else with my family, my feelings about the store are complicated. "But not forever."

Mason nods. "You're right. I'm sorry."

"You have nothing to be sorry for."

"I always say the wrong thing." He scratches the back of his neck.

I grab his bicep and give it a gentle squeeze. A forlorn expression spreads over his face, and my insides ache at the fact that I'm the one who caused it.

"You didn't say anything wrong," I insist. "I'm sure I sound like I hate my job. But it's more that I hate that I never got to decide on my own. College or no college, furniture or something else, my parents carved out those paths for me."

Mason avoids looking at my face as he traces the steering wheel with his index finger. The absence of his gaze is like pulling off a stack of blankets in the middle of a winter's night: empty, cold, unbearable. I want to take his chin in my hand and draw his face to mine, but I don't. "Have you thought any more about your princess story?" he asks.

I turn fully toward him. "Um, absolutely. Like, what if she finds a fallen angel on one of her hunts? And she has to protect him."

"And they fall in love?" he asks.

I roll my eyes playfully. "Obviously."

"Fable Industry hasn't done anything with angels before."

I beam. "I know. It could be another edge to help sell the story. A kick-ass, plus-size princess who saves an angel."

A car behind us honks, forcing Mason to loop around. This time, he parks as far back in the lane as possible so people are less likely to queue up behind us.

"Have you tried to talk to your parents about it?"

I shake my head hard. His face and the trees outside the truck twist and blur with the force of my movement. "I can't. They built that store for me. It would kill them if I rejected their plans. They've sacrificed so much."

"But if you've never asked them, how do you know—"

I hold up my hand to quiet him. "I don't need to ask. They have been working toward this for me since I was born. As far as they're concerned, this is my future." My stomach sours, and I pick at a thread on the hem of my tank top. That trapped feeling sinks over me, the doors of the truck inching closer, the roof lowering with every breath.

"What if you win?" Mason asks.

That's the part I don't like to think about. "Then I'll have to tell them. I'll have the money to do it myself if they don't support me." I scrub at my forehead with the heel of my hand. "I know it doesn't really make sense, but without the prize money, there's no point in breaking their hearts. Not yet, at least."

He cups my chin with one hand and brushes a few strands of hair from my eyes with the other. "It makes perfect sense." He kisses me softly. "Just promise me one thing. Even if you don't win, don't give up on this."

This time I lean forward to kiss him. My phone tumbles to the floor as I stretch across the console to press my lips to his. "Only if you promise the same."

Nodding, he eases the truck back in front of the hotel. We kiss one more time, long and slow.

I look back to him as I open the passenger door. "But one of us is definitely winning."

"Hey, Mrs. B."

"Hi, Mr. Baker."

I step out of the bathroom to hear Tess and Issy answering their phones at the same time.

My heart freezes in my chest. It's almost nine o'clock. I missed a check-in *again*.

I'm swearing under my breath as I hustle toward Issy. I press her phone to my ear before it's even fully in my hand. "I was waiting for my phone to charge and I needed a shower. I was about to call you, I swear."

"Your mother was beside herself," my dad says. "She said this happened earlier too."

"Dad. We only have two days left here, we're just trying to make the most of them. I've been checking in"—I have to stop myself from saying *more than enough*—"a ton."

He sighs. "I know, Amelia. I'm doing my best to make this work for all of us."

I wish that didn't mean leaving me still strangled by my mom's anxiety. "Could we maybe stop with the scheduled check-ins if I promise I'll call more? I think it's too much for her to be watching the clock. If I'm a second late, she spirals."

Even though I can't see him, I know he's nodding. "Call a lot," he says.

"Deal."

He gives the phone to my mom, and for the next few minutes, I answer every one of her questions about where my friends and I were and what we did. I try my best to only tell the truth, but I have to make up stuff about dinner and the last few hours, since I was with Mason. "Yep. We went back to Phoenix's Landing after dinner because Tess seems to enjoy torturing us with rides that flip upside down postmeals."

"I'm helping you develop an iron stomach!" Tess yells from her bed.

By the time I've finished talking to my mom, she seems calmer. I hand Issy her phone as I flop back onto the bed.

"Sorry that they're dragging you two into it now," I mumble.

"It's no big deal," Issy says, "but why didn't they call you first?"

Tess thumps my head lightly with her socked foot. "Did you not learn your lesson from the last time you silenced your phone?"

"It's not sil— Shit." I jerk up into a sitting position. I don't remember bringing my phone with me back to the room. Jumping up, I rush to the bathroom and check the pockets of my shorts.

I tear through my luggage next, tossing clothes everywhere.

"When do you last remember having it?" Tess asks. She's following me around, picking up the clothes and folding them on the bed.

"In the truck when Mason dropped me off." I claw my hands through my hair. "I have no way of letting him know I might have left it there." I stare from Issy to Tess in horror. "How am I going to solve the next clue if I can't get it back?"

"He'll have to come back tomorrow to get his own clues. You can make sure to grab it then." Issy speaks softly and slowly like I'm liable to combust at a loud noise.

I shake my head. "It's not his truck, it's his dad's." Closing my eyes, I try to remember what Mason had said about his dad leaving to gamble. Was it just for today? Would Mason still have the truck tomorrow? But my mind's too full of our kissing and everything he shared about his life to recall those tiny details. "I could lose. There are fifty contestants left, and half of us will be cut tomorrow. I won't have any time to plan or figure things out ahead of time. And I was ranked too low for the special hints. This could be it."

My stomach lurches, and for a second, I'm afraid I'm going to be sick. Confiding in Mason about my princess story, seeing the look on his face as he listened, made that dream feel closer. Almost within my grasp. But now it might as well be floating into space. Headed toward one of those stars that's millions of light-years away.

"Hey." Tess stops balling up my orphaned socks to lay a hand on my arm. "I'll text Carter. He'll text Mason. Mason will get your phone."

She pulls out her phone and types, then returns to picking up my mess.

Issy pats the bed beside her. "How was it with Mason? Did you guys talk?"

I tip my head back to stare at the ceiling. "Yes. But not about anything we needed to talk about."

"So you still don't know what you'll do when you get to the end of the contest?" she asks.

I shake my head.

"Or what happens after you leave?"

I shake my head harder.

Tess has four of my shirts draped over her arms. "Okay, but what about you?"

"What do you mean?"

"What do you want?" She sets my shirts down one by one in my suitcase and lowers the top, then comes to sit across from me. "If you could decide what happens, what would that be?"

"I'd win." Tess nods. "I'd move here. And Mason and I would be together."

It's the first time that I've really thought about us this way. As something that could be concrete. Real. Not some nebulous after.

I hate how much I want it as soon as I make it a possibility.

"What if you don't win?" she asks softly.

My arms fold over my chest. "That's not—"

She holds up her hands in surrender. "I know. I know. You're the queen of Fableland. You're obviously going to win. But humor me. What if you don't win?"

I grab a nearby pillow and scream into it. Then I mumble, "I still want to be with Mason."

The bed undulates beneath me as Issy claps with excitement.

Lowering the pillow from my face, I clutch it to my chest.

"I'm starting to think I need to tell my parents about all of this. Mason, wanting to work here, everything."

"Hallelujah." Tess throws her hands in the air like she's at church. "Finally."

I kick her shins (somewhat) gently.

Issy knocks her shoulder into mine. "They'll understand."

I hope she's right. But I'm worried that my mom will fall apart. That she won't be able to get past her anxiety enough to see what all this means to me.

That thought still hasn't left my head an hour later when Carter texts Tess back.

"All set on your phone," she announces. "Mason will meet you at the gate with it in the morning.

"And the first clue is **This culinary delight is a winter's treat wrapped in a buttery blanket.**"

CHAPTER 24

June 23

Phoenix's Landing, Fableland
Orlando, FL

Very little is known about Sam Casterman's world outside of Fable Industry. His only brother died of cancer when the boys were in their teens, and his parents were killed in a car accident when Casterman was in college. Although he never married, he was rumored to have maintained a long-distance relationship with a woman named Ava for most of his life. Many rumors have sprung up about who Ava might have been and why they lived apart, but the identity of this mystery woman has never been unveiled.

—The Unofficial Biography of Sam Casterman, Magic Maker

"I HATE THIS THING."

Mason mutters the words as he follows me into one of the cars for the Phoenix Rising Ferris wheel. Every movement causes it to swing like a boat on choppy waters.

He sits down across from me, and our feet tangle between us. It's been like that since he met me at the park entrance this morning, some part of us always connecting. As if our bodies recognize we only have so much time left together.

I pull out my phone to text my mom a picture, since Ferris wheels are her favorite. Anything to stay in her good graces after missing two check-ins in one day. I can't help but smile as the screen lights up. My text chain with Mason is still open to the messages he sent me last night, forgetting I wouldn't get them. Most are descriptions of whatever nutty thing Waffles and Toast were doing, but the last one simply says, "I wish you were still here," with a photo of the empty pillow my head lay on for hours yesterday while we talked.

I shove my phone back in my pocket after texting Mom and grin at Mason. "Buckle up, buttercup. We're going to have to move around when we reach the top."

"You're taking the picture for both of us."

The second clue for today requires contestants to snap a photo of the elaborate phoenix mosaic crafted at the bottom of the man-made lake that sits on the eastern edge of the park. The top of the Ferris wheel is the only spot in Phoenix's Landing that provides a clear view of the whole bird in all its fiery glory. We then have to show the image to the cast member dressed in a bird suit to get the QR code.

I tilt my head. "You've been on a bazillion roller coasters this week. Why is this so scary?"

"The other rides don't feel like they're seconds from falling apart." His watercolor eyes flick toward the gondola above us as it rocks back and forth. "Plus roller coasters move. You're not sitting still, forced to confront how squishy you really are and how far a fall it would be."

The ride creaks along its slow upward climb, and Mason grips one of the bars on the window, his knuckles turning white. "Why couldn't this have been another food thing like earlier?" he mumbles.

We started the day at the royal dining room on the third floor of Reddingshire Castle for the first clue, the park's renowned hot-chocolate croissants. Though the riddle wasn't hard, accessing the pastries was, because they're only served in one spot, and guests need an invitation or the secret code to gain entrance.

Thankfully, I'd watched the rerelease of *Percivel Night* recently enough to know the code. In the post-credits scene, Percivel stares up at the sky from the balcony of the castle and whispers, "Thank the stars for my royal jewel," before hurrying to join Regina for dinner. I whispered those words to the cast member stationed at the top of the stairs in full military regalia, and he let us pass.

I couldn't help but shoot Mason a triumphant grin as we pushed through the elaborate French doors. Who was helping whom now? Without me, he would have been milling around with the five or six other contestants we saw, trying to find the answer online.

Even Tess looked impressed as she'd shoved a croissant in her mouth. "Maybe you're not such a nerd after all," she joked.

She and Issy both share Mason's distaste for Ferris wheels, so they'd left us to finish the clues for the day while they met Carter in Hero's Quest to explore the Land of Plenty, the pavilion with food demonstrations and re-creations from all of Fable Industry's films.

Mason sucks in a sharp breath and shuts his eyes tight as our gondola rises higher.

I tuck a sneaker against his ankle in the hopes of comforting him. "Have you really never been on this? The view is supposed to be spectacular."

"You're the first one to even get me in line."

"Would you have come without the contest?"

He sneaks open one eye to peer at me. "If you asked, probably."

My heart leaps in my chest.

"Why don't you check the leaderboard while we wait?" Clearly, he could use the distraction.

I get my phone back out as well. Unlike most Ferris wheels, the Phoenix is unpredictable. Sometimes you'll sit in the same spot for five minutes; sometimes it will loop around three times without stopping. I need to be ready to snap those pictures at the first opportunity. The last thing we want to do is have to ride this again when so many people are being cut.

"No one is finished yet, but there's at least five of us on clue two and four on clue three," Mason says.

"We should be fine, then," I muse. But my leg keeps bouncing anyway. Mason and I have ended the day in the top twenty-five only once. If we don't make that happen today, we're screwed.

"As long as we don't die on this thing, sure," Mason quips.

The next time the wheel turns, we find ourselves at the top. Mason presses his head to his knees with a groan, while I angle sideways in my seat, doing my best not to rock the car. A gasp escapes my lips as I peer over the side. I've never seen anything like this mosaic. Thousands of glass tiles in endless shades of blue and gray and white are shaped into a phoenix that looks frozen in ice. At the center of the lake, a fountain shoots sprays of water, creating restless waves that make the creature's blue flames appear to dance in a phantom breeze.

I snap photo after photo, then take Mason's phone to do the same.

"You can't tell me there isn't a little magic here," I murmur as I stare down at the water.

Mason *hmm*s in agreement.

When I glance over at him, his eyes are open. But they're on me, not the lake below.

Here lies a rose that can stretch across oceans.

My smile widens each time I read the final clue. I know this one, and it's one of my favorite things about the entire resort.

"How do you know where we're going?" Mason asks. Despite our height difference, he has to jog a little to keep up with me. Nothing makes me faster than being excited. Tess says I could have been a track star if Elorra and Oliver Cray were waiting for me at the end of every race. "The only rose I can think of is in Hero's Quest."

"The one in Annie DoGood's hat?"

"Yeah. But it doesn't cross any oceans, so I'm not sure what they're getting at."

"It's not a movie. It's Casterman lore."

"Like the unicorn?"

I nod.

Getting back to Reddingshire Castle from Phoenix Rising means walking the circumference of half the lake, and it feels like it's taking us ages. I swear every person we pass has a contestant pin, until I look more closely, and I can't help but check the leaderboard every few minutes to see how many people are ahead of us. Tomorrow's the last day. The cash prize is legitimately in reach for me or Mason. It's not a pipe dream anymore. All I have to do is stay calm and focused and trust in my knowledge of the park.

And in Mason.

I had my doubts at the beginning of the week but he's been a real teammate and ally, and so much more. As much as I can't wait to get my hands on that prize money, I also don't want to rush the clock. I want every second with him I can get. Even if we're just standing next to each other, fingers woven together, breathing in silence. I don't know how I'm going to go back to my old life now, not when he's carved a space for himself in it.

Two people have completed the clues for the day (Ember and Erica, of course), but otherwise, the stats look the same as the last time I checked. We're still numbers five and six, respectively. I don't know how many people are aware of Reddingshire Castle's dungeons, so it may take the other contestants longer than usual to secure their spots. Which means a better chance for Mason and me to reach the top ten.

I switch over to my texts before I put my phone away. I send off a quick message to Issy and Tess updating them on where Mason and I are. Then I open my text chain with Mom to send her a picture of the phoenix. It's been more than twenty minutes since I sent her the last photo, and I can't believe she hasn't responded. Mom never lets go of her phone when I'm not home.

Maybe she's having an extra-good day. For that to happen while I'm away would be amazing. It would show that her meds are working.

I lead Mason around the left side of the castle, in the opposite direction from where we went to find Smokey on the first day.

"No one does the dungeon walk-through anymore," he notes as we reach the entrance. "It's boring as hell. Most people have forgotten it's even here."

From what I've read, there aren't anything but empty cells and flickering lights down here, because Casterman didn't want to scare the kids. But we're not going to the dungeons to be entertained.

"Just trust me," I say, smiling at him over my shoulder.

Our hands still hooked together, we duck beneath the low doorway into the first twisting hallway.

"Given your love of murder tunnels, I figured you'd be totally into this place," I joke.

Mason shakes his head, that little smile I love so much tipping up.

The space around us is cavernous and dark, except for a few sconces on the wall painted to look like torches, complete with swaying flames. The dungeon walls are stone, and I drag the fingers of my free hand along their bumpy surface as we turn down a hallway that leads us deeper into the castle.

"The clues today have been so much harder," I say. Maybe not for me, but in general. Not one of them has been something widely known.

"It's going to get worse from here."

"Oh?" I arch an eyebrow.

"I have it on good authority that one of the clues tomorrow is timed."

"Carter told you?"

Mason snorts. "We have to access Alistair's workshop during the creature parade. That's all I know."

"That happens at eleven in the morning."

"And the doors close about ten minutes after the creatures emerge."

That means we'll need to be there and ready when the parade starts. It'll be the first time since the welcome party that all the contestants will be in the same place at the same time.

"I'll wear my running shoes," I mutter.

We loop in descending circles, the tunnel narrowing as we go. Around the fourth one the tunnel branches in two. To the right is a set of stairs that lead up to the queue for the castle walk-through, according to F^3. Going left should lead us to the rose. Except it's blocked by yellow construction tape.

"Shit."

"What?"

"We need to go that way." I gesture at the tape.

Mason steps closer and squints into the dark. "I don't know why they'd be doing work down here without closing the whole attraction." He pulls out his phone and sends a text.

A second later, a notification dings.

"Carter says he hasn't heard about any construction over here."

My eyes narrow. "Can you get this kind of tape anywhere?"

Mason shrugs. "Sure."

"Erica." I widen my eyes at him. "Yesterday we ran into her at Elorra's lab, and she tried to convince me, Issy, and Tess that the last clue wasn't there."

"And she's one of the only people that's done for today," he says.

"Yep. Apparently she's not above conniving and cheating." I yank down the tape and step into the hall.

"She's a regular Sora Shadowblood."

I snort. "Look at you speaking Fableland with the best of us."

Those watercolor eyes squint as he smiles. "I blame you."

"Then just wait for this." I take his hand again and lead him down the hallway. At the far end, just where the forums said it would be, so low we both have to crouch to see it properly, is a rose etched elaborately into a block of pure gold that has been set into one of the stones.

"Do you know what this is?" I ask quietly. Reverently.

Mason shakes his head.

We both scan the QR code mounted beside it, then put our

phones away as soon as we hear the trumpet that confirms we've moved on. Neither of us checks the leaderboard or what our bonus reward is for the day. Neither of us acknowledges that we've officially made it to the last day of the scavenger hunt. That we're three clues away from the money to make one of our dreams come true. It's like we both know that this moment—this place—is special.

I settle down beside the stone and pat the space next to me. As soon as he's close enough, Mason circles my waist with his arms and pulls me back against his chest.

"This is Ava's rose," I say.

"Who's Ava?" His lips brush the shell of my ear.

"The love of Casterman's life."

"I thought he never got married."

"He didn't, because Ava lived in France," I say softly.

"She never moved here? He never moved there?" The rumble of his voice reverberates from his chest down my spine.

"No."

"But they stayed together?"

I let my head fall back against his chest. "They did."

None of the sounds of the park reach us here, so only our soft breathing breaks the silence.

I've always loved this story about Casterman. This idea that he was able to create amazing love stories because he'd had his own, that his and Ava's love was so strong they'd been able to sustain it across a vast distance. That even though they were both long dead, it survived in their roses.

But as I sit here with Mason, folded in the warmth of his

arms and the comfort of his presence, knowing that I only get another day of this, the rose's story suddenly means so much more.

"He wanted a way to be with Ava all the time, and she grew roses, so he 'grew' one for her here, in her favorite part of the park. There's supposed to be a matching gold block built into the wall that surrounded her garden, wherever that was. The story goes that every day, the two of them would touch their roses at the same time so they were always joined, even when they weren't."

"Wow," Mason mumbles. His cheek nestles against my hair.

I wish I could chisel the rose from the wall and hold it in my hands. I wish I could take it with me when I leave, that I could give one to Mason too. *This* is the Fableland magic I want. The promise of a connection that can't be broken. A tether that won't snap no matter how hard you pull on it.

"I can't imagine how tough it is to be apart that much, but I'm willing to try," I say. "If you are." These were the things we needed to say yesterday. We can't keep dancing around this. "I want to give us a chance, no matter what happens tomorrow."

"Lia."

I turn to face him. "I was thinking about this last night. If we make it to the end, what would happen if we both scanned the last code at once? Maybe we could tie? Or both win?"

"There's no way to scan a code at exactly the same time. One will register before the other."

"Okay, but we could try." My voice sharpens. I wasn't expecting him to shut me down like this.

Mason's mouth yanks tight. "At best we'd probably split the prize."

"That's still something."

His whole body stiffens, his muscles and tendons like dominoes in reverse, straightening one by one until he's rigid. A statue. "Barely enough to cover two years at a state school. Not nearly enough to get you settled and secure in a whole new state, away from your family."

Every word he speaks feels like an arrow skewering my hope. "Well, what if you win and I don't, what then? Or"—this is the option I've barely been able to let myself consider—"what if neither of us wins?"

"What?" That one syllable is more gravel than voice.

I shift to my knees so I can peer into his face. "What is this? What's going on between us? What happens when I leave?"

All this time, I've been assuming that we would figure this out. That we'd be like Casterman and Ava. We'd find a way to make this work. But from the look on Mason's face, it seems he doesn't feel the same.

He looks so genuinely confused that my stomach plummets. I feel like I'm falling, too.

I scoot away from him fast, my back slamming hard into the opposite wall. "You haven't thought about this at all, have you?" My fingers curl into fists. "Tomorrow's the last day of the contest. Then I leave. That's it."

My words hit him like a boulder. I see him jerk. See his shoulders roll forward. "I thought we were hanging out. Enjoying each other's company. Working together to win this contest."

"Then why did you ask about my parents? Why did you take me to your house? Let me meet your dogs? Introduce me to Nora?" My left hand crashes into the wall behind me as I fling my arms out. My knuckles drag across rough stone and I feel the skin break, but I barely register the pain through the other emotions clouding my head.

None of this makes any sense. Yesterday, it felt like we'd taken a step forward, connected in a way that meant something. Now he's staring at me like I imagined the whole thing.

"I like seeing you happy."

"Do I look happy now?" I clamp my eyes shut against tears I refuse to shed. I have to cough to clear a sob from my throat. All the time I wasted, thinking this was something. All the lies to my parents, the time with Tess and Issy I gave up, the contest I could have won on my own.

Fableland isn't magic.

Neither is Mason.

It's all painted grass. I should have listened to him the first time he tried to tell me.

"I got caught up," he says, leaning back against the wall. "In this"—he waves his hand between us—"in the magic you see everywhere."

"But?"

"But I don't have any answers." When he looks at me, his eyes are glassy. "I've barely slept since the day we met, trying to find some way this works. But it doesn't exist unless you win and move here."

"There are a lot of good schools in Boston. Maybe you could

get a scholarship if neither of us wins?" The words slice my tongue. Like I'm throwing knives and holding them by the sharp end. It's such a selfish thing to say. There's no way for me to uproot my life for him, so here I am, hoping he might do it for me.

His face hardens as creases appear in his brow. I know his answer before he says it. He can't choose me. He never could.

I hear his words as if through a howling blizzard. "I never had the grades for scholarships. It would take me three times as long to save up the money for out-of-state tuition, even at the cheapest school in Massachusetts." He doesn't look at me as he says it. "I don't want to have to wait that long. I can't wait that long."

My stomach curdles, like I've eaten something rotten. It's not fair, but he's right. And even at my most selfish, I won't demand he make a different choice.

"I don't want to make you impossible promises, Lia."

If only I could spill his laughs from my pockets. Throw his moments back in his face. Peel his kisses from my lips. But they're a part of me now. I feel the way they've changed me, rewritten my DNA, restructured me on a molecular level. Now that I've met Mason, I will never be the same. I'd need a sharp knife to carve him out.

But I don't have a knife. Or an answer. Or anything at all.

Only two days' worth of seconds that can't fix any of this.

I push myself to my feet with shaking arms. "I should go."

He stands, too. "Not like this." I try to ignore the way his voice cracks, but it's like a chisel, breaking me open, creating new fissures that will never close.

I face the wall for a minute. Count my breaths. I get to fifty before I find the steadiness to turn around. "I think we should say goodbye." I can't believe how calm I sound.

"Until tomorrow?" He says it like a small child hoping whoever told him Santa doesn't exist was kidding.

"Just goodbye."

"But the contest—"

"Good luck." My words are clipped, pointed. I hope they hurt. "May the best one of us win."

CHAPTER 25

June 23

Starshatter Hotel, Fableland
Orlando, FL

>   OLIVER
>   We need real magic right now, Princess.
>   Not some chemical reactions.
>   ELORRA
> (pours a boiling substance over some loose gunpowder)
>   Not even magic can fix what's already broken.
>
>   But science can transform it into something new.
>
>   —*Sunspark (01:28:13)*

I DON'T REMEMBER SHOVING THROUGH STARSHATTER'S OSCIL-lating front doors.

I don't remember taking the elevator to the ninth floor.

I don't remember inserting my keycard into the door reader.

I don't remember texting my mother for our next check-in.

I don't remember shucking my clothes.

I don't remember slipping on new ones.

I don't remember tearing my notebooks in half. Once, then again, and again, and again.

I don't remember pulling the comforter off my bed and wrapping it around my shoulders.

I don't remember sliding open the door to the balcony.

I don't remember lying down on the small lounger overlooking the pool.

I don't remember my heart shattering into such small pieces that I will never be able to find them all.

I'm lying on my side, wrapped in a blanket despite the ninety-degree weather.

I stare at my phone screen, but there's nothing on it.

Not from Mom.

Not from Mason.

Not from my friends.

Although I don't remember it, I must have fallen asleep at some point because the sun has swung toward the west, and my phone says it's two-thirty.

Everything seems to be behind a screen, happening in a fog.

Sitting up, I pull up the Scavenger Hunt app. It opens to the leaderboard, showing Mason and me right under Ember and

Erica, positions three and four. It should make me feel better, to know I'm still in this, with my highest ranking ever, that my preparation and planning and knowledge haven't gone to waste. But all that oscillates in my center is something hot, burning. Flicking the app closed, I press on it, staring at the delete option. It would be so easy to do. Erase all of this. Wipe these five days away so they're no more real than what Mason and I had.

I throw my phone beside me, a new wave of tears pouring from my eyes.

My stomach cramps, and I slap my hand over my mouth, afraid I'm going to be sick. My last boyfriend and I broke up long enough ago that the feelings have gone fuzzy, but I remember more emptiness than pain. Like I was a house after the furniture had been removed.

But this is like the house has been razed to the ground. And I'm whatever was left inside. Crushed beyond repair.

The underside of the balcony above mine is painted black and strung with tiny lights like stars. Because of course it is. Mason was right: there isn't a corner of this place that's real. I squeeze my eyes shut. If it weren't for Fableland and its supposed magic, I wouldn't feel so awful right now. For the first time since we got here, I want to go home.

And just like that, I sob louder. Because my home is not a sanctuary, it's a prison I'm trying hard to escape. With this resort, with this contest, maybe even with Mason. And none of it has worked.

It takes me a while to cry myself out. Then I stare dumbly at the false sky above me. My tears dry itchy on my cheeks and neck in the heat, and my eyes burn. I should get up, but my body has that feeling like when you swim for a long time, my muscles dense as cement and out of sorts, like I'm put together wrong.

Maybe I am. Maybe after this trip I'll never be put back right again.

A few hours ago, I would have said I liked it that way—that I didn't want to be the old version of Lia anymore—but now I wish I'd never come here. That I'd never tried to do something for myself. That I'd never met Mason. It's easier not to want things. Your heart might not feel anything, but at least it can't get broken. There's nothing to break.

I hear muffled voices and then the door opening. I turn toward the cushions.

"The light's on," Tess says.

"Lia, are you here?" Issy calls out.

I don't get up.

"It looks like she brought a tornado with her."

"Tess, shut it."

"Shit, those are her research notes. Lia, did you not get the clues in time?"

The glass door groans on its track. "There you are." Issy's soft voice. I don't look at her. "Why didn't you— Hey, are you okay?"

She kneels in front of me, her coffee-brown eyes wide. Her hand is so close, the tips of her fingers touch my arm, and from somewhere in me, a new well of tears brims my lashes. They're hot, and as they fall, they draw raw, stinging paths down my face. I don't wipe them away.

"Tess, get over here," Issy says.

Tess's platinum-blond head appears around the door. "Have you been sitting out here the whole . . ." She takes a good look at me, and her last words wither on her tongue.

"How was the pavilion?" I ask weakly.

Worry wrinkles Issy's features. "Fun."

"You should have seen all the food," Tess adds. "And there was this chef who was drooling over Is like she was a five-star dessert."

"You give the restaurants stars, not the meals." Issy rolls her eyes, then focuses back on me. "Stop deflecting. Tell us what's wrong," she presses. "Did you lose the contest?"

I shake my head. It's as heavy as a boulder on my neck. "Mason—" I choke. His name is like ice in my mouth. Or fire. Poison. Something that hurts.

I pull my knees as close to my chest as I can and lock my gaze on the pool below. I suddenly feel too big for this lounger, this balcony, this room. This park. This whole world.

I want to disappear.

"It's done," I croak.

"Oh, Lia." Issy frowns. "What happened?"

I drop my chin to my chest. I don't really want to say it out loud. But they're my friends. I should talk to them. "He doesn't want to try to be together."

"What?" Tess rears back in surprise. "That makes no sense. That boy is so into you."

Issy squeezes my arm. "Maybe you misunderstood him?"

I yank my arm away. "It's pretty hard to misunderstand

'I don't see any way this can work.' We're over. We're nothing." Each word causes a bit more of that anger I'm forever forcing down to flare in my chest. But for once I'm not mad at the situation, at the things I can't control. I'm mad at my friends. "I can't believe you two weren't here. I had to deal with this all alone. *Again*." My gaze flits between Tess and Issy. "Just like with everything else lately." If they were as invested in this trip as me, if they'd actually tried to help with the contest, if they'd wanted to spend time with me for real, I wouldn't have been so distracted by Mason. I wouldn't be sitting here trying to hold myself together. We'd be at one of the parks celebrating that I was one of the top ten contestants with one day left. "It's like neither of you gives a crap about me anymore." It's almost a relief to have somewhere to put these emotions before they tear through me.

Tess stares at me, dumbfounded, her mouth actually hanging open. "What are you talking about?" Once she regains her composure, she points her phone screen at me. It's our group chat. The last message was from this morning at breakfast when Issy was complaining about the poor caramelization on the French toast. "I don't see any messages here from you telling us you need us." Her hand drops to her side. "We would have come. You know that. But you don't ever ask for help. You just . . . run away and get mad. You don't deal with things."

My ears are ringing, and anger surges like lighting in my veins. All these things she's saying, they aren't what I need to hear right now. I say as much out loud as I snatch my phone from the chair and storm inside.

Issy and Tess follow. "What do you need to hear then?" Tess asks.

I whirl on her. "You're sitting here telling me that I should lean on you, talk to you, when in two months, neither of you will be here anymore. What's the point of that? I might as well get used to being on my own."

"Is that what this is about?" Tess drops onto the bed. "Us going to college?"

I growl and start pacing in a circle. It's like I'm speaking a different language. My hands fist so hard that I can feel the sting of my nails as I tighten my fingers.

"No. It's about the way you diminish everything that matters to me. 'Fableland's childish, you're never going to win this contest, you're the only one who thinks you're fat, you should appreciate the job you parents are giving you.' Nothing I'm feeling seems to be a big deal to you. You brush it all away. Like you get to control what hurts me, what I think."

"What—"

I cut her off before she can tell me I'm wrong. "I have the right to feel abandoned. The whole time we've been here, you both keep leaving me when we're supposed to be making memories, the three of us. It feels like you're already gone." And now Mason is too.

Tess is as pale as her hair. Her phone has tumbled from her fingers. Issy's crying. "We knew you liked Mason. We wanted you to get some time with him. We thought it would make you happy," Tess whispers.

That's the second time I've heard that today. And the second time it's been a wrecking ball through my middle.

"Do I look happy?"

Issy sniffles.

"Maybe you should have asked me what *I* wanted, before deciding that for yourself."

I walk out the door, slamming it behind me. I don't know how I'm crying again, but new tears leak down my face as I stalk toward the elevator.

Stopping in front of the up and down buttons, I pause, unsure what to do. My first instinct is to text Mason, and that makes my stomach heave. He should never be my first call. We're nothing to each other. Just a blip, a pencil scratch across a long piece of paper, a summer drizzle. Nothing substantial. Nothing that would ever last.

I text my mom, and when she doesn't immediately answer, I cry harder. I've never felt so alone.

With shaking hands, I do the only thing I can think of: I dial my home number. As I listen to the phone ring, I make the decision. I'm going to ask my parents how to change a flight. I'm coming home.

I won't win the contest. I don't feel ready to talk to them about my future. But I can't be here anymore. It's not helping. It doesn't feel like freedom. It feels like a mirror, reflecting everything I want that I can't have.

No one picks up. I try three more times with the same result.

Everything about this trip was a bad idea. Thinking I could win a contest against so many other people, believing a week with my friends would somehow make up for them leaving me behind for college, letting myself give in to feelings for a guy I just met, hoping some amusement park would be enough to change the last eighteen years of my life.

Maybe the things I want *are* childish. Maybe *I* am.

Frustrated, I jam my finger into the down button. My hand is wet from my tears and my fingertip slips against the smooth metal. Sobbing has given me the hiccups. I don't know where I'm going until the elevator opens in the lobby.

I see the oscillating glass doors. Outside. Fresh air. More distance.

It takes all my willpower not to run. I don't even do my plus-size geometry before slipping between the rotating panes.

Away. Out. It's all I can think.

The muggy Florida afternoon drapes over my skin like a damp towel as the door opens onto the sidewalk. I don't care. I suck in wet breaths like they're refreshing. Like I've never tasted such fantastic air before.

As I push out onto the pavement, I stumble into someone tall and solid.

I mumble, "I'm sorry," and try to angle out of their way, but a hand gently grasps my arm. As I glance up, angry words are already rushing to my lips. But then the whole world starts to spin, and I think I might faint.

Because there's my father, holding my wrist.

CHAPTER 26

June 23

Starshatter Hotel, Fableland
Orlando, FL

~~Fableland, the place where dreams happen.~~
~~Fableland, bring your imagination to life.~~
~~Fableland, a bridge to your imagination.~~
~~Fableland, where dreams come true.~~
~~Fableland, fall into your imagination.~~
Fableland, bringing you closer to your imagination.

—Excerpt from Sam Casterman's "Ideas" notebook

I WAS IN EIGHTH GRADE WHEN MY MOTHER'S ANXIETY PUT HER IN the hospital.

It was the day after Thanksgiving, and the store was having Black Friday sales, so Dad was at work from open to close.

I found Mom on the couch when I woke up, but she was sometimes a morning napper, so I made myself breakfast without thinking much of it. Two hours later, though, she still hadn't moved.

I knelt by the couch and touched her arm. "Mom?" I whispered.

Her face was a mess of dried tears and snot when she turned it from the pillow.

"Are you okay?"

"It's too much," she said.

"What is?"

"Everything."

I tugged on her wrist. "I think you should get up, Mom." My knees had started to wobble, but I forced myself to stand. To be steady.

"I just don't want to be here right now, Lia."

"Mom, where?" Fear was a thunderstorm in my stomach. "At home?"

"Here." She kept saying those words. It was all she would respond with, no matter what I asked her. *I don't want to be here. I don't want to be here.* They circled in my head like an awful song.

I called my father, but he didn't answer. And somewhere in me, I just . . . I *knew*. If I didn't do something right now, I might lose my mother.

So I called 911.

The ambulance came and transported us both to the hospital. The emergency room was quiet, and I sat in an uncomfortable plastic chair by myself, doing my best not to listen as the triage nurse asked my mother scary questions with even scarier answers. Soon Mom disappeared behind doors that screamed Authorized Personnel Only in red block letters.

The music playing in the waiting area was from some soft rock station—sad songs about love and loss that tugged like a rope at my chest. I tried to tune them out by playing games on my phone, but every time the battery line dropped I'd panic it would die before I heard from my father. My muscles were coiled metal springs, so when the nurse called for me, I tripped and cracked my knees on the linoleum.

Following the nurse through those doors, I tiptoed like I was in a graveyard, though machines beeped and people yelled. Someone laughed.

The nurse gestured toward a bed in the middle of the ER, and there she was, my mom. She looked so small. They had her in green scrubs, the color of Christmas trees. No one else was wearing them. It was like some kind of scarlet letter. So everyone knew why she was there.

A woman sat beside Mom's bed. There was a chart on a clipboard on the end. Someone was monitoring my mother's behavior, scribbling notes every fifteen minutes. I wondered, ridiculously, if she was passing whatever test she was taking.

She cried when I hugged her, whispering she was sorry so many times the words lost meaning.

My father arrived a few minutes later. He had called Tess's mother to come take me home. When I said goodbye to Mom, I was afraid I'd never see her again, and the four days she was gone felt like an eternity. I'd almost forgotten her smell, the feel of her in the house.

She was smiling when she came home. Dad said she was much better.

The hospital prescribed her medication and helped her find a therapist. She never had another day like that Black Friday.

But even so, every time I look at her, I see a shattered mirror. So full of cracks it might fall apart again at any second.

I count those fault lines now as I stand across from her.

She's kneading her hands like they're bread. Dark circles rim her eyes. I wonder when she last slept, and my stomach wrings itself out because this is my fault. I did this to her by leaving. That must be why they're here. It was too much for her, even with Dad around.

My very existence is too much for her sometimes.

I fold my arms across my chest like I can be my own fortress.

She keeps saying my name, but the lobby is loud, and I let her voice get lost in the din. They've both been bombarding me with questions for the last ten minutes. I haven't answered any of them.

Instead, I ask my own. "What are you doing here?"

I can't do this right now. I just screamed at my friends. Mason and I are done. The scavenger hunt isn't over. A moment ago, I wanted desperately to go home, but now that I'm gaping at my parents, I know I'm not ready for them. For this.

It's too much.

"Let's go to your room and we'll talk. There's a lot of noise here." Dad grabs the handle of their suitcase. "Lead the way."

They have a *suitcase*. They aren't going anywhere. RIP Operation Freedom, or whatever this was.

It's like I'm at the peak of Valyrad's Flight, about to be dropped over the top. Except this time Mason's not beside me, solid and secure. I have no one's hand to hold. I'm alone, the darkness looming ahead, and I realize as the brakes let go that my safety harness isn't locked.

Falling, falling, falling. I'm not sure I'll ever stop falling today.

I didn't bring my keycard, so I have to knock on the door when we get to the room. Tess is already talking as she swings it open. "Listen, if we're going to fight you have to at least give us a fair chance by—" Her words die on her lips. "Um, hi, Mr. and Mrs. B."

"Tess, sweetie, how are you?" Mom pats my friend on the cheek as she slips past Tess and into the room. Her eyes dart around, taking it in, seeing how many ways it fails her checklist.

Dad trails in her wake, the suitcase's wheels *thump, thump, thump*ing on the carpet.

Tess clutches my arm and squeezes as I shut the door behind me. "I know," I mumble.

"Did you call them?" She, at least, has the sense to keep her voice low.

I shake my head. "They were just . . . here."

"How many check-ins did you miss?"

"None today."

I hug Tess. She doesn't hesitate to hug me back. "I'm sorry—" I start to say.

"We'll worry about it later." She's talking out of the corner of her mouth like a cartoon character. "We have bigger fish to fry."

I can't help it. I laugh. At this point, what else am I going to do? You can't stop the apocalypse once it's started. Thanos has snapped his fingers. Half the Avengers are gone. We're screwed.

"Girls," Mom says as she gives Issy a side hug, "Mr. Baker and I need to talk to Amelia. There's a restaurant here, right?"

"And a movie theater and a bowling alley and an arcade," Tess lists.

"And an ice cream shop," Issy adds.

Dad pulls his wallet out of his pocket and fetches some twenties. He hands them to Tess. "Give us a little bit, okay? We'll be out of your hair soon."

Tess and Issy stop on either side of me. Issy offers an encouraging smile. Tess bear-hugs me. "We'll see you later."

They're gone too fast, and I'm standing in the room alone with my parents.

My parents. How are they here? Why?

I stare at them from my place by the door. "I don't understand. I checked in every time you wanted me to today. You're"—I point at my mother—"the one who hasn't answered any of my texts. Who didn't pick up when I called."

Dad sits on my friends' bed, facing me. Mom pulls the chair out from the desk and slides it next to the footboard. She beckons me over.

My feet are traitors. They drag me to my own bed and drop

me down on the coverlet even though all I want to do is cling to the doorknob. Whatever's about to happen, I can't handle it.

It's all too much. Too much. Too much. Too much.

"You weren't where you said you were yesterday," Mom says once I'm seated.

My heart hiccups. "What are you talking about?"

"You told me you were with your friends, in the park. But that's not where your phone was. You were out of the resort for most of the day."

Of course. I shake my head. She was tracking me. It's been so long since there was any kind of break in our normal routine that I forgot she could do that. Anger kindles hot and thick at my center. "Why were you tracking my phone? You promised to trust me." All this time, I thought I was getting some real distance. I thought I was able to make some choices on my own. But they've been watching. Checking in. Controlling me, even from a plane ride away.

"I had to know you were keeping your phone on like you promised."

My head falls into my hands. I don't have the energy for this. My anger licks out as quickly as it blazed.

"Where were you, Amelia?" my father asks.

There doesn't seem to be much point in lying. "With a guy."

"Doing what?" My mother's voice is shrill. When I glance up at Dad, his expression is blank, like he's trying not to judge.

"Meeting his dogs."

Mom wrings her hands in her lap. Her right foot taps against the chair's wheel erratically. Dad places a soothing hand on her knee. "Is that code for something?" he says gruffly.

It's so ridiculous I laugh, inviting a flash of irritation into his eyes. I sigh. After all his warnings about "no boys," I guess I shouldn't expect him to find this amusing. "Yes. It's code for meeting his dachshunds, Waffles and Toast."

"Amelia."

"Nothing happened, Dad."

Mom reaches across the space between us to take my hand. "You promised us you wouldn't leave Fableland."

I meet her eyes. They're blue like mine, but darker, more distinct. Sapphires shining in the evening light. Freckles dust her nose. My mother is delicate and beautiful. I wish I saw more of myself in her. "It was only for a few hours. He wanted to show me a little of his life before I left." Tears hot as coals press against the backs of my eyelids. I don't want to talk about Mason. It reopens wounds that haven't closed yet.

"Amelia, your phone was out of the resort all night," Mom reminds me.

"I forgot it in the truck when he dropped me off here."

Her lips purse in doubt.

I look at Dad. "Remember, I talked to you from Issy's phone."

He begrudgingly confirms it. I don't know why this is what sets me off, but a sob blubbers out of me at his angry *hmph*.

"None of this matters anyway."

"What happened?" Mom squeezes my hand.

I shrug hard. "He lives here. I don't."

"Why didn't you tell us about him, instead of all these lies?" she asks.

"Because you would have been on the first plane out here to collect me."

My father shakes his head. "Untrue."

I gape at him, flourishing my hands to indicate their presence.

"We're here because you lied, Amelia," Dad says. "I know it probably doesn't seem like it, but we trust you. You could have told us."

Trust me? I almost laugh. My parents have never shown me anything but endless worry. And that's basically the opposite of trust.

Near Mom's chair, a scrap of paper peeks out from the mussed comforter. A piece of one of my notebooks that I tore up. Tess and Issy must have cleaned up the rest. I jolt to my feet and grab the paper, turning it over in my hands like it's some kind of lifeline. But both sides are blank; it's just a corner. I can't believe I did this to my research. What if I need these notes tomorrow?

I crush the paper between my fingers, and its edges drag along the skin of my palm.

The whole purpose of this trip, of this contest, was to help me find a new future. One that didn't involve me living at home forever. Living buried beneath my mom's worries forever. The contest isn't over yet, but I've seen the mermaids at Neptune's Launch. I've eaten desserts good and gross at the Cursed Apple. I've walked through Elorra's laboratory and watched the shadows dance in Atalantia. I touched the fountain of rings. I saw Casterman's unicorn and Dudley's stash.

I've done so many things I never thought I would. And I vividly remember how each made me feel—that kernel of excitement that bloomed in my chest. That strong urge to find more. To *do* more.

To *want* more.

And with Mason, I gave in to that. I kissed the hottest guy I've ever seen. I confided in him because my heart told me to. I laid my feelings bare for him, even though I was scared.

Now my parents are here. I need to keep following that push toward something new. I have to tell them what I'm feeling.

Yet the words catch in my throat like they have claws. Clinging to my windpipe, my tongue. Anything not to leave my mouth.

I try to take a deep breath, but the air won't slip past the giant lump in my throat. Instead, I choke, and my mother's on her feet reaching for me, panic flaring in her eyes.

I jerk away. "*No.* I can't . . . I can't do this anymore." Every word is a splinter drawing blood as it yanks out of me.

"You can't do what?" Mom's still on her feet, her hands extended. Her fingers are long and thin and tense, like they might crack at the knuckles at any moment. Every part of her is so breakable.

I have to repeat the words in my head four times before I can form them out loud. "I don't want to work at the store." I stare at the carpet, at the scuffed toes of my sneakers, anywhere but at my parents. My hands are clenched in the hem of my T-shirt so they won't shake. "That scavenger hunt I came down here for? The prize is fifty thousand dollars."

My father nods. "We know."

"What?" I stare between him and my mother in shock. "How?"

"I had to know everything about this contest before I could let you go," my mom says.

"But you still did?"

"It didn't seem likely you'd win," she explains. "And we know how much you love this place."

"It seemed harmless," my father adds. "A good chance for you to have time with your friends before they leave."

Their doubt should probably hurt more than it does, but I'm too drained to feel anything else. "I'm still in it. There's only twenty-five of us left."

"And if you win?" My father's voice is low. Scratchy.

"I want to move down here. Get a job here. Do something that *I* want."

They're quiet for way too long. If not for the sound of their breathing and the weight of their gazes on me, I would have believed they'd up and walked out.

Nothing about this feels like relief. I'm not lighter or freer. Instead, my body's filled with lead. Anchoring me forever to the ground. To this awful moment.

When my dad clears his throat, the sound ripples off me like he's thrown a stone.

"I see." That's all he says. Two words.

Next to him, my mother sucks in a puff of air.

I sink to the floor. Dig my fingers in the plush carpet. "You never asked me if I wanted to spend my life selling furniture."

Mom grasps the sleeve of Dad's button-down shirt. Her fist is a bouquet of white knuckles. "We did that for you, sweetie."

"I know, b—"

"So you would have something to take care of you. To keep you secure." Dad's face is stricken.

This is what I didn't want to do: hurt them.

I cover my eyes with my hands. "I know. And I love you guys for wanting to take care of me. But I was a baby when you made these decisions. You had no idea who I would be. What I would want. And because you'd already made those choices, I didn't bother to find out either."

"Amelia." Dad settles on his knees in front of me. He carefully pries my hands from my face, then holds them in his.

"Everyone I know has these big dreams. Tess wants to be some kind of CFO. Issy wants to have a restaurant. M—" I catch myself before saying his name. "Other people want to teach or study languages or write books or whatever. And even if they don't want to make a career out of it, they have things they love, like art or TV or animals or whatever. I have nothing like that. Nothing but this place." I open my hand, and the crumpled paper tumbles onto the carpet. Dad watches it roll away. "And like, Tess and Issy, they think it's this one thing, the store, my job, but that's connected to everything else."

"Sweetie, calm down," Mom says.

I keep talking. "I did so many things this week. I found all these park secrets I always wanted to see. I told my friends how I feel about them leaving me. I met this boy. I started to want things. And it's like, before all this, there was one path. And now suddenly there's these smaller ones branching off, but I can't follow any of them because I'm chained to the main path. I can't change my future. I can't breathe in our house. I can't . . . I can't keep going like this. If I do, I'm afraid it'll break me."

I take the deepest breath I can muster, letting the air fill my mouth, my throat.

Mom's staring at me like I've slapped her, but Dad's directly beside me now. We sit crisscross applesauce, our knees touching. He rubs his hands together. "What are you saying? You don't want your job at the store?"

Tears prick at my eyes as I shake my head. I tilt my chin toward the ceiling and try to blink them away. "I want to work here. They have a storytelling department. It's where they write the movies and come up with the parks' lore. I want to do that. Help other people fall in love with this place like I did. I can't do that working full-time for you guys."

Dad's eyes sink closed, and he nods. When he opens them again, he's got his bargaining face on. "If you don't win, what's the plan?"

"*Eli.*" Mom's voice is shrill. Two beats away from a spiral. It cuts right through me.

"What do you mean, what's the plan?" I say.

"You're done with high school. You can't come home and do nothing. So how are you going to get what you want?"

I rock back. "You're not mad?"

He tilts his head, surprise in his eyes. "Why would I be mad? It's your life. You need to be happy."

I wrap the hem of my shirt around my fingers. No matter how much I tense my muscles, I can't stop my hands from trembling. My parents, the hotel room, everything seems out of focus and unfamiliar. As if the world just blinked out of existence and returned as something entirely new. And I don't know where I fit in this world yet.

"Can I . . . can I think about it?" I ask.

Dad pats my leg. "Of course."

My mother's face is the color of snow before anyone's stepped in it, and her eyes are glassy with tears. "I had no idea we made you feel this way. That *I* made you feel this way." She can barely get the words out, her chin wobbling visibly. "I just want you to be safe." She reaches for the box of tissues on the nightstand. Grabbing five or six, she crushes them in her hand and blots her eyes.

"But what you see as safe is suffocating to me." I speak as gently as I can. "I know it's not your fault, so I've tried to push down all this stuff. But it's not helping. I walk around feeling like I'm seconds from erupting." I rub my temples as I blink back tears. When my mom hands me the tissue box, I take one. "I don't want to keep feeling this way."

She cups my cheek with her hand. "I don't want you to feel this way." Sniffling hard, she shakes her head. "But I don't know how to fix this. I can't just turn off my anxiety."

My father takes her free hand. "I don't think that's what Lia's asking."

"I'm not." I drag the tissue over my eyes. It burns. At this point, every part of my face feels like it's on fire. "The fact that you're listening, that you understand I need things to change, that's something." I blow out a breath. "It's somewhere to start."

Mom nods, then stands and kisses my temple. "Maybe we should go check in."

Dad's eyes are sad, but he gives her a soft smile. "Betsy, I don't think we need to stay. It's pretty clear Lia has things under control."

Her eyes flit to me. I see the panic in them. I also see her trying to fight it.

"I'll keep calling and texting," I promise. As much as I hate doing it, I know she needs it. And I can give her that much after everything my father's offered. Everything she hasn't fought against today.

My parents agree to stay at a hotel outside the parks and let me finish the trip alone with my friends. Mom even smiles for a second as she gathers her purse to go to the business center. "We haven't had a vacation in ages, Eli. Just the two of us."

As she closes the door behind her, she stares back at me, unblinking, like she thinks she'll never see me again. I guess, she won't—not like this, anyway. By the time I get home, I'll be someone new. Someone who gets to make choices.

Maybe that will be a good thing for both of us.

Dad and I study the door for a long time after it clicks shut. I'm the one who finally breaks the silence. "Is it really okay that I don't want the store?"

He sighs. "I'm sorry you feel like it isn't a possibility you could explore."

"The store's your life. You love it. You're so proud of it. You've both worked so hard and have given up so much to make it a success. I never wanted to destroy your legacy or let you down."

"Amelia, the store's always going to be yours. But it can be something you have—that you inherit when we're gone—not something you do. We can find someone else to run it."

I scrub my hands over my face, the rough movement making my tearstained skin sting. "What if I win? Will you let me come down here to stay? Would Mom be able to handle it?"

Dad scratches at the shadow of dark stubble on his jaw. "You heard her. She wants you to be happy. It will take time, but whatever happens, she'll be okay. I promise. It's not your job to manage her anxiety. I know sometimes I put that on you, and that's not fair. You have to live your life." He slings an arm around my shoulders and pulls me against him. "I *want* you to live your life. And so does your mom."

Live your life. The words are still echoing in my head when he stands and kisses my head. When he tells me he'll see me Sunday. When his suitcase *thump, thump, thump*s out the door behind him.

I find the torn slip of my notes and smooth it out against the carpet. For what feels like ages, I stare down at the wrinkled white surface.

Blank. Empty. New.

Just like me.

CHAPTER 27

June 23

Tanglewood Heights Hotel, Fableland
Orlando, FL

OC + ET = OTP

—A carving on the Sunspark tree

THE SUN IS A BLAZING BALL OF ORANGE ON THE HORIZON WHEN I reach the copse of trees behind the Tanglewood Heights Hotel.

It's five past six. My parents are on their way to their hotel in central Orlando. Issy and Tess won't be here for dinner until seven.

I'm alone. But it's not the burden it usually is, bending my shoulders, pressing on my insides. Instead, it feels light. Full of possibility, like the untrodden path now laid out before me. For once, I can do anything. And right now that means finding the Sunspark tree.

This particular park landmark was created by a fan: Rachel Eaton (MyCatIsOliverCray on the F^3 forums). When she visited Fableland ten years ago, she found a tree behind the Tanglewood Heights Hotel that looked identical to the one Oliver cuts his and Elorra's initials into at the end of *Sunspark*. As a love letter to the movie, Rachel dug the symbol—a heart with an arrow through it, *ET + OC* at its center—in the exact same place on the bark of this tree. Other guests have come and added their own carvings: some *Sunspark* themed, others memorializing great loves from their own lives. The tree is said to be covered in markings and yet somehow there's always room for more.

Another hint of Fableland magic.

The tree sits at the center of a large grove. Most of the others are weeping willows, trailing long curtains of branches and leaves toward the green grass, but the Sunspark tree is a royal poinciana in full bloom, its branches, laden with bright-red blossoms, arching like an umbrella over a thick, split trunk.

I find the tree as if I have a map that leads right to it. Or maybe as if it is waiting for me.

This part of the garden is empty, and the tendrils of the weeping willows sway in a soft wind as I pass through them. It feels like climbing into Narnia's wardrobe or falling down Alice's rabbit hole or jumping through Dr. Strange's portals. Crossing into somewhere new.

Behind the willows it's cool; the sunlight only reaches through in small patches of light that slip through the gaps between the branches of the royal poinciana's thick canopy. Everything smells of flowers and dew and a crisp summer day. When I inhale, I trap the air in my lungs for as long as possible before letting it go.

Approaching the Sunspark tree, I run my fingers over the various markings. They're all different, carved by hands of varying sizes and strengths. Some grooves are sliced deep into the bark, the outer layer peeling and exposing the raw wood beneath. A few are written in black marker, and others have barely broken the skin, time and weather stealing them away.

Right at the center is Rachel's, the lines thick and distinct. The curve of the heart sits under where the royal poinciana's trunk splits into its series of branches that create the tree's crown of blossoms, as if her carving is holding all the flowers up. She's managed to match Oliver's scraggly penmanship perfectly, so much so I'd believe that he had stepped out of the film to guide her hand.

Pulling out my phone, I snap picture after picture: up close, far away, from every angle.

Since I've got time to kill and nothing left to do, I take some time to scroll through my photos.

All the clues are there: Dudley's stash, Smokey, the mermaids, Casterman's unicorn, the fountain of rings, the dancing shadows. Issy's perfect shots of our tasting menu at the Curséd Apple, along with a few I snuck of her and Tess stuffing their faces. Tess has cream on her nose in one, Issy's lips are painted in chocolate in another. I smile broader with each image that slides across my screen.

I had forgotten about the photos of Mason's bookcases until

they pop up next, and I bristle at the sight of them. It's been only a few hours since I left him at Ava's rose, but so much has happened it feels like years stretch between us. My stomach cramps, and my hands shake, and I wonder how long it will be before the thought of him doesn't tear up my insides. Leave them as shredded as my research.

I don't expect the pictures that follow because I didn't take them. Mason did. Like they were new treasures for me to find when he returned my phone. Candid shots of Toast and Waffles lounging on his bed. His copy of *The Hammer of God* next to the rings we got from the fountain, the empty Death by Chocolate bowl, and an anchor from Neptune's Launch. Things we saw and did together, displayed on his shelf like priceless artifacts.

The final image is of him, staring at the camera the same way he always looked at me. Unblinking and thoughtful, his eyes peering well beyond what you want him to see.

My heart slams against my rib cage, and my head is spinning. After our conversation earlier, I was sure that I didn't matter to him. That we weren't worth the headache of trying to make things work. That *I* wasn't. But these pictures, everything he's showed me, suggests he's holding on every bit as tightly as I am. I just didn't see it.

This is my conversation with my dad all over again. Another instance of me making assumptions about people's expectations and reacting to them without knowing if they're true. Maybe the last few days would have gone entirely differently if I'd stopped jumping to conclusions about *everyone*.

But my parents listened. Does that mean Mason might, too?

Flicking open our text conversation, I upload the photo of him. I found your pictures, I type below it. Then I hit Send.

Dad said I should live my life. I'm not sure what that's going to mean for my future yet, but I know what I want right now.

Another chance to talk to Mason. To fix whatever this is between us.

The small letters under the photo and message immediately flip to Read, and ellipses appear on the screen. They blink, one dot after another. Over and over again. I stare at them, the phone's white light growing brighter as the sun sets.

Then they disappear.

My heart drops to my stomach, and my stomach sails toward the ground. I follow it, spine dragging down the scratchy bark of the tree trunk as I sit on the grass.

I type another message.

Lia
You were busy last night.
(6:36 PM)

It gets read with no response, but that doesn't stop me from sending more.

Lia
I'm sorry about earlier. I don't want this to be how we say goodbye, either.
(6:38 PM)

Lia
Can we try again?
(6:40 PM)

More ellipses. Followed by more stretches of blank screen. More silence.

I wait ten minutes more, then pull myself to my feet. I can't keep sitting here hoping he'll answer. Soon, Tess and Issy will be expecting me, and I don't want to be late. Not for the two of them, who always forgive me. Who always let me try again.

Once I'm standing, I brush my hands along the royal poinciana's bark one last time. There's a small spot right beneath the arch of a branch that hasn't been filled. I fish in my purse for the small scissors I brought for this occasion.

Pressing their points against the tree, I dig in and start carving.

When I'm done, my hands are scratched, deep enough in some places to draw blood, and flecks of bark speckle my black T-shirt.

Still, I smile at my handiwork.

TR+IM+LB=BFFS 4EVA

I don't know if Mason and I will ever talk again, and if we do, what will happen when I leave. I have no idea if we could even last.

What Tess, Issy, and I have, though, even on our worst days, *that's* worth memorializing. True, real, honest-to-goodness friendship—that's not something you find every day.

CHAPTER 28

June 24

Hero's Quest, Fableland
Orlando, FL

At the top of Sun's Peak, overlooking the entirety of Hero's Quest, is a small snatch of grass teeming with sunspark blossoms. Each morning they're replenished so a new crop of visitors can follow Elorra Tanglewood's trek up the mountain to find the spray of flowers that will save her kingdom. Most days all the sprigs are picked by noon, so, my advice? Get there early if you want your own.

—*MyCatIsOliverCray, Fabler Fanatics' Forum*

"IT'S TOO HOT FOR THIS."

Tess stops to lean over the railing that guards the steep turn of steps. Panting, she lifts her shirt to swipe the sweat from her forehead.

"You ran track for four years," I point out.

She narrows her eyes at me. "I did not run track *up stairs*."

I meet Issy's gaze, and we both shake our heads, grinning. Nothing can tame Tess's melodrama. Not even a hike to the top of Sun's Peak.

Mason was right about the first clue of the day taking place at the Alistair's Labyrinth attraction. Instead of a riddle, instructions arrived at midnight, explaining that for the first event of the day, contestants would have to find three items hidden in Alistair's workshop. We were also warned that some of us would be eliminated.

Thank God I was in the top ten yesterday, which means I'll get some extra hints to give me an advantage. The instructions said they'd be revealed when the hunt at Alistair's Labyrinth begins.

In the meantime, Tess, Issy, and I have a good two hours to pick some sunspark before we head to Vale of Villainy.

This was one of our biggest dreams as kids, and I'm so excited that we get to make it come true. On some other plane of the space-time continuum, the twelve-year-old versions of us are screaming like fans at a boy-band concert right now as we get closer to the top of the peak.

"We're almost there," Issy says, offering Tess her water bottle.

Tess takes it, dumping the water over her head instead of sipping it.

I grab my phone to take a picture of her, but I can't resist the urge to check my texts. Mason still hasn't responded.

Issy frowns at me. "If he can't be bothered to answer, he doesn't deserve you. Don't waste the rest of the trip pining for him."

I know she's right, at least about not wasting our trip. But I'm not ready to give up. Not quite yet. Mason's worth it. I still believe that. And though it may be all we get, I want the time we have left. I want the chance for one of us to win this contest. To get more than we're used to for once.

A family of four skirts us on the stairs. The older son looks about our age, tall with a boyish face, chin-length bronze hair, and big brown eyes. They catch on Issy as he passes by and he smiles shyly at her.

She returns his grin, but then quickly feigns interest in her unpainted nails.

Tess groans as he moves out of earshot. "Is, he was adorable."

"And with his parents," Issy points out. I can see the tension in her jaw, and the way her shoulders rise toward her ears.

I press my arm against hers to remind her that I'm here. Maybe with me for support, she can finally tell Tess the truth.

Tess sighs. "Everyone here is with their parents. Even Lia for a while yesterday."

I squawk, wishing I had something to toss at her head. "Too soon."

Tess and I laugh, but Issy's frown remains. Her eyes flit around our surroundings, the stairs, the top of the peak a few feet away, the clusters of people trailing up the path behind us.

She waits until the next group goes by, then clears her throat.

"Tess." She says her name so softly Tess has to get closer to hear her.

"Is?"

Issy presses her spine against the metal railing as she blows out a long breath. "I need to talk to you about something." She swallows, then rubs at her eyes with the heel of her hand. "Or . . . I guess . . . tell you something." Her voices catches.

She doesn't need an audience for this, so I wander a little farther up the stairs and take in the view.

After a few long moments, I see Tess pull Issy into a hug. The moment Issy accepts it, I rush toward them and join in, wrapping my arms around my friends.

They hug me right back.

"Can you be done playing matchmaker now?" Issy asks gently.

"You got it." Tess tightens her embrace. "I just wanted you both to be okay. Everything's about to change, and, honestly, it's kind of terrifying."

I gape at her. "Wait. This is about next year?"

Tess nods. "It helps having someone else in your corner. Like I have Grace. I want you both to have that." She cuts her eyes to Issy. "But not if you don't want it. I just want you to be good. I want us all to be good."

"We are. We will be." I blink against the emotions stinging my eyes. "If this week has taught us anything, I think it's that the three of us don't break so easily."

For months, the space between us has been shifting and taking on new shapes. But since we've been at Fableland, it's become more pronounced, as if all those changes are solidifying. Becoming real. This is the first time I've been honest with my parents. It's the first time I've seen Issy truly speak up for herself. It's the first time either of us have pushed back against Tess's need to make everything just so.

Stepping back, I run my hand along my pocket, feeling for my notes about Alistair's Labyrinth. Tess and Issy found the research I'd torn up after my fight with Mason and taped the papers back together. Then Tess threw out her precious schedule. Literally. Tossed it right over the balcony. Most of the pages landed in the pool. From all the way on the ninth floor, I could see her perfectly symmetrical handwriting bleed across the paper.

It's like we've come full circle. Back to the start of the week, when it was the three of us exploring the parks. But we're all a little different now. A little clearer. Maybe a little brighter, too.

Quietly, we climb the last few flights of stairs and reach the top of Sun's Peak. Between the mountain's peaks is a plateau smothered in grass so green it looks like it recently soaked up a good spring rain. Small rocks poke out among its thick tufts, their flecks of silver and bronze winking in the morning sunshine. Circling them like wreaths are sprays of golden flowers identical to the one we saw in Elorra's lab.

Sunspark. So much sunspark.

An attendant wearing a wide-brimmed hat and a khaki button-down over shorts the same color greets us. With a flourish of his hands, he says, "Welcome to Sun's Peak. Feel free to wander as long as you like. But no climbing on the fence and only one flower per guest." When we nod in understanding, he disappears back into his kiosk, which boasts empty mason jars and small hollow terrarium necklaces, all cowering from the direct sunlight under a giant umbrella.

I walk to the edge of the plateau and lean against the metal fence to stare down at the park. Its bold primary colors look muted from so far up, and even the tallest roller coasters seem a little less daunting, like they're nothing but big toy train tracks.

I close my eyes as a warm breeze kisses my cheeks. "Thanks for doing this," I say to my friends.

Tess nudges me. "Like we'd miss this."

"After yesterday—"

"I can't believe your parents were here," she interrupts. "And that they *left*. Sort of, at least."

Issy nods. "I was afraid they were going to make you go home."

I sniff. "Me too. I honestly can't believe everything I said to them." I frown. "Or to you guys." We still haven't talked about what happened before my parents showed up. All the things I said. Every time I try, they wave me off, but I'm determined to get the words out. They need to know I'm sorry.

"Yesterday sucked," Issy says. "We get it."

"I was upset about Mason, and I took it out on you two. I shouldn't have." I tap my toe against one of the steel posts. "You're allowed to go to college. You're not abandoning me. I'm sorry I said all that."

Tess clears her throat. "I'm sorry, too," she says, glancing between Issy and me. "I *swear* I'm going to listen more. Sometimes I forget there are other opinions in the world besides mine."

Her words remind me of what Issy and I talked about earlier in the week. That Tess has become so much *more* . . . well . . . Tess-like these past few months. She's always so confident and organized and in control that we don't check in with her like we should. It's too easy to assume she's fine.

But if the past few days have taught me anything, it's how damaging assumptions can be. I set my hand on her arm. "What's going on with that?"

Her eyebrows press together. "What do you mean?"

"Lately, you've seemed more . . ."

"Intense," Issy offers.

I nod.

"How?" Tess's voice is a little sharp.

"Think about it," Issy says softly. "The decor for our dorm room, the schedule for this trip, the endless finals study sessions, the way we had to coordinate our dresses for prom and the afterparty and our courses for next year and our morning schedule every day this past semester—out by seven, coffee at exactly seven-fifteen, in the parking lot by seven-twenty-five. You cried the day the barista screwed up Lia's order and we were off by three minutes."

"I did not."

"I saw you wiping your eyes," I say.

"So what? You know I've always been a planner."

"But this is more than planning." Issy's voice hasn't lost its gentleness, but it's firmer.

Tess crosses her arms and walks backward a few paces. "What are you trying to say? That you don't want to be roommates or like my plans?"

Issy mirrors her stance but holds her ground. "I want to know what changed this year."

Tess's eyes shoot to me.

I shake my head, eyes widening slightly.

"Tess, come on," Issy urges. "What happened?"

Tess digs her hands through her hair. "Things are kind of . . . tough . . . right now." She treads in a circle around a nearby bunch of sunspark, careful not to crush the delicate buds of light. "My mom's hours got reduced at work last fall, and we've been trying to save ever since, but I don't know if I'm going to have enough money for college."

No wonder she's been so fixated on the cost of things this week. "Why didn't you tell us?"

"Money's weird. And I feel like people don't really understand what it's like to not have any if you haven't been through it. I might have to take out loans, and it just feels like I have no idea what's going to happen and that makes me"—she holds her hands out in front of her and shakes them—"I don't know . . . out of control. The only way I feel better is when everything else is taken care of."

"What about your dad?" Issy asks. "Can't he help?"

Tess stares up at the sky, blinking rapidly. "I asked him. I begged. He told me he paid child support and that was his only obligation." Her hands are fists now. The same way they'd been when she came running out the blue door of his one-story home this past winter, her face red and splotchy. She could barely unfold her fingers to grab the steering wheel. We'd listened to her mom's only rock CD, some very loud band called Disturbd, the whole ride home. Every time I tried to talk to her, she turned the radio up louder.

Issy drops her chin to her chest. "I didn't know," she says softly.

"I didn't tell you."

"You should have."

"I know." Tess looks at us. "I'm sorry if I've been unbearable."

"I'm sorry if I've been frustrating," I say. "And yell-y."

Issy sighs. "I'm sorry I haven't been more up-front."

Tess narrows her eyes. "About the aromantic stuff? You have the right to tell us when you're ready."

Issy blows out a breath. "I know. But I wish I hadn't waited so long."

"We're glad you told us now." I give Issy a squeeze then pull Tess into us. "And you're going to be okay."

Tess nods confidently, though her eyes are a little glassy. "I'm going to work a ton while I'm in school and hopefully be able to pay some of the loans off right after I graduate." Her shoulders square. I'm willing to bet there are three spreadsheets on her laptop with all this planned out.

"I'm sure my parents will give you a job in the summers if you want," I offer. "They pay more than minimum wage."

"Really?"

"Um, they love you. Plus they're going to have a position to fill now that I might not be working there for long."

I thought about it all last night. If I don't win this contest, I'm going to come back to Orlando anyway. I'll need to work for my parents to build up some savings first, but then I'm going to try to get one of the paid writing internships in Fableland's storytelling department. And if that doesn't work out, there's tons of other positions in different departments. I'll find something. I will make my way back here. Even if Mason and I never see each other again, even if that day at Ava's rose was the end for us, I can't let go of my new dream. Now that I have Princess Caelyssa's story in my head, it has to find its way into Fableland's lore. I owe it to all the people who look like me who want to find themselves in Fable Industry's stories.

I owe it to myself.

I tell my friends all this. For once, I don't hold it in. And all they do is smile. Like it makes the most sense in the world.

Like they've never expected anything else from me.

"Time to make your own magic," Tess whispers.

I nod. That's exactly it.

I crouch beside a particularly vivid spray of sunspark, and a second later, Tess and Issy flank me. I run my hands gently over the threads of light that spray out of it. They're supple and thick, like really good leather, and even though I know they can't be real, it's impossible to see where the facade ends. They give off the same soft fragrance as actual flowers, and when I release the blossom, pollen dusts my life lines. The plants are even rooted in the ground; a small clump of dirt clings to Issy's as she plucks it from the grass.

It takes me longer than the two of them to pick my own sunspark. I circle one patch, then another, until I see it, one lone sprig huddled by itself under a curve in the stone. It's as vibrant as its sisters, but the blossom of light curves toward the ground. When I see it, I can't help but think of me my first few days here: crushed under the burden of what I thought was everyone else's expectations for me.

I tug the flower from the soil and cradle it gently as I head toward the kiosk. Tess and Issy opt for mason jars, but I select a terrarium necklace, one with a long chain so the sunspark will hang close to my heart. Before the attendant stoppers it closed, I pull out my notes and tear off a blank corner, then drop it into the tiny glass globe. It settles like a backdrop against the golden rays of the sunspark. My old ties to Fableland mixing with the new ones to come.

I'm still clutching the necklace in my hand when we head back to the stairs.

"Going down had *better* be easier or I'm calling a manager," Tess grumbles.

Issy checks the time on her phone. "We should head over to Vale of Villainy," she says. "You want to be at the front of that line of people rushing for the labyrinth."

Tess bumps my shoulder. "Is Mason going to be there?"

I shrug, that ache at my center yawning open at the thought of him. "I'm sure he will." I blow out a breath. "Just not . . . for me."

Tess tips her small chin toward the sky. "Good, because you don't need him. You carried his ass through this whole scavenger hunt."

The truth was, we were pretty much neck and neck. But I like Tess's version better.

Today is the first time the contestants will be pitted against each other in the same place. And the first time not everyone will have the chance to make it to the end of the day. Tension is high. The stakes are even higher.

Mason and I can't both win the money. But we're close enough to the end that one of us might, and I'm not sure that whatever we had would have survived that. The two of us want this prize too badly. We need it too much.

I let my friends lead me to the interpark tram. My pulse thumps against my eardrums and my knees are shaking. I force myself to take a long, deep breath.

I took a chance on Mason. I made a choice by opening myself up to him, by trying to make this work. He broke my heart when he couldn't reciprocate, and everything in me still hurts. But for the first time since I walked away from Ava's rose yesterday, I know I'll be okay.

CHAPTER 29

June 24

Vale of Villainy, Fableland
Orlando, FL

Alistair and His Monsters was Fable Industry's attempt to tell a Frankenstein story. Except Alistair is a lonely thirteen-year-old who makes a wish in the wrong magic fountain and ends up bringing to life all the mismatched toys he's cobbled together from his older brother's castoffs. Its companion attraction in Vale of Villainy remains a fan favorite. Riders are taken on a tour of the labyrinth in the basement of Alistair's grandparents' ancient mansion, where he has trapped his toys before they cause more chaos. And every day at eleven on the dot, the labyrinth opens up, allowing the creatures a chance to stretch their legs and wander the park to spook a few guests.

—Buzzworthy, "Fableland Rides Not to Miss"

"WHAT DO YOU THINK YOU'LL HAVE TO FIND IN THERE?" ISSY ASKS.

The three of us stare up at the gigantic metal doors where lines would normally form for Alistair's Labyrinth. In fifteen minutes, they'll open up and release the creations, and I'll need to run for the stairs to the workshop. Usually, guests can only peer into this space through windows in the queue, but the remaining scavenger hunt contestants get to go inside and see Alistair's experiments up close.

"I don't know," I mumble. "Maybe tools he used to make his monsters? Or Easter eggs from the film?"

"I always hated that movie," Issy points out as she links her arm with mine.

Tess does the same on my left. "You would. There's no love story."

"Nah, you know Issy shipped those two hybrid robot-Barbie dolls," I joke.

Issy's laugh echoes around us. "Maybe a little. But those creatures he made were so . . ." She shudders without finishing her sentence.

"Creepy?" I suggest.

"Awesome?" Tess adds. No one loves a good horror story like Tess.

"Yes." Issy points at me. "And no," she says to Tess. "I'm very *not* excited to see them come to life while Lia rummages around in there."

"We'll miss you when you never find your way out." Tess nudges me.

I roll my eyes. "You get lost in one corn maze in the fifth grade and you never hear the end of it." Sure, I was crying by the time they found me, but no one needs to discuss that part.

After days of having to jump straight into every clue, the downtime this morning has rubbed off some of the edge of this moment. But now that I'm here, eclipsed by the shadow of this massive attraction, it hits me hard.

This is it. The beginning of the end. The final set of clues. Some of us are going to walk out of the labyrinth eliminated. In a few hours, one of us is going to win the money and it could very well be me. I survey my surroundings. The delicious smells, the happy people, the perfect re-creation of the mansion where Alistair hides his creatures that blocks off this section of Vale of Villainy, one of the million ways that this resort immerses its visitors in Fable Industry's stories.

This could be my future.

Maybe Rowan Sunsgrace, Princess Caelyssa's nemesis, could have an attraction here someday. Right next to Alistair's. Winged chariots that fly as high as Pillager's Peak, that fall as fast and as far as Valyrad's Flight.

Maybe this is the beginning of my dreams coming true.

My body is buzzing and itchy, the same feeling I get when my mom stresses me out. Time to keep moving.

With Tess and Issy in tow, I make my way over to the right

side of the attraction, where a group of people mill around near a sign with the same design as our contestant pin. At this point, a bunch of their faces look familiar from the leaderboard photos and from seeing them wandering the park. Ember and Erica, not surprisingly, are both at the head of the pack.

Slightly apart from the rest of the contestants, I spot Mason. He's so tall, and so damned good-looking, it's impossible to miss him. My heart speeds up, and I must make some kind of noise because Tess and Issy follow my gaze.

Tess practically growls in his direction. "How dare he show his face here."

"I'm actually glad he came," I say. And I mean it. "He deserves a chance at that money as much as I do." I would never want to be the reason Mason didn't try to win the future he wants.

Issy nudges me. "Kick his ass in there."

"Scavenger hunt the hell out of that place!" Tess pumps her fist.

I hug them both, then join the group.

As I mix in with the other contestants, my eyes drift toward Mason. Our gazes catch for a moment before I glance away.

I dig my heels into the asphalt. I can't think about him right now. None of us will know what we need to look for until we're in the workshop. And not all of us will be able to find the objects and scan the codes. I have to have my knowledge of this movie and this ride at my fingertips. There's no time for hesitation. No room for Mason to take up space in my head.

A siren blasts, drowning out the other noises of the park, and in front of us, the iron doors of the labyrinth creak open achingly slowly. Alistair's squeaky voice belts out from speakers mounted on the labyrinth roof. "Today's a special day. While my creatures step out to make some new friends"—he pauses to chuckle—"twenty-five of our parks' biggest fans will get a one-of-a-kind look at my workshop." He lets out a loud cackle. "And only fifteen of them will emerge."

My body loses all sense of gravity. *Fifteen?* That's just over half of the remaining contestants.

"Get ready, superfans," Alistair continues. "Once my hippogator leaves the gate, it will be time for you to enter." With that, the PA system goes silent, and the first creature stumbles into the light.

Part rabbit, part race car, it zooms toward the first kid it sees, and the small child squeals with delight. After that, creature after creature lumbers forward. They clearly spared no expense because every monster is here, even the ones that seem like they would have been impossible to re-create in real life. A beautiful doll in a prom dress with the legs of a robot. Her male counterpart with a human body and a mechanical head. Crab claws on a dog. A cat with eight legs. As the crowd reacts with joyful screams at each new member added to the procession, I swear I can hear Tess above them all, hollering like her favorite band just took the stage.

I take a deep breath and shake out my limbs. I can do this. I didn't come this far to fail. I can practically feel the money in my hand, see my apartment nearby, envision myself at a desk collaborating with artists to bring Princess Caelyssa to life. Curves, thick thighs, round stomach, and all.

A cast member dressed like Alistair's grandfather steps to the head of our group. "The hippogator will come out next. Once he does, please follow me single file through the labyrinth doors." He uses a wireless microphone so we can hear him. "The event will not begin until you are in the workshop, so there's no need to rush or shove or to put anyone at risk. Please line up now so we're ready to go."

Everyone obeys, shuffling into place. Ember and Erica hold the first two spots in line. I file in toward the back.

Despite being on the opposite side of the group, Mason somehow ends up behind me.

His stare causes the hairs on the back of my neck to rise. I can feel it there, pressed against me, as palpable as any hand.

I keep my eyes on the parade. The hippogator's broad snout pushes out into the sun, and immediately, our line moves forward.

"Good luck," I hear Mason whisper as the dark chasm of the labyrinth's entrance looms ahead.

I glance back at him once. Let my eyes linger for only a second. "You too," I murmur.

Alistair's face appears on the large screen mounted outside the door to the workshop.

"Welcome, superfans!" he bellows, throwing his arms up. "You are about to see something no visitor at Fableland ever has: the inside of my workshop, where I create all my friends." A slightly manic smile takes over his acne-scarred face. Abruptly, he surges forward so his eyes and the bridge of his nose overtake the screen. "Careful not to become one yourself." His laugh sounds more like a banshee screaming.

After a moment, he quiets, and the camera eases back. "In exchange for giving you this supersecret access to my lair, I need your help. Granddad has locked me out after my last experiment went . . . sideways. But I can't stop it from destroying the town without my tools. Can you get them for me?" A list appears beside his head. "I need my needle, my thread of life, and the jar of magic well water. Scan the code beside each item to return it to me. The fifteen of you that find all three first get to escape."

I repeat the items in my head. Needle, thread, jar of water. They're prominent items from *Alistair and His Monsters,* but that doesn't mean they'll be easy to locate in the workshop. Alistair is wily. In the movie, he's always hiding things that matter to him so no one else can find them.

Mason is still behind me, but when I sneak a glimpse at him over my shoulder, his eyes are fixed on the screen, his jaw a hard line. I don't know how familiar he is with this film. It's pretty recent—just five years old—and Mason gave up on Fableland long before that. He might have no idea what the three items look like or where to start searching for them.

Part of me itches to tell him, but I turn away. We're not a team anymore. I'm on my own.

And so is he.

Alistair's chilling laugh pulls my attention back to the screen. "One last thing, superfans. A recent experiment of mine might have gotten . . . loose . . . in the workshop. Be careful when you're in there. If it catches you, you lose." A graphic replaces his face: the silhouette of a monster pressing its hand on the shoulder of a person. Next to it reads: **If you are tagged by the monster, you are automatically eliminated.**

Another obstacle. Another way to whittle us down. They really aren't going to make this last day easy. I can't imagine what the clues will look like after this.

The screen goes dark, and the metal door of the workshop eases open. All twenty-five of us hurry inside. There are no lights and I can barely see two inches in front of my face. Around me, people mumble in confusion.

"This is impossible."

"Is there a light switch somewhere?"

"This is a lawsuit waiting to happen."

I reach out, cautiously feeling for whatever furniture or other obstacles might be in the vicinity. If we have to find Alistair's tools in the dark, then that's what I'll do.

A second later, the door to the workshop *snick*s shut behind us, and bright fluorescents snap on overhead, bathing the antiseptic room in harsh light.

I blink against the glare as I take in my surroundings. The walls are white; the cabinets, counters, and other fixtures stainless steel. The floors are black tile, and at the center of the room is what looks like a giant operating table.

The workshop stretches about half the length of my house before breaking off into three darkened corridors. Given the lockers that line them, we're probably going to have to venture that way.

There's a monitor mounted above the door, and it begins counting down the seconds from ninety. At the same time, my phone beeps with a notification from the contest app. Ember, Erica, Mason, and a few others look at their phones as well.

The hint for this clue has come in.

I tap the icon: **Alistair's thread of life is stitched, not spooled.**

My gaze cuts back to the room. I notice that there are multiple shelves stocked with spools of thread in a variety of colors. Most people will probably head there immediately, but now I know not to waste my time.

My heart batters my chest as I watch the numbers pass. Six . . . *five* . . . *four* . . . *three* . . . *two* . . . *one.*

I hold my breath. The room is so silent that it feels like everyone else is doing the same.

After the buzzer sounds, there is one last beat of quiet, as if we are all frozen in place, then pandemonium. Everyone rushes in different directions, and the room is full of loud, anxious breathing and the intermittent slamming of doors and drawers as Erica and some others ransack the room. They're so intent on finding the items that no one is really paying attention to anyone else unless they bump into one another. Like we're all here in this room, and yet somehow each of us is alone.

I want to be a little more methodical, so I stand still and take in the space. Above my head, the monitor now holds a leaderboard, and I see the zero beside the name Jorge switch to a one as a contestant scans an item somewhere in the workshop.

My pulse races, but I need to be smart about this. Patience and efficiency will help me win. The tortoise and the hare and all that.

Since I have information about the thread of life, I decide to start there. In the film, it's an iridescent silver, and I know from the hint that it won't be on a spool. So where could it be? Probably not just cast away in a cabinet or locker. Not when Alistair needed it for every experiment.

Toward the back of the room, there are metal drawers in rows of three that look like something out of a morgue. To house Alastair's creations, I guess. Maybe he was in the middle of one when he lost his thread.

That guess is as good as any other, so I hurry over there.

Most of the other contestants are focused on the supply cabinets or have disappeared down the hallways, so I'm alone as I yank open the top row of drawers. Thankfully, they're empty. I could barely reach the handle to release them—I would have needed a step stool if there'd been something in them to inspect.

It takes every bit of strength I have to heave open the center drawer in the next row. I swallow back a screech as the drawer slides out, revealing a life-size crocodile prone on it. On each side, what looks like leopard legs have been stitched in place of the crocodile's own limbs. Shimmering next to one of the furry black leopard spots is a strand of silver thread. And beside it, fixed to the crocodile's scaly back, the QR code.

My hands tremble as I fumble to scan it. As soon as I hear the beep, I whip my head around to check the monitor.

I'm in third. I need to protect this head start.

Shoving the drawer back in, I waste no time dashing across the room to hunt through the cabinets and drawers for the needle. I don't really have a strategy this time, but there are a ton of medical supplies in the cabinets on the right side of the room, so I target them first. I find only sterile-looking silver syringes, nothing like the thick, crooked black needle Alistair uses to sew together his monsters.

Crap. Where else could it be? Closing my eyes, I think back to the movie. Where did Alistair keep his needle? He always had it with him.

And he was usually wearing his lab coat in the workshop.

I spin around, looking for anything tall enough to store a coat.

Between hallways I notice two closet doors. My hands are shaking as I throw one, then the other, open. But neither closet has a lab coat. Just cleaning equipment and stacks of jars full of cloudy liquids with who knows what suspended in them.

Ducking around a cluster of contestants emptying the trash bins, I sprint into the first hallway. There are maybe ten or fifteen lockers, and as I peer into each one only to discover they're empty, it feels like a countdown, ticking me closer to losing everything I've worked so hard for this week.

By the time I reach the last locker, a thick blanket of doubt has settled over me. Maybe I'm remembering the movie wrong? Did Alistair *have* a lab coat? Could I be confusing him with a scientist from one of Fable Industry's sci-fi features?

I yank the metal door open and let out a yelp as something thin and white billows toward me. For a full minute, I'm convinced it's a ghost and I'm about to be possessed. I don't recognize the outline of the lab coat until my heart settles.

Sometimes, this place is a little *too* immersive. Forget "fall into your imagination." More like, "careful it doesn't scare you to death."

Saying a little prayer to Sam Casterman for help, I dive my hand into one pocket, then the other. From the second one, I fish out a plastic bag. It cradles Alistair's needle, a QR code affixed to the outside.

I'm practically yelling as I scan the black-and-white box.

There's one tool left to find. I'm kicking ass. Scavenger hunting the hell out of this place, as Tess would say.

I might *truly* win.

On weightless legs, I dash back toward the workshop. My path crosses Mason's as I reach the brightly lit lab. I skip my gaze to my feet and angle my shoulder to slip past him, but he stops, blocking me.

"Seven people are already through," he says.

My eyes search out the monitor for confirmation. Sure enough, seven names have *completed* beside them. I'm shocked to see that both Ember and Erica still need one more item to finish. I thought for sure they'd be at the top of the chart.

I nod to Mason in thanks, but then I'm off running again before he disrupts my focus. There's something in the movie about the well water needing darkness to maintain its magic. It could be hidden in one of the cabinets.

I'm passing the operating table when the lights flicker out. Several people yell out in surprise, and I hear what sounds like someone tripping.

The air around me feels thicker, the room fuller somehow, like more people have crowded in. Someone screams.

The lights blaze on again, and I discover we aren't alone. In the middle of the room stands one of Alistair's creatures. It's almost as big as me and jet black, with the wings and beak of a bird. Its legs look like they belong to a goat, and antlers grow from the top of its head. When it turns my way, I realize the beak has teeth. Sharp, pointed teeth.

This must be the creature Alistair warned us about in the video. I shudder. If someone told me right now that I'd slipped into a horror movie, I'd one hundred percent believe them. That thing looks way too real.

I back toward the sink, hoping to stay off the creature's radar. If it tags one of us, we're out. I can't let that happen.

Thankfully, it lunges at the first person who runs, and chases him down the far hallway.

Everyone seems to see this as a sign to hustle, and a fervor of frantic movement fills the room. I beeline for the sink and throw open the surrounding cabinets. They're full of odds and ends, anything Alistair could use to fuse his creations together.

Under the basin, I notice something red and white with a handle. I shove aside chemicals and cleaning solutions to shimmy the object out. It's a cooler, white on the bottom and red on the top, like the one my mom would send me on school field trips with.

I can't imagine Alistair would hide precious magic water in something like this, but it's cool and dark, so I set it on the counter to check.

I don't even have time to open it. The bird-deer-goat thing has crashed back into the room, its sights set on Erica. She's screaming like the monster might actually kill her, elbowing aside anyone who gets in her way.

Barreling straight for me, she grabs the handle of the cooler and jerks it off the counter. I'm still holding it, so the force sends me flying between her and the creature. She wrenches the cooler from my hands and then knocks me back into Alistair's monster.

I feel its wing settle on my shoulder.

My body freezes as if the thing has ice powers.

The creature tagged me. I'm out.

I can barely function as it gestures for me to scan the code under its wing, confirming my elimination. I stand in the middle of the room, shock numbing everything but my burning eyes. My vision is blurry as I watch Erica tip open the cooler and pull a jar out from inside. It's an opaque mason jar with liquid that twinkles like stars.

I was right. I had the well water in my hand until Erica stole it from me. I should have been on that leaderboard. I should be one step closer to winning. I glance at the monitor. All the spots but two are full now. And I won't be one of them.

My stomach cramps, and I feel like I'm going to throw up. But I also want to scream. And break something. My hands clutch at the hem of my shorts, my nails stabbing into the weave of the denim like knives.

Erica sets the jar down to get her phone, and a part of me—the part that refuses to accept I've lost—considers rushing forward and scanning it anyway. Maybe giving her a good push in the process. Screw the rules. It's not as if Erica has followed them either. And now she's going to get the chance to win.

But before I can move, Mason is in front of her. He plucks the jar from her hand.

"What the hell are you doing?" she screeches. Her face is bright red, her eyes wide and unblinking.

"Making sure you lose," he says softly.

He's just standing there, holding the jar.

"Mason! Finish this. Win!" I holler. Why the hell isn't he scanning the code?

Erica swats at him, even tries to tackle him. She's threatening him with everything from lawsuits to being doxed.

Mason remains statue-still. Only his eyes move, searching me out, clinging to me, as if there aren't twenty-three other people around us. As if Erica isn't trying to knock him over. "None of this is worth it without you," he says.

On the monitor above his head, I watch another name blink onto the list. We're down to one spot. What is he doing? "No," I insist. "Get the money for school."

Mason turns away from me. I see his eyes land on Ember. They're rifling through stacks of file folders, their movements frantic. Dodging another swipe from Erica, Mason calls out to them. When they face him, he tosses Ember the jar.

Ember catches it, surprise creasing their brow. "Uh, thanks, dude."

Mason nods. "Win the whole thing," he tells them.

Ember scans the code. A wide smile brightens their face when their name pops up in the last spot on the leaderboard.

A moment later, my phone dings. The event is over.

For Mason and me, so is the contest.

Erica fires an impressive string of curses at Mason, then storms off, demanding to talk to a manager.

I'm shaking as I step toward him. My heart has two holes now—one from him, and one from losing this contest. If either gets any bigger, I'm afraid I'll fall to pieces.

"Why would you do that?" I demand.

"I never expected to win." His watercolor eyes settle on me. Drink me in. Devour me whole.

"But you could have." I want to pound on his chest the same way Erica did. It almost hurts worse knowing we both lost.

"School's not going anywhere."

"Mason."

"Lia. Yesterday, that was the worst mistake I've ever made. Letting you walk away like that. Then not answering you." He shakes his head. "I was scared. I couldn't see an answer, so instead of trying to find one, I gave up." He reaches out like he wants to take my hand, but then lets his fall back to his side. "I've had tunnel vision for so long. School is all I've been working toward. I couldn't wrap my head around the idea of having two dreams. I didn't think I could want two things. That the universe would let me have them both."

I'm trying to listen to him, to let his words sink in, even as my brain repeats, *Lost, lost, lost.* "You can still have them."

"I can keep working toward school, sure. But you leave tomorrow." His mouth tenses, and a muscle in his jaw ripples as he swallows. "Lia, I'm not good with words. I needed a way to show you that I'm not ready to let go either. I want us to try to figure this out together."

"Another alliance?" I offer him a small smile.

He doesn't respond, but he reaches for me again. Slowly. Hesitantly.

This time, I let my fingers find his. And as his warm palm presses against mine, I feel one of those holes in my heart shrink a little.

CHAPTER 30

June 24

A random stretch of road
Outside Hero's Quest, Fableland

Near Orlando, FL

Cloud Kingdom was Fableland's biggest failure. The park was barely open eight years and almost every major injury that has ever happened at the resort occurred within its gates. Rumors blame ghosts, but most likely it was due to Fable Industry's attempts to build the park quickly and bring in extra revenue during the recession years. No one has accessed the park in decades. It remains standing but nonoperating at the eastern edge of the resort.

—FablelandFacts.com

MASON HOLDS OPEN A PADLOCKED GATE, WAITING FOR ME TO slip through the gap.

This part of the street is shaded by a row of overgrown trees, and their branches shudder with the force of cars zipping by. The smell of exhaust burns the inside of my nose.

It's after dinner, and the sun's light has softened against the clusters of clouds overhead. After we left Alistair's workshop, Mason, Carter, Tess, Issy, and I spent the next few hours making the most of the parks, bleeding those FOTL passes for everything they're worth. Yet every end to a ride, every new treat that passed between my lips, every piece of swag I purchased, felt like a consolation prize. A bunch of small Band-Aids trying to cover the gaping wound that was the cash I'll never have.

Now Mason and I are alone for what little time we have left.

As I get closer to the fence, I fight the urge to do another round of plus-size geometry. I want to trust that Mason will make sure I fit. When I duck through the gate, he guides me forward with a hand on my elbow. "Where are we going?" I ask.

"You'll see."

"You know, when Tess insisted we have one last date, she didn't mean take me somewhere to murder me."

"You have an unhealthy preoccupation with murder."

I grin. "I blame all the true crime podcasts."

"Let me give you this one last piece of magic, okay?" His mouth is drawn tight, but I see the softness in his watercolor eyes.

This feels too much like an end. My fingers itch to grab him, to tow him back through the gate and all the way to Phoenix's Landing, where everything started. As if that could reset the clock or defuse this ticking time bomb. Give us a chance to begin again. Or at least continue.

But all I can do is take his hand when he offers it.

The road ahead looks like it was once a part of the resort that nature has since reclaimed. Weeds snake through cracks in the cement and clog the gaps of storm grates, and neglected trees arch over our heads, their branches heavy from lack of pruning. The green blots out the sun and sketches creeping shadows across the pavement.

My mind swirls as we walk in silence. It feels like Tess, Issy, and I just got here. That I've barely finished the first clue. That Mason and I have only recently held hands for the first time. But already, everything's over. And without that cash prize to cushion my moving expenses, I don't know when I'll get back here. When I'll see him again.

It could be months. Who knows how long it will take for me to save up, to find a job at Fableland? Without the contest, the path ahead of me is completely undefined, overgrown like the one we're walking now.

But at least, for once, it's mine.

It's a mile or so before we encounter another fence, and Mason holds my hand the whole way. Tight, like if his grip is strong enough, I'll never go anywhere.

I want him to be that powerful.

The chain-link fence bows close enough to the ground that we can climb over it easily. On the other side, through a thicket of bushes that scrape at my skin and tug loose threads from my shirt, I find myself staring at the butt end of a dilapidated roller coaster.

"Cloud Kingdom," I say, my voice soft with awe.

This abandoned park makes every Fableland top ten secrets list. Not because no one can prove its existence—there are pictures of it all over the internet from people who've snuck in—but because there are so many stories about why it was shut down. It opened in the '80s, not long after Atalantia, but by 1992, it was no longer accessible to the public because there had been too many catastrophes and issues with the rides. Tons of people think it's haunted, but the more realistic explanation is that it was built during a time when Fable Industry's movies weren't performing well and they had to rein in their spending, which meant they sacrificed due diligence and safety precautions for the quick revenue of a new park opening.

It probably didn't help that everyone hated the *Cloud Kingdom* movie.

The dips and curves of the coaster are a wooden mountain range looming before us. My eyes run up and down them as if I have to look at every piece of it to make it real.

Advancing, I rest my palm against one of the crisscrossed wooden slats of the structure. It's warm from the sun. Small slivers of white paint cling to the corners, but most of the paint has flecked away, exposing the grayed-out, faded pine beneath.

"I still can't believe we lost," I mumble to the wood. "And that I go home tomorrow."

"I'm not sorry I stopped Erica from making it through, though," Mason says adamantly.

"Me either. She sucked."

He huffs out a low laugh.

A few feet ahead, on an incline that dips low to the ground, one of the cars sits imprisoned by the brush and weeds that have clustered around its wheels and up over its sides. Mason stares at it as we pass it.

I sigh. "But I wish you could have still won." I wanted one of us to get to hold our dreams in our hands. Erica ensured it wouldn't be me, but Mason had made his choice by giving the jar of well water to Ember.

"Right now, walking here with you is more important to me. Besides," he adds, tugging me closer to his side, "think of everything you got to do this week. All those smaller dreams you made come true. Your trip wasn't for nothing."

I know that in my heart. If I hadn't come here, I probably never would have found the courage to tell my parents the truth about how I feel and what I want for my future. Tess, Issy, and I might have grown farther apart, rather than closer.

"And I met you," I say softly. The biggest piece of Fableland magic, standing warm and solid beside me.

We pick our way around the base of the coaster. Every few feet, planks are missing, exposing holes that peer down into an endless sea of leaves and grass and insects. Twice, the wood buckles beneath me, but Mason catches me smoothly before I fall.

After passing between two more motionless carts and turnstiles with no arms, we're standing at the top of a tall set of open concrete steps.

From here, we can see out over the whole park. Thirty years of neglect have turned the space into a muddle of green and gray and brown, a sea of cement disrupted only by weeds and bushes choking any rides close to the ground. Small pops of color strain from under the leaves, as if the carts call out to remind us of their presence.

Rising above it all is the pristine skeleton of the Hurricane. One of those steel roller coasters full of twists and turns. I point at it.

"I want to go there."

"Where did you think we're headed?" Mason asks, offering me his signature smile. I reach out and tap the dimple that flares in his cheek. I wish I could imprint it on my fingertip. Hold on to it, to him, forever.

The grass is up to our knees in places as we approach the Hurricane, and my mother's voice sings a litany of dangers in my head: *poison ivy, ticks, snakes, spiders, needles.*

"My mother would die right now if she saw me." I shake my head. "Of course, she'd also die if she saw me sitting quietly on a bench, so I guess that's not saying much." Before scaling the next thatch of weeds, I pause and peer up at Mason. The slowly setting sun backlights him in shades of pink and Creamsicle. "I talked to her, you know. To both of them."

He arches an eyebrow. "Yeah?" he asks.

"Apparently they were tracking my phone, and when it was with you all day instead of at the resort, they just . . . showed up."

"Oh shit."

"It was actually a good 'oh shit' moment, though. I was so upset from our talk, then from yelling at Tess and Issy, that I blurted out everything I was feeling."

"How did they take it?" He guides me up the steps to the

roller coaster's loading area. An old sign reads WELCOME TO THE HURRICANE with the image of blowing wind swirling beneath it.

"Surprisingly well. This whole time, they thought working at the store was what I wanted because I never said anything." I squeeze my eyes closed and pretend I'm at the top of this broken roller coaster, ready to slip over the first hill. "They said we'll figure it out when I get home."

His arms find me, strong and solid and real as they wrap around my waist. "So what's the new plan?" His breath blows hot against my neck.

"Work at the store to save some money. Apply for jobs here. Come back once I get one."

"In the story department?"

I press my forehead to his chest and nod. "I've already bookmarked the application to fill out when I get home. But if not that, something else." For a moment, I breathe Mason in. "I don't know how long it will take, but I'm coming back."

His chin settles on the crown of my head and he whispers, "Good," into my hair.

My heart dances against my ribs. I hate that every touch tonight feels like the last one, that even as I promise to come back, it feels like we're saying goodbye.

Pulling away, I stare up at the track curling above us. It's so tall it feels like you could touch the sky if you climbed to the top.

"Want to go higher?" he asks.

Using an abandoned roller coaster as a jungle gym doesn't seem like the wisest of decisions, but I nod anyway. I want to see every piece of Fableland, accept every touch of magic it's willing to give me.

Mason steps onto the edge of the Hurricane's curved track and helps me up beside him. We scoot along the edge like we're walking a tightrope, him first, me clinging to the back of his shirt.

When the steel rails turn into giant strands of DNA spiraling around us, we use the various bars and ladders to climb from piece to piece, pointing out birds' nests and trash and random shoes and a doll (creepy) caught in the loops.

There's something serene in Mason's face as he leans down to pull me onto the next straight shot of track. His eyes siphon off the blue of the sky, and his jaw doesn't clench the way it usually does. As if up here, where it feels as though all we'd have to do to brush the clouds is stretch up our arms, the weight of the world can't touch him.

"Lia, what happens when you leave tomorrow?" He stops, still holding my hand at the small of his back, where he's been using it to shepherd me along behind him.

"I was going to ask you the same thing," I say quietly. "If I'd won that money, this would be so much easier. I'd have a timeline. A real sense of when I would be back."

I want concrete answers. I want to be able to make solid promises. But all either of us have are maybes and somedays. I can feel that buzzy feeling threatening my limbs again. Brushing past him, I mount the metal stairway beside the Hurricane's first descent. I scale it about halfway to the top, then sit. A minute later, Mason settles beside me.

The sun is moving across the horizon, and it gilds the plants and metal around us, melting them to burnished gold. Ahead, the steeples of Reddingshire Castle jut into the sky as if they're level with us. The corners of other roller coasters curl around the castle like clouds.

Clenching my hands into fists, I jam them into my lap and turn to him. "I know you don't do magic and promises and all that, but it feels like there's no version of me you're not a part of now. So if we say goodbye, then you're going to be this absence I carry with me like a ghost. I don't want a ghost, Mason. Especially not yours." I take a deep breath to steady myself. I'm sitting at the top of a roller coaster and it's not nearly as scary as the thoughts in my head right now, the things I need to say to him so I can leave here with no regrets. "I think . . . I think that I could love you someday." I swallow hard. I've never said those words to a guy before, and yet, with every step we've taken through Cloud Kingdom tonight, I've become more certain they're true. "I feel like this thing with us could really become something."

He closes his eyes. "Lia, it already has." When his eyes open, they catch on the top of Reddingshire Castle, the point farthest from us.

Even though there's still an hour until it's dark, the lights in the parks have begun to pop on, casting everything in the distance in a hazy, ethereal glow.

This week, I've spoken my mind more times than I thought I ever could. And every time, it has helped change something. With my parents, with Tess, even with Mason, though it hurt. But this time, I need him to be the one to tell me what he wants. He already knows where I stand.

"What do you want to do?" I ask.

He faces me, his gaze locking with mine. "I want us to be together. I don't care how far away you live. I can't let you leave tomorrow and know I'll never see you smile again, that you'll never make me laugh again, that I won't have you to talk to, to make me see the world in a more magical way." He brushes a few strands of my hair off my temple. "I don't want to say goodbye. I can't."

I rest my chin on his shoulder so I'm staring into his profile. I can feel the rise and fall of each breath move through him and into me. "Then we won't. We'll text and call and email." A burst of wind shakes the structure beneath us and tries to snatch the words from my mouth. "We'll find our own path." The same way I've done with everything else this week.

This thing with Mason and me, it was never what I thought. We weren't rivals. Or allies. We weren't a summer fling. From the moment our eyes met, he was always so much more.

I don't know if he'll still be that once I go home, once our lives move forward, once he's no longer a car ride away and there's more than a breath's space between our skin.

But I'm not ready to let go. To fall without him.

And it's clear he's not either. Which is all the promise I need right now.

I angle my head, tipping my chin up so my mouth finds his. His body melts against mine as we sink into a deep kiss. As if he's finally letting go of all the fears he's been grasping so tightly.

I let him tug me closer, let him kiss me with abandon, my own lips just as urgent on his. I don't know when I'll see him again. I need to imprint his touch, his mouth, onto my skin. I need to remember every sensation, every word we spoke to each other. Every smile that broke across his face. It's all proof that this was real, in case the distance between us ever starts to feel like too much.

Mason's mouth drifts to the shell of my ear. "We'll make our own magic," he whispers against my cheek.

I draw him back into another kiss. "We already have."

CHAPTER 31

June 24

Starshatter Hotel, Fableland
Orlando, FL

Each night at Phoenix's Landing ends with a fireworks display around the turrets of Reddingshire Castle. Instrumental renditions of Fable Industry's most famous tunes sing out in the background as color overcomes the night sky. The entire show is spectacular, but it seems to be the final series that sticks with guests most: when dozens of fireworks sketch a giant rainbow-colored circle above the castle, a reminder that the magic at Fableland never ends. That tomorrow, the parks will open and magic will fill the air once again.

—Fableland, 50th-Anniversary Documentary

MASON AND I MEET CARTER AND MY FRIENDS BACK AT THE STAR-shatter at the end of the night.

Beyond the domed pool, there's a grassy knoll with some benches and a few umbrella-covered tables that look out over the enormous lake that separates the hotel from Vale of Villainy. We order mozzarella sticks and nachos from the snack bar and take them out to wait for the closing fireworks. Even though all the travel sites say this is one of the best spots for viewing, we're alone, probably because of the chill that's set in following an evening rainstorm.

Mason and I sit sideways on the picnic table bench so I'm leaning back against his chest, my legs stretched out in front of me, both of us huddled in his old gray sweatshirt for warmth. Tess and Issy lie across the benches of the next table, and Carter sits on his jacket in the damp grass.

"Did you hear who won the scavenger hunt?" he asks us.

"Not Erica," I mutter, earning a laugh from Mason.

"I'd like to have a conversation with that girl if our paths ever cross," Tess declares.

Issy snorts. "Someone warn her. Tess is out for blood."

Carter shakes his head, amused as ever at Tess's brand of drama. "It was Ember."

I smile. "Good. They dominated the entire contest." I lean forward so I can see Carter. "What was the final clue?" Even though I know Fable Industry has other, more popular movies, I hope it was *Sunspark* related.

"The two final contestants had to remember Oliver Cray's *actual* backstory, find those Easter eggs in the various parks, and scan the codes in the right order. The last clue was in the hull of the Fool's Gambit, and there was this whole obstacle course the contestants had to make it through that mirrored the mutiny on the ship that stranded Oliver in Elorra's kingdom."

Epic. As always, this place doesn't disappoint.

"Oliver tells, like, four different stories about his life before he met Elorra," Tess points out.

"That's the challenge. You have to remember what pieces from each of the stories are actually true." I can hear the wistfulness in my voice, and an ache echoes at my center. I would have loved a chance to walk in Oliver's shoes that way. To practically get to *be* in my favorite movie for a minute.

We fall silent as the fireworks display begins.

The colorful lights paint rainbows in Tess's platinum-blond hair and turn Issy's dark eyes into starlit galaxies.

I capture this moment and tuck it straight into my heart. These six days have been magic. Today has been magic. These last moments are magic.

My friends are always magic. Mason's just another dose. And no matter what happens to the two of us, I'll never forget our time together here.

I'll never forget *him*.

"Thank you for all of this," I say.

Issy peeks up over the table, cocking her head in question.

"You guys gave me exactly what I needed."

Tess doesn't look away from the burst of color streaking like paint across the sky. "We love you, Lia. And you better visit us every weekend next year."

I snort. "Mom will love that." Then I blow them both kisses as the final series of fireworks race for the moon. Enough explode at once that their booms shake the ground. I sink deeper into Mason, inhaling his pine scent and memorizing the feel of him solid and steady against my back.

I'm not sure if there's a point to wishing on fireworks, but I do it anyway. With my eyes closed and my breath held and my hands folded in my lap.

For once, I don't wish for time to stand still. I'm ready to move forward. To see where the new paths I've laid will take me.

But I never want to forget this moment and exactly how I feel. I hope Fableland and its magic will give me that one last gift.

CHAPTER 32

June 25

Lia's phone
Boston, MA

Lia
We just landed!
(3:48 PM)

Mason
I miss you already.
(3:49 PM)

Lia
Same.
(3:49 PM)

July 6
Lia's phone
Waterville, MA

Mason
Okay. I watched this Captain America movie you keep yelling about.
(12:09 PM)

Lia
AHHH. FINALLY.
(12:11 PM)

Mason
I have bad news for you.
(12:13 PM)

This is not science fiction. It's magic dressed up to look like science.
(12:15 PM)

Lia
Didn't one of your author people say something about how magic is just science we haven't come up with yet?
(12:18 PM)

Mason
"Any sufficiently advanced technology is indistinguishable from magic."
(12:20 PM)

Lia
Potato. Potahto.
(12:25 PM)

Mason
I wish you could see how hard I'm laughing right now.
(12:27 PM)

Lia

(12:27 PM)

> **July 14**
> **Lia's phone**
> **Waterville, MA**

FaceTime call from Mason Clarke
(11:40 PM)

> **July 28**
> **Lia's phone**
> **Waterville, MA**

Lia
OH MY GOD.
(2:41 PM)

Mason
WHAT?
(3:10 PM)

Lia
I just got an email from Fableland's storytelling department. They want to talk to me about a writer's assistant job. They loved my Princess Caelyssa story!
(3:40 PM)

Mason
I'm crossing all my fingers.
(3:42 PM)

August 2
Lia's phone
Waterville, MA

Mason
I signed up for my first class in the fall.
(8:01 AM)

Lia
Shut. Up. I AM SO PROUD OF YOU.
(8:05 AM)

Mason
It's just a first-year writing class.
(8:05 AM)

Lia
Like that matters. It is still amazing.
(8:06 AM)

YOU'RE amazing.
(8:07 AM)

Mason
I love you.
(8:08 AM)

Calling Mason Clarke . . .
(8:09 AM)

August 15
Lia's phone
Waterville, MA

Lia
Tess and Issy just left.
(11:10 AM)

Lia
We hugged for like ten minutes.
(11:12 AM)

Lia
And I know I'm going to see them at the end of September.
(11:12 AM)

But I still can't stop crying.
(11:12 AM)

FaceTime call from Mason Clarke
(11:13 AM)

> **August 16**
> **Lia's phone**
> **Waterville, MA**

Lia
YOU MADE ME A ROSE.
(1:38 PM)

Mason
Carved it with my own hands.
(1:46 PM)

Image sent
(1:48 PM)

I have one too.
(1:49 PM)

Lia
OMG WE'RE CASTERMAN AND AVA
(1:52 PM)

Mason
No. We're Lia and Mason. We have our own story to tell.
(1:53 PM)

August 18
Lia's phone
Waterville, MA

Lia
Image sent
(9:53 AM)

Lia
Guess who's officially a writer's assistant for Fableland's storytelling department!!!
(9:57 AM)

Mason
What???? You're incredible.
(9:57 AM)

When does it start?
(9:57 AM)

Lia
Not until October but I have to go down there before that for an orientation session.
(9:59 AM)

Image sent
(10:01 AM)

Mason
Wait. This plane ticket is for next week.
(10:03 AM)

Lia
See you soon. 🩶
(10:05 AM)

Acknowledgments

I conceptualized *Love at Full Tilt* in 2017 after a family trip to Disney World with my in-laws. When I started it, I was writing the story for the sixteen-year-old version of me who had always dreamed of meeting a cute guy in line for an amusement park ride and having a whirlwind romance (but never did). Yet in the end, it turned out to be so much more—the book I needed as a plus-size teen to remind me that I was worthy of love; the book I needed at twenty-eight as I received rejection after rejection on the first project I queried; the book I needed at thirty-nine when I stepped away from writing YA to try a new genre and age category, believing I'd never fulfill my dream of writing for teens. And it's the book I needed in 2023 to 2024, when revising it offered me pockets of joy in what was an incredibly difficult year. I hope it finds its readers exactly when they need it too.

One of the themes of *Love at Full Tilt* is that we can make our dreams come true, and the fact that this book exists is a testament to that. I am so deeply appreciative of everyone who walked with me on the path to get here.

To my literary agent, Katelyn Detweiler, thank you for not hesitating even for a second when I randomly asked you about putting this book on sub. Your boundless confidence in me and my writing keeps me going, and there's no one else I'd want to be on this journey with (which is why I secretly call you my "lobster agent" to my friends, lol). Thank you for everything you do, always.

To my editor, Hannah Hill, thank you for loving this book as much as I do (and for reading it as many times as I have! Lol). I knew from the first second of our call that you saw to the heart of Lia's story (and I love that we had the exact same thought for how to revise it!). With every draft you've helped me make it everything I knew it could be. I am so grateful for all your insight and for the ways I have grown as a writer over this past year with your feedback and guidance, and for how much you've embraced the importance of Lia's story and getting it out in the world. I can't wait for us to tell more stories together!

I am so grateful to my critique partners and friends who have read *Love at Full Tilt* in its many iterations over the years: (in no particular order) Courtney Kae, Renée Reynolds, Samantha Eaton, Annette Christie, Kelsey Rodkey, Jessica James, Leanne Schwartz, Rachel Griffin, Sonia Hartl, Carlyn Greenwald, Alechia Dow, and Katie DeLuca. Without your feedback, I never would have gotten this book off the ground, and without your unbridled enthusiasm and belief in it, I never would have kept putting it out there until it found its home.

My biggest thanks to the team at Delacorte Romance. *Love at Full Tilt* would not be the book it is today without all your support. And a special shoutout to my copy editors Colleen Fellingham and Heather Hughes for catching all the mistakes my eyes could no longer see! I'm sorry for my misplaced hyphens and commas, and for never knowing the difference between *past* and *passed*.

One of my biggest publishing dreams has been to have a cover by Leni Kauffman, and Leni surpassed my already-high expectations with this one. Thank you for bringing my story to life, Leni, and for always rendering plus-size characters so beautifully.

I am also so grateful to Ray Shappell for the beautiful cover design, to Cathy Bobak for the wonderful interior layout, and to J. S. Dykes for bringing Fableland to life with the unbelievable map. I might wallpaper my house with this book, I love it so much.

To all of the wonderful booksellers, librarians, and readers who have discovered me through my adult romance books, thank you always for your support and enthusiasm. You make me want to keep telling stories, even when it feels hard. I hope you love this one as much as I do!

To my husband, Kevin, thank you for being that love story I dreamed about when I was writing this book. And for always flirting with me while we wait in line for rides at the many amusement parks I drag you to. I know you never doubted that I'd be sitting here writing acknowledgments for a YA book, and every time you've dealt with the dogs, the dishes, the meals, the cleaning, every time you've let me vent and cry, every time you've helped me work out logic issues or listened to me talk through a plot point, you've proven that you meant it. I love you to the moon and back. Thank you for being my partner on this and every other adventure.

Mom, you told me that I could be whatever I wanted to be, and I took you seriously. And now here we are at BOOK NUMBER FOUR. Thank you for teaching me to believe in myself and for being my first (and biggest) fan! I love you.

Finally, to every writer who picks up this book, remember that your shelved stories are never gone. They're just waiting for their moment. 😊